D0918765

BENEATH THE MOORS AND DARKER PLACES

TOR BOOKS BY BRIAN LUMLEY

The Necroscope Series

Necroscope
Necroscope II: Vamphyri!
Necroscope III: The Source
Necroscope IV: Deadspeak
Necroscope V: Deadspawn
Blood Brothers
The Last Aerie
Bloodwars
Necroscope: The Lost Years
Necroscope: Resurgence
Necroscope: Invaders
Necroscope: Defilers
Necroscope: Avengers

The Titus Crow Series

Titus Crow, Volume One: The Burrowers Beneath & Transition
Titus Crow, Volume Two: The Clock of Dreams & Spawn of the Winds
Titus Crow, Volume Three: In the Moons of Borea & Elysia

The Psychomech Trilogy

Pyschomech
Psychosphere
Psychamok

Other Novels

Demogorgon
The House of Doors
Maze of Worlds

Short Story Collections

Beneath the Moors and Darker Places
Fruiting Bodies and Other Fungi
The Whisperer and Other Voices

TOR®

A TOM DOHERTY ASSOCIATES BOOK
NEW YORK

BENEATH THE MOORS AND DARKER PLACES

BRIAN LUMLEY

This is a work of fiction. All the characters and events portrayed in this collection are either fictitious or are used fictitiously.

BENEATH THE MOORS AND DARKER PLACES

Copyright © 2002 by Brian Lumley

All rights reserved, including the right to reproduce this book, or portions thereof, in any form.

This book is printed on acid-free paper.

Design by Heidi Eriksen

A Tor Book
Published by Tom Doherty Associates, LLC
175 Fifth Avenue
New York, NY 10010

www.tor.com

Tor® is a registered trademark of Tom Doherty Associates, LLC.

ISBN 0-312-87694-7

First Edition: February 2002

Printed in the United States of America

0 9 8 7 6 5 4 3 2 1

This collection copyright © Brian Lumley, 2002. "David's Worm," copyright © Brian Lumley 1972, first published in *Year's Best Horror* No. 2, ed. Richard Davis, Sphere Books, 1972. "Dagon's Bell," copyright © Brian Lumley 1988, first published in *Weirdbook 23/24*, 1988. "The Sun, the Sea, and the Silent Scream," copyright © Brian Lumley 1988, first published in *F&SF*, February 1988. "The Second Wish," copyright © Brian Lumley 1980, first published in *New Tales of the Cthulhu Mythos*, ed. Ramsey Campbell, Arkham House, 1980. "A *Thing* About Cars!," copyright © Brian Lumley 1971, from *The Caller of the Black*, Arkham House, 1971. "Rising with Surtsey," copyright © Brian Lumley 1971, first published in *Dark Things*, ed. August Derleth, Arkham House, 1971. "Big 'C'," copyright © Brian Lumley 1990, first published in *Lovecraft's Legacy*, TOR Books, 1990. "The Fairground Horror," copyright © Brian Lumley 1976, first published in *Disciples of Cthulhu*, ed. E. P. Berglund, DAW Books, 1976. "Beneath the Moors," copyright © Brian Lumley 1974, from *Beneath the Moors*, Arkham House, 1974.

For Lelia Loban,
who had no axe to grind

CONTENTS

INTRODUCTION   13

DAVID'S WORM   19

DAGON'S BELL   29

THE SUN, THE SEA, AND THE SILENT SCREAM   77

THE SECOND WISH   121

A *THING* ABOUT CARS!   153

RISING WITH SURTSEY   167

BIG 'C'   205

THE FAIRGROUND HORROR   231

BENEATH THE MOORS   273

INTRODUCTION

I HAVE BEEN A WRITER now for a third of a century, and across the years, other than my "series" short stories and novels (such as the Necroscope series, the Titus Crow stories, and the Hero and Primal Land series), I have written a good many stand-alone novels and short stories hitherto uncollected in mass-market paperback in the U.S. Here TOR Books has given me the opportunity to present some of these in two large companion volumes, *Beneath the Moors* and *The Whisperer.*

The following introductions to the stories in the present volume, *Beneath the Moors,* may give the reader some insight as to how, why, or when they were written, and why they are included here.

My first selection, "David's Worm," was written in 1969 and was among the earliest of my stories. At first I couldn't find a buyer, then it went into *The Year's Best Horror Stories,* and from there must have found its way into translation; eventually it was adapted for both German and Italian radio. "David's Worm" hasn't received much coverage in the U.S., however, which makes it ideal, not to mention topical, as a taster here—well, depending on your taste buds. For in the light of the current European "Mad Cow" disease scare, it might be well to remember what the nutritionists have been telling us for years: we are what we eat. . . .

As for "Dagon's Bell":

H. P. Lovecraft's Cthulhu mythology—especially his Deep Ones, those batrachian dwellers in fathomless ocean employed so effectively in *The Shadow over Innsmouth,* and frequently hinted at elsewhere in HPL's fiction—always fascinated me, as it has fascinated many a writer before and after, and as it will doubtless continue to do. In 1978 I wrote a full-length novel based on the Deep Ones, entitled (with brilliant originality!) *The Return of the Deep Ones.* It may be found in this book's companion volume. Looking back, it was probably an error to set the story in a locale with which I wasn't overly familiar, but I covered as best I could. The current story, however, makes use of a location with which I'm *very* familiar; in fact it's the northeast coast of England, where I was raised. If you should find that "Dagon's Bell" rings true, that's probably the reason.

The third inclusion is one of my personal favourites. "The Sun, the Sea, and the Silent Scream" was written, along with "Fruiting Bodies," "The Picnickers," "The Pit Yakker," "No Sharks in the Med," and a handful of others, in 1987–88. These were very good years for me since they also saw first publication of *Wamphyri!* and *The Source* in the U.K., and *Necroscope* in the U.S. And they were especially good when for two consecutive years I even managed to indulge my passion for the Greek Islands—but not, I hasten to add, on the island in this story!

Then we have "The Second Wish," which I'd like to talk about at greater length. Among horror classics, "The Monkey's Paw" must rank with the very best. I don't think "Paw" inspired the present tale, though certainly both stories share a similar macabre motif. My *first* wish when I set about to write this story was to reiterate the theme of "the warning ignored" and the resultant "payment exacted"; that's what it's about. It's also a Cthulhu Mythos story, but despite the usual (or unusual? or obligatory?) references, it isn't typically Lovecraftian.

As for *my* second wish:

Twenty years ago when this story was written, I was still a soldier. I wasn't dependent upon earnings from my literary efforts; writing was only a hobby, while the Army was my real bread and butter. Which meant I wouldn't kick and scream if an editor wanted to suggest some small change in a manuscript. At that time the important thing was to get my stuff into print.

In order to comply with just such editorial requirements, I rewrote the *original* ending in a style that never entirely satisfied me: a case of "who pays the piper calls the tune," so to speak. This time around I've put the matter right. It's only a small thing—just a paragraph, that's all—but I can now consider "The Second Wish" in its entirety published the way I want it.

My *third* wish is that it should give you the creeps . . .

The fifth *tale* herein was the very first story in my very first book. "A *Thing* About Cars!" was written back in the summer of 1969, when I was a Military Policeman. I think the idea took root from something a friend said to me at the scene of a bad traffic accident: that in the hands of some people "motor vehicles are projectiles that are *aimed* along the roads, badly—and then let loose!" In light of the carnage I agreed with him. Later, however, when I thought about it—well personally I was always a lateral thinker . . .

"Rising with Surtsey" goes a long way back. It was written in December 1967, revised in '68, and got a further (slight) revision when editor James Turner wanted to use it in an updated, excellent *Tales of the Cthulhu Mythos* (1990). H. P. Lovecraft's influence is very strong here, but since this was only my tenth story ever from my very first year of writing, that's hardly surprising. I think it was also my most ambitious story to date: an homage, most certainly, to HPL, but also to August Derleth of Arkham House, without whose dedication HPL's work might have languished in the brown and crumbling pages of ancient copies of *Weird Tales* forever. Wherefore, what would the story be without its purple prose?

One last thing:

Unlike Gustaf Johansen's narrative concerning R'lyeh's upheaval from the sea floor, the details of Surtsey's rising are very well documented . . .

When I started to put "Big 'C' " together, I didn't have a Lovecraftian thought in my head, and I wasn't even certain it would turn out to be a horror story. For some time I had been playing around with ideas for weird SF tales, and "Big 'C' " was a bunch of ideas left over from another story. Later, when I was asked to write a story for a book called *Lovecraft's Legacy*, I remembered "Big 'C' " and wondered if I could maybe rework it into something HPL might have inspired . . . only to discover that he sure as hell had inspired it! So while "Big 'C' " isn't pastiche—while it wasn't consciously written "after" HPL—nevertheless he does seem to have had a hand in it. There are no prizes for matching this up with Lovecraft's original masterpiece. That would be too easy, for they're both pretty much the same alien colour . . .

The penultimate story, "The Fairground Horror," was written twenty-three years ago and appeared in an anthology called *The Disciples of Cthulhu* along with stories by Lin Carter, Fritz Leiber, Ramsey Campbell, and others, with an introduction by Robert Bloch—a book which at once vanished,* hasn't been seen since, and now commands a high price in the collector's market. More recently, to celebrate Lovecraft's centenary year, there has appeared a handful of books, any one of which might easily be mistaken for *Disciples*, which to my mind corroborates what I said elsewhere about the fascination of the Mythos. Of course, it also means that there's a whole generation of Mythos freaks (not a derogatory term, I promise; I'm a Mythos freak myself!) out there who don't know that this story exists. So here it is as it first appeared in 1976.

And that leaves us with the title story, in fact a novel, *Beneath*

---

*Lo and behold! A new revised edition of *Disciples* has recently appeared from Chaosium . . . which only goes to prove what I said about the durability of the Cthulhu Mythos.

the Moors. Long out of print in its original, blackbound, Arkham House edition, *BTM* has only ever seen reprint in British paperback format. Now TOR has given me the opportunity—and the space, for the novel is an odd length—to bring it back into print in the U.S. I hope the new generation of Cthulhu enthusiasts will find it sufficiently Lovecraftian, and the rest of the stories in this volume sufficiently weird, to merit a place on the shelf with their other Horror and Mythos fiction volumes.

Brian Lumley
Devon, England
July 2001

DAVID'S
WORM

Professor Lees, chief radiobiologist at the Kendall nuclear research and power station, was showing his son some slides he had prepared weeks earlier from pond and seawater in irradiated test tubes. David was only seven, but already he could understand much of what his famous father said.

"Look," the professor explained as the boy peered eagerly into the microscope. "That's an *amoeba*, quite dead, killed off by radiation. Just like a little jellyfish, isn't it? And this . . ." he swapped slides, ". . . is a tiny wee plant called a *diatom*. It's dead too—they all are—that's what hard radiation does to living things . . ."

"What's this one?" David asked, changing the slides himself.

"That's a young flatworm, David. It's a tiny freshwater animal. Lives in pools and streams. Funny little thing. That one's a type with very strange abilities. D'you know, when one *planarian* (that's what they're called) eats another—" David looked up sharply at his father, who smiled at the boy's expression. "Oh, no! They're not cannibals—at least I don't think so—but if a dead worm is chopped up and fed to another, why! the live worm 'inherits' the knowledge of the one it's eaten!"

"Knowledge?" David looked puzzled. "Are they clever, then?"

"Noooo, not strictly *clever*, but they can be taught simple things like how a drop in temperature means it's feeding time, stuff like that. And, as I've said, when one of them is dead and chopped up, whatever he knew before he died is passed on to the planarian who eats him."

"And they're not cannibals?" David still looked puzzled.

"Why, no," the professor patiently explained. "I don't suppose for one minute they'd eat each other if they *knew* what they were eating—we do chop them up first!" He frowned. "I'm not absolutely sure though. . . . You could, I suppose, call them *unwilling* cannibals if you wished. Is it important?"

But David was not listening. Suddenly his attention seemed riveted on the tiny creature beneath the microscope.

"He moved—!"

"No he didn't, David. That's just your imagination. He *couldn't* move, he's dead." Nonetheless the scientist pulled his son gently to one side to have a look himself. It wasn't possible—no, of course not. He had been studying the specimens for three weeks, since the experiment, watching them all die off, and since then there had not been a sign of returning life in any of them. Certainly there could be none now. Even if the sustained blast of hard radiation had not killed them off proper (which of course it had), then colouring them and fixing them to the slides certainly must have. No, they were dead, all of them, merely tiny lumps of useless gelatin . . .

The next day was Saturday and David was not at school. He quit the house early saying he was going fishing at the pool. Shortly after he left, his father cleaned off his many slides, hardly missing the one with the tiny planarium worm, the one in David's pocket!

David *knew* he had seen the worm move under the microscope—a stiff, jerky movement, rather like the slug he had pinned to the garden with a twig through its middle one evening a few weeks earlier . . .

David's pool was his own. It lay in the grounds of the house, set far back from the road, in the copse that marked the boundary of his father's land. In fact it was a runoff from the river, filled nine months of the year by high waters flooding the creek running to it. There were fish, but David had never caught any of the big ones, not with his bent pin. He had seen them often enough in the reeds—even a great pike—but his catches were never any bigger than the occasional newt or minnow. That Saturday it was not even his intention to fish; that had only been an excuse to his mother to allow him to get down to the pool.

The truth was that David was a very humane boy really and the idea that the flatworm had been *alive* on that slide, no matter how, was abhorrent to him. His father had said that the creature was a freshwater dweller; well, if it *was* alive, David believed it should be given another chance. Immersion in water, its natural habitat, might just do the trick!

He put the slide down on a stone in a part of the pool not quite so shaded by the surrounding trees, so that the creature upon it might benefit from what was left of the late summer sun. There he could see it just beneath the surface of the water. He kept up a watch on the tiny speck on the slide for almost an hour before growing tired of the game. Then he went home to spend the rest of the day in the library boning up on planarian worms.

In defiance of everything the books said, "Planny" (as David christened the creature the day after he saw it detach itself from the slide and swim almost aimlessly away) grew up very strangely indeed. Instead of adopting a worm shape as it developed, with a lobey, spade-shaped head, it took on one more like that of an amoeba. It was simply a shapeless blob—or, at best, a roundish blob.

Now one might ask: "Just how did David manage, in such a large pool, to follow the comings and goings of such a small animal?" And the answer would be that Planny did not stay small for very long. Indeed, no, for even on that morning when he got loose from the slide he trebled his size: that is, he *converted* many times his own weight in less wily, even smaller denizens of David's pool. In just a day or two he was as big as a Ping-Pong ball, and David had taken to getting up very early, before school, so that he could go down to the copse to check the creature's rate of growth.

Two weeks later there was not a single minnow left in the pool, nor a stickleback, and even the numbers of the youngest of the larger fish were on a rapid decline.

David never discovered just how Planny swam. He could see that there were no fins or anything, no legs, yet somehow the animal managed quite nimbly in the water without such extensions—and especially after dining on the first of the larger fish. It had been noticeable, certainly, how much the freakish flatworm "learned" from the minnows: how to hunt and hide in the reeds, how to sink slowly to the bottom if ever anything big came near, things like that. Not that Planny really *needed* to hide, but he was not aware of that yet; he only had the experience ("inherited" of course) of the minnows and other fish he had eaten. Minnows, being small, have got to be careful . . . so David's worm was careful too! Nor did he get much from the bigger fish; though they did help his self-assurance somewhat and his speed in the water, for naturally, they had the bustling attitude of most aquatic adults.

Then, when Planny was quite a bit bigger, something truly memorable happened! He was all of five weeks reborn when he took the pike: David was lucky enough to see the whole bit. That old pike had been stalking Planny for a week, but the radiation-transformed worm had successfully managed to avoid him right until the best possible moment: that is, until their sizes were more or less equal . . . in mass if not in shape.

David was standing at the poolside, admiring Planny as he gently undulated through the water, when the ugly fish came sliding out of the reed patch, its wicked eyes fixed firmly on the vaguely globular, greyish-white thing in the water. David's worm had eyes too, two of them, and they were fixed equally firmly on the pike.

The boy gawked at the way it happened. The fish circled once, making a tight turn about his revolving "prey," then flashed in to the attack at a speed which left David breathless. The boy knew all about this vicious species of fish, especially about the powerful jaws and great teeth, but the pike in question might never have had any teeth at all—might well have been a caviar sandwich—for all Planny worried! He simply *opened up*, seeming to split down the middle and around his circumference until David, still watching from the poolside, thought he must tear himself in two. But he did not. David saw a flash of rapidly sawing rows of rasplike teeth marching in columns along Planny's insides, and then the creature's two almost-halves ground shut on the amazed pike.

Planny seemed to go mad then, almost lifting himself (or being lifted) out of the water as the fish inside him thrashed about. But not for long. In a few seconds his now somewhat *elongated* shape became very still, then wobbled tiredly out of sight into deeper water to sleep it off . . .

For a full four days after this awesome display David's worm was absent from its rebirth-place. There had been some rain and the creek was again swollen, which was as well for the oddly mutated flatworm, for there were no fish left in the pool. In fact, there was not much of *anything* left in the pool—at least, not until the after-noon of the pike's vanquishment, when heavy rain brought the river waters to restock the Planny-depleted place. For that ugly, sadly vulnerable fish had been the pool's last natural inhabitant, and until the rain came it would have been perfectly true to say of David's pool that it was the most sterile stretch of open water in the whole world!

Now it is probably just as well that the majority of tales told by fishermen are usually recognized for what they usually are, for certainly a few strange stories wafted up from the riverside during that four-day period, and not *all* of them from rod-and-liners. Who can say what the result might have been had anyone really tried to check these stories out?

For Planny was coming along nicely, thank you, and in no time at all he had accumulated all the nastiness of quite a large number of easily devoured pike of all sizes. He had developed a taste for them. Also, he had picked up something of the unreasonable antagonism of a particularly unfriendly, yappy little dog whose master called for him in vain from the riverbank until late into the fourth night.

On the fifth morning, having almost given up hope of ever seeing the curious creature again, David went down to the pool as usual. Planny was back, and much bigger! Not only had he put on a lot of weight but his capacity for learning had picked up, too. The little dog had gone down (or rather *in*!) almost without a burp, and Planny's very efficient digestive system had proved only slightly superior to his "natural" talent for, well, *picking* brains.

But while the animal's hidden abilities were not so obvious, his growth assuredly was!

David gaped at the creature's size—almost two feet in diameter now—as it came sliding out of the reed patch with the top three inches of its spongy, greyish-white bulk sticking up out of the water. The eyes were just below the surface, peering out liquidly at the boy on the bank. It is not difficult to guess what was going on in Planny's composite knowledge-cells . . . or brain . . . or ganglia . . . or whatever! The way he had been hiding in the reeds and the way he carefully came out of them undoubtedly highlighted a leftover characteristic from his earlier, minnow period. The gleam in his peculiar eyes (of which David was innocently unaware) was suspiciously like that glassiness, intense and snide, seen in the eyes of doggies as they creep up on the backsides of postmen, and there was also something of a very real and greedy *intent* in there somewhere. Need we mention the pike?

Up into the shallows Planny came, flattening a little as his body edged up out of the water, losing something of its buoyancy, and David—innocent David—mistakenly saw the creature's approach as nothing if not natural. After all, had he not saved the poor thing's life?—and might he not therefore expect Planny to display friendship and even loyalty and gratitude? Instinctively he reached out his hand . . .

Now dogs are usually loyal only to their rightful masters, and minnows are rarely loyal at all, except perhaps to other minnows. But pike? Why the pike is a notoriously unfriendly fish, showing never a trace of gratitude or loyalty to anyone . . .

Approximately one hundred and thirty yards away and half an hour later, Professor Lees and his wife rose up from their bed and proceeded to the kitchen where they always had breakfast. A rather pungent, stale-water smell had seemingly invaded the house, so that the scientist's wife, preceding her husband, sniffed suspiciously at the air, dabbing at her nose with the hem of her dressing gown as she opened the kitchen door and went in.

Her throbbing scream of horror and disbelief brought her husband in at the run through the open kitchen door a few seconds later. There was his wife, crouched defensively in a corner, fending off a hideously wobbly *something* with her bleeding, oddly dissolved and pulpy hands.

David's father did not stop to ponder what or why, fortunately he was a man of action. Having seen at a glance the destructive properties of Planny's weird acid make-up, he jumped forward, snatching the patterned cloth from the table as he went. Flinging the tablecloth over the bobbing, roughly globular thing on the floor, he hoisted it bodily into the air. Fortunately for the professor, Planny had lost much of his bulk in moisture-seepage during his journey from the pool, but even so the creature was heavy. Three quick steps took the scientist to the kitchen's great, old-fashioned all-night fire. Already feeling the acid's sting through the thin linen, he kicked open the heavy iron fire-door and bundled his wobbly, madly pulsating armful—tablecloth and all—straight in atop the glowing coals, slamming the door shut on it. Behind him his wife screamed out something ridiculous and fainted, and almost immediately—even though he had put his slippered foot against it— the door burst open and an awfully wounded Planny leapt forth in a hissing cloud of poisonous steam. Slimy and dripping, shrunken and mephitic, the creature wobbled drunkenly, dementedly about the floor, only to be bundled up again in the space of a few seconds, this time in the scientist's sacrificed dressing gown, and hurled once more to the fire. And this time, so as to be absolutely sure, David's father put his hands to the hot iron door, holding it firmly shut. He threw all his weight into the job, staying his ground until his fingers and palms, already blistered through contact with Planny's singular juices, blackened and cracked. Only then, and when the pressures from within ceased, did he snatch his steaming, monstrously damaged hands away . . .

It was only in some kind of blurred daze that Professor Lees managed to set the wheels of action in motion from that time onwards. Once the immediate panic had subsided a sort of shocked lethargy crept over him, but in spite of this he cleaned up his unconscious wife's bubbly hands as best he could, and his own— though that proved so painful he almost fainted himself—and then, somehow, he phoned for the doctor and the police.

Then, after another minute or so, still dazed but remembering something of the strange things his wife had screamed before she fainted, David's father went upstairs to look for his son. When he found the boy's room empty he became once more galvanized into frantic activity. He began rushing about the house calling David's name before remembering his son's odd habit of the last month or so—how he would get up early in the morning and go off down to the pool before school.

As he left the house a police car was just pulling up on the drive outside. He shouted out to the two constables, telling them they would find his wife in the house . . . would they look after her? Then, despite the fact that they called out after him for an explanation, he hurried off toward the copse.

At first the policemen were appalled by the loathsome stench issuing undiluted from the house; then, fighting back their nausea, they went in and began doing what they could to improve Mrs. Lees's lot. The doctor arrived only a moment later. He could see instantly what was wrong: there had been some sort of accident with acid. Relieved at the arrival of this sure-handed professional, the bewildered policemen followed the scientist's tracks to the pool.

There they found him sitting at the poolside with his head in his tattily bandaged hands. He had seen the slide on the stone in the pool, and, in a dazed sort of fashion, he had noted the peculiar, flattened *track* in the grass between the house and the copse. And then, being clever, totalling up these fragile facts, he had finally arrived at the impossible solution . . .

It all hinged, of course, on those mad things his wife had screamed before fainting. Now, thinking back on those things, David's father could see the connections. He *remembered* now that there had been a slide missing from his set. He recalled the way in which David had declared the flatworm—the *planarian* worm—on a certain slide to be alive.

Quite suddenly he took one hand from his face and shoved it into his mouth right up to the bandaged knuckles. Just for a moment his eyes opened up very wide, and then he let both his hands fall and turned his face up to the patient policemen.

"God . . . God . . . *God-oh-God!*" he said then. "My wife! She said . . . she said . . ."

"Yes, sir—" one of the officers prompted him, "what did she say?"

Aimlessly the professor got to his feet. "She said that—that it was sitting at the breakfast table—sitting there in David's chair— *and she said it called her Mummy!*"

DAGON'S
BELL

I

DEEP KELP

It strikes me as funny sometimes how scraps of information fragments of seemingly dissociated fact and half-seen or -felt fancies
and intuitions, bits of local legend and immemorial myth, can suddenly connect and expand until the total is far greater than the sum
of the parts, like a jigsaw puzzle. Or perhaps not necessarily *funny*
. . . odd.

Flotsam left high and dry by the tide, scurf of the rolling sea;
a half-obliterated figure glimpsed on an ancient, well-rubbed coin
through the glass of a museum's showcase; old-wives' tales of hauntings and hoary nights, and the ringing of some sepulchral, sunken
bell at the rising of the tide; the strange speculations of sea-coal
gatherers supping their ale in old North-East pubs, where the sound
of the ocean's wash is never far distant beyond smoke-yellowed
bull's-eye windowpanes. Items like that, apparently unconnected.

But in the end there was really much more to it than that. For
these things were only the *pieces* of the puzzle; the picture, complete,
was vaster far than its component parts. Indeed cosmic . . .

I long ago promised myself that I would never again speak or even think of David Parker and the occurrences of that night at Kettlethorpe Farm (which formed, in any case, a tale almost too grotesque for belief), but now, these years later . . . well, my promise seems rather redundant. On the other hand it is possible that a valuable warning lies inherent in what I have to say, for which reason, despite the unlikely circumstance that I shall be taken at all seriously, I now put pen to paper.

My name is William Trafford, which hardly matters, but I had known David Parker at school—a Secondary Modern in a colliery village by the sea—before he passed his college examinations, and I was the one who would later share with him Kettlethorpe's terrible secret.

In fact I had known David well: the son of a miner, he was never typical of his colliery contemporaries but gentle in his ways and lacking the coarseness of the locality and its guttural accents. That is not to belittle the North-Easterner in general (after all, I became one myself!), for in all truth they are the salt of the earth, but the nature of their work, and what that work has gradually made of their environment, has molded them into a hard and clannish lot. David Parker, by his nature, was not of that clan, that is all, and neither was I at that time.

My parents were Yorkshire born and bred, only moving to Harden in County Durham when my father bought a newsagent's shop there. Hence the friendship that sprang up between us, born not so much out of straightforward compatibility as of the fact that we both felt outsiders. A friendship which lasted for five years from a time when we were both eight years of age, and which was only renewed upon David's release from his studies in London twelve years later. That was in 1951.

Meanwhile, in the years flown between . . .

My father was now dead and my mother more or less confined, and I had expanded the business to two more shops in Hartlepool, both of them under steady and industrious managers, and several smaller but growing concerns much removed from the sale of magazines and newspapers in the local colliery villages. Thus my time was mainly taken up with business matters, but in the highest capacity, which hardly consisted of backbreaking work. What time remained I was pleased to spend, on those occasions when he was available, in the company of my old school friend.

And he too had done well, and would do even better. His studies had been in architecture and design, but within two short years of his return he expanded these spheres to include interior decoration and landscape gardening, setting up a profitable business of his own and building himself an enviable reputation in his fields.

And so it can be seen that the war had been kind to both of us. Too young to have been involved, we had made capital while the world was fighting; now while the world licked its wounds and rediscovered its directions, we were already on course and beginning to ride the crest. Mercenary? No, for we had been mere boys when the war started and were little more than boys when it ended.

But now, eight years later . . . We were, or saw ourselves as being, very nearly sophisticates in a mainly unsophisticated society, that is to say part of a very narrow spectrum, and so once more felt drawn together. Even so, we made odd companions. At least externally, superficially. Oh, I suppose our characters, drives, and ambitions were similar, but physically we were poles apart. David was dark, handsome, and well proportioned; I was sort of dumpy, sandy, pale to the point of being pallid. I was not unhealthy, but set beside David Parker I certainly looked it!

On the day in question, that is to say the day when the first unconnected fragment presented itself—a Friday in September '53, it was, just a few days before the Feast of the Exaltation, sometimes called Roodmas in those parts, and occasionally by a far older name—we met in a bar overlooking the sea on old Hartlepool's headland. On those occasions when we got together like this we would normally try to keep business out of the conversation, but there were times when it seemed to intrude almost of necessity. This was one such.

I had not noticed Jackie Foster standing at the bar upon entering, but certainly he had seen me. Foster was a foreman with a small fleet of sea-coal–gathering trucks of which I was co-owner, and he should not have been there in the pub at that time but out and about his work. Possibly he considered it prudent to come over and explain his presence, just in case I *had* seen him, and he did so in a single word.

"Kelp?" David repeated, looking puzzled, so that I felt compelled to explain.

"Seaweed," I said. "Following a bad blow, it comes up on the beach in thick drifts. But—" and I looked at Foster pointedly, "I've never before known it to stop the sea-coalers."

The man shuffled uncomfortably for a moment, took off his cap, and scratched his head. "Oh, once or twice ah've known it almost this bad, but before your time in the game. It slimes up the rocks an' the wheels of the lorries slip in the stuff. Bloody arful! An' stinks like death. It's lying' feet thick on arl the beaches from here ta Sunderland!"

"Kelp," David said again, thoughtfully. "Isn't that the weed people used to gather up and cook into a soup?"

Foster wrinkled his nose. "Hungry folks'll eat just about owt, ah suppose, Mr. Parker, but they'd not eat this muck. We carl it 'deep kelp.' It's not unusual this time of year—Roodmas time or thereabouts—and generally hangs about for a week or so until the tides clear it or it rots away."

David continued to look interested and Foster continued: "Funny stuff. Ah mean, you'll not find it in any book of seaweeds—not that ah've ever seen. As a lad ah was daft on nature an' arl. Collected birds' eggs, took spore prints of mushrooms an' toadstools, pressed leaves an' flowers in books—arl that daft stuff—but

in arl the books ah read ah never did find a mention of deep kelp."
He turned back to me. "Anyway, boss, there's enough of the stuff
on the beach ta keep the lorries off. It's not that they canna get
onto the sands, but when they do they canna see the coal for weed.
So ah've sent the lorries south ta Seaton Carew. The beach is pretty
clear down there, ah'm told. Not much coal, but better than nowt."

My friend and I had almost finished eating by then. As Foster
made to leave, I suggested to David: "Let's finish our drinks, climb
down the old seawall, and have a look."

"Right!" David agreed at once. "I'm curious about this stuff."
Foster had heard and he turned back to us, shaking his head con-
cernedly. "It's up ta you, gents," he said, "but you won't like it.
Stinks man! *Arful!* There's kids who play on the beach arl the live-
long day, but you'll not find them there now. Just the bloody weed,
lyin' there an' turnin' ta rot!"

II

A WEDDING AND A WARNING

In any event, we went to see for ourselves, and if I had doubted
Foster, then I had wronged him. The stuff *was* awful, and it *did*
stink. I had seen it before, always at this time of year, but never in
such quantities. There had been a bit of a blow the night before,
however, and that probably explained it. To my mind, anyway. David's mind was a fraction more inquiring.

"Deep kelp," he murmured, standing on the weed-strewn rocks,
his hair blowing in a salty, stenchy breeze off the sea. "I don't see
it at all."

"What don't you see?"

"Well, if this stuff comes from the deeps—I mean from really
deep down—surely it would take a real upheaval to drive it onto

the beaches like this. Why, there must be thousands and thousands of tons of the stuff! All the way from here to Sunderland? Twenty miles of it?"

I shrugged. "It'll clear, just like Foster said. A day or two, that's all. And he's right: with this stuff lying so thick, you can't see the streaks of coal."

"How about the coal?" he said, his mind again grasping after knowledge. "I mean, where does it come from?"

"Same place as the weed," I answered. "Most of it. Come and see." I crossed to a narrow strip of sand between waves of deep kelp. There I found and picked up a pair of blocky, fist-sized lumps of ocean-rounded rock. Knocking them together, I broke off fragments. Inside, one rock showed a greyish-brown uniformity; the other was black and shiny, finely layered, pure coal.

"I wouldn't have known the difference," David admitted.

"Neither would I!" I grinned. "But the sea-coalers rarely err. They say there's an open seam way out there," I nodded toward the open sea. "Not unlikely, seeing as how this entire county is riddled with rich mines. Myself, I believe a lot of the coal simply gets washed out of the tippings, the stony debris rejected at the screens. Coal is light and easily washed ashore. The stones are heavy and roll out— downhill, as it were—into deeper water."

"In that case it seems a pity," said David. "—That the coal can't be gathered, I mean."

"Oh?"

"Why, yes. Surely, if there is an open seam in the sea, the coal would get washed ashore with the kelp. Underneath this stuff, there's probably tons of it just waiting to be shovelled up!"

I frowned and answered: "You could well be right . . ." But then I shrugged. "Ah, well, not to worry. It'll still be there after the weed has gone." And I winked at him. "Coal doesn't rot, you see?"

He wasn't listening but kneeling, lifting a rope of the offensive stuff in his hands. It was heavy, leprous white in the stem or body, deep dark green in the leaf. Hybrid, the flesh of the stuff was—well, fleshy—more animal than vegetable. Bladders were present every-where, large as a man's thumbs. David popped one and gave a disgusted grunt, then came to his feet.

"God!" he exclaimed, holding his nose. And again: "*God!*"

I laughed and we picked our way back to the steps in the old sea wall.

And that was that: a fragment, an incident unconnected with anything much. An item of little real interest. One of Nature's pe-riodic quirks, affecting nothing a great deal. Apparently . . .

It seemed not long after the time of the deep kelp that David got tied up with his wedding plans. I had known, of course, that he had a girl—June Anderson, a solicitor's daughter from Sunderland, which boasts the prettiest girls in all the land—for I had met her and found her utterly charming, but I had not realized that things were so advanced.

I say it did not seem a long time, and now looking back I see that the period was indeed quite short—the very next summer. Perhaps the span of time was foreshortened even more for me by the suddenness with which their plans culminated. For all was brought dramatically forward by the curious and unexpected va-cancy of Kettlethorpe Farm, an extensive property on the edge of Kettlethorpe Dene.

No longer a farm proper but a forlorn relic of another age, the great stone house and its out-buildings were badly in need of repair, but in David's eyes the place had an Olde Worlde magic all its own, and with his expertise he knew that he could soon convert it into a modern home of great beauty and value. And the place was going remarkably cheap.

As to the farm's previous tenant: here something peculiar. And here too the second link in my seemingly unconnected chain of occurrences and circumstances.

Old Jason Carpenter had not been well liked in the locality, in fact not at all. Grey-bearded, taciturn, cold, and reclusive—with eyes grey as the rolling North Sea and never a smile for man or beast— he had occupied Kettlethorpe Farm for close on thirty years. Never a wife, a manservant, or maid, not even a neighbour had entered the place on old Jason's invitation. No one strayed onto the grounds for fear of Jason's dog and shotgun; even tradesmen were wary on those rare occasions when they had to make deliveries.

But Carpenter had liked his beer and rum chaser, and twice a week would visit The Trust Hotel in Harden. There he had used to sit in the smoke room and linger over his tipple, his dog Bones alert under the table and between his master's feet. And customers had used to fear Bones a little, but not as much as the dog feared his master.

And now Jason Carpenter was gone. Note that I do not say dead, simply gone, disappeared. There was no evidence to support any other conclusion—not at that time.

It had happened like this: over a period of several months various tradesmen had reported Jason's absence from Kettlethorpe, and eventually, because his customary seat at The Trust had been vacant over that same period, members of the local police went to the farm and forced entry into the main building. No trace had been found of the old hermit, but the police had come away instead with certain documents—chiefly a will, of sorts—which had evidently been left pending just such a search or investigation.

In the documents the recluse had directed that in the event of his "termination of occupancy," the house, attendant buildings, and grounds "be allowed to relapse into the dirt and decay from which they sprang," but since it was later shown that he was in considerable debt, the property had been put up for sale to settle his various accounts. The house had in fact been under threat of the bailiffs.

All of this, of course, had taken some considerable time, during which a thorough search of the rambling house, its outbuildings, and grounds had been made for obvious reasons. But to no avail.

Jason Carpenter was gone. He had not been known to have relatives; indeed, very little had been known of him at all—it was almost as if he had never been. And to many of the people of Harden, that made for a most satisfactory epitaph.

One other note: it would seem that his "termination of occupancy" had come about during the Roodmas time of the deep kelp . . .

And so to the wedding of David Parker and June Anderson, a sparkling affair held at the Catholic Church in Harden, where not even the drab, near-distant background of the colliery's chimneys and cooling towers should have been able to dampen the gaiety and excitement of the moment. And yet even here, in the steep, crowd-packed streets outside the church, a note of discord. Just one, but one too many.

For as the cheering commenced and the couple left the church to be showered with confetti and jostled to their car, I overheard as if they were spoken directly into my ear—or uttered especially for my notice—the words of a crone in shawl and pinafore, come out of her smoke-grimed miner's terraced house to shake her head and mutter: "Aye, an' he'll take that bonnie lass ta Kettlethorpe, will he? Arl the bells are ringin' now, it's true, but what about the *other* bell, eh? It's only rung once or twice arl these lang years—since old Jason had the house—but now there's word it's ringin' again, when nights are dark an' the sea has a swell ta it."

I heard it as clearly as that, for I was one of the spectators. I would have been more closely linked with the celebrations but had expected to be busy, and only by the skin of my teeth managed to be there at all. But when I heard the guttural imprecation of the old lady I turned to seek her out, even caught a glimpse of her, before being engulfed by a horde of Harden urchins leaping for a handful of hurled pennies, threepenny bits, and sixpences as the newlyweds' car drove off.

By which time summer thunderclouds had gathered, breaking at the command of a distant flash of lightning, and rain had begun to pelt down. Which served to put an end to the matter. The crowd rapidly dispersed and I headed for shelter.

But . . . I would have liked to know what the old woman had meant . . .

III

GHOST STORY

"Haunted?" I echoed David's words.

I had bumped into him at the library in Hartlepool some three weeks after his wedding. A voracious reader, an "addict" for hard-boiled detective novels, I had been on my way in as he was coming out.

"Haunted, yes!" he repeated, his voice half-amused, half-excited. "The old farm—haunted!"

The alarm his words conjured in me was almost immediately relieved by his grin and wide-awake expression. Whatever ghosts they were at the farm, he obviously didn't fear them. Was he having a little joke at my expense? I grinned with him, saying: "Well, I shouldn't care to have been your ghosts. Not for the last thirty years, at any rate. Not with old man Carpenter about the place. That would be a classic case of the biter bit!"

"Old Jason Carpenter," he reminded me, smiling still but less brilliantly, "has disappeared, remember?"

"Oh!" I said, feeling a little foolish. "Of course he has." And I followed up quickly with: "But what do you mean, haunted?"

"Local village legend," he shrugged. "I heard it from Father Nicholls, who married us. He had it from the priest before him, and so on. Handed down for centuries, so to speak. I wouldn't have known if he hadn't stopped me and asked how we were getting on up at the farm. If we'd seen anything—you know—odd? He wouldn't have said anything more but I pressed him."

"And?"

"Well, it seems the original owners were something of a fishy bunch."

"Fishy?"

"Quite literally! I mean, they *looked* fishy. Or maybe froggy? Protuberant lips, wide-mouthed, scaly-skinned, pop-eyed—you name it. To use Father Nicholls's own expression, 'ichthyic.' "

"Slow down," I told him, seeing his excitement rising up again. "First of all, what do you mean by the 'original' owners? The people who built the place?"

"Good heavens, no!" he chuckled, and then he took me by the elbow and guided me into the library and to a table. We sat. "No one knows—no one can remember—who actually built the place. If ever there were records, well, they're long lost. God, it probably dates back to Roman times! It's likely as old as the Wall itself—even older. Certainly it has been a landmark on maps for the last four hundred and fifty years. No, I mean the first *recorded* family to live there. Which was something like two and a half centuries ago."

"And they were—" I couldn't help frowning "—odd-looking, these people?"

"Right! And odd not only in their looks. That was probably just a case of recessive genes, the result of indiscriminate inbreeding.

Anyway, the locals shunned them—not that there were any real 'locals' in those days, you understand. I mean, the closest villages or towns then were Hartlepool, Sunderland, Durham, and Seaham Harbour. Maybe a handful of other, smaller places—I haven't checked. But this country was wild! And it stayed that way, more or less, until the modern roads were built. Then came the railways, to service the pits, and so on."

I nodded, becoming involved with David's enthusiasm, finding myself carried along by it. "And the people at the farm stayed there down the generations?"

"Not quite," he answered. "Apparently there was something of a hiatus in their tenancy around a hundred and fifty years ago, but later, about the time of the American Civil War, a family came over from Innsmouth in New England and bought the place up. They, too, had the degenerate looks of earlier tenants; might even have been an offshoot of the same family, returning to their ancestral home, as it were. They made a living farming and fishing. Fairly industrious, it would seem, but surly and clannish. Name of Waite. By then, though, the 'ghosts' were well established in local folklore. *They* came in two manifestations, apparently."

"Oh?"

He nodded. "One of them was a gigantic, wraithlike, nebulous figure rising from the mists over Kettlethorpe Dene, seen by travellers on the old coach road or by fishermen returning to Harden along the cliff-top paths. But the interesting thing is this: if you look at a map of the district, as I've done, you'll see that the farm lies in something of a depression directly between the coach road and the cliffs. Anything seen from those vantage points could conceivably be emanating from the farm itself!"

I was again beginning to find the nature of David's discourse disturbing. Or if not what he was saying, his obvious *involvement* with the concept. "You seem to have gone over all of this rather thoroughly," I remarked. "Any special reason?"

"Just my old thirst for knowledge," he grinned. "You know I'm never happy unless I'm tracking something down—and never happier than when I've finally got it cornered. And after all, I do live at the place! Anyway, about the giant mist-figure: according to the legends, it was half-fish, half-man!"

"A merman?"

"Yes. And now—" He triumphantly took out a folded sheet of rubbing parchment and opened it out onto the table. "*Ta-rah!* And what do you make of that?"

The impression on the paper was perhaps nine inches square, a charcoal rubbing taken from a brass of some sort, I correctly imagined. It showed a mainly anthropomorphic male figure seated upon a rock-carved chair or throne, his lower half obscured by draperies of weed bearing striking resemblance to the deep kelp. The eyes of the figure were large and somewhat protuberant; his forehead sloped; his skin had the overlapping scales of a fish, and the fingers of his one visible hand where it grasped a short trident were webbed. The background was vague, reminding me of nothing so much as cyclopean submarine ruins.

"Neptune," I said. "Or at any rate, a merman. Where did you get it?"

"I rubbed it up myself," he said, carefully folding the sheet and replacing it in his pocket. "It's from a plate on a lintel over a door in one of the outbuildings at Kettlethorpe." And then for the first time he frowned. "Fishy people and a fishy symbol . . ."

He stared at me strangely for a moment and I felt a sudden chill in my bones—until his grin came back and he added: "And an entirely fishy story, eh?"

We left the library and I walked with him to his car. "And what's your real interest in all of this?" I asked. "I mean, I don't remember you as much of a folklorist?"

His look this time was curious, almost evasive. "You just won't believe that it's only this old inquiring mind of mine, will you?" But then his grin came back, bright and infectious as ever.

He got into his car, wound down the window and poked his head out. "Will we be seeing you soon? Isn't it time you paid us a visit?"

"Is that an invitation?"

He started up the car. "Of course—any time."

"Then I'll make it soon," I promised.

"Sooner!" he said.

Then I remembered something he had said. "David, you mentioned two manifestations of this—this ghostliness. What was the other one?"

"Eh?" he frowned at me, winding up his window. Then he stopped winding. "Oh, that. The bell, you mean . . ."

"Bell?" I echoed him, the skin of my neck suddenly tingling. "What bell?"

"A ghost bell!" he yelled as he pulled away from the kerb. "What else? It tolls underground or under the sea, usually when there's a mist or a swell on the ocean. I keep listening for it, but—"

"No luck?" I asked automatically, hearing my own voice almost as that of a stranger.

"Not yet."

And as he grinned one last time and waved a farewell, pulling away down the street, against all commonsense and logic I found myself remembering the old woman's words outside the church: "What about the *other* bell, eh?"

What about the other bell, indeed . . .

IV

"MIASMA"

Half-way back to Harden it dawned on me that I had not chosen a book for myself. My mind was still full of David Parker's discoveries, about which, where he had displayed that curious excitement, I still experienced only a niggling disquiet.

But back at Harden, where my home stands on a hill at the southern extreme of the village, I remembered where once before I had seen something like the figure on David's rubbing. And sure enough it was there in my antique, illustrated two-volume family Bible, pages I had not looked into for many a year, which had become merely ornamental on my bookshelves.

The item I refer to was simply one of the many small illustrations in Judges XIII: a drawing of a piscine deity on a Philistine coin or medallion. Dagon, whose temple Samson toppled at Gaza. Dagon . . .

With my memory awakened, it suddenly came to me where I had seen one other representation of this same god. Sunderland has a fine museum and my father had often taken me there when I was small. Amongst the museum's collection of coins and medals I had seen . . .

"Dagon?" the curator answered my telephone inquiry with interest. "No, I'm afraid we have very little of the Philistines; no coins that I know of. Possibly it was a little later than that. Can I call you back?"

"Please do, and I'm sorry to be taking up your time like this."

"Not at all, a pleasure. That's what we're here for."

And ten minutes later he was back. "As I suspected, Mr. Trafford. We do have that coin you remembered, but it's Phoenician, not Philistine. The Phoenicians adopted Dagon from the Philistines and called him Oannes. That's a pattern that repeats all through history. The Romans in particular were great thieves of other people's gods. Sometimes they adopted them openly, as with Zeus becoming Jupiter, but at other times—where the deity was especially dark or ominous, as in Summanus—they were rather more covert in their worship. Great cultists, the Romans. You'd be surprised at how many secret societies and cults came down the ages from sources such as these. But . . . there I go again . . . lecturing!"

"Not at all," I assured him. "That's all very interesting. And thank you very much for your time."

"And is that it? There's no other way in which I can assist?"

"No, that's it. Thank you again."

And indeed that seemed to be that. . . .

I went to see them a fortnight later. Old Jason Carpenter had not had a telephone, and David was still in the process of having one installed, which meant that I must literally drop in on them.

Kettlethorpe lies to the north of Harden, between the modern coast road and the sea, and the view of the dene as the track dipped down from the road and wound toward the old farm was breathtaking. Under a blue sky, with seagulls wheeling and crying over a distant, fresh-ploughed field, and the hedgerows thick with honeysuckle and the droning of bees, and sweet smells of decay from the streams and hazelnut-shaded pools, the scene was very nearly idyllic. A far cry from midnight tales of ghouls and ghosties!

Then to the farm's stone outer wall—almost a fortification, reminiscent of some forbidding feudal structure—which encompassed all of the buildings including the main house. Iron gates were open, bearing the legend "Kettlethorpe" in stark letters of iron. Inside . . . things already were changing.

The wall surrounded something like three and a half to four acres of ground, being the actual core of the property. I had seen several rotting "Private Property" and "Trespassers Will Be Prosecuted" notices along the road, defining Kettlethorpe's exterior boundaries, but the area bordered by the wall was the very heart of the place.

In layout, there was a sort of geometrical regularity to the spacing and positioning of the buildings. They formed a horseshoe, with the main house at its apex; the open mouth of the horseshoe faced the sea, unseen, something like a mile away beyond a rise which boasted a dense-grown stand of oaks. All of the buildings were of local stone, easily recognizable through its tough, flinty-grey texture. I am no geologist and so could not give that stone a name, but I knew that in years past it had been blasted from local quarries or cut from outcrops. To my knowledge, however, the closest of these sources was a good many miles away; the actual building of Kettlethorpe must therefore have been a Herculean task.

As this thought crossed my mind, and remembering the words of the curator of Sunderland's museum, I had to smile. Perhaps not Herculean but something later than the Greeks. Except that I couldn't recall a specific Roman strongman!

And approaching the house, where I pulled up before the stone columns of its portico, I believed I could see where David had got his idea of the age of the place. Under the heat of the sun the house was redolent of the centuries; its walls massive, structurally Romanesque. The roof, especially, low-peaked and broad, giving an impression of strength and endurance.

What with its outer wall and horseshoe design, the place might well be some strange old Roman temple. A temple, yes, but wavery for all its massiveness, shimmering as smoke and heat from a small bonfire in what had been a garden drifted lazily across my field of vision. A temple—ah!—but to what strange old god?

And no need to ponder the source of *that* thought, for certainly the business of David's antiquarian research was still in my head; and while I had no intention of bringing that subject up, still I wondered how far he had progressed. Or perhaps by now he had discovered sufficient of Kettlethorpe to satisfy his curiosity. Perhaps, but I doubted it. No, he would follow the very devil to hell, that one, in pursuit of knowledge.

"Hello, there!" He slapped me on the back, causing me to start as I got out of my old Morris and closed its door. I started . . . reeled . . .

He had come out of the shadows of the porch so quickly . . . I had not seen him . . . My eyes . . . the heat and the glaring sun and the drone of bees . . .

"*Bill!*" David's voice came to me from a million miles away, full of concern. "What on earth . . . ?"

"I've come over queer," I heard myself say, leaning on my car as the world rocked about me.

"Queer? Man, you're pale as death! It's the bloody sun! Too hot by far. And the smoke from the fire. And I'll bet you've been driving with your windows up. Here, let's get you into the house."

Hanging onto his broad shoulder, I was happy to let him lead me staggering indoors. "The hot sun," he mumbled again, half to me, half to himself. "And the honeysuckle. Almost a miasma. Nauseating, until you get used to it. June has suffered in exactly the same way."

V

THE ENCLOSURE

"Miasma?" I let myself fall into a cool, shady window seat.

He nodded, swimming into focus as I quickly recovered from my attack of—of whatever it had been. "Yes, a mist of pollen, invisible, borne on thermals in the air, sweet and cloying. Enough to choke a horse!"

"Is that what it was? God!—I thought I was going to faint."

"I know what you mean. June has been like it for a week. Conks out completely at high noon. Even inside it's too close for her liking. She gets listless. She's upstairs now, stretched out flat!"

As if the very mention of her name were a summons, June's voice came down to us: "David, is that Bill? I'll be down at once."

"Don't trouble yourself on my account," I called out, my voice still a little shaky. "And certainly not if you don't feel too well."

"I'm fine!" her voice insisted. "I was just a little tired, that's all."

I was myself again, gratefully accepting a scotch and soda, swilling a parched dryness from my mouth and throat.

"There," said David, seeming to read my thoughts. "You look more your old self now."

"First time that ever happened to me," I told him. "I suppose your 'miasma' theory must be correct. Anyway, I'll be up on my feet again in a minute." As I spoke I let my eyes wander about the interior of what would be the house's main living room.

The room was large, for the most part oak-panelled, almost stripped of its old furniture and looking extremely austere. I recalled the bonfire, its pale flames licking at the upthrusting, worm-eaten leg of a chair. . . .

One wall was of the original hard stone, polished by the years, creating an effect normally thought desirable in modern homes but perfectly natural here and in no way contrived. All in all a charming room. Ages-blackened beams bowed almost imperceptibly toward the centre, where they crossed the low ceiling wall to wall.

"Built to last," said David. "Three hundred years old at least, those beams, but the basic structure is—" he shrugged "—I'm not sure, not yet. This is one of five lower rooms, all about the same size. I've cleared most of them out now, burnt up most of the old furniture, but there were one or two pieces worth renovation. Most of the stuff I've saved is in what used to be old man Carpenter's study. And the place is—will be—beautiful. When I'm through with it. Gloomy at the moment, yes, but that's because of the windows.

I'm afraid most of these old small-panes will have to go. The place needs opening up."

"Opening up, yes," I repeated him, sensing a vague irritation or tension in him, a sort of urgency.

"Here," he said, "are you feeling all right now? I'd like you to see the plate I took that rubbing from."

"The Dagon plate," I said at once, biting my tongue a moment too late.

He looked at me, stared at me, and slowly smiled. "So you looked it up, did you? Dagon, yes—or Neptune, as the Romans called him. Come on, I'll show you." And as we left the house he yelled back over his shoulder: "June, we're just going over to the enclosure. Back soon."

"Enclosure?" I followed him toward the mouth of the horseshoe of buildings. "I thought you said the brass was on a lintel?"

"So it is, over a doorway, but the building has no roof and so I call it an enclosure. See?" and he pointed. The mouth of the horseshoe was formed by a pair of small, rough stone buildings set perhaps twenty-five yards apart, which were identical in design but for the one main discrepancy David had mentioned, namely that the one on the left had no roof.

"Perhaps it fell in?" I suggested as we approached the structure. David shook his head. "No," he said, "there never was a roof. Look at the tops of the walls. They're flush. No gaps to show where roof support beams might have been positioned. If you make a comparison with the other building you'll see what I mean. Anyway, whatever its original purpose, old man Carpenter filled it with junk: bags of rusty old nails, worn-out tools, that sort of thing. Oh, yes and he kept his firewood here, under a tarpaulin."

I glanced inside the place, leaning against the wall and poking my head in through the vacant doorway. The wall stood in its own shadow and was cold to my touch. Beams of sunlight, glancing in over the top of the west wall, filled the place with dust motes that drifted like swarms of aimless microbes in the strangely musty air. There was a mixed smell of rust and rot, of some small dead thing, and of . . . the sea? The last could only be a passing fancy, no sooner imagined than forgotten.

I shaded my eyes against the dusty sunbeams. Rotted sacks spilled nails and bolts upon a stone-flagged floor; farming implements red with rust were heaped like metal skeletons against one wall; at the back, heavy blocks of wood stuck out from beneath a mold-spotted tarpaulin. A dead rat or squirrel close to my feet seethed with maggots.

I blinked in the hazy light, shuddered—not so much at the sight of the small corpse as at a sudden chill of the psyche—and hastily withdrew my head.

"There you are," said David, his matter-of-fact tone bringing me back down to earth. "The brass."

Above our heads, central in the stone lintel, a square plate bore the original of David's rubbing. I gave it a glance, an almost involuntary reaction to David's invitation that I look, and at once looked away. He frowned, seemed disappointed. "You don't find it interesting?"

"I find it . . . disturbing," I answered at length. "Can we go back to the house? I'm sure June will be up and about by now."

He shrugged, leading the way as we retraced our steps along sun-splashed, weed-grown paths between scrubby fruit trees and dusty, cobwebbed shrubbery. "I thought you'd be taken by it," he said. And, "How do you mean, 'disturbing?' "

I shook my head, had no answer for him. "Maybe it's just me," I finally said. "I don't feel at my best today. I'm not up to it, that's all."

"Not up to what?" he asked sharply, then shrugged again before I could answer. "Suit yourself." But after that he quickly became distant and a little surly. He wasn't normally a moody man, but I knew him well enough to realize that I had touched upon some previously unsuspected, exposed nerve, and so I determined not to prolong my visit.

I did stay long enough to talk to June, however, though what I saw of her was hardly reassuring. She looked pinched, her face lined and pale, showing none of the rosiness one might expect in a newly-wed, or in any healthy young woman in summertime. Her eyes were red-rimmed, their natural blue seeming very much watered-down; her skin looked dry, deprived of moisture; even her hair, glossy black and bouncy on those previous occasions when we had met, seemed lacklustre now and disinterested.

It could be, of course, simply the fact that I had caught her at a bad time. Her father had died recently, as I later discovered, and of course that must still be affecting her. Also, she must have been working very hard, alongside David, trying to get the old place put to rights. Or again it could be David's summer "miasma"—an allergy, perhaps.

Perhaps . . .

But why any of these things—David's preoccupation, his near-obsession (or mine?) with occurrences and relics of the distant past; the old myths and legends of the region, of hauntings and misty phantoms and such; and June's queer malaise—why any of these things should concern me beyond the bounds of common friendship I did not know, could not say. I only knew that I felt as if somewhere a great wheel had started to roll, and that my friend and his wife lay directly in its path, not even knowing that it bore down upon them . . .

VI

DAGON'S BELL

Summer rolled by in warm lazy waves; autumn saw the trees shamelessly, mindlessly stripping themselves naked (one would think they'd keep their leaves to warm them through the winter). My businesses presented periodic problems enough to keep my nose to the grindstone, and so there was little spare time in which to ponder the strangeness of the last twelve months. I saw David in the village now and then, usually at a distance; saw June, too, but much less frequently. More often than not he seemed haggard—or if not haggard, hagridden, nervous, agitated, *hurried*—and she was . . . well, spectral. Pale and willow-slim, and red-eyed (I suspected) behind dark spectacles. Married life? Or perhaps some other problem? None of my business.

Then came the time of the deep kelp once more, which was when David made it my business.

And here I must ask the reader to bear with me. The following part of the story will seem hastily written, too thoughtlessly prepared and put together. But this is how I remember it: blurred and unreal, and patterned with mismatched dialogue. It *happened* quickly; I see no reason to spin it out . . .

David's knock was urgent on a night when the sky was black with falling rain and the wind whipped the trees to a frenzy, and yet he stood there in shirt sleeves, shivering, gaunt in aspect and almost vacant in expression. It took several brandies and a thorough rubdown with a warm towel to bring him to a semblance of his old self, by which time he seemed more ashamed of his behaviour than eager to explain it. But I was not letting him off that lightly. The time had come, I decided, to have the thing out with him; get it out in the open, whatever it was, and see what could be done about it while there was yet time.

"Time?" he finally turned his gaze upon me from beneath his mop of tousled hair, a towel over his shoulders while his shirt steamed before my open fire. "*Is* there yet time? Damned if I know . . ." He shook his head.

"Well then, *tell* me," I said, exasperated. "Or at least try. Start somewhere. You must have come to me for something. Is it you and June? Was your getting married a mistake? Or is it just the place, the old farm?"

"Oh, come on, Bill!" he snorted. "You know well enough what it is. Something of it, anyway. You experienced it yourself. Just the place?" The corners of his mouth turned down, his expression souring. "Oh, yes, it's the place, all right. What the place was, what it might be even now . . ."

"Go on," I prompted him, and he launched into the following:

"I came to ask you to come back with me. I don't want to spend another night alone there."

"Alone? But isn't June there?"

He looked at me for a moment and finally managed a ghastly grin. "She is and she isn't," he said. "Oh, yes, yes, she's there—but still I'm alone. Not her fault, poor love. It's that bloody awful place!"

"Tell me about it," I urged.

He sighed, bit his lip, and after a moment: "I think," he began, "—I think it was a temple. And I don't think the Romans had it first. You know, of course, that they've found Phoenician symbols on some of the stones at Stonehenge? Well, and what else did the ancients bring with them to old England, eh? What did we worship in those prehistoric times? The earth-mother, the sun, the rain— the sea? We're an island, Bill. The sea was everywhere around us! And it was bountiful. It still is, but not like it was in those days. What more natural than to worship the sea—and what the sea brought?"

"Its bounty?" I said.

"That, yes, and something else. Cthulhu, Pischa, the Kraken, Dagon, Oannes, Neptune. Call him—it—what you will. But it was worshipped at Kettlethorpe, and it still remembers. Yes, and I think it comes, in certain seasons, to seek the worship it once knew and perhaps still . . . still . . ."

"Yes?"

He looked quickly away. "I've made . . . discoveries."

I waited.

"I've found things out, yes, yes—and—" His eyes flared up for a moment in the firelight, then dulled.

"And?"

"*Damn it!*" He turned on me and the towel fell from his shoulders. Quickly he snatched it up and covered himself—but not before I had seen how thin mere months had made him. "Damn it!" he mumbled again, less vehemently now. "Must you repeat everything I say? God, I do enough of that myself! I go over everything—over and over and over . . ."

I sat in silence, waiting. He would tell it in his own time.

And eventually he continued. "I've made discoveries, and I've heard . . . things." He looked from the fire to me, peered at me, ran trembling fingers through his hair. And did I detect streaks of grey in that once jet mop? "I've heard the bell!"

"Then it's time you got out of there!" I said at once. "Time you got June out, too."

"I know, I *know!*" he answered, his expression tortured. He gripped my arm. "But I'm not finished yet. I don't know it all, not yet. It lures me, Bill. I have to know . . ."

"Know what?" It was my turn to show my agitation. "What do you need to know, you fool? Isn't it enough that the place is evil? You know *that* much. And yet you stay on there. Get out, that's my advice. Get out now!"

"*No!*" His denial was emphatic. "I'm not finished. There has to be an end to it. The place must be cleansed." He stared again into the fire.

"So you do admit it's evil?"

"Of course it is. Yes, I know it is. But leave, get out? I can't, and June—"

"Yes?"

"She *won't!*" He gave a muffled sob and turned watery, searching eyes full upon me. "The place is like . . . like a magnet! It has a genius loci. It's a focal point for God-only-knows-what forces. Evil? Oh, yes! An evil come down all the centuries. But I bought the place and I shall cleanse it—end it forever, whatever it is."

"Look," I tried reasoning with him, "let's go back, now, the two of us. Let's get June out of there and bring her back here for the night. How did you get here anyway? Surely not on foot, not on a night like this?"

"No, no," he shook his head. "Car broke down halfway up the hill. Rain must have got under the bonnet. I'll pick it up tomorrow." He stood up, looked suddenly afraid, wild-eyed. "I've been away too long. Bill, will you run me back? June's there—alone! She was sleeping when I left. I can fill you in on the details while you drive."

VII

MANIFESTATION

I made him take another brandy, threw a coat over his shoulders, bustled him out to my car. Moments later we were rolling down into Harden and he was telling me all that had happened between times. As best I remember, this is what he said:

"Since that day you visited us I've been hard at work. Real work, I mean. Not the other thing, not delving—not all of the time, anyway. I got the grounds inside the walls tidied up, even tried a little preliminary landscaping. And the house: the old windows out, new ones in. Plenty of light. But still the place was musty. As the summer turned I began burning old Carpenter's wood, drying out the house, ridding it of the odour of centuries—a smell that was always thicker at night. And fresh paint, too, lots of it. Mainly white, all bright and new. June picked up a lot; you must have noticed how down she was? Yes, well, she seemed to be on the mend. I thought I had the—the 'miasma' on the run. *Hah!*" He gave a bitter snort. "A 'summer miasma,' I called it. Blind, blind!"

"Go on," I urged him, driving carefully through the wet streets.

"Eventually, to give myself room to sort out the furniture and so on, I got round to chucking the old shelves and books out of Carpenter's study. That would have been okay, but . . . I looked into some of those books. That was an error. I should have simply burned the lot, along with the wormy old chairs and shreds of carpet. And yet, in a way, I'm glad I didn't." I could feel David's fevered eyes burning me in the car's dark interior, fixed upon me as he spoke.

"The *knowledge* in those books, Bill. The dark secrets, the damnable mysteries. You know, if anyone does, what a fool I am for a mystery. I was hooked; work ceased. I had to know! But those books and manuscripts: the *Unter-Zee Kulten* and *Hydrophinnae*. Doorfen's treatise on submarine civilizations and the *Johansen Narrative* of 1925. A great sheaf of notes purporting to be from American government files for 1928, when federal agents 'raided' Innsmouth, a decaying, horror-haunted town on the coast of New England; and other scraps and fragments from all the world's mythologies, all of them concerned with the worship of a great god of the sea."

"Innsmouth?" My ears pricked up. I had heard that name mentioned once before. "But isn't that the place—?"

"The place which spawned that family, the Waites, who came over and settled at Kettlethorpe about the time of the American

Civil War? That's right," he nodded an affirmative, stared out into the rain-black night. "And old Carpenter who had the house for thirty years, he came from Innsmouth, too!"

"He was of the same people?"

"No, not him. The very opposite. He was at the farm for the same reason I am—now. Oh, he was strange, reclusive—who wouldn't be? I've read his diaries and I understand. Not everything, for even in his writing he held back, didn't explain too much. Why should he? His diaries were for him, aids to memory. They weren't meant for others to understand, but I fathomed a lot of it. The rest was in those government files.

"Innsmouth prospered in the time of the clipper ships and the old trade routes. The captains and men of some of those old ships brought back wives from Polynesia—and also their strange rites of worship, their gods. There was queer blood in those native women, and it spread rapidly. As the years passed the entire town became infected. Whole families grew up tainted. They were less than human, amphibian, creatures more of the sea than the land. Merfolk, yes! Tritons, who worshipped Dagon in the deeps: 'Deep Ones,' as old Carpenter called them. Then came the federal raid of '28. But it came too late for old Carpenter.

"He had a store in Innsmouth, but well away from the secret places—away from the boarded-up streets and houses and churches where the worst of them had their dens and held their meetings and kept their rites. His wife was long dead of some wasting disease, but his daughter was alive and schooling in Arkham. Shortly before the raid she came home, little more than a girl. And she became—I don't know—lured. It's a word that sticks in my mind. A very real word, to me.

"Anyway, the Deep Ones took her, gave her to something they called out of the sea. She disappeared. Maybe she was dead, maybe something worse. They'd have killed Carpenter then, because he'd learned too much about them and wanted revenge, but the government raid put an end to any personal reprisals or vendettas. Put an end to Innsmouth, too. Why, they just about wrecked the town! Vast areas of complete demolition. They even depth-charged a reef a mile out in the sea . . .

"Well, after things quieted down Carpenter stayed on a while in Innsmouth—what was left of it. He was settling his affairs, I suppose, and maybe ensuring that the evil was at an end. Which must have been how he learned that it wasn't at an end but spreading like some awful blight. And because he suspected the survivors of the raid might seek haven in old strongholds abroad, finally he came to Kettlethorpe."

"Here?" David's story was beginning to make connections, was starting to add up. "Why would he come here?"

"Why? Haven't you been listening? He'd found something out about Kettlethorpe, and he came to make sure the Innsmouth horror couldn't spread here. Or perhaps he knew it was already here, waiting, like a cancer ready to shoot out its tentacles. Perhaps he came to stop it spreading further. Well, he's managed that these last thirty years, but now—"

"Yes?"

"Now he's gone, and I'm the owner of the place. Yes, and I have to see to it that whatever he was doing gets finished!"

"But what *was* he doing?" I asked. "And at what expense? Gone, you said. Yes, old Carpenter's gone. But gone where? What will all of this cost you, David? And more important by far, what will it cost June?"

My words had finally stirred something in him, something he had kept suppressed, too frightened of it to look more closely. I could tell by the way he started, sat bolt upright beside me. "June? But—"

"But nothing, man! Look at yourself. Better still, take a good look at your wife. You're going down the drain, both of you. It's something that started the day you took that farm. I'm sure you're right about the place, about old Carpenter, all that stuff you've dredged up, but now you've got to forget it. Sell Kettlethorpe, that's my advice, or better still, raze it to the ground! But whatever you do—"

"*Look!*" He started again and gripped my arm in a suddenly claw-hard hand.

I looked, applied my brakes, brought the car skidding to a halt in the rain-puddled track. We had turned off the main road by then, where the track winds down to the farm. The rain had let up and the air had gone still as a shroud. Shroudlike, too, the silky mist that lay silently upon the near-distant dene and lapped a foot deep about the old farm's stony walls. The scene was weird under a watery moon, but weirder by far was the morbid *manifestation* which was even now rising up like a wraith over the farm.

A shape, yes, billowing up, composed of mist, writhing huge over the ancient buildings. The shape of some monstrous merman— the ages-evil shape of Dagon himself!

I should have shaken David off and driven on at once, of course I should, down to the farm and whatever waited there, but the sight of that figure mushrooming and firming in the dank night air was paralysing. And sitting there in the car, with the engine slowly ticking over, we shuddered as one as we heard, quite distinctly, the first muffled gonging of some damned and discordant bell. A tolling whose notes might on another occasion be sad and sorrowful, which now were filled with a menace out of the eons.

"The bell!" David's gasp galvanized me into action.

"I hear it," I said, throwing the car into gear and racing down that last quarter-mile stretch to the farm. It seemed that time was frozen in those moments, but then we were through the iron gates and slewing to a halt in front of the porch. The house was bright with lights, but June—

While David tore desperately through the rooms of the house, searching upstairs and down, crying her name, I could only stand by the car and tremblingly listen to the tolling of the bell, its dull, sepulchral summons seeming to me to issue from below, from the very earth beneath my feet. And as I listened so I watched that writhing figure of mist shrink down into itself, seeming to glare from bulging eyes of mist one final ray of hatred in my direction, before spiralling down and disappearing—into the shell of that roofless building at the mouth of the horseshoe!

David, awry and babbling as he staggered from the house, saw it too. "There!" he pointed at the square, mist-wreathed building. "That's where it is. And that's where she'll be. I didn't know she knew . . . she must have been watching me. Bill—" he clutched at my arm, "—are you with me? Say you are, for God's sake!" And I could only nod my head.

Hearts racing, we made for that now ghastly edifice of reeking mist—only to recoil a moment later from a figure that reeled out from beneath the lintel with the Dagon plate to fall swooning into David's arms. June, of course—but how could it be? How could *this* be June?

Not the June I had known, no, but some other, some revenant of that June . . .

VIII

"THAT PLACE BELOW . . ."

She was gaunt, hair coarse as string, skin dry and stretched over features quite literally, shockingly altered into something . . . different. Strangely, David was not nearly so horrified by what he could see of her by the thin light of the moon; far more so after we had taken her back to the house. For quite apart from what were to me undeniable alterations in her looks in general—about which, as yet, he had made no comment—it then became apparent that his wife had been savaged and brutalized in the worst possible manner.

I remember, as I drove them to the emergency hospital in Hartlepool, listening to David as he cradled her in his arms in the back of the car. She was not conscious, and David barely so (certainly he was oblivious to what he babbled and sobbed over her during that nightmare journey) but my mind was working overtime as I listened to his crooning, utterly distraught voice:

"She must have watched me, poor darling, must have seen me going to that place. At first I went for the firewood—I burned up all of old Jason's wood—but then, beneath the splinters and bits of bark, I found the millstone over the slab. The old boy had put that stone there to keep the slab down. And it had done its job, by God! Must have weighed all of two hundred and forty pounds. Impossible to shift from those slimy, narrow steps below. But I used a lever to move it, yes, and I lifted the slab and went down. Down those ancient steps—down, down, down. A maze, down there. The Earth itself, honeycombed! . . .

"What were they for, those burrows? What purpose were they supposed to fulfill? And *who* dug them? I didn't know, but I kept it from her anyway—or thought I had. I couldn't say why, not then, but some instinct warned me not to tell her about . . . about that place below. I swear to God I meant to close it up forever, choke the mouth of that—that pit! with concrete. And I'd have done it, I swear it, once I'd explored those tunnels to the full. But that millstone, June, that great heavy stone. How did you shift it? *Or were you helped?*

"I've been down there only two or three times on my own, and I never went very far. Always there was that feeling that I wasn't alone, that things moved in the darker burrows and watched me where I crept. And that sluggish stream, bubbling blindly through airless fissures to the sea. That stream which rises and falls with the tides. And the kelp all bloated and slimy. Oh, my God! My God!" . . .

And so on. But by the time we reached the hospital David had himself more or less under control again. Moreover, he had dragged from me a promise that I would let him—indeed help him—do things his own way. He had a plan which seemed both simple and faultless, one which must conclusively write *finis* on the entire affair. That was to say *if* his fears for Kettlethorpe and the conjectural region he termed "that place below" were soundly based.

As to why I so readily went along with him—why I allowed him to brush aside unspoken any protests or objections I might have entertained—quite simply, I had seen that mist-formed shape with my own eyes, and with my own ears had heard the tolling of that buried and blasphemous bell. And for all that the thing seemed fantastic, the conviction was now mine that the farm was a seat of horror and evil as great and maybe greater than any other these British Isles had ever known . . .

We stayed at the hospital through the night, gave identical, falsified statements to the police (an unimaginative tale of a marauder, seen fleeing under cover of the mist towards the dene), and in between sat together in a waiting area drinking coffee and quietly conversing. Quietly now, yes, for David was exhausted both physically and mentally, and much moreso after he had attended that examination of his wife made imperative by her condition and by our statements.

As for June: mercifully she stayed in her traumatized state of deepest shock all through the night and well into the morning. Finally, around 10:00 A.M. we were informed that her condition, while still unstable, was no longer critical, and then, since it was very obvious that we could do nothing more, I drove David home with me to Harden.

I bedded him down in my guest room, by which time all I wanted to do was get to my own bed for an hour or two, but about 4:00 P.M. I was awakened from uneasy dreams to find him on the telephone, his voice stridently urgent. As I went to him he put the phone down, turned to me haggard and red-eyed, his face dark with stubble. "She's stabilized," he said, and: "Thank God for that! But she hasn't come out of shock—not completely. It's too deep-seated. At least that's what they told me. They say she could be like it for weeks . . . maybe longer."

"What will you do?" I asked him. "You're welcome to stay here, of course, and—"

"Stay here?" he cut me short. "Yes, I'd like that—afterwards."

I nodded, biting my lip. "I see. You intend to go through with it. Very well, but there's still time to tell the police, you know. You could still let them deal with it."

He uttered a harsh, barking laugh. "Can you really imagine me telling all of this to your average son-of-the-sod Hartlepool bobby? Why, even if I showed them that . . . the place below, what could they do about it? And should I tell them about my plan, too? What!—mention dynamite to the law, the local authorities? Oh, yes, I can just see that! Even if they didn't put me in a straight jacket it would still take them an age to get round to doing anything. And meanwhile, if there is something down there under the farm—and Bill, we know there is—what's to stop it or them from moving on to fresh pastures?"

When I had no answer, he continued in a more controlled, quieter tone. "Do you know what old Carpenter was doing? I'll tell you: he was going down there in the right seasons, when he heard the bell ringing—going down below with his shotgun and blasting all hell out of what he found in those foul black tunnels! Paying them back for what they did to him and his in Innsmouth. A madman who didn't know what he wrote in those diaries of his? No, for we've *seen* it, Bill, you and I. And we've heard it—heard Dagon's bell ringing in the night, summoning that ancient evil up from the sea.

"Why, that was the old man's sole reason for living there: so that he could take his revenge! Taciturn? A recluse? I'll say he was! He lived to kill—*to kill them*! Tritons, Deep Ones, amphibian abortions born out of a timeless evil, inhuman lust, and black, alien nightmare. Well, now I'll finish what he started, only I'll do it a damn sight faster! It's my way or nothing." He gazed at me, his eyes steady now and piercing, totally sane, strong as I had rarely seen him. "You'll come?"

"First," I said, "there's something you must tell me. About June. She—her looks—I mean . . ."

"I know what you mean," his voice contained a tremor, however tightly controlled. "It's what makes the whole thing real for me. It's proof positive, as if that were needed now, of all I've suspected and discovered of the place. I told you she wouldn't leave the farm, didn't I? But did you know it was her idea to buy Kettlethorpe in the first place?"

"You mean she was . . . lured?"

"Oh, yes, that's exactly what I mean—but by what? By her blood, Bill! She didn't know, was completely innocent. Not so her forebears. Her great-grandfather came from America—New England. That's as far as I care to track it down, and no need now to take it any further. But you must see why I personally have to square it all away?"

I could only nod.

"And you will help?"

"I must be mad," I answered, nodding again, "—or at best an idiot—but it seems I've already committed myself. Yes, I'll come."

"Now?"

"Today? At this hour? That *would* be madness! Before you know it, it'll be dark, and—"

"Dark, yes!" he broke in on me. "But what odds? It's *always* dark down there, Bill. We'll need electric torches, the more the better. I have a couple at the farm. How about you?"

"I've a good heavy-duty torch in the car," I told him. "Batteries, too."

"Good! And your shotguns—we'll need them, I think. But we're not after pheasant this time, Bill."

"Where will you get the dynamite?" I asked, perhaps hoping that this was something which, in his fervor, he had overlooked.

He grinned—not his old grin but a twisted, vicious thing and said: "I've already got it. Had it ever since I found the slab two weeks ago and first went down there. My gangers use it on big landscaping jobs. Blasting out large boulders and tree stumps saves a lot of time and effort. Saves money, too. There's enough dynamite at the farm to demolish half of Harden!"

David had me, and he knew it. "It's now, Bill, now!" he said. And after a moment's silence he shrugged. "But if you haven't the spit for it . . ."

"I said I'd come," I told him, "and so I will. You're not the only one who loves a mystery, even one as terrifying as this. Now that I know such a place exists, of course I want to see it. I'm not easy about it, no, but . . ."

He nodded. "Then this is your last chance, for you can be sure it won't be there for you to see tomorrow!"

IX

DESCENT INTO MADNESS

Within the hour we were ready. Torches, shotguns, dynamite, and fuze wire—everything we would need—all was in our hands. And as we made our way from the house at Kettlethorpe along the garden paths to the roofless enclosure, already the mists were rising and beginning to creep. And I admit here and now that if David had offered me the chance again, to back out and leave him to go it alone, I believe I might well have done so.

As it was, we entered under the lintel with the plate, found the slab as David had described it, and commenced to lever it up from its seatings.

As we worked my friend nodded his head towards a very old and massive millstone lying nearby. "That's what Jason Carpenter used to seal it. And do you believe June could have shifted that on her own? Never! She was helped—must have been helped from below!"

At that moment the slab moved, lifted, was awkward for a moment, but at our insistence slid gratingly aside. I don't know what I expected, but the blast of foul, damp air that rushed up from below took me completely by surprise. It blew full into my face, jetting up like some noxious, invisible geyser, a pressured stench of time and ocean, darkness and damp, and alien things. And I knew it at once: that tainted odour I had first detected in the summer, which David had naively termed "a miasma."

Was this the source, then, of that misty phantom seen on dark nights, that bloating spectre formed of fog and the rushing reek of inner earth? Patently it was, but that hardly explained the shape the thing had assumed . . .

In a little while the expansion and egress of pent-up gases subsided and became more a flow of cold, salty air. Other odours were there, certainly, but however alien and disgusting they no longer seemed quite so unbearable.

Slung over our shoulders we carried partly filled knapsacks which threw us a little off balance. "Careful," David warned, descending ahead of me, "it's steep and slippery as hell!" Which was no exaggeration.

The way was narrow, spiralling, almost perpendicular—a stair-well through solid rock which might have been cut by some huge and eccentric drill. Its steps were narrow in the tread, deep in the rise, and slimy with nitre and a film of moisture clammy as sweat. And our powerful torches cutting the way through darkness deep as night, and the walls winding down, down, ever down.

I do not know the depth to which we descended; there was an interminable sameness about that corkscrew of stone which seemed to defy measurement. But I recall something of the characters carved almost ceremoniously into its walls. Undeniably Roman, some of them, but I was equally sure that these were the most recent! The rest, having a weird, almost glyphic angularity and coarseness—a barbaric simplicity of style—must surely have pre-dated any Roman incursion into Britain.

And so down to the floor of that place, where David paused to deposit several sticks of dynamite in a dark niche. Quickly he fitted a fuze, and while he worked so he spoke to me in a whisper which echoed sibilantly away and came rustling back in decreasing sus-surations. "A long fuze for this one. We'll light it on our way out. And at least five more like this before we're done. I hope it's enough. God, I don't even know the extent of the place! I've been this far before and farther, but you can imagine what it's like to be down here on your own . . ."

Indeed I could imagine it, and shuddered at the thought.

While David worked I stood guard, shotgun under my arm, cocked, pointing it down a black tunnel that wound away to God-knows-where. The walls of this horizontal shaft were curved inward at the top to form its ceiling, which was so low that when we com-menced to follow it we were obliged to stoop. Quite obviously the tunnel was no mere work of nature; no, for it was far too regular for that, and everywhere could be seen the marks of sharp tools used to chip out the stone. One other fact which registered was this: that the walls were of the same stone from which Kettlethorpe

Farm—in what original form?—must in some dim uncertain time predating all memory, myth, and legend have been constructed.

And as I followed my friend, so in some dim recess of my mind I made note of these things, none of which lessened in the slightest degree the terrific weight of apprehension resting almost tangibly upon me. But follow him I did, and in a little while he was showing me fresh marks on the walls, scratches he had made on previous visits to enable him to retrace his steps.

"Necessary," he whispered, "for just along here the tunnels begin to branch, become a maze. Really, a maze! Be a terrible thing to get lost down here . . ."

My imagination needed no urging, and after that I followed more closely still upon his heels, scratching marks of my own as we went. And sure enough, within a distance of perhaps fifty paces more, it began to become apparent that David had in no way exaggerated with regard to the labyrinthine nature of the place. There were side tunnels, few at first but rapidly increasing in number, which entered into our shaft from both sides and all manner of angles, and shortly after this we came to a sort of gallery wherein many of these lesser passages met.

The gallery was in fact a cavern of large dimensions with a domed ceiling perhaps thirty feet high. Its walls were literally honeycombed with tunnels entering from all directions, some of which descended steeply to regions deeper and darker still. Here, too, I heard for the first time the sluggish gurgle of unseen waters, of which David informed: "That's a stream. You'll see it shortly."

He laid another explosive charge out of sight in a crevice, then indicated that I should once more follow him. We took the tunnel with the highest ceiling, which after another seventy-five to one hundred yards opened out again onto a ledge that ran above a slow-moving, blackly gleaming rivulet. The water gurgled against our direction of travel, and its surface was some twenty feet lower than the ledge; this despite the fact that the trough through which it coursed was green and black with slime and incrustations almost fully up to the ledge itself. David explained the apparent ambiguity.

"Tidal," he said. "The tide's just turned. It's coming in now. I've seen it fifteen feet deeper than this, but that won't be for several hours yet." He gripped my arm, causing me to start. "And look! Look at the kelp . . ."

Carried on the surface of the as yet sluggish stream, great ropes of weed writhed and churned, bladders glistening in the light from our torches. "David," my voice wavered, "I think . . ."

"Come on," he said, leading off once more. "I know what you think, but we're not going back. Not yet." Then he paused and turned to me, his eyes burning in the darkness. "Or you can go back on your own, if you wish . . . ?"

"David," I hissed, "that's a rotten thing to—"

"My *God*, man!" he stopped me. "D'you think you're the only one who's afraid?"

However paradoxically, his words buoyed me up a little, following which we moved quickly on and soon came to a second gallery. Just before reaching it the stream turned away, so that only its stench and distant gurgle stayed with us. And once more David laid charges, his actions hurried now, nervous, as if in addition to his admitted fear he had picked up something of my own barely subdued panic.

"This is as far as I've been," he told me, his words coming in a sort of rapid gasping or panting. "Beyond here is fresh territory. By my reckoning we're now well over a quarter-mile from the entrance." He flashed the beam of his torch around the walls, causing the shadows of centuries-formed stalactites to flicker and jump. "There, the big tunnel. We'll take that one."

And now, every three or four paces, or wherever a side tunnel opened into ours, we were both scoring the walls to mark a fresh and foolproof trail. Now, too, my nerves really began to get the better of me. I found myself starting at every move my friend made;

I kept pausing to listen, my heartbeat shuddering in the utter still-ness of that nighted place. Or was it still? Did I hear something just then? The echo of a splash and the soft *flop, flop* of furtive footsteps in the dark?

It must be pictured: we were in a vast subterranian warren. A place hollowed out centuries ago by . . . by whom? By what? And what revenants lurked here still, down here in these terrible caverns of putrid rock and festering, sewagelike streams?

Slap, slap, slap . . .

And that time I definitely had heard something. "David—" my voice was thin as a reedy wind. "For God's sake—"

"*Shh!*" he warned, his cautionary hiss barely audible. "I heard it, too, and they might have heard us! Let me just get the rest of this dynamite planted—one final big batch, it'll have to be—and then we'll get out of here." He used his torch to search the walls but could find no secret place to house the explosives. "Round this next bend," he said. "I'll find a niche there. Don't want the stuff to be found before it's done its job."

We rounded the bend, and ahead: a glow of rotten, phospho-rescent light, a luminescence almost sufficient to make our torches redundant. We saw, and we began to understand.

The roofless building up above—the enclosure that was merely the entrance. This place here, far underground, was the actual place of worship, the subterranean temple to Dagon. We knew it as soon as we saw the great nitre-crusted bell hanging from the centre of the ceiling—the bell and the rusted iron chain which served as its rope, hanging down until its last link dangled inches above the surface and centre of a black and sullenly rippling lake of scum and rank weed.

For all the horror that might follow on our very heels, still we found ourselves pulled up short by the sight of that fantastic final gallery.

It was easily a hundred feet wall to wall, roughly circular, domed over and shelved around, almost an amphitheatre in the shape of its base, and obviously a natural, geological formation. Stalactites hung down from above, as in the previous gallery, and stalagmitic stumps broke the weed pool's surface here and there, showing that at some distant time in our planet's past the cave had stood well above sea level.

As to the source of the pool itself: this could only be the sea. The deep kelp alone was sufficient evidence of that. And to justify and make conclusive this observation, the pool was fed by a broad expanse of water which disappeared under the ledge beneath the far wall, which my sense of direction told me lay toward the sea. The small ripples or wavelets we had noted disturbing the pool's surface could only be the product of an influx of water from this source, doubtless the flow of the incoming tide.

Then there was the light: that same glow of putrescence or organic decomposition seen in certain fungi—an unhealthy illumination which lent the cave an almost submarine aspect. So that even without the clean light of our electric torches, still the great bell in the ceiling would have remained plainly visible.

But that bell . . . who could say where it came from? Not I. Not David. Certainly this was that bell whose sepulchral tolling had penetrated even to the surface, but as to its origin . . .

In that peculiar way of his, David, as if reading my thoughts, confirmed: "Well, it'll not ring again, not after this lot goes off!" And I saw that he had placed his knapsack full of dynamite out of sight beneath a low, shallow ledge in the wall and was even now uncoiling a generous length of fuze wire. Finishing the task, he glanced at me once, struck a match and set sputtering fire to the end of the wire, pushing it, too, out of sight.

"There," he grunted, "and now we can get—" But here he paused, and I knew why.

The echo of a voice—a *croak?*—had come to us from somewhere not too far distant. And even as our ears strained to detect other than the slow gurgle of weed-choked waters, so there echoed again that damnably soft and furtive *slap, slap, slap* of nameless feet against slimy stone . . .

X

DEEP ONES!

At that panic gripped both of us anew, was magnified as the water of the pool gurgled more loudly yet and ripples showed that could *not* be ascribed solely to an influx from the sea. Perhaps at this very moment something other than brine and weed was moving towards us along that murky and mysterious watercourse.

My limbs were trembling, and David was in no better condition as, throwing caution to the wind, we commenced scramblingly to retrace our steps, following those fresh marks where we had scratched them upon the walls of the maze. And behind us the hidden fuze slowly sputtering its way to that massive charge of dynamite, and approaching the great pool, some entirely conjectural thing whose every purpose we were sure must be utterly alien and hostile. While ahead . . . who could say?

But one thing was certain: our presence down here had finally stirred something up—maybe many somethings—and now their noises came to us even above our breathless panting, the hammering of our hearts, and the clattering sounds of our flight down those black tunnels of inner earth. Their *noises*, yes, for no man of the sane upper world of blue skies and clean air could ever have named those echoing, glutinous bursts of sporadic croaking and clotted, inquiring gurgles and grunts as speech, and no one could mistake the slithering, slapping, *flopping* sounds of their pursuit for anything remotely human. Or perhaps they were remotely human, but so sunken into hybrid degeneracy as to seem totally alien to all human expectations. And all of this without ever having seen these Deep Ones—"Tritons," as David had named them—or at least, not yet!

But as we arrived at the central gallery and paused for breath, and as David struck a second match to light the fuze of the charge previously laid there, that so far merciful omission commenced to resolve itself in a manner I shall never forget to my dying day.

It started with the senses-shattering gonging of the great bell, whose echoes were deafening in those hellish tunnels, and it ended . . . but I go ahead of myself.

Simultaneous with the ringing of the bell, a renewed chorus of croaking and grunting came to us from somewhere dangerously close at hand, so that David at once grabbed my arm and half-dragged me into a small side tunnel leading off at an angle from the gallery. This move had been occasioned not alone by the fact that the sounds we had heard were coming closer, but also that they issued from the very burrow by which we must make our escape! But as the madly capricious gods of fate would have it, our momentary haven proved no less terrifying in its way than the vulnerable position we had been obliged to quit.

The hole into which we had fled was no tunnel at all but an L-shaped cave which, when we rounded its single corner, laid naked to our eyes a hideous secret. We recoiled instinctively from a discovery grisly as it was unexpected, and I silently prayed that God—if indeed there was any good, sane God—would give me strength not to break down utterly in my extreme of horror.

In there, crumpled where he had finally been overcome, lay the ragged and torn remains of old Jason Carpenter. It could only be him; the similarly broken body of Bones, his dog, lay across his feet. And all about him on the floor of the cave, spent shotgun cartridges; and clasped in his half-rotted, half-mummied hand, that weapon which in the end had not saved him.

But he had fought—how he had fought! Jason, and his dog, too.

Theirs were not the only corpses left to wither and decay in that tomb of a cave. No, for heaped to one side was a pile of quasi-human—*debris*—almost beyond my powers of description. Suffice to say that I will not even attempt a description, but merely confirm that these were indeed the very monstrosities of David's tale of crumbling Innsmouth. And if in death the things were loathsome, in life they would yet prove to be worse by far. That was still to come . . .

And so, with our torches reluctantly but necessarily switched off, we crouched there in the fetid darkness amidst corpses of man, dog, and nightmares, and we waited. And always we were full of that awful awareness of slowly burning fuzes, of time rapidly running out. But at last the tolling of the bell ceased and its echoes died away, and the sounds of the Deep Ones decreased as they made off in a body towards the source of the summoning, and finally we made our move.

Switching on our torches we ran crouching from the cave into the gallery—and came face to face with utmost terror! A lone member of that flopping, frog-voiced horde had been posted here and now stood central in the gallery, turning startled, bulging batrachian eyes upon us as we emerged from our hiding place.

A moment later and this squat obscenity—this part-man, part-fish, part-frog creature—threw up webbed hands before its terrible face, screamed a hissing, croaking cry of rage and possibly agony, and finally hurled itself at us . . .

. . . Came frenziedly lurching, flopping, and floundering, head-long into a double-barrelled barrage from the weapon I held in fingers which kept on uselessly squeezing the trigger long after the face and chest of the monster had flown into bloody tatters and its body was lifted and hurled away from us across the chamber.

Then David was yelling in my ear, tugging at me, dragging me after him, and . . . and all of the rest is a chaos, a madness, a nightmare of flight and fear.

I seem to recall loading my shotgun—several times, I think—and I have vague memories of discharging it a like number of times; and I believe that David, too, used his weapon, probably more successfully. As for our targets: it would have been difficult to miss them. There were clutching claws and eyes bulging with hatred and lust; there was foul, alien breath in our faces, slime and blood and bespattered bodies obstructing our way where they fell; and always a swelling uproar of croaking and flopping and slithering as that place below became filled with the spawn of primal oceans.

Then . . . the Titan blast that set the rock walls to trembling, whose reverberations had no sooner subsided when a yet more ominous rumbling began . . . Dust and stony debris rained down from the tunnel ceilings, and a side tunnel actually collapsed into ruin as we fled past its mouth, but finally we arrived at the foot of those upward-winding stone steps in the fluelike shaft which was our exit.

Here my memory grows more distinct, too vivid if anything—as if sight of our salvation sharpened fear-numbed senses—and I see David lighting the final fuze as I stand by him, firing and reloading, firing and reloading. The sharp smell of sulphur and gunpowder in a haze of dust and flickering torch beams, and the darkness erupting anew in shambling shapes of loathsome fright. The shotgun hot in my hands, jamming at the last, refusing to break open.

Then David taking my place and firing point-blank into a mass of mewling horror, and his voice shrill and hysterical, ordering me to climb, climb and get out of that hellish place. From above I look down and see him dragged under, disappearing beneath a clawing, throbbing mass of bestiality; and their frog-eyes avidly turning upwards to follow my flight, fangs gleaming in grinning, wide-slit mouths, an instant's pause before they come squelching and squalling up the steps behind me!

And at last . . . at last I emerge into moonlight and mist. And with a strength born of madness I hurl the slab into place and weight it with the millstone. For David is gone now and no need to ponder over his fate. It was quick, I saw it with my own eyes, but at least he has done what he set out to do. I know this now, as I feel from far below that shuddering concussion as the dynamite finishes its work.

Following which I stumble from the roofless building and collapse on a path between stunted fruit trees and unnaturally glossy borders of mist-damp shrubbery. And lying there I know the sensation of being shaken, of feeling the earth trembling beneath me, and of a crashing of masonry torn from foundations eaten by the ages.

And at the very end, sinking into a merciful unconsciousness, at last I am rewarded by a sight which will allow me, with the dawn, to come awake a sane, whole man. That sight which is simply this: a great drifting mass of mist, dissipating as it coils away over the dene, melting down from the shape of a rage-tormented merman to a thin and formless fog.

For I know that while Dagon himself lives on—as he has "lived" since time immemorial—the seat of his worship which Kettlethorpe has been for centuries is at last no more . . .

That is my story, the story of Kettlethorpe Farm, which with the dawn lay in broken ruins. Not a building remained whole or standing as I left the place, and what has become of it since I cannot say for I never returned and I have never inquired. Official records will show, of course, that there was "a considerable amount of pit subsidence" that night, sinkings and shiftings of the earth with which colliery folk the world over are all too familiar; and despite the fact that there was no storm as such at sea, still a large area of the ocean-fringing cliffs were seen to have sunken down and fallen onto the sands or into the sullen water.

What more is there to say? There was very little deep kelp that year, and in the years since the stuff has seemed to suffer a steady decline. This is hearsay, however, for I have moved inland and will never return to any region from which I might unwittingly spy the sea or hear its wash.

As for June: she died some eight months later giving premature birth to a child. In the interim her looks had turned even more strange, ichthyic, but she was never aware of it for she had become a happy little girl whose mind would never be whole again. Her doctors said that this was just as well, and for this I give thanks.

As well, too, they said, that her child died with her . . .

THE SUN, THE SEA, AND THE SILENT SCREAM

This time of year, just as you're recovering from Christmas, they're wont to appear, all unsolicited, *plop* on your welcome mat. I had forgotten that fact, but yesterday I was reminded.

Julie was up first, creating great smells of coffee and frying bacon. And me still in bed, drowsy, thinking how great it was to be nearly back to normal. Three months she'd been out of *that* place, and fit enough now to be first up, running about after me for a change.

Her sweet voice called upstairs: "Post, darling!" And her slippers flip-flopping out onto the porch. Then those long moments of silence—until it dawned on me what she was doing. I knew it instinctively, the way you do about someone you love. She was screaming—but silently. A scream that came drilling into all my bones to shiver into shards right there in the marrow. Me out of bed like a puppet on some madman's strings, jerked downstairs so as to break my neck, while the silent scream went on and on.

And Julie standing there with her head thrown back and her mouth agape, and the unending scream not coming out. Her eyes starting out with their pupils rolled down, staring at the thing in her white, shuddering hand—

A travel brochure, of course . . .

Julie had done Greece fairly extensively with her first husband. That had been five or six years ago, when they'd hoped and tried for kids a lot. No kids had come; she couldn't have them; he'd gone off and found someone who could. No hard feelings. Maybe a few soft feelings.

So when we first started going back to Greece, I'd suggested places they'd explored together. Maybe I was looking for faraway expressions on her face in the sunsets, or a stray tear when a familiar *bousouki* tune drifted out on aromatic taverna exhalations. Somebody had taken a piece of my heart, too, once upon a time; maybe I wanted to know how much of Julie was really mine. As it happened, all of her was.

After we were married, we left the old trails behind and broke fresh ground. That is, we started to find new places to holiday. Twice yearly we'd pack a few things, head for the sunshine, the sea, and sometimes the sand. Sand wasn't always a part of the package, not in Greece. Not the golden or pure white varieties, anyway. But pebbles, marble chips, great brown and black slabs of volcanic rock sloping into the sea—what odds? The sun was always the same, and the sea . . .

The sea. Anyone who knows the Aegean, the Ionian, the Mediterranean in general, in between and around Turkey and Greece, knows what I mean when I describe those seas as indescribable. Blue, green, mother-of-pearl, turquoise in that narrow band where the sea meets the land—fantastic! Myself, I've always liked the colours *under* the sea the best. That's the big bonus I get, or got, out of the islands: the swimming, the amazing submarine world just beyond the glass of my face mask, the spearfishing.

And this time—last time, the very last time—we settled for Makelos. But don't go looking for it on any maps. You won't find it; much too small, and I'm assured that the British don't go there any more. As a holiday venue, it's been written off. I'd like to think I had something, everything, to do with that, which is why I'm writing this. But a warning: if you're stuck on Greece anyway, and willing to take your chances come what may, read no further. I'd hate to spoil it all for you.

So . . . what am I talking about? Political troubles, unfinished hotel apartments, polluted swimming pools? No, nothing like that. We didn't take that sort of holiday, anyway. We were strictly "off-the-beaten-track" types. Hence Makelos.

We couldn't fly there direct; the island was mainly a flat-topped mountain climbing right out of the water, with a dirt landing strip on the plateau suitable only for Skyvans. So it was a packed jet to Athens, a night on the town, and in the mid-morning a flying Greek matchbox the rest of the way. Less than an hour out of Athens and into the Cyclades, descending through a handful of cotton-wool clouds, that was our first sight of our destination.

Less than three miles long, a mile wide—that was it. Makelos. There was a "town," also called Makelos, at one end of the island where twin spurs formed something of a harbour; and the rest of the place around the central plateau was rock and scrub and tiny bays, olive groves galore, almonds and some walnuts, prickly pears, and a few lonely lemons. Oh, and lots of wildflowers, so that the air seemed scented.

The year before, there'd been a few apartments available in Makelos town. But towns weren't our scene. This time, however, the island had something new to offer: a lone taverna catering for just three detached, cabin-style apartments, or "villas," all nestling in a valley two miles down the coast from Makelos town itself. Only one or two taxis on the entire island (the coastal road was little more than a track), no fast-food stands, and no packed shingle beaches where the tideless sea would be one-third sun oil and two-thirds tourist pee!

We came down gentle as a feather, taxied up to a windblown shack that turned out to be the airport, deplaned, and passed in front of the shack and out the back, and boarded our transport.

There were other holiday makers, but we were too excited to pay them much attention; also a handful of dour-faced island Greeks—Makelosians, we guessed. Dour, yes. Maybe that should have told us something about their island.

Our passports had been stamped over the Athens stamp with a local variety as we passed through the airport shack, and the official doing the job turned out to be our driver. A busy man, he also introduced himself as the mayor of Makelos! The traction end of our "transport" was a three-wheeler: literally a converted tractor, hauling a four-wheeled trolley with bucket seats bolted to its sides. On the way down from the plateau, I remember thinking we'd never make it; Julie kept her eyes closed for most of the trip; I gave everyone aboard an A for nerve. And the driver-mayor sang a doleful Greek number all the way down.

The town was very old, with nowhere the whitewashed walls you become accustomed to in the islands. Instead, there was an air of desolation about the place. Throw in a few tumbleweeds, and you could shoot a Western there. But fishing boats bobbed in the harbour; leathery Greeks mended nets along the quayside; old men drank muddy coffee at wooden tables outside the tavernas; and bottles of Metaxa and ouzo were very much in evidence. Crumbling fortified walls of massive thickness proclaimed, however inarticulately, a one-time Crusader occupation.

Once we'd trundled to a halt in the town's square, the rest of the passengers were home and dry; Julie and I still had a mile and a half to go. Our taxi driver (transfer charges both ways, six pounds sterling: I'd wondered why it was so cheap!) collected our luggage from the tractor's trolley, stowed it away, waited for us while we dusted ourselves down and stretched our legs. Then we got into his "taxi."

I won't impugn anyone's reputation by remarking on the make of that old bus; come to think of it, I could possibly *make* someone's name, for anywhere else in the world this beauty would have been off the road in the late sixties! Inside—it was a shrine, of course. The Greek sort, with good-luck charms, pictures of the saints, photos of Mum and Dad, and iconlike miniatures in silver frames hanging and jangling everywhere. And even enough room for the driver to see through his windscreen.

"Nichos," he introduced himself, grave-faced, trying to loosen my arm in its socket with his handshake where he reached back from the driver's seat. And to Julie, seated beside him up front: "Nick!" and he took her hand and bowed his head to kiss it. Fine, except we were already mobile and leaving the town, and holiday makers and villagers alike were scattering like clucking hens in all directions in our heavy blue exhaust smoke.

Nichos was maybe fifty, hard to tell: bright brown eyes, hair greying, upwards-turned moustache, skin brown as old leather. His nicotine-stained teeth and ouzo breath were pretty standard. "A fine old car," I opined, as he jarred us mercilessly on nonexistent suspension down the patchy, pot-holed tarmacadam street.

"Eh?" He raised an eyebrow.

"The car," I answered. "She goes, er, well!"

"Very well, thank you. The car," he apparently agreed.

"Maybe he doesn't speak it too well, darling." Julie was straight-faced.

"Speaks it," Nichos agreed with a nod. Then, registering understanding: "Ah—*speak* it! I am speaking it, yes, and slowly. Very *slooowly*! Then is understanding. Good morning, good evening, welcome to my house—exactly! I am in Athens. Three years. Speaks it much, in Athens."

"Great!" I enthused, without malice. After all, I couldn't speak any Greek.

"You stay at Villas Dimitrios, yes?" He was just passing the time. Of course we were staying there; he'd been paid to take us there, hadn't he? And yet at the same time, I'd picked up a note of genuine enquiry, even something of concern in his voice, as if our choice surprised or dismayed him.

"Is it a nice place?" Julie asked.

"Nice?" he repeated her. "Beautiful!" He blew a kiss. "Beautiful sea—for swim, *beautiful!*" Then he shrugged, said: "All Makelos same. But Dimitrios water—water for drink—him not so good. You drinking? OK—you drink Coke. You drink beer. Drinking water in bottle. Drinking wine—very cheap! Not drinking water. Is big hole in Dimitrios. Deep, er—well? Yes? Water in well bad. All around Dimitrios bad. Good for olives, lemons; no good for the people."

We just about made sense of everything he said, which wasn't quite as easy as I've made it sound here. As for the water situation: that was standard, too. We never drank the local water anyway. "So it's a beautiful place," I said. "Good."

Again he glanced at me over his shoulder, offered another shrug. "Er, beautiful, yes." He didn't seem very sure about it now. The Greeks are notoriously vague.

We were out of Makelos, heading south round the central plateau, kicking up the dust of a narrow road where it had been cut through steep, seaward-sloping strata of yellow-banded, dazzling white rock to run parallel with the sea on our left. We were maybe thirty or forty feet above sea level, and down there through bights in the shallow sea cliffs, we were allowed tantalizing glimpses of white pebble beaches scalloping an ocean flat as a millpond. The fishing would be good. Nothing like the south coast of England (no Dover sole basking on a muddy bottom here), but that made it more of a challenge. You had to be *good* to shoot fish here!

I took out a small paper parcel from my pocket and unwrapped it: a pair of gleaming trident spearheads purchased in Athens. With luck these heads should fit my spears. Nichos turned his head. "You like to fish? I catch plenty! *Big* fisherman!" Then that look was back on his face. "You fish in Dimitrios? No eat. You like the fishing—

good! Chase him, the fish—shoot, maybe kill—but no eat. OK?"

I began to feel worried. Julie, too. She turned to stare at me. I leaned forward, said: "Nichos, what do you mean? Why shouldn't we eat what I catch?"

"My house!" he answered as we turned a bend through a stand of stunted trees. He grinned, pointed.

Above us, the compacted scree slope was green with shrubs and Mediterranean pines. There was a garden set back in ancient, gnarled olives, behind which a row of white-framed windows reflected the late-morning sunlight. The house matched the slope rising around and beyond it, its ochre-tiled roof seeming to melt into the hillside. Higher up there were walled, terraced enclosures; higher still, where the mountain's spur met the sky, goats made gravity-defying silhouettes against the dazzle.

"I show you!" said Nichos, turning right onto a track that wound dizzily through a series of hairpins to the house. We hung on as he drove with practised ease almost to the front door, parking his taxi in the shade of an olive tree heavy with fruit. Then he was opening doors for us, calling out to his wife: "Katrin—hey, Katrin!"

We stayed an hour. We drank cold beer, ate a delicious sandwich of salami, sliced tomatoes, and goat's milk cheese. We admired the kids, the goats and chickens, the little house. It had been an effective way of changing the subject. And we didn't give Nichos's reticence (was that what it had been, or just poor communication?) another thought until he dropped us off at Villas Dimitrios.

The place was only another mile down the road, as the crow flies. But that coastal road knew how to wind. Still, we could probably have walked it while Katrin made us our sandwiches. And yet the island's natural contours kept it hidden from sight until the last moment.

We'd climbed up from the sea by then, maybe a hundred feet, and the road had petered out to little more than a track as we crested the final rise and Nichos applied his brakes. And there we sat in that oven of a car, looking down through its dusty, fly-specked windows on Villas Dimitrios. It was . . . idyllic!

Across the spur where we were parked, the ground dipped fairly steeply to a bay maybe a third of a mile point to point. The bay arms were rocky, formed by the tips of spurs sloping into the sea, but the beach between them was sand. *White* sand, Julie's favourite sort. Give her a book, a white beach, and a little shade, and I could swim all day. The taverna stood almost at the water's edge: a long, low house with a red-tiled roof, fronted by a wooden framework supporting heavy grapevines and masses of bougainvillaea. Hazy blue woodsmoke curled up from its chimney, and there was a garden to its rear. Behind the house, separate from it and each other and made private by screening groves of olives, three blobs of shimmering white stone were almost painful to look at. The chalets or "villas."

Nichos merely glanced at it; nothing new to him. He pointed across the tiny valley to its far side. Over there, the scree base went up brown and yellow to the foot of sheer cliffs, where beneath a jutting overhang the shadows were so dark as to be black. It had to be a cave. Something of a track had been worn into the scree, leading to the place under the cliff.

"In there," said Nichos with one of his customary shrugs, "the well. Water, him no good . . ." His face was very grave.

"The water was poisoned?" Julie prompted him.

"Eh?" he cocked his head, then gave a nod. "Now is poison!"

"I don't understand," I said. "What is it—" I indicated the dark blot under the cliff "—over there?"

"The well," he said again. "Down inside the cave. But the water, he had, er—like the crabs, you know? You understand the crabs, in the sea?"

"Of course," Julie told him. "In England we eat them."

He shook his head, looked frustrated. "Here, too," he said. "But this thing not crab. Very small." He measured an inch between thumb and forefinger. "And no eat him. Very bad! People were . . . sick. They died. Men came from the government in Athens. They bring, er, chemicals? They put in well. Poison for the crabs." Again his shrug. "Now is OK—maybe. But I say, no drink the water."

Before we could respond, he got out of the car, unloaded our luggage onto the dusty track. I followed him. "You're not taking us down?"

"Going down OK." he shrugged, this time apologetically. "Come up again difficult! Too—how you say?" He made an incline with his hand.

"Too steep?"

"Is right. My car very nice—also very old! I sorry." I picked up the cases; Julie joined us and took the travel bags. Nichos made no attempt to help; instead he gave a small, awkward bow, said: "You see my house? Got the problem, come speak. Good morning." Then he was into his car. He backed off, turned around, stopped, and leaned out his window. "Hey, mister, lady!"

We looked at him.

He pointed. "Follow road is long way. Go straight down, very easy. Er, how you say—shortcut? So, I go. See you in two weeks."

We watched his tyres kicking up dust and grit until he was out of sight. Then: Taking a closer look at the terrain, I could see he was right. The track followed the ridge of the spur down to a sharp right turn, then down a hard-packed dirt ramp to the floor of the valley. It was steep, but a decent car should make it—even Nichos's taxi, I thought. But if we left the track here and climbed straight down the side of the spur, we'd cut two or three hundred yards off the distance. And actually, even the spur wasn't all that steep. We made it without any fuss, and I sat down only once when my feet shot out from under me.

As we got down onto the level, our host for the next fortnight came banging and clattering from the direction of the taverna, bumping over the rough scrub in a Greek three-wheeler with a cart at the back. Dimitrios wore a wide-brimmed hat against the sun, but still he was sweating just as badly as we were. He wiped his brow as he dumped our luggage into his open-ended cart. We hitched ourselves up at the rear and sat with our feet dangling. And he drove us to our chalet.

We were hot and sticky, all three of us, and maybe it wasn't so strange we didn't talk. Or perhaps he could see our discomfort and preferred that we get settled in before turning on the old Greek charm. Anyway, we said nothing as he opened the door for us, gave me the key, helped me carry our bags into the cool interior. I followed him back outside again while Julie got to the ritual unpacking.

"Hot," he said then. "Hot, the sun . . ." Greeks have this capacity for stating the obvious. Then, carrying it to extreme degrees, he waved an arm in the direction of the beach, the sea, and the taverna. "Beach. Sea. Taverna. For swimming. Eating. I have the food, drinks. I also selling the food for you the cooking . . ." The chalet came with its own self-catering kit.

"Fine," I smiled. "See you later."

He stared at me a moment, his eyes like dull lights in the dark shadow of his hat, then made a vague sort of motion halfway between a shrug and a nod. He got back aboard his vehicle and started her up, and as his clatter died away, I went back inside and had a look around.

Julie was filling a pair of drawers with spare clothing, at the same time building a teetering pyramid of reading material on a chair. Where books were concerned, she was voracious. She was like that about me, too. No complaints here.

Greek island accommodation varies from abominable to half decent. Or, if you're willing to shell out, you might be lucky enough to get good, but rarely better than that. The Villas Dimitrios chalets were . . . well, OK. But we'd paid for it, so it was what we expected.

I checked the plumbing first. Greek island plumbing is never better than basic. The bathroom was tastefully but totally tiled, even the ceiling! No bathtub, but a good shower and, at the other end of the small room, the toilet and washbasin. Enclosed in tiles, you could shower and let the water spray where-the-heck; if it didn't end up in the shower basin, it would end up on the floor, which sloped gently from all directions to one corner where there was a hole going—where? That's the other thing about Greek plumbing: I've never been able to figure out where everything goes.

But the bathroom did have its faults: like, there were no plugs for the washbasin and shower drainage, and no grilles in the plug holes. I suppose I'm quirky, but I like to see a grille in there, not just a black hole gurgling away to nowhere. It was the same in the little "kitchen" (an alcove under an arch, really, with a sink and drainer unit, a two-ring gas stove, a cupboard containing the cylinder, and a wall-mounted rack for crockery and cutlery; all very nice and serviceable and equipped with a concealed overhead fan-extractor): no plug in the sink and no grille in the plug hole.

I complained loudly to Julie about it.

"Don't put your toe down and you won't get stuck!" was her advice from the bedroom.

"Toe down?" I was already miles away, looking for the shaver socket.

"Down the shower plug hole," she answered. And she came out of the bedroom wearing sandals and the bottom half of her bikini. I made slavering noises, and she turned coyly, tossed back her bra straps for me to fasten. "Do me up."

"You were quick off the mark," I told her.

"All packed away, too," she said with some satisfaction. "And the big white hunter's kit neatly laid out for him. And all performed free of charge—while he examines plug holes!" Then she picked up a towel and tube of lotion and headed for the door. "Last one in the sea's a pervert!"

Five minutes later I followed her. She'd picked a spot halfway
between the chalet and the most northerly bay arm. Her red towel
was like a splash of blood on the white sand two hundred yards
north of the taverna. I carried my mask, snorkel, flippers, some
strong string, and a tatty old blanket with torn corners; that was all.
No spear gun. First I'd take a look-see, and the serious stuff could
come later. Julie obviously felt the same as I did about it: no book,
just a slim, pale white body on the red towel, green eyes three-
quarters shuttered behind huge sunglasses. She was still wet from
the sea, but that wouldn't last long. The sun was a furnace, steaming
the water off her body.

On my way to her, I'd picked up some long, thin, thorny
branches from the scrub; when I got there, I broke off the thorns
and fixed up a sunshade. The old blanket's torn corners showed
how often we'd done this before. Then I took my kit to the water's
edge and dropped it, and ran gasping, pell-mell into the shallows
until I toppled over! My way of getting into the sea quickly. Following which I outfitted myself and finned for the rocks where the
spur dipped below the water.

As I've intimated, the Mediterranean around the Greek islands
is short on fish. You'll find red mullet on the bottom, plenty of
them, but you need half a dozen to make a decent meal. And grey
mullet on top, which move like lightning and cause you to use up
more energy than eating them provides—great sport, but you
couldn't live on it. But there's at least one fish of note in the Med,
and that's the grouper.

Groupers are territorial: a family will mark out its own patch,
usually in deep water where there's plenty of cover, which is to say
rock or weeds. And they love caves. Where there are plenty of rocks
and caves, there'll also be groupers. Here, where the spur crumbled
into the sea, this was ideal grouper ground. So I wasn't surprised

to see this one, especially since I didn't have my gun! Isn't that always the way of it?

He was all of twenty-four inches long, maybe seven across his back, mottled red and brown to match his cave. When he saw me, he headed straight for home, and I made a mental note to mark the spot. Next time I came out here, I'd have my gun with me, armed with a single flap-nosed spear. The spear goes into the fish, the flap opens, and he's hooked, can't slip off. Tridents are fine for small fish, but not for this bloke. And don't talk to me about cruel; if I'm cruel, so is every fisherman in the world, and at least I eat what I catch. But it was then, while I was thinking these things, that I noticed something was wrong.

The fish had homed in on his cave all right, but as his initial reaction to my presence wore off, so his spurt of speed diminished. Now he seemed merely to drift toward the dark hole in the rock, lolling from side to side like some strange, crippled sub, actually missing his target to strike *against* the weedy stone! It was the first time I'd seen a fish collide with something underwater. This was one very sick grouper.

I went down to have a closer look. He was maybe ten feet down, just lolling against the rock face. His huge gill flaps pulsed open and closed, open and closed. I could have reached out and touched him. Then, as he rolled a little on one side, I saw—

I backed off, felt a little sick—felt sorry for him. And I wished I had my gun with me, if only to put him out of his misery. Under his great head, wedging his gill slits half open, a nest of fish lice or parasites of some sort were plainly visible. Not lampreys or remora or the like, for they were too small, only as big as my thumbs. Crustaceans, I thought—a good dozen of them—and they were hooked into him, leeching on the raw red flesh under his gills.

God, I have a *loathing* of this sort of thing! Once in Crete I'd come out of the sea with a suckerfish in my armpit. I hadn't noticed it until I was toweling myself dry and it fell off me. It was only three or four inches long but I'd reacted like I was covered with leeches! I had that same feeling now.

Skin crawling, I drifted up and away from the stricken fish, and for the first time got a good look at his eyes. They were dull, glazed, bubbly as the eyes of a fatally diseased goldfish. And they followed me. And then *he* followed me!

As I floated feet first for the surface, that damned grouper finned lethargically from the rocks and began drifting up after me. Several of his parasites had detached themselves from him and floated alongside him, gravitating like small satellites about his greater mass. I pictured one of them with its hooked feet fastened in my groin, or over one of my eyes. I mean, I knew they couldn't do that—their natural hosts are fish—but the thoughts made me feel vulnerable as hell.

I took off like Tarzan for the beach twenty-five yards away, climbed shivering out of the water in the shadow of the declining spur. As soon as I was out, the shudders left me. Along the beach my sunshade landmark was still there, flapping a little in a light breeze come up suddenly off the sea, but no red towel, no Julie. She could be swimming. Or maybe she'd felt thirsty and gone for a drink under the vines where the taverna fronted onto the sea.

Kit in hand, I padded along the sand at the dark rim of the ocean, past the old blanket tied with string to its frame of branches, all the way to the taverna. The area under the vines was maybe fifty feet along the front by thirty deep, a concrete base set out with a dozen small tables and chairs. Dimitrios was being a bit optimistic here, I thought. After all, it was the first season his place had been in the brochures. But . . . maybe next year there'd be more chalets, and the canny Greek owner was simply thinking well ahead.

I gave the place the once-over. Julie wasn't there, but at least I was able to get my first real look at our handful of fellow holiday makers.

A fat woman in a glaring yellow one-piece splashed in eighteen inches of water a few yards out. She kept calling to her husband, one George, to come on in. George sat half in, half out of the shade; he was a thin, middle-aged, balding man not much browner than myself, wearing specs about an inch thick that made his eyes look like marbles. "No, no, dear," he called back. "I'm fine watching you." He looked frail, timid, tired—I thought: *Where the hell are marriages like this made?* They were like characters off a seaside postcard, except he didn't even seem to have the strength to ogle the girls—if there'd been any! His wife was twice his size.

George was drinking beer from a glass. A bottle, three-quarters empty and beaded with droplets of moisture, stood on his table. I fancied a drink but had no money on me. Then I saw that George was looking at me, and I felt that he'd caught me spying on him or something. "I was wondering," I said, covering up my rudeness, "If you'd seen my wife? She was on the beach there, and—"

"Gone back to your chalet," he said, sitting up a bit in his chair. "The girl with the red towel?" And suddenly he looked just a bit embarrassed. So he was an ogler after all. "Er, while you were in the sea . . ." He took off his specs and rubbed gingerly at a large red bump on the lid of his right eye. Then he put his glasses on again, blinked at me, held out the beer bottle. "Fancy a mouthful? To wash the sea out of your throat? I've had all I want."

I took the bottle, drained it, said: "Thanks! Bite?"

"Eh?" He cocked his head on one side.

"Your eye," I said. "Mosquito, was it? Horsefly or something?"

"Dunno." He shook his head. "We got here Wednesday, and by Thursday night this was coming up. Yesterday morning it was like this. Doesn't hurt so much as irritates. There's another back of my knee, not fully in bloom yet."

"Do you have stuff to dab on?"

He nodded in the direction of his wallowing wife and sighed, "She has *gallons* of it! Useless stuff! It will just have to take its own time."

"Look, I'll see you later," I said. "Right now I have to go and see what's up with Julie." I excused myself.

Leaving the place, I nodded to a trio of spinsterish types relaxing in summer frocks at one of the tables further back. They looked like sisters, and the one in the middle might just be a little retarded. She kept lolling first one way, then the other, while her companions propped her up. I caught a few snatches of disjointed, broad Yorkshire conversation:

"Doctor? . . . sunstroke, I reckon. Or maybe that melon? . . . taxi into town will fix her up . . . bit of shopping . . . pull her out of it . . . Kalamari?—*yechhh!* Don't know what decent grub is, these foreign folks . . ." They were so wrapped up in each other, or in complaint of the one in the middle, that they scarcely noticed me at all.

On the way back to our chalet, at the back of the house/taverna, I looked across low walls and a row of exotic potted plants to see an old Greek (male or female I couldn't determine, because of the almost obligatory floppy black hat tilted forward and flowing black peasant clothes) sitting in a cane chair in one corner of the garden. He or she sat dozing in the shade of an olive tree, chin on chest, all oblivious of the world outside the tree's sun-dappled perimeter. A pure white goat, just a kid, was tethered to the tree; it nuzzled the oldster's dangling fingers like they were teats. Julie was daft for young animals, and I'd have to tell her about it. As for the figure in the cane chair: he/she had been there when Julie and I went down to the beach. Well, getting old in this climate had to be better than doing it in some climates I could mention. . . .

I found Julie in bed, shivering for all she was worth! She was patchy red where the sun had caught her, cold to the touch but filmed with perspiration. I took one look, recognized the symptoms, said: "Oh-oh! Last night's moussaka, eh? You should have had the chicken!" Her tummy *always* fell prey to moussaka, be it good or bad. But she usually recovered quickly, too.

"Came on when I was on the beach," she said. "I left the blanket . . ."

"I saw it," I told her. "I'll go get it." I gave her a kiss.

"Just let me lie here and close my eyes for a minute or two, and I'll be OK," she mumbled. "An *hour* or two, anyway." And as I was going out the door: "Jim, this isn't Nichos's bad water, is it?"

I turned back. "Did you drink any?"

She shook her head.

"Got crabs?"

She was too poorly to laugh, so merely snorted.

I pocketed some money. "I'll get the blanket, buy some bottled drinks. You'll have something to sip. And then . . . will you be OK if I go fishing?"

She nodded. "Of course. You'll see; I'll be on my feet again tonight."

"Anyway, you should see the rest of them here," I told here. "Three old sisters, and one of 'em not all there—a little man and fat woman straight off a postcard! Oh, and I've a surprise for you."

"Oh?"

"When you're up," I smiled. I was talking about the white kid. Tonight or tomorrow morning I'd show it to her.

Feeling a bit let down—not by Julie but by circumstances in general, even by the atmosphere of this place, which was somehow odd—I collected the sunscreen blanket and poles, marched resolutely back to the taverna. Dimitrios was serving drinks to the spinsters. The "sunstruck" one had recovered a little, sipped Coke through a straw. George and his burden were nowhere to be seen. I sat down at one of the tables, and in a little while Dimitrios came over. This time I studied him more closely.

He was youngish, maybe thirty, thirty-five, tall if a little stooped. He was more swarthy peasant Greek than classical or cosmopolitan; his natural darkness, coupled with the shadow of his hat (which he wore even here in the shade), hid his face from any really close inspection. The one very noticeable thing about that face, however, was this: it didn't smile. That's something you get to expect in the islands, the flash of teeth. Even badly stained ones. But not Dimitrios's teeth.

His hands were burned brown, lean, almost scrawny. Be that as it may, I felt sure they'd be strong hands. As for his eyes: they were the sort that make you look away. I tried to stare at his face a little while, then looked away. I wasn't afraid, just concerned. But I didn't know what about.

"Drink?" he said, making it sound like "dring." "Melon? The melon he is free. I give. I grow plenty. You like him? And water? I bring half-melon and water."

He turned to go, but I stopped him. "Er, no!" I remembered the conversation of the spinsters, about the melon. "No melon, no water, thank you." I tried to smile at him, found it difficult. "I'll have a cold beer. Do you have bottled water? You know, in the big plastic bottles? And Coke? Two of each, for the refrigerator. OK?"

He shrugged, went off. There was this lethargy about him, almost a malaise. No, I didn't much care for him at all. . . .

"Swim!" the excited voice of one of the spinsters reached me. "Right along there, at the end of the beach. Like yesterday. Where there's no one to peep."

God! You'll be lucky, I thought.

"Shh!" one of her sisters hushed her, as if a crowd of rapacious men were listening to every word. "Don't tell the whole world, Betty!"

A Greek girl, Dimitrios's sister or wife, came out of the house carrying a plastic bag. She came to my table, smiled at me—a little nervously, I thought. "The water, the Coke," she said making each definite article sound like "thee." *But at least she can speak my language,* I had to keep reminding myself. "Four hundred drachmas, please," she said. I nodded and paid up. About two pounds sterling.

Cheap, considering it all had to be brought from the mainland. The bag and the bottles inside it were tingling cold in my hand.

I stood up, and the girl was still there, barring my way. The three sisters made off down the beach, and there was no one else about. The girl glanced over her shoulder toward the house. The hand she put on my arm was trembling and now I could see that it wasn't just nervousness. She was afraid.

"Mister," she said, the word very nearly sticking in her dry throat. She swallowed and tried again. "Mister, please. I—"

"Elli!" a low voice called. In the doorway to the house, dappled by splashes of sunlight through the vines, Dimitrios.

"Yes?" I answered her. "Is there—?"

"*Elli!*" he called again, an unspoken warning turning the word to a growl.

"Is all right," she whispered, her pretty face suddenly thin and pale. "Is—nothing!" And then she almost ran back to the house.

Weirder and weirder! But if they had some husband-and-wife thing going, it was no business of mine. I'm no Clint Eastwood—and they're a funny lot, the Greeks, in an argument.

On my way back to the chalet, I looked again into the garden. The figure in black, head slumped on chest, sat there as before; it hadn't moved an inch. The sun had, though, and was burning more fiercely down on the drowsing figure in black. The white kid had got loose from its tether and was on its hind legs, eating amazing scarlet flowers out of their tub. "You'll get hell, mate," I muttered, "when he/she wakes up!"

There were a lot of flies about. I swatted at a cloud of the ugly, buzzing little bastards as I hurried, dripping perspiration, back to the chalet.

Inside, I took a long drink myself, then poured ice-cold water into one glass, Coke into another. I put both glasses on a bedside table within easy reach of Julie, stored the rest of the stuff in the fridge. She was asleep: bad belly complicated by a mild attack of sunstroke. I should have insisted that Nichos bring us right to the door. He could have, I was sure. Maybe he and Dimitrios had a feud or something going. But ... Julie was sleeping peacefully enough, and the sweat was off her brow.

Someone tut-tutted, and I was surprised to find it was I. Hey!—this was supposed to be a holiday, wasn't it?

I sighed, took up my kit, including the gun, went back into the sun. On impulse I'd picked up the key. I turned it in the lock, withdrew it, stooped, and slid it under the door. She could come out, but no one could go in. If she wasn't awake when I got back, I'd simply hook the key out again with a twig.

But right now it was time for some serious fishing!

There was a lot of uneasiness building up inside me, but I put it all out of my head (what was it anyway but a set of unsettling events and queer coincidence?) and marched straight down to the sea. The beach was empty here, not a soul in sight. No, wrong: at the far end, near the foot of the second spur, two of the sisters splashed in the shallows in faded bathing costumes twenty years out of date, while the third one sat on the sand watching them. They were all of two or three hundred yards away, however, so I wouldn't be accused of ogling them.

In a little while I was outfitted, in the water, heading straight out to where the sandy bottom sloped off a little more steeply. At about eight or nine feet, I saw an octopus in his house of shells—a big one, too, all coiled pink tentacles and cat eyes wary—but in a little while I moved on. Normally I'd have taken him, gutted him, and beaten the grease out of him, then handed him in to the local taverna for goodwill. But on this occasion that would be Dimitrios. Sod Dimitrios!

At about twelve feet the bottom levelled out. In all directions I saw an even expanse of golden, gently rippled sand stretching away: beautiful but boring. And not a fish in sight! Then ... the silvery flash of a belly turned side-on—no, two of them, three!—caught my eye. Not on the bottom but on the surface. Grey mullet, and of course they'd seen me before I saw them. I followed their darting shapes anyway, straight out to sea as before.

In a little while a reef of dark, fretted rocks came in view. It seemed fairly extensive, ran parallel to the beach. There was some weed but not enough to interfere with visibility. And the water still only twelve to fifteen feet deep. Things were looking up.

If a man knows the habits of his prey, he can catch him, and I knew my business. The grey mullet will usually run, but if you can surprise him, startle him, he'll take cover. If no cover's available, then he just keeps on running, and he'll very quickly outpace any man. But here in this pock-marked reef, there *was* cover. To the fish, it would seem that the holes in the rocks were a refuge, but in fact they'd be a trap. I went after them with a will, putting everything I'd got into the chase.

Coming up fast behind the fish, and making all the noise I could, I saw a central school of maybe a dozen small ones, patrolled by three or four full-grown outriders. The latter had to be two-pounders if they were an ounce. They panicked, scattered; the smaller fish shot off in all directions, and their big brothers went to ground! Exactly as I'd hoped they would. Two into one outcrop of honeycombed rock, and two into another.

I trod water on the surface, getting my breath, making sure the rubbers of my gun weren't tangled with the loose line from the spear, keeping my eyes glued to the silvery grey shapes finning nervously to and fro in the hollow rocks. I picked my target, turned on end, thrust my legs up, and let my own weight drive me to the bottom; and as my impetus slowed, so I lined up on one of the two holes. Right on cue, one of the fish appeared. He never knew what hit him.

I surfaced, freed my vibrating prize from the trident where two of the tines had taken him behind the gills, hung him from a gill ring on my belt. By now his partner had made off, but the other pair of fish was still there in the second hole. I quickly reloaded, made a repeat performance. My first hunt of the season, and already I had two fine fish! I couldn't wait to get back and show them to Julie.

I was fifty yards out. Easing the strain on muscles that were a whole year out of practice, I swam lazily back to the beach and came ashore close to the taverna. Way along the beach, two of the sisters were putting their dresses on over their ancient costumes, while the third sat on the sand with her head lolling. Other than these three, no one else was in sight.

I made for the chalet. As I went, the sun steamed the water off me and I began to itch; it was time I took a shower, and I might try a little protective after-sun lotion, too. Already my calves were turning red, and I supposed my back must be in the same condition. Ugly now, but in just a few days' time . . .

Passing the garden behind the house, this time I didn't look in. The elderly person under the tree would be gone by now, I was sure, but I did hear the lonely bleating of the kid.

Then I saw Dimitrios. He was up on the roof of the central chalet, and from where I padded silently between the olives, I could see him lifting a metal hatch on a square water tank. The roofs were also equipped with solar panels. So the sun heated the water, but . . . where did the water come from? Idiot question, even to oneself! From a well, obviously. But which well?

I passed under the cover of a clump of trees, and the Greek was lost to sight. When I came out again into the open, I saw him descending a ladder propped against the chalet's wall. He carried a large galvanized bucket—empty, to judge from its swing and bounce. He hadn't seen me, and for some hard-to-define reason, I didn't want him to. I ran the rest of the way to our chalet.

The door was open; Julie was up and about in shorts and a halter. She greeted me with a kiss, *oohed* and *aahed* at my catch. "Supper," I told her with something of pride. "No moussaka tonight. Fresh fish done over charcoal, with a little Greek salad and a filthy great bottle of retsina—or maybe two filthy great bottles!"

I cleaned the fish into the toilet, flushed their guts away. Then I washed them, tossed some ice into the sink unit, and put the fish in the ice. I didn't want them to stiffen up in the fridge, and they'd keep well enough in the sink for a couple of hours.

"Now you stink of fish," Julie told me without ceremony. "Your forearms are covered in scales. Take a shower and you'll feel great. I did."

"Are you OK?" I held her with my eyes.

"Fine now, yes," she said. "System flushed while you were out—you don't wish to know that—and now the old tum's settled down nicely, thank you. It was just the travel, the sun—"

"The moussaka?"

"That, too, probably." She sighed. "I just wish I didn't love it so!"

I stripped and stepped into the shower basin, fiddled with the knobs. "What'll you do while I shower?"

"Turn 'em both on full," she instructed. "Hot and cold both. Then the temperature's just right. Me? I'll go and sit in the shade by the sea, start a book."

"In the taverna?" Maybe there was something in the tone of my voice.

"Yes. Is that OK?"

"Fine," I told her, steeling myself and spinning the taps on. I didn't want to pass my apprehension on to her. "I'll see you there—*ahh!*—shortly." And after that, for the next ten minutes, it was hissing, stinging jets of water and blinding streams of medicated shampoo . . .

Towelling myself dry, I heard the clattering on the roof. Maintenance? Dimitrios and his galvanized bucket? I dressed quickly in lightweight flannels and a shirt, flip-flops on my feet, went out, and locked the door. Other places like this, we'd left the door open.

Here I locked it. At the back of the chalet, Dimitrios was coming down his ladder. I came round the corner as he stepped down. If anything, he'd pulled his hat even lower over his eyes, so that his face was just a blot of shadow with two faint smudges of light for eyes. He was lethargic as ever, possibly even more so. We stood looking at each other.

"Trouble?" I eventually ventured.

Almost imperceptibly, he shook his head. "No troubles," he said, his voice a gurgle. "I just see all OK." He put his bucket down, wiped his hands on his trousers.

"And is it?" I took a step closer. "I mean, is it all OK?"

He nodded and at last grinned. Briefly a bar of whiteness opened in the shadow of his hat. "Now is OK," he said. And he picked up his bucket and moved off away from me.

Surly bastard! I thought. And: *What a dump! God, but we've slipped up this time, Julie, my love!*

I started toward the taverna, remembered I had no cigarettes with me, and returned to the chalet. Inside, in the cool and shade, I wondered what Dimitrios had been putting in the water tanks. Some chemical solution, maybe? To purify or purge the system? Well, I didn't want my system purified, not by Dimitrios. I flushed the toilet again. And I left the shower running full blast for all of five minutes before spinning the taps back to the off position. I would have done the same to the sink unit, but my fish were in there, the ice almost completely melted away. And emptying another tray of ice into the sink, I snapped my fingers: *Hah!* A blow for British eccentricity!

By the time I got to the taverna, Dimitrios had disappeared, probably inside the house. He'd left his bucket standing on the garden wall. Maybe it was simple curiosity, maybe something else— I don't know—but I looked into the bucket. Empty. I began to turn away, looked again. No, not empty, but almost. Only a residue remained. At the bottom of the bucket, a thin film of . . . jelly? That's what it looked like: grey jelly.

I began to dip a finger. Hesitated, thought: *What the hell! It's nothing harmful.* It couldn't be, or he wouldn't be putting it in the water tanks. Would he? I snorted at my mind's morbid fancies. Surly was one thing, but homicidal—?

I dipped, held my finger up to the sun where that great blazing orb slipped down toward the plateau's rim. Squinting, I saw . . . just a blob of goo. Except—black dots were moving in it, like microscopic tadpoles.

Urgh! I wiped the slime off my finger onto the rough concrete of the wall. Wrong bucket, obviously, for something had gone decidedly wrong in this one. Backing uncertainly away, I heard the doleful bleating of the white kid.

Across the garden, he was chewing on the frayed end of a rope hanging from the corner of a tarpaulin where it had been thrown roughly over the chair under the olive tree. The canvas had peaked in the middle, so that it seemed someone with a pointed head was still sitting there. I stared hard, felt a tic starting up at the corner of my eye. And suddenly I knew that I didn't want to be here. I didn't want it one little bit. And I wanted Julie to be here even less.

Coming round the house to the seating area under the vines, it became noisily apparent that I wasn't the only disenchanted person around here. An angry, booming female voice, English, seemed matched against a chattering wall of machine-gun-fire Greek. I stepped quickly in under the vines and saw Julie sitting in the shade at the ocean's edge, facing the sea. A book lay open on her table. She looked back over her shoulder, saw me, and even though she wasn't involved in the exchange, still relief flooded over her face.

I went to her, said, "What's up?" She looked past me, directing her gaze toward the rear of the seating area.

In the open door of the house, Dimitrios made a hunched silhouette, stiff as a petrified tree stump; his wife was a pale shadow behind him, in what must be the kitchen. Facing the Greek, George's wife stood with her fists on her hips, jaw jutting. "How *dare* you?" she cried, outraged at something or other. "What do you mean, you can't help? No phone? Are you actually telling me there's no telephone? Then how are we to contact civilization? I have to speak to someone in the town, find a doctor. My husband, George, *needs* a doctor! Can't you understand that? His lumps are moving. *Things are alive under his skin!*"

I heard all of this, but failed to take it in at once. George's lumps moving? Did she mean they were spreading? And still, Dimitrios stood there, while his wife squalled shrilly at him (at *him*, yes, not at George's wife as I'd first thought) and tried to squeeze by him. Whatever was going on here, someone had to do something, and it looked like I was the one.

"Sit tight," I told Julie, and I walked up behind the furious fat lady. "Something's wrong with George?" I said.

All eyes turned in my direction. I still couldn't see Dimitrios's face too clearly, but I sensed a sudden wariness in him. George's wife pounced on me. "Do you know George?" she said, grasping my arm. "Oh, of course! I saw you talking to him when I was in the sea."

I gently prized her sweaty, iron-band fingers from my arm. "His lumps?" I pressed. "Do you mean those swollen stings of his? Are they worse?"

"Stings?" I could see now that her hysteria had brought her close to the point of tears. "Is that what they are? Well, God only knows what stung him! Some of them are opening, and there's movement in the wounds! And George just lies there, without the will to do anything. He must be in agony, but he says he can't feel a thing. There's something terribly wrong . . ."

"Can I see him?"

"Are you a doctor?" She grabbed me again.

"No, but if I could see how bad it is—"

"A waste of *time!*" she cut me off. "He needs a doctor now!"

"I take you to Makelos." Dimitrios had apparently snapped out of his rigor-mortis mode, taken a jerky step toward us. "I take, find doctor, come back in taxi."

She turned to him. "Will you? Oh, *will* you, really? Thank you, oh, thank you! But . . . *how* will you take me?"

"Come," he said. They walked round the building to the rear, followed the wall until it ended, crossed the scrub to a clump of olives, and disappeared into the trees. I went with them part of the way, then watched them out of sight: Dimitrios stiff as a robot, never looking back, and Mrs. George rumbling along massively behind him. A moment later there came the clattering and banging of an engine, and his three-wheeler bumped into view. It made for the packed-dirt incline to the road where it wound up the spur. Inside, Dimitrios at the wheel behind a flyspecked windscreen, almost squeezed into the corner of the tiny cab by the fat lady where she hunched beside him.

Julie had come up silently behind me. I gave a start when she said: "Do you think we should maybe go and see if this George is OK?"

I took a grip of myself, shrugged, said: "I was speaking to him just—oh, an hour and a half ago. He can't have got really bad in so short a time, can he? A few horsefly bites, he had. Nasty enough, but you'd hardly consider them as serious as all that. She's just got herself a bit hot and bothered, that's all."

Quite suddenly, shadows reached down to us from the high brown and purple walls of the plateau. The sun had commenced to sink behind the island's central hump. In a moment it was degrees cooler, so that I found myself shivering. In that same moment the cicadas stopped their frying-fat onslaught of sound, and a strange silence fell over the whole place. On impulse, quietly, I said: "We're out of here tomorrow."

That was probably a mistake. I hadn't wanted to get Julie going. She'd been in bed most of the time; she hadn't experienced the things I had, hadn't felt so much of the strangeness here. Or maybe she had, for now she said: "Good," and gave a little shudder of her own. "I was going to suggest just that. I'm sure we can find cheap lodging in Makelos. And this place is such—I don't know—such a dead and alive hole! I mean, it's beautiful, but it's also very ugly. There's just something morbid about it."

"Listen," I said, deciding to lighten the atmosphere if I could. "I'll tell you what we'll do. You go back to the taverna, and I'll go get the fish. We'll have the Greek girl cook them for us and dish them up with a little salad—and a bottle of retsina, as we'd planned. Maybe things will look better after a bite to eat, eh? Is your tummy up to it?"

She smiled faintly in the false dusk, leaned forward, and gave me a kiss. "You know," she said, "whenever you start worrying about me—and using that tone of voice—I always know that there's something you're worrying about yourself. But actually, you know, I do feel quite hungry!"

The shadows had already reached the taverna. Just shadows— in no way night, for it wasn't properly evening yet, though certainly the contrast was a sort of darkness—and beyond them the vast expanse of the sea was blue as ever, sparkling silver at its rim in the brilliant sunlight still striking there. The strangeness of the place seemed emphasized, enlarged . . .

I watched Julie turn right and disappear into the shade of the vines, and then I went for our fish.

The real nightmare began when I let myself into the chalet and went to the sink unit. Doubly shaded, the interior really was quite dark. I put on the light in the arched-over alcove that was the kitchen, and picked up the two fish, one in each hand—and dropped them, or rather tossed them back into the sink! The ice was all melted; the live-looking glisten of the scales had disappeared with the ice, and the mullets themselves had been—infected!

Attached to the gill flap of one of them, I'd seen a parasite exactly like the ones on the big grouper; the second fish had had one of the filthy things clamped half over a filmed eye. My hair actually prickled on my head; my scalp tingled; my lips drew back from my teeth in a silent snarl. The things were something like sheep ticks, in design if not in dimension, but they were pale, blind, spiky, and looked infinitely more loathsome. They were only—crustaceans? Insects? I couldn't be sure, but there was that about them which made them more horrific to me than any creature has a right to be.

Anyone who believes you can't go cold, break out in gooseflesh, on a hot, late afternoon in the Mediterranean is mistaken. I went so cold I was shaking, and I kept on shaking for long moments, until it dawned on me that just a few seconds ago, I'd actually handled these fish!

Christ!

I turned on the hot tap, thrust my hands forward to receive the cleansing stream, snatched them back again. God, no! I couldn't wash them, for Dimitrios had been up there putting something in the tank! Some kind of spawn. But that didn't make sense: hot water would surely kill the things. If there was any hot water . . .

The plumbing rattled, but no hot water came. Not only had Dimitrios interfered with the water, introduced something into it, but he'd also made sure that from now on we could use only the *cold* water!

I wiped my trembling hands thoroughly on sheets from a roll of paper towel, filled the kettle with water from a refrigerated bottle, quickly brought the water toward boiling. Before it became unbearable, I gritted my teeth, poured a little hot water first over one hand, then the other. It stung like hell, and the flesh of my hands went red at once, but I just hugged them and let them sting. Then, when the water was really boiling, I poured the rest of the contents of the kettle over the fish in the sink.

By that time the parasites had really dug themselves in. The one attached to the gill flap had worked its way under the gill, making it bulge; the other had dislodged its host's eye and was halfway into the skull. Worse, another had clawed its way up the plug hole and was just now emerging into the light! The newcomer was white, whereas the others were now turning pink from the ingestion of fish juices.

But up from the plug hole? This set me shuddering again, and again I wondered: *what's down there, down in the slop under the ground? Where does everything go?*

These fish had been clean when I caught them; I'd gutted them, and so I ought to know. But their scent had drawn these things up to the feast. Would the scent of human flesh attract them the same way?

As the boiling water hit them, the things popped like crabs tossed into a cooking pot. They seemed to hiss and scream, but it was just the rapid expansion and explosion of their tissues. And the stench that rose up from the sink was nauseating. God!—would I ever eat fish again?

And the thought kept repeating over and over in my head: what was down below?

I went to the shower recess, put on the light, looked in, and at once shrank back. The sunken bowl of the shower was crawling with them! Two, three dozen of them at least. And the toilet? And the cold-water system? And all the rest of the bloody plumbing? There'd be a cesspit down there, and these things were alive in it in their thousands! And the maniac Dimitrios had been putting their eggs in the water tanks!

But what about the spinsters? They had been here before us, probably for the past three or four days at least. And what about

George? George and his lumps! And Julie: she wouldn't have ordered anything yet, would she! She wouldn't have *eaten* anything!

I left the door of the chalet slamming behind me, raced for the taverna.

The sun was well down now, with the bulk of the central mountain throwing all of the eastern coastline into shadow; halfway to the horizon, way out to sea, the sun's light was a line ruled across the ocean, beyond which silver-flecked blueness seemed to reach up to the sky. And moment by moment the ruled line of deeper blue flowed eastward as the unseen sun dipped even lower. On the other side of the island, the west coast, it would still be sweltering hot, but here it was noticeably cooler. Or maybe it was just my blood.

As I drew level with the garden at the back of the house, something came flopping over the wall at me. I hadn't been looking in that direction or I'd have seen her: Julie, panic-stricken, her face a white mask of horror. She'd seemed to fly over the wall—jumped or simply bundled herself over I couldn't say—and came hurtling into my arms. Nor had she seen me, and she fought with me a moment when I held her. Then we both caught our breath, or at least I did. Julie had a harder time of it. Even though I'd never heard her scream before, there was one building up in her, and I knew it.

I shook her, which served to shake me a little, too, then hugged her close. "What were you doing in the garden?" I asked, when she'd started to breathe again. I spoke in a whisper, and that was how she answered me, but drawing breath raggedly between each burst of words:

"The little goat . . . he was bleating . . . so pitifully . . . frightened! I heard him . . . went to see . . . got in through a gate on the other side." She paused and took a deep breath. "Oh *God*, Jim!"

I knew without asking. A picture of the slumped figure in the chair, under the olive tree, had flashed momentarily on my mind's eye. But I asked anyway: "The tarpaulin?"

She nodded, gulped. "Something had to be dead under there. I had no idea it would be a . . . a . . . a man!"

"English?" That was a stupid question, so I tried again: "I mean, did he look like a tourist, a holiday maker?"

She shook her head. "An old Greek, I think. But there are— *ugh!*—these things all over him. Like . . . like—"

"Like crabs?"

She drew back from me, her eyes wide, terror replaced by astonishment. "How did you know that?"

Quickly, I related all I knew. As I was finishing, her hand flew to her mouth. "Dimitrios? Putting their eggs in the tanks? But Jim, we've taken showers—both of us!"

"Calm down," I told her. "We had our showers *before* I saw him up there. And we haven't eaten here, or drunk any of the water."

"Eaten?" her eyes opened wider still. "But if I hadn't heard the kid bleating, I might have eaten!"

"What?"

She nodded. "I ordered wine and . . . some melon. I thought we'd have it before the fish. But the Greek girl dropped it, and—"

She was rapidly becoming incoherent. I grabbed her again, held her tightly. "Dropped it? You mean she dropped the food?"

"She dropped the melon, yes." She nodded jerkily. "The bottle of wine, too. She came out of the kitchen and just let everything drop. It all smashed on the floor. And she stood there wringing her hands for a moment. Then she ran off. She was crying: 'Oh Dimitrios, Dimitrios!' "

"I think he's crazy," I told her. "He has to be. And his wife— or sister, or whatever she is—she's scared to death of him. You say she ran off? Which way?"

"Toward the town, the way we came. I saw her climbing the spur."

I hazarded a guess: "He's pushed her to the edge, and she's

slipped over. Come on, let's go and have a look at Dimitrios's kitchen."

We went to the front of the building, to the kitchen door. There on the floor by one of the tables, I saw a broken wine bottle, its dark red contents spilled. Also a half-melon, lying in several softly jagged chunks. And in the melon, crawling in its scattered seeds and pulpy red juices—

"Where are the others?" I said, wanting to speak first before Julie could cry out, trying to forestall her.

"Others?" she whispered. She hadn't really heard me, hadn't even been listening; she was concentrating on backing away from the half-dozen crawling things that moved blindly on the floor.

I stamped on them, crushed them in a frenzy of loathing, then scuffed the soles of my flip-flops on the dusty concrete floor as if I'd stepped in something nasty—which is one hell of an understatement. "The other people," I said. "The three sisters and . . . and George." I was talking more to myself than to Julie, and my voice was hoarse.

My fear transferred itself instantly. "Oh Jim, Jim!" she cried. She threw herself into my arms, shivering as if in a fever. And I felt utterly useless—no, defenceless—a sensation I'd occasionally known in deep water, without my gun, when the shadow of a rock might suddenly take on the aspect of a great, menacing fish.

Then there came one of the most dreadful sounds I've ever heard in my life: the banging and clattering of Dimitrios's three-wheeler on the road cut into the spur, echoing down to us from the rocks of the mountainside. "My spear gun," I said. "Come on, quickly!"

She followed at arm's length, half running, half dragged. "We're too vulnerable," I gasped as we reached the chalet. "Put clothes on, anything. Cover up your skin."

"What?" She was still dazed. "What?"

"*Cover yourself!*" I snapped. Then I regained control. "Look, he tried to give us these things. He gave them to George, and to the sisters for all I know. And he may try again. Do you want one of those things on your flesh, maybe laying its eggs in you?"

She emptied a drawer onto the floor, found slacks, and pulled them on; good shoes, too, to cover her feet. I did much the same: pulled on a long-sleeved pullover, rammed my feet into decent shoes. And all in a sort of frenzied blur, fingers all thumbs, heart thumping. And: "*Oh shit!*" she sobbed. Which wasn't really my Julie at all.

"Eh?" She was heading for the small room at the back.

"Toilet!" she said. "I have to."

"*No!*" I jumped across the space between, dragged her away from the door to the toilet-*cum*-shower unit. "It's crawling with them in there. They come up the plug holes." In my arms, I could feel that she was also crawling. Her flesh. Mine, too. "If you must go, go outside. But first let's get away from here." I picked up my gun, loaded it with a single flap-nosed spear.

Leaving the chalet, I looked across at the ramp coming down from the rocky spur. The clatter of Dimitrios's three-wheeler was louder. It was there, headlight beams bobbing as the vehicle trundled lurchingly down the rough decline. "Where are we going?" Julie gasped, following me at a run across the scrub between clumps of olives. I headed for the other chalets.

"Safety in numbers," I answered. "Anyway, I want to know about George, and those three old spinsters."

"What good will they be, if they're old?" She was too logical by half.

"They're not that old." Mainly, I wanted to see if they were all right. Apart from the near-distant racket Dimitrios's vehicle was making, the whole valley was quiet as a tomb. Unnaturally quiet. It had to be a damned funny place in Greece where the cicadas keep their mouths shut.

Julie had noticed that, too. "They're not singing," she said. And I knew what she meant.

"Rubbing," I answered. "They rub their legs together or something."

"Well," she panted, "whatever it is they do, they're not."

It was true evening now, and a half-moon had come up over the central mountain's southern extreme. It's light silvered our way through thorny shrubs and tall, spiked grasses, under the low grey branches of olives and across their tangled, groping roots.

We came to the first chalet. Its lights were out, but the door stood ajar. "I think this is where George is staying," I said. And calling ahead, "George, are you in?," I entered and switched on the light. He was in—in the big double bed, stretched out on his back. But he turned his head toward us as we entered. He blinked in the sudden, painful light. One of his eyes did, anyway. The other couldn't . . .

He stirred himself, tried to sit up. I think he was grinning. I can't be sure, because one of the things, a big one, was inside the corner of his mouth. They were hatching from fresh lumps down his neck and in the bend of his elbow. God knows what the rest of his body was like. He managed to prop himself up, hold out a hand to me—and I almost took it. And it was then that I began to understand something of the nature of these things. For there was one of them in his open palm, its barbed feet seeming poised, waiting.

I snatched back my hand, heard Julie's gasp. And there she was, backed up against the wall, screaming her silent scream. I grabbed her, hugged her, dragged her outside. For of course there was nothing we could do for George. And, afraid she would scream, and maybe start *me* going, I slapped her. And off we went again, reeling in the direction of the third and last chalet.

Down by the taverna, Dimitrios's three-wheeler had come to a halt, its engine stilled, its beams dim, reaching like pallid hands along the sand. But I didn't think it would be long before he was on the move again. And the nightmare was expanding, growing vaster with every beat of my thundering heart.

In the third chalet . . . it's hard to describe all I saw. Maybe there's no real need. The spinster I'd thought was maybe missing something was in much the same state as George: she, too, was in bed, with those god-awful things hatching in her. Her sisters . . . at first I thought they were both dead, and . . . But there, I've gone ahead of myself. That's how it always happens when I think about it, try to reconstruct it again in my own mind: it speeds up until I've outstripped myself. You have to understand that the whole thing was kaleidoscopic.

I went inside ahead of Julie, got a quick glimpse, an indistinct picture of the state of things fixed in my brain, then turned and kept Julie from coming in. "Watch for him." I forced the words around my bobbing Adam's apple and returned to take another look. I didn't want to, but I thought the more we knew about this monster, the better we'd know how to deal with him. Except that in a little while, I guessed there would be only one possible way to deal with him.

The sister in the bed moved and lolled her head a little; I was wary, suspicious of her, and left her strictly alone. The other two had been attacked. With an axe or a machete or something. One of them lay behind the door, the other on the floor on the near side of the bed. The one behind the door had been sliced twice, deeply, across the neck and chest and lay in a pool of her own blood, which was already congealing. Tick-things, coming from the bathroom, had got themselves stuck in the darkening pool, their barbed legs twitching when they tried to extricate themselves. The other sister . . .

Senses swimming, throat bobbing, I stepped closer to the bed with its grimacing, hag-ridden occupant, and I bent over the one on the floor. She was still alive, barely. Her green dress was a sodden red under the rib cage, torn open in a jagged flap to reveal her gaping wound. And Dimitrios had dropped several of his damned pets onto her, which were burrowing in the raw, dark flesh.

She saw me through eyes already filming over, whispered something. I got down on one knee beside her, wanted to hold her hand, stroke her hair, do something. But I couldn't. I didn't want those bloody things on me. "It's all right," I said. "It's all right." But we both knew it wasn't.

"The . . . the Greek," she said, her voice so small I could scarcely hear it.

"I know, I know," I told her.

"We wanted to . . . to take Flo into town. She was . . . was so *ill*! He said to wait here. We waited, and . . . and . . ." She gave a deep sigh. Her eyes rolled up, and her mouth fell open.

Something touched my shoulder where I knelt, and I leapt erect, flesh tingling. The one on the bed, Flo, had flopped an arm in my direction—deliberately! Her hand had touched me. Crawling slowly down her arm, a trio of the nightmare ticks or crabs had been making for me. They'd been homing in on me like a bee targeting a flower. But more slowly, thank God, far more slowly.

Horror froze me rigid, but in the next moment, Julie's sobbing cry—"Jim, he's coming!"—unfroze me at once.

I staggered outside. A dim, slender, dark, and reeling shape was making its way along the rough track between the chalets. Something glinted dully in his hand. Terror galvanized me. "Head for the high ground," I said. I took Julie's hand, began to run.

"High ground?" she panted. "Why?" She was holding together pretty well. I thanked God I hadn't let her see inside the chalet.

"Because then we'll have the advantage. He'll have to come up at us. Maybe I can roll rocks down on him or something."

"You have your gun," she said.

"As a last resort," I told her, "yes. But this isn't a John Wayne western, Julie. This is real! Shooting a man isn't the same as shoot-

ing a fish . . ." And we scrambled across the rough scrubland toward
the goat track up the far spur. Maybe ten minutes later and halfway
up that track, suddenly it dawned on both of us just where we were
heading. Julie dug in her heels and dragged me to a halt.

"But the cave's up there!" she panted. "The well!"

I looked all about. The light was difficult, made everything seem
vague and unreal. Dusk is the same the world over: it confuses
shapes, distances, colours, and textures. On our right, scree rising
steeply all the way to the plateau—too dangerous by far. And on
our left a steep, in places sheer, decline to the valley's floor. All you
had to do was stumble once, and you wouldn't stop sliding and
tumbling and bouncing till you hit the bottom. Up ahead the track
was moon-silvered, to the place where the cliff overhung, where the
shadows were black and blacker than night. And behind . . . behind
us came Dimitrios, his presence made clear by the sound his boots
made shoving rocks and pebbles out of his way.

"Come on," I said, starting on up again.

"But where to?" Hysteria was in her whisper.

"That clump of rocks there." Ahead, on the right, weathered
out of the scree, a row of long boulders like leaning graveyard slabs
tilted at the moon. I got between two of them, pulled Julie off the
track, and jammed her behind me. It was last-ditch stuff; there was
no way out other than the way we'd come in. I loaded my gun,
hauling on the propulsive rubbers until the spear was engaged. And
then there was nothing else to do but wait.

"Now be quiet," I hissed, crouching down. "He may not see us,
go straight on by."

Across the little valley, headlights blazed. Then came the echoing roar of revving engines. A moment more, and I could identify
humped silhouettes making their way like beetles down the ridge
of the far spur toward the indigo sea, then slicing the gloom with
scythes of light as they turned onto the dirt ramp. Two cars and a
motorcycle. Down on the valley's floor, they raced for the taverna.

Dimitrios came struggling out of the dusk, up out of the darkness, his breathing loud, laboured, gasping as he climbed in our tracks. His silhouette where he paused for breath was scarecrowlean, and he'd lost his floppy, wide-brimmed hat. But I suspected a strength in him that wasn't entirely his own. From where she peered over my shoulder Julie had spotted him too. I heard her sharp intake of breath, breathed *"Shh!"* so faintly I wasn't even sure she'd hear me.

He came on, the thin moonlight turning his eyes yellow, and turning his machete silver. Level with the boulders he drew, and almost level with our hiding place, and paused again. He looked this way and that, cocked his head, and listened. Behind me, Julie was trembling. She trembled so hard I was sure it was coming right through me, through the rocks, too, and the earth, and right through the soles of his boots to Dimitrios.

He took another two paces up the track, came level with us. Now he stood out against the sea and the sky, where the first pale stars were beginning to switch themselves on. He stood there, looking up the slope toward the cave under the cliff, and small, dark silhouettes were falling from the large blot of his head. Not droplets of sweat, no, for they were far too big, and too brittle-sounding when they landed on the loose scree.

Again Julie snatched a breath, and Dimitrios's head slowly came round until he seemed to be staring right at us.

Down in the valley the cars and the motorcycle were on the move again, engines revving, headlight beams slashing here and there. There was some shouting. Lights began to blaze in the taverna, the chalets. Flashlights cut narrow searchlight swaths in the darkness.

Dimitrios seemed oblivious to all this; still looking in our direction, he scratched at himself under his right armpit. His actions rapidly became frantic, until with a soft, gurgling cry, he tore open his shirt. He let his machete fall clattering to the track and clawed wildly at himself with both hands! He was shedding tick-things as a dog sheds fleas. He tore open his trousers, dropped them, staggered as he stepped out of them. Agonized sulphur eyes burned yellow in his blot of a face as he tore at his thighs.

I saw all of this, every slightest action. And so did Julie. I felt her swell up behind me, scooping in air until she must surely burst—and then she let it out again. But silently, screaming like a maniac in the night—and nothing but air escaping her!

A rock slid away from under my foot, its scrape a deafening clatter to my petrified mind. The sound froze Dimitrios, too, but only for a moment. Then he stooped, regained his machete. He took a pace toward us, inclined his head. He couldn't see us yet, but he knew we were there. Then—*God*, I shall dream of this for the rest of my life!

He reached down a hand and stripped a handful of living, crawling filth from his loins, and lobbed it in our direction as casually as tossing crumbs to starveling birds!

The next five seconds were madness.

I stumbled out from cover, lifted my gun, and triggered it. The spear struck him just below the rib cage, went deep into him. He cried out, reeled back, and yanked the gun from my hand. I'd forgotten to unfasten the nylon cord from the spear. Behind me, Julie was crumpling to the ground; I was aware of the latter, turned to grab her before she could sprawl. There were tick-things crawling about, and I mustn't let her fall on them.

I got her over my shoulder in a fireman's lift, went charging out onto the track, skipping and stamping my feet, roaring like a maddened bull. And I was mad: mad with shock, terror, loathing. I stamped and kicked and danced, never letting my feet stay in one place for more than a fraction of a second, afraid something would climb up onto me. And the wonder is I didn't carry both of us flying down the steep scree slope to the valley's floor.

Dimitrios was halfway down the track when I finally got myself under a semblance of control. Bouncing toward our end of the valley, a car came crunching and lurching across the scrub. I fancied it was Nichos's taxi. And sure enough, when the car stopped and its headlight beams were still, Nichos's voice came echoing up, full of concerned enquiry:

"Mister, lady—you OK?"

"Look out!" I shouted at the top of my voice, but only at the second attempt. "He's coming down! Dimitrios is coming down!"

And now I went more carefully, as in my mind the danger receded, and in my veins the adrenalin raced less rapidly. Julie moaned where she flopped loosely across my shoulder, and I knew she'd be all right.

The valley seemed alight with torches now, and not only the electric sort. Considering these people were Greeks, they seemed remarkably well organized. That was a thought I'd keep in mind, something else I would have to ask about. There was some shouting down there, too, and flaring torches began to converge on the area at the foot of the goat track.

Then there echoed up to me a weird, gurgled cry: a cry of fear, protestation—relief? A haunting, sobbing shriek cut off at highest pitch by the dull boom of a shot fired, and a moment later by a blast that was the twin of the first. From twin barrels, no doubt.

When I got down, Julie was still out of it, for which I was glad. They'd poured gasoline over Dimitrios's body and set fire to it. Fires were burning everywhere: the chalets, taverna, gardens. Cleansing flames leaping. Figures moved in the smoke and against a yellow roaring background, searching, burning. And I sat in the back of Nichos's taxi, cradling Julie's head. Mercifully, she remained unconscious right through it.

Even with the windows rolled up, I could smell something of the smoke, and something that wasn't smoke . . .

———

In Makelos town, Julie began to stir. I asked for her to be sedated, kept down for the night. Then, when she was sleeping soundly and safely in a room at the mayor's house, I began asking questions. I was furious at the beginning, growing more furious as I started to get the answers.

I couldn't be sorry for the people of Makelos, though I did feel something for Elli, Dimitrios's wife. She'd run to Nichos, told him what was happening. And he'd alerted the townspeople. Elli had been a sort of prisoner at the taverna for the past ten days or so, after her husband had "gone funny." Then, when she'd started to notice things, he'd told her to keep quiet and carry on as normal, or she'd be the loser. And he meant she'd lose all the way. She reckoned he'd got the parasites off the goats, accidentally, and she was probably right, for the goats had been the first to die. Her explanation was likely because the goats used to go up there some-times, to the cave under the mountain. And that was where the things bred, in that cave and in the well it contained, which now and then overflowed, and found its way to the sea.

But Elli, poor peasant that she was, on her way to alert Nichos, she'd seen her husband kill George's wife and push her over the cliffs into the sea. Then she'd hid herself off the road until he'd turned his three-wheeler round and started back toward the taverna.

As for the corpse under the tarpaulin: that was Dimitrios's grandfather, who along with his grandson had been a survivor of the first outbreak. He'd been lucky that time, not so lucky this time.

And the tick things? They were . . . a *disease*, but they could never be a plague. The men from Athens had taken some of them away with them that first time. But away from their well, away from the little shaded valley and from Makelos, they'd quickly died. This was their place, and they could exist nowhere else. Thank God!

Last time the chemicals hadn't killed them off, obviously, or maybe a handful of eggs had survived to hatch out when the poisons had dissolved away. For they *were* survivors, these creatures, the last of their species, and when they went, their secret would go with them. But a disease? I believe so, yes.

Like the common cold, or rabies, or any other disease, but far worse because they're visible, apparent. The common cold makes you sneeze, so that the disease is propagated, and hydrophobia, which makes its victims claw and bite, gets passed on in their saliva. The secret of the tick-things was much the same sort of thing: they made their hosts pass them on. It was the way their intelligent human hosts did it that made them so much more terrible.

In the last outbreak, only Greeks—Makelosians—had been involved; this time it was different. This time, too, the people would take care of the problem themselves: they'd pour hundreds of gallons of gasoline and fuel oil into the well, set the place on fire. And then they'd dynamite the cliff, bring it down to choke the well for ever, and they'd never, *ever*, let people go into that little valley again. That was their promise, but I'd made myself a couple of promises, too. I was angry and frightened, and I knew I was going to stay that way for a long time to come.

We were out of there first thing in the morning, on the first boat to the mainland. There were smart-looking men to meet us at the airport in Athens, Greek officials from some ministry or other. They had interpreters with them, and nothing was too much trouble. They, too, made promises, offers of compensation, anything our hearts desired. We nodded and smiled wearily, said yes to this, that, and the other, anything so that we could just get aboard that plane. It had been our shortest holiday ever: we'd been in Greece just forty-eight hours, and all we wanted now was to be out of it as quickly as possible. But when we were back home again—*that* was when we told our story!

It was played down, of course: the Common Market, international tensions, a thousand other economic and diplomatic reasons. Which is why I'm now telling it all over again. I don't want anybody to suffer what we went through, what we're still going through. And so if you happen to be mad on the Mediterranean islands . . . well, I'm sorry, but that's the way it was.

As for Julie and me: we've moved away from the sea, and come summer, we won't be going out in the sun too much or for too long. That helps a little. But every now and then, I'll wake up in the night, in a cold sweat, and find Julie doing her horrible thing: nightmaring about Dimitrios, hiding from him, holding her breath so that he won't hear her—

—And sometimes screaming her silent screams . . .

THE SECOND WISH

The scene was awesomely bleak: mountains gauntly grey and black towered away to the east, forming an uneven backdrop for a valley of hardy grasses, sparse bushes, and leaning trees. In one corner of the valley, beneath foothills, a scattering of shingle-roofed houses, with the very occasional tiled roof showing through, was enclosed and protected in the Old European fashion by a heavy stone wall.

A mile or so from the village—if the huddle of timeworn houses could properly be termed a village—leaning on a low rotting fence that guarded the rutted road from a steep and rocky decline, the tourists gazed at the oppressive bleakness all about and felt oddly uncomfortable inside their heavy coats. Behind them their hired car—a black Russian model as gloomy as the surrounding countryside, exuding all the friendliness of an expectant hearse—stood patiently waiting for them.

He was comparatively young, of medium build, dark-haired, unremarkably good-looking, reasonably intelligent, and decidedly idle. His early adult years had been spent avoiding any sort of real industry, a prospect which a timely and quite substantial inheritance had fortunately made redundant before it could force itself upon him. Even so, a decade of living at a rate far in excess of even his ample inheritance had rapidly reduced him to an almost penniless, unevenly cultured, high-ranking rake. He had never quite lowered himself to the level of a gigolo, however, and his womanizing had been quite deliberate, serving an end other than mere fleshly lust.

They had been ten very good years by his reckoning and not at all wasted, during which his expensive lifestyle had placed him in intimate contact with the cream of society, but while yet surrounded by affluence and glitter he had not been unaware of his own steadily dwindling resources. Thus, towards the end, he had set himself to the task of ensuring that his tenuous standing in society would not suffer with the disappearance of his so carelessly distributed funds; hence his philandering. In this he was not as subtle as he might have been, with the result that the field had narrowed down commensurately with his assets, until at last he had been left with Julia.

She was a widow in her middle forties but still fairly trim, rather prominently featured, too heavily made-up, not a little calculating, and very well-to-do. She did not love her consort—indeed she had never been in love—but he was often amusing and always thoughtful. Possibly his chief interest lay in her money, but that thought did not really bother her. Many of the younger, unattached men she had known had been after her money. At least Harry was not foppish, and she believed that in his way he did truly care for her.

Not once had he given her reason to believe otherwise. She had only twenty good years left and she knew it; money could only buy so much youth . . . Harry would look after her in her final years and she would turn a blind eye on those little indiscretions which must surely come—provided he did not become too indiscreet. He had asked her to marry him and she would comply as soon as they returned to London. Whatever else he lacked he made up for in bed. He was an extremely virile man and she had rarely been so well satisfied . . .

Now here they were together, touring Hungary, getting "far away from it all."

"Well, is this remote enough for you?" he asked, his arm around her waist.

"Umm," she answered. "Deliciously barren, isn't it?"

"Oh, it's all of that. Peace and quiet for a few days—it was a good idea of yours, Julia, to drive out here. We'll feel all the more like living it up when we reach Budapest."

"Are you so eager, then, to get back to the bright lights?" she asked. He detected a measure of peevishness in her voice.

"Not at all, darling. The setting might as well be Siberia for all I'm concerned about locale. As long as we're together. But a girl of your breeding and style can hardly—"

"Oh, come off it, Harry! You can't wait to get to Budapest, can you?"

He shrugged, smiled resignedly, thought: *You niggly old bitch!* and said, "You read me like a book, darling, but Budapest is just a wee bit closer to London, and London is that much closer to us getting married, and—"

"But you have me anyway," she again petulantly cut him off. "What's so important about being married?"

"It's your friends, Julia," he answered with a sigh. "Surely you know that?" He took her arm and steered her towards the car. "They see me as some sort of cuckoo in the nest, kicking them all out of your affections. Yes, and it's the money, too."

"The money?" she looked at him sharply as he opened the car door for her. "What money?"

"The money I haven't got!" he grinned ruefully, relaxing now that he could legitimately speak his mind, if not the truth. "I mean, they're all certain it's your money I'm after, as if I was some damned gigolo. It's hardly flattering to either of us. And I'd hate to think they might convince you that's all it is with me. But once we're married I won't give a damn what they say or think. They'll just have to accept me, that's all."

Reassured by what she took to be pure naïveté, she smiled at him and pulled up the collar of her coat. Then the smile fell from her face, and though it was not really cold she shuddered violently as he started the engine.

"A chill, darling?" he forced concern into his voice.

"Umm, a bit of one," she answered, snuggling up to him. "And a headache, too. I've had it ever since we stopped over at—oh, what's the name of the place? Where we went up over the scree to look at that strange monolith?"

"Stregoicavar," he answered her. "The 'Witch-Town.' And that pillar-thing was the Black Stone. A curious piece of rock that, eh? Sticking up out of the ground like a great black fang! But Hungary is full of such things: myths and legends and odd relics of forgotten times. Perhaps we shouldn't have gone to look at it. The villagers shun it . . ."

"Mumbo jumbo," she answered. "No, I think I shall simply put the blame on *this* place. It's bloody depressing, really, isn't it?"

He tut-tutted good humouredly and said: "My God!—the whims of a woman, indeed!"

She snuggled closer and laughed in his ear. "Oh, well, that's what makes us so mysterious, Harry. Our changeability. But seriously, I think maybe you're right. It is a bit late in the year for wandering about the Hungarian countryside. We'll stay the night at the inn as planned, then cut short and go on tomorrow into Budapest. It's a drive of two hours at the most. A week at Zjhack's place, where we'll be looked after like royalty, and then on to London. How does that sound?"

"Wonderful!" He took one hand from the wheel to hug her. "And we'll be married by the end of October."

The inn at Szolyhaza had been recommended for its comforts and original Hungarian cuisine by an innkeeper in Kecskemét. Harry had suspected that both proprietors were related, particularly when he first laid eyes on Szolyhaza. That had been on the previous evening as they drove in over the hills.

Business in the tiny village could hardly be said to be booming. Even in the middle of the season, gone now along with the summer, Szolyhaza would be well off the map and out of reach of the ordinary tourist. It had been too late in the day to change their minds, however, and so they had booked into the solitary inn, the largest building in the village, an ancient stone edifice of at least five and a half centuries.

And then the surprise. For the proprietor, Herr Debrec, spoke near-perfect English; their room was light and airy with large windows and a balcony (Julia was delighted at the absence of a television set and the inevitable "Kultur" programs); and later, when they came down for a late evening meal, the food was indeed wonderful!

There was something Harry had wanted to ask Herr Debrec that first evening, but sheer enjoyment of the atmosphere in the little dining-room—the candlelight, the friendly clinking of glasses coming through to them from the bar, the warm fire burning bright in an old brick hearth, not to mention the food itself and the warm red local wine—had driven it from his mind. Now, as he parked the car in the tiny courtyard, it came back to him. Julia had returned it to mind with her headache and the talk of ill-rumoured Stregoicavar and the Black Stone on the hillside.

It had to do with a church—at least Harry suspected it was or had been a church, though it might just as easily have been a castle or ancient watchtower—sighted on the other side of the hills beyond gaunt autumn woods. He had seen it limned almost as a silhouette against the hills as they had covered the last few miles to Szolyhaza from Kecskemét. There had been little enough time to study the distant building before the road veered and the car climbed up through a shallow pass, but nevertheless Harry had been left with a feeling of—well, almost of—déjà vu, or perhaps presentiment. The picture of sombre ruins had brooded obscurely in his mind's eye until Herr Debrec's excellent meal and luxurious bed, welcome after many hours of driving on the poor country roads, had shut the vision out.

Over the midday meal, when Herr Debrec entered the dining room to replenish their glasses, Harry mentioned the old ruined church, saying he intended to drive out after lunch and have a closer look at it.

"That place, mein Herr? No, I should not advise it."

"Oh?" Julia looked up from her meal. "It's dangerous, is it?"

"Dangerous?"

"In poor repair—on the point of collapsing on someone?"

"No, no. Not that I am aware of, but—" he shrugged half apologetically.

"Yes, go on," Harry prompted him.

Debrec shrugged again, his short fat body seeming to wobble uncertainly. He slicked back his prematurely greying hair and tried to smile. "It is . . . very old, that place. Much older than my inn. It has seen many bad times, and perhaps something of those times still—how do you say it?—yes, 'adheres' to it."

"It's haunted?" Julia suddenly clapped her hands, causing Harry to start.

"No, not that—but then again—" the Hungarian shook his head, fumbling with the lapels of his jacket. He was obviously finding the conversation very uncomfortable.

"But you must explain yourself, Herr Debrec," Harry demanded. "You've got us completely fascinated."

"There is . . . a dweller," the man finally answered. "An old man—a holy man, some say, but I don't believe it—who looks after . . . things."

"A caretaker, you mean?" Julia asked.

"A keeper, madam, yes. He terms himself a 'monk,' I think, the last of his sect. I have my doubts."

"Doubts?" Harry repeated, becoming exasperated. "But what about?"

"Herr, I cannot explain," Debrec fluttered his hands. "But still I advise you, do not go there. It is not a good place."

"Now wait a min—" Harry began, but Debrec cut him off.

"If you insist on going, then at least be warned: do not touch . . . anything. Now I have many duties. Please to excuse me." He hurried from the room.

Left alone they gazed silently at each other for a moment. Then Harry cocked an eyebrow and said: "Well?"

"Well, we have nothing else to do this afternoon, have we?" she asked.

"No, but—oh, I don't know," he faltered, frowning. "I'm half inclined to heed his warning."

"But why? Don't tell me you're superstitious, Harry?"

"No, not at all. It's just that—oh, I have this feeling, that's all."

She looked astounded. "Why, Harry, I really don't know which one of you is trying hardest to have me on: you or Debrec!" She tightened her mouth and nodded determinedly. "That settles it then. We *will* go and have a look at the ruins, and damnation to all these old wives' tales!"

Suddenly he laughed. "You know, Julia, there might just be some truth in what you say—about someone having us on, I mean. It's just struck me: you know this old monk Debrec was going on about? Well, I wouldn't be surprised if it turned out to be his uncle or something! All these hints of spooky goings-on could be just some sort of put-on, a con game, a tourist trap. And here we've fallen right into it! I'll give you odds it costs us five pounds a head just to get inside the place!" And at that they both burst out laughing.

The sky was overcast and it had started to rain when they drove away from the inn. By the time they reached the track that led off from the road and through the grey woods in the direction of the ruined church, a ground mist was curling up from the earth in white drifting tendrils.

"How's this for sinister?" Harry asked, and Julia shivered again and snuggled closer to him. "Oh?" he said, glancing at her and smiling. "Are you sorry we came after all, then?"

"No, but it is eerie driving through this mist. It's like floating on milk! . . . Look, there's our ruined church directly ahead."

The woods had thinned out and now high walls rose up before them, walls broken in places and tumbled into heaps of rough moss-grown masonry. Within these walls, in grounds of perhaps half an acre, the gaunt shell of a great Gothic structure reared up like the tombstone of some primordial giant. Harry drove the car through open iron gates long since rusted solid with their massive hinges. He pulled up before a huge wooden door in that part of the building which still supported its lead-covered roof.

They left the car to rest on huge slick centuried cobbles, where the mist cast languorous tentacles about their ankles. Low over distant peaks the sun struggled bravely, trying to break through drifting layers of cloud.

Harry climbed the high stone steps to the great door and stood uncertainly before it. Julia followed him and said, with a shiver in her voice: "Still think it's a tourist trap?"

"Uh? Oh! No, I suppose not. But I'm interested anyway. There's something about this place. A feeling almost of—"

"As if you'd been here before?"

"Yes, exactly! You feel it too?"

"No," she answered, in fine contrary fashion. "I just find it very drab. And I think my headache is coming back."

For a moment or two they were silent, staring at the huge door.

"Well," Harry finally offered, "nothing ventured, nothing gained." He lifted the massive iron knocker, shaped like the top half of a dog's muzzle, and let it fall heavily against the grinning metal teeth of the lower jaw. The clang of the knocker was loud in the misty stillness.

"Door creaks open," Julia intoned, "revealing Bela Lugosi in a black high-collared cloak. In a sepulchral voice he says: 'Good evening . . .' " For all her apparent levity, half of the words trembled from her mouth.

Wondering how, at her age, she could act so stupidly girlish, Harry came close then to telling her to shut up. Instead he forced a grin, reflecting that it had always been one of her failings to wax witty at the wrong time. Perhaps she sensed his momentary annoyance, however, for she frowned and drew back from him fractionally. He opened his mouth to explain himself but started violently instead as, quite silently, the great door swung smoothly inward.

The opening of the door seemed almost to pull them in, as if a vacuum had been created . . . the sucking rush of an express train through a station. And as they stumbled forward they saw in the gloom, the shrunken, flame-eyed ancient framed against a dim, musty-smelling background of shadows and lofty ceilings.

The first thing they really noticed of him when their eyes grew accustomed to the dimness was his filthy appearance. Dirt seemed ingrained in him! His coat, a black full-length affair with threadbare sleeves, was buttoned up to his neck where the ends of a grey tattered scarf protruded. Thin grimy wrists stood out from the coat's sleeves, blue veins showing through the dirt. A few sparse wisps of yellowish hair, thick with dandruff and probably worse, lay limp on the pale bulbous dome of his head. He could have been no more than sixty-two inches in height, but the fire that burned behind yellow eyes, and the vicious hook of a nose that followed their movements like the beak of some bird of prey, seemed to give the old man more than his share of strength, easily compensating for his lack of stature.

"I . . . that is, we . . ." Harry began.

"Ah!—*English!* You are English, yes? Or perhaps American?" His heavily accented voice, clotted and guttural, sounded like the gurgling of a black subterranean stream. Julia thought that his throat must be full of phlegm, as she clutched at Harry's arm.

"Tourists, eh?" the ancient continued. "Come to see old Möhrsen's books? Or perhaps you don't know why you've come?" He clasped his hands tightly together, threw back his head, and gave a short coughing laugh.

"Why, we . . . that is . . ." Harry stumbled again, feeling foolish, wondering just why they *had* come.

"Please enter," said the old man, standing aside and ushering them deeper, irresistibly in. "It is the books, of course it is. They all come to see Möhrsen's books sooner or later. And of course there is the view from the tower. And the catacombs . . ."

"It was the ruins," Harry finally found his voice. "We saw the old building from the road, and—"

"Picturesque, eh. The ruins in the trees . . . Ah!—but there are other things here. You will see."

"Actually," Julia choked it out, fighting with a sudden attack of nausea engendered by the noisome aspect of their host, "we don't have much time . . ."

The old man caught at their elbows, yellow eyes flashing in the gloomy interior. "Time? No time?" his hideous voice grew intense in a moment. "True, how true. Time is running out for all of us!"

It seemed then that a draught, coming from nowhere, caught at the great door and eased it shut. As the gloom deepened Julia held all the more tightly to Harry's arm, but the shrunken custodian of the place had turned his back to guide them on with an almost peremptory: "Follow me."

And follow him they did.

Drawn silently along in his wake, like seabirds following an ocean liner through the night, they climbed stone steps, entered a wide corridor with an arched ceiling, finally arrived at a room with a padlocked door. Möhrsen unlocked the door, turned, bowed, and ushered them through.

"My library," he told them, "my beautiful books."

With the opening of the door, light had flooded the corridor, a beam broad as the opening in which musty motes were caught, drifting, eddying about in the disturbed air. The large room—bare except for a solitary chair, a table, and tier upon tier of volume-weighted shelves arrayed against the walls—had a massive window composed of many tiny panes. Outside the sun had finally won its battle with the clouds; it shone wanly afar, above the distant mountains, its autumn beam somehow penetrating the layers of grime on the small panes.

"Dust!" cried the ancient. "The dust of decades—of decay! I cannot keep it down." He turned to them. "But see, you must sign."

"Sign?" Harry questioned. "Oh, I see. A visitors' book."

"Indeed, for how else might I remember those who visit me here? See, look at all the names . . ."

The old man had taken a leather-bound volume from the table. It was not a thick book, and as Möhrsen turned the parchment leaves they could see that each page bore a number of signatures, each signature being dated. Not one entry was less than ten years old. Harry turned back the pages to the first entry and stared at it. The ink had faded with the centuries so that he could not easily make out the ornately flourished signature. The date, on the other hand, was still quite clear: "Frühling, 1611."

"An old book indeed," he commented, "but recently, it seems, visitors have been scarce . . ." Though he made no mention of it, frankly he could see little point in his signing such a book.

"Sign nevertheless," the old man gurgled, almost as if he could read Harry's mind. "Yes, you must, and the madam too." Harry reluctantly took out a pen, and Möhrsen watched intently as they scribbled their signatures.

"Ah, good, good!" he chortled, rubbing his hands together. "There we have it—two more visitors, two more names. It makes an old man happy, sometimes, to remember his visitors . . . And sometimes it makes him sad."

"Oh?" Julia said, interested despite herself. "Why sad?"

"Because I know that many of them who visited me here are no more, of course!" He blinked great yellow eyes at them.

"But look here, look here," he continued, pointing a grimy sharp-nailed finger at a signature. "This one: 'Justin Geoffrey, 12 June, 1926.' A young American poet, he was. A man of great promise. Alas, he gazed too long upon the Black Stone!"

"The Black Stone?" Harry frowned. "But—"

"And here, two years earlier: 'Charles Dexter Ward'—another American, come to see my books. And here, an Englishman this time, one of your own countrymen, 'John Kingsley Brown.'" He let the pages flip through filthy fingers. "And here another, but much more recently. See: 'Hamilton Tharpe, November, 1959.' Ah, I remember Mr. Tharpe well! We shared many a rare discussion here in this very room. He aspired to the priesthood, but—" He sighed. "Yes, seekers after knowledge all, but many of them ill-fated, I fear . . ."

"You mentioned the Black Stone," Julia said. "I wondered—?"

"Hmm? Oh, nothing. An old legend, nothing more. It is believed to be very bad luck to gaze upon the stone."

"Yes," Harry nodded. "We were told much the same thing in Stregoicavar."

"Ah!" Möhrsen immediately cried, snapping shut the book of names, causing his visitors to jump. "So you, too, have seen the Black Stone?" He returned the volume to the table, then regarded them again, nodding curiously. Teeth yellow as his eyes showed as he betrayed a sly, suggestive smile.

"Now see here—" Harry began, irrational alarm and irritation building in him, welling inside.

Möhrsen's attitude, however, changed on the instant. "A myth, a superstition, a fairy story!" he cried, holding out his hands in the manner of a conjurer who has nothing up his sleeve. "After all, what is a stone but a stone?"

"We'll have to be going," Julia said in a faint voice. Harry noticed how she leaned on him, how her hand trembled as she clutched his arm.

"Yes," he told their wretched host, "I'm afraid we really must go."

"But you have not seen the beautiful books!" Möhrsen protested. "Look, look—" Down from a shelf he pulled a pair of massive antique tomes and opened them on the table. They were full of incredible, dazzling, illuminated texts; and despite themselves, their feelings of strange revulsion, Harry and Julia handled the ancient works and admired their great beauty.

"And this book, and this." Möhrsen piled literary treasures before them. "See, are they not beautiful. And now you are glad you came, yes?"

"Why, yes, I suppose we are," Harry grudgingly replied.

"Good, good! I will be one moment—some refreshment— please look at the books. Enjoy them . . ." And Möhrsen was gone, shuffling quickly out of the door and away into the gloom.

"These books," Julia said as soon as they were alone. "They must be worth a small fortune!"

"And there are thousands of them," Harry answered, his voice awed and not a little envious. "But what do you think of the old boy?"

"He—frightens me," she shuddered. "And the way he smells!"

"Ssh!" he held a finger to his lips. "He'll hear you. Where's he gone, anyway?"

"He said something about refreshment. I certainly hope he doesn't think I'll eat anything he's prepared!"

"Look here!" Harry called. He had moved over to a bookshelf near the window and was fingering the spines of a particularly musty-looking row of books. "Do you know, I believe I recognize some of these titles? My father was always interested in the occult, and I can remember—"

"The occult?" Julia echoed, cutting him off, her voice nervous again. He had not noticed it before, but she was starting to look her age. It always happened when her nerves became frazzled, and then all the makeup in the world could not remove the stress lines.

"The occult, yes," he replied. "You know, the 'mystic arts,' the 'supernatural,' and what have you. But what a collection! There are books here in Old German, in Latin, Dutch—and listen to some of the titles: '*De Lapide Philosophico* ... *De Vermis Mysteriis* ... *Othuum Omnicia* ... *Liber Ivonis* ... *Necronomicon.*' " He gave a low whistle, then: "I wonder what the British Museum would offer for this lot? They must be near priceless!"

"They *are* priceless!" came a guttural gloating cry from the open door. Möhrsen entered, bearing a tray with a crystal decanter and three large crystal glasses. "But please, I ask you not to touch them. They are the pride of my whole library."

The old man put the tray upon an uncluttered corner of the table, unstoppered the decanter, and poured liberal amounts of wine. Harry came to the table, lifted his glass, and touched it to his lips. The wine was deep, red, sweet. For a second he frowned, then his eyes opened in genuine appreciation. "Excellent!" he declared.

"The best," Möhrsen agreed, "and almost one hundred years old. I have only six more bottles of this vintage. I keep them in the catacombs. When you are ready you shall see the catacombs, if you so desire. Ah, but there is something down there that you will find most interesting, compared to which my books are dull, uninteresting things."

"I don't really think that I care to see your—" Julia began, but Möhrsen quickly interrupted.

"A few seconds only," he pleaded, "which you will remember for the rest of your lives. Let me fill your glasses."

The wine had warmed her, calming her treacherous nerves. She could see that Harry, despite his initial reservations, was now eager to accompany Möhrsen to the catacombs.

"We have a little time," Harry urged. "Perhaps—?"

"Of course," the old man gurgled, "time is not *so* short, eh?" He threw back his own drink and noisily smacked his lips, then shepherded his guests out of the room, mumbling as he did so: "Come, come—this way—only a moment—no more than that."

And yet again they followed him, this time because there seemed little else to do, deeper into the gloom of the high-ceilinged corridor, to a place where Möhrsen took candles from a recess in the wall and lit them; then on down two, three flights of stone steps into a nitrous vault deep beneath the ruins; and from there a dozen or so paces to the subterranean room in which, reclining upon a couch of faded silk cushions, Möhrsen's revelation awaited them.

The room itself was dry as dust, but the air passing gently through held the merest promise of moisture, and perhaps this rare combination had helped preserve the object on the couch. There she lay—central in her curtain-veiled cave, behind a circle of worn, vaguely patterned stone tablets, reminiscent of a miniature Stonehenge—a centuried mummy-parchment figure, arms crossed over her abdomen, remote in repose. And yet somehow . . . unquiet.

At her feet lay a leaden casket, a box with a hinged lid, closed, curiously like a small coffin. A design on the lid, obscure in the poor light, seemed to depict some mythic creature, half-toad, half-dog. Short tentacles or feelers fringed the thing's mouth. Harry traced the dusty raised outline of this chimera with a forefinger.

"It is said she had a pet—a companion creature—which slept

beside her in that casket," said Möhrsen, again anticipating Harry's question.

Curiosity overcame Julia's natural aversion. "Who is . . . who *was* she?"

"The last true Priestess of the Cult," Möhrsen answered. "She died over four hundred years ago."

"The Turks?" Harry asked.

"The Turks, yes. But if it had not been them . . . who can say? The cult always had its opponents."

"The cult? Don't you mean the order?" Harry looked puzzled. "I've heard that you're—ah—a man of God. And if this place was once a church—"

"A man of God?" Möhrsen laughed low in his throat. "No, not of your God, my friend. And this was not a church but a temple. And not an order, a cult. I am its priest, one of the last, but one day there may be more. It is a cult which can never die." His voice, quiet now, nevertheless echoed like a warning, intensified by the acoustics of the cave.

"I think," said Julia, her own voice weak once more, "that we should leave now, Harry."

"Yes, yes," said Möhrsen, "the air down here, it does not agree with you. By all means leave—but first there is the legend."

"Legend?" Harry repeated him. "Surely not another legend?"

"It is said," Möhrsen quickly continued, "that if one holds her hand and makes a wish . . ."

"*No!*" Julia cried, shrinking away from the mummy. "I couldn't touch that!"

"Please, please," said Möhrsen, holding out his arms to her, "do not be afraid. It is only a myth, nothing more."

Julia stumbled away from him into Harry's arms. He held her for a moment until she had regained control of herself, then turned to the old man. "All right, how do I go about it? Let me hold her hand and make a wish—but then we *must* be on our way. I mean, you've been very hospitable, but—"

"I understand," Möhrsen answered. "This is not the place for a gentle, sensitive lady. But did you say that you wished to take the hand of the priestess?"

"Yes," Harry answered, thinking to himself: "if that's the only way to get the hell out of here!"

Julia stepped uncertainly, shudderingly back against the curtained wall as Harry approached the couch. Möhrsen directed him to kneel; he did so, taking a leathery claw in his hand. The elbow joint of the mummy moved with surprising ease as he lifted the hand from her withered abdomen. It felt not at all dry but quite cool and firm. In his mind's eye Harry tried to look back through the centuries. He wondered who the girl had really been, what she had been like. "I wish," he said to himself, "that I could know you as you were . . ."

Simultaneous with the unspoken thought, as if engendered of it, Julia's bubbling shriek of terror shattered the silence of the vault, setting Harry's hair on end and causing him to leap back away from the mummy. Furthermore, it had seemed that at the instant of Julia's scream, a tingle as of an electrical charge had travelled along his arm into his body.

Now Harry could see what had happened. As he had taken the mummy's withered claw in his hand, so Julia had been driven to clutch at the curtains for support. Those curtains had not been properly hung but merely draped over the stone surface of the cave's walls; Julia had brought them rustling down. Her scream had originated in being suddenly confronted by the hideous bas-reliefs which completely covered the walls, figures and shapes that seemed to leap and cavort in the flickering light of Möhrsen's candles.

Now Julia sobbed and threw herself once more into Harry's

arms, clinging to him as he gazed in astonishment and revulsion at the monstrous carvings. The central theme of these was an octopodal creature of vast proportions—winged, tentacled, and dragonlike, and yet with a vaguely anthropomorphic outline—and around it danced all the demons of hell. Worse than this main horror itself, however, was what its attendant minions were doing to the tiny but undeniably human figures which also littered the walls. And there, too, as if directing the nightmare activities of a group of these small, horned horrors, was a girl—with a leering dog-toad abortion that cavorted gleefully about her feet!

Hieronymus Bosch himself could scarcely have conceived such a scene of utterly depraved torture and degradation, and horror finally burst into livid rage in Harry as he turned on the exultant keeper of this nighted crypt. "A temple, you said, you old devil! A temple to what?—to that obscenity?"

"To Him, yes!" Möhrsen exulted, thrusting his hook nose closer to the rock-cut carvings and holding up the candles the better to illuminate them. "To Cthulhu of the tentacled face, and to all his lesser brethren."

Without another word, more angry than he could ever remember being, Harry reached out and bunched up the front of the old man's coat in his clenched fist. He shook Möhrsen like a bundle of moth-eaten rags, cursing and threatening him in a manner which later he could scarcely recall.

"God!" he finally shouted. "It's a damn shame the Turks didn't raze this whole nest of evil right down to the ground! You . . . you can lead the way out of here right now, at once, or I swear I'll break your neck where you stand!"

"If I drop the candles," Möhrsen answered, his voice like black gas bubbles breaking the surface of a swamp, "we will be in complete darkness!"

"No, please!" Julia cried. "Just take us out of here . . ."

"If you value your dirty skin," Harry added, "you'll keep a good grip on those candles!"

Möhrsen's eyes blazed sulphurous yellow in the candlelight and he leered hideously. Harry turned him about, gripped the back of his grimy neck, and thrust him ahead, out of the blasphemous temple. With Julia stumbling in the rear, they made their way to a flight of steps that led up into daylight, emerging some twenty-five yards from the main entrance.

They came out through tangled cobwebs into low decaying vines and shrubbery that almost hid their exit. Julia gave one long shudder, as if shaking off a nightmare, and then hastened to the car. Not once did she look back.

Harry released Möhrsen who stood glaring at him, shielding his yellow eyes against the weak light. They confronted each other in this fashion for a few moments, until Harry turned his back on the little man to follow Julia to the car. It was then that Möhrsen whispered:

"Do not forget: I did not force you to do anything. I did not make you touch anything. You came here of your own free will."

When Harry turned to throw a few final harsh words at him, the old man was already disappearing down into the bowels of the ruins.

In the car as they drove along the track through the sparsely clad trees to the road, Julia was very quiet. At last she said: "That was quite horrible. I didn't know such people existed."

"Nor did I," Harry answered.

"I feel filthy," she continued. "I need a bath. What on earth did that creature want with us?"

"I haven't the faintest idea. I think he must be insane."

"Harry, let's not go straight back to the inn. Just drive around for a while." She rolled down her window, breathing deeply of the fresh air that flooded in before lying back in the seat and closing her eyes. He looked at her, thinking: "God!—but you're certainly showing your age now, my sweet" . . . but he couldn't really blame her.

There were two or three tiny villages within a few miles of Szolyhaza, centres of peasant life compared to which Szolyhaza was a veritable capital. These were mainly farming communities, some of which were quite picturesque. Nightfall was still several hours away and the rain had moved on, leaving a freshness in the air and a beautiful warm glow over the hills, so that they felt inclined to park the car by the roadside and enjoy a drink at a tiny *Gasthaus*.

Sitting there by a wide window that overlooked the street, while Julia composed herself and recovered from her ordeal, Harry noticed several posters on the wall of the building opposite. He had seen similar posters in Szolyhaza, and his knowledge of the language was just sufficient for him to realize that the event in question— whatever that might be—was taking place tonight. He determined, out of sheer curiosity, to question Herr Debrec about it when they returned to the inn. After all, there could hardly be very much of importance happening in an area so out of the way. It had already been decided that nothing should be said about their visit to the ruins, the exceedingly unpleasant hour spent in the doubtful company of Herr Möhrsen.

Twilight was settling over the village when they got back. Julia, complaining of a splitting headache, bathed and went straight to her bed. Harry, on the other hand, felt strangely restless, full of physical and mental energy. When Julia asked him to fetch her a glass of water and a sleeping pill, he dissolved two pills, thus ensuring that she would remain undisturbed for the night. When she was asleep he tidied himself up and went down to the bar.

After a few drinks he buttonholed Herr Debrec and questioned him about the posters; what was happening tonight? Debrec told him that this was to be the first of three nights of celebration. It was the local shooting carnival, the equivalent of the German *Schützenfest*, when prizes would be presented to the district's best rifle shots.

There would be sideshows and thrilling rides on machines specially brought in from the cities, members of the various shooting teams would be dressed all in hunter's green, beer and wine would flow like water, and there would be good things to eat—oh, and all the usual trappings of a festival. This evening's main attraction was to be a masked ball, held in a great barn on the outskirts of a neighbouring village. It would be the beginning of many a fine romance. If the Herr wished to attend the festivities, Debrec could give him directions . . . ?

Harry declined the offer and ordered another drink. It was odd the effect the brandy was having on him tonight: he was not giddy—it took a fair amount to do that—but there seemed to be a peculiar *excitement* in him. He felt much the same as when, in the old days, he'd pursued gay young debutantes in the Swiss resorts or on the Riviera.

Half an hour and two drinks later he checked that Julia was fast asleep, obtained directions to the *Schützenfest,* told Herr Debrec that his wife was on no account to be disturbed, and drove away from the inn in fairly high spirits. The odds, he knew, were all against him, but it would be good fun and there could be no possible comeback; after all, they were leaving for Budapest in the morning, and what the eye didn't see the heart wouldn't grieve over. He began to wish that his command of the language went a little further than "good evening" and "another brandy, please." Still, there had been plenty of times in the past when language hadn't mattered at all, when talking would have been a positive hindrance.

In no time at all he reached his destination, and at first glance

he was disappointed. Set in the fields beside a hamlet, the site of
the festivities was noisy and garishly lit, in many ways reminiscent
of the country fairgrounds of England. All very well for teenage
couples, but rather gauche for a civilized, sophisticated adult. Nevertheless, that peculiar tingling with which Harry's every fibre
seemed imbued had not lessened, seemed indeed heightened by the
whirling machines and gaudy, gypsyish caravans and sideshows, and
so he parked the car and threaded his way through the swiftly gathering crowd.

Hung with bunting and festooned with balloons like giant ethereal multihued grapes, the great barn stood open to the night. Inside, a costumed band tuned up while masked singles and couples
in handsome attire gathered, preparing to dance and flirt the night
away. Framed for a moment in the huge open door, frozen by the
camera of his mind, Harry saw among the crowd the figure of a
girl—a figure of truly animal magnetism—dressed almost incon-
gruously in peasant's costume.

For a second masked eyes met his own and fixed upon them
across a space of only a few yards, and then she was gone. But the
angle of her neck as she had looked at him, the dark unblinking
eyes behind her mask, the fleeting, knowing smile on her lips before
she turned away—all of these things had spoken volumes.

That weird feeling, the tingling that Harry felt, suddenly suf-
fused his whole being. His head reeled and his mouth went dry; he
had consciously to fight the excitement rising from within; following
which he headed dizzily for the nearest wine tent, gratefully to slake
his thirst. Then, bolstered by the wine, heart beating fractionally
faster than usual, he entered the cavernous barn and casually cast
about for the girl whose image still adorned his mind's eye.

But his assumed air of casual interest quickly dissipated as his
eyes swept the vast barn without sighting their target, until he was
about to step forward and go among the tables in pursuit of his
quarry. At that point a hand touched his arm, a heady perfume

reached him, and a voice said: "There is an empty table on the balcony. Would you like to sit?"

Her voice was not at all cultured, but her English was very good; and while certainly there was an element of peasant in her, well, there was much more than that. Deciding to savour her sensuous good looks later when they were seated, he barely glanced at her but took her hand and proceeded across the floor of the barn. They climbed wooden stairs to an open balcony set with tables and cane chairs. On the way he spoke to a waiter and ordered a bottle of wine, a plate of dainties.

They sat at their tiny table overlooking the dance floor, toying with their glasses and pretending to be interested in completely irrelevant matters. He spoke of London, of skiing in Switzerland, the beach at Cannes. She mentioned the mountains, the markets of Budapest, the bloody history of the country, particularly of this region. He was offhand about his jet-setting, not becoming ostentatious; she picked her words carefully, rarely erring in pronunciation. He took in little of what she said and guessed that she wasn't hearing him. But their eyes—at first rather fleetingly—soon became locked; their hands seemed to meet almost involuntarily atop the table.

Beneath the table Harry stretched out a leg towards hers, felt something cold and hairy arching against his calf as might a cat. A cat, yes, it must be one of the local cats, fresh in from mousing in the evening fields. He edged the thing to one side with his foot . . . but she was already on her feet, smiling, holding out a hand to him.

They danced, and he discovered gypsy in her, and strangeness, and magic. She bought him a red mask and positioned it over his face with fingers that were cool and sure. The wine began to go down that much faster . . .

———

It came almost as a surprise to Harry to find himself in the car, in the front passenger seat, with the girl driving beside him. They were just pulling away from the bright lights of the *Schützenfest*, but he did not remember leaving the great barn. He felt more than a little drunk—with pleasure as much as with wine.

"What's your name?" he asked, not finding it remarkable that he did not already know. Only the sound of the question seemed strange to him, as if a stranger had spoken the words.

"Cassilda," she replied.

"A nice name," he told her awkwardly. "Unusual."

"I was named after a distant . . . relative."

After a pause he asked: "Where are we going, Cassilda?"

"Is it important?"

"I'm afraid we can't go to Szolyhaza—" he began to explain.

She shrugged, "My . . . home, then."

"Is it far?"

"Not far, but—"

"But?"

She slowed the car, brought it to a halt. She was a shadowy silhouette beside him, her perfume washing him in warm waves. "On second thoughts, perhaps I had better take you straight back to your hotel—and leave you there."

"No, I wouldn't hear of it," he spoke quickly, seeing his hopes for the night crumbling about him, sobered by the thought that she could so very easily slip out of his life. The early hours of the morning would be time enough for slipping away—and *he* would be doing it, not the girl. "You'd have to walk home, for one thing, for I'm afraid I couldn't let you take the car . . ." To himself he added: And I know that taxis aren't to be found locally.

"Listen," he continued when she made no reply, "you just drive yourself home. I'll take the car from there back to my hotel."

"But you do not seem steady enough to drive."

"Then perhaps you'll make me a cup of coffee?" It was a terribly juvenile gambit, but he was gratified to see her smiling behind her mask.

Then, just as quickly as the smile had come, it fell away to be replaced by a frown he could sense rather than detect in the dim glow of the dashboard lights. "But you must not see where I live."

"Why on earth not."

"It is not . . . a rich dwelling."

"I don't care much for palaces."

"I don't want you to be able to find your way back to me afterward. This can be for one night only . . ."

Now this, Harry thought to himself, is more like it! He felt his throat going dry again. "Cassilda, it can't possibly be for more than one night," he gruffly answered. "Tomorrow I leave for Budapest."

"Then surely it is better that—"

"Blindfold me!"

"What?"

"Then I won't be able to see where you live. If you blindfold me I'll see nothing except . . . your room." He reached across and slipped his hand inside her silk blouse, caressing a breast.

She reached over and stroked his neck, then pulled gently away. She nodded knowingly in the darkness: "Yes, perhaps we had better blindfold you, if you insist upon handling everything that takes your fancy!"

She tucked a black silk handkerchief gently down behind his mask, enveloping him in darkness. Exposed and compromised as she did this, she made no immediate effort to extricate herself as he fondled her breasts through the silk of her blouse. Finally, breathing the words into his face, she asked:

"Can you not wait?"

"It's not easy."

"Then I shall make it easier." She took his hands away from her body, sat back in her seat, slipped the car into gear and pulled away. Harry sat in total darkness, hot and flushed and full of lust.

"We are there," she announced, rousing him from some peculiar torpor. He was aware only of silence and darkness. He felt just a trifle queasy and told himself that it must be the effect of being driven blindfolded over poor roads. Had he been asleep? What a fool he was making of himself!

"No," she said as he groped for the door handle. "Let's just sit here for a moment or two. Open a bottle, I'm thirsty."

"Bottle? Oh, yes!" Harry suddenly remembered the two bottles of wine they had brought with them from the *Schützenfest*. He reached into the back seat and found one of them. "But we have no glasses. And why should we drink here when it would be so much more comfortable inside?"

She laughed briefly. "Harry, I'm a little nervous . . ."

Of course! French courage!—or was it Dutch? What odds? If a sip or two would help her get into the right frame of mind, why not? Silently he blessed the manufacturers of screw-top bottles and twisted the cap free. She took the wine from him, and he heard the swishing of liquid. Her perfume seemed so much stronger, heady as the scent of poppies. And yet beneath it he sensed . . . something tainted?

She returned the bottle to him and he lifted it to parched lips, taking a long deep draft. His head immediately swam, and he felt a joyous urge to break into wild laughter. Instead, discovering himself the victim of so strange a compulsion, he gave a little grunt of surprise.

When he passed the bottle back to her, he let his hand fall to her breast once more—and gasped at the touch of naked flesh, round and swelling! She had opened her blouse to him—or she had removed it altogether! With trembling fingers he reached for his mask and the handkerchief tucked behind it.

"No!" she said, and he heard the slither of silk. "There, I'm covered again. Here, finish the bottle and then get out of the car. I'll lead you . . ."

"Cassilda," he slurred her name. "Let's stop this little game now and—"

"You may not take off the blindfold until we are in my room, when we both stand naked." He was startled by the sudden coarseness of her voice—the lust he could now plainly detect—and he was also fired by it. He jerked violently when she took hold of him with a slender hand, working her fingers expertly, briefly, causing him to gabble some inarticulate inanity.

Momentarily paralysed with nerve-tingling pleasure and shock, when finally he thought to reach for her she was gone. He heard the whisper of her dress and the click of the car door as she closed it behind her.

Opening his own door he almost fell out, but her hand on his shoulder steadied him. "The other bottle," she reminded him.

Clumsily he found the wine, then stumbled as he turned from the car. She took his free hand, whispering: "Ssh! Quiet!" and gave a low guttural giggle.

Blind, he stumbled after her across a hard, faintly familiar surface. Something brushed against his leg, cold, furry, and damp. The fronds of a bushy plant, he suspected.

"Lower your head," she commanded. "Carefully down the steps. This way. Almost there . . ."

"Cassilda," he said, holding tightly to her hand. "I'm dizzy."

"The wine!" she laughed.

"Wait, wait!" he cried, dragging her to a halt. "My head's swimming." He put out the hand that held the bottle, found a solid surface, pressed his knuckles against it and steadied himself. He leaned against a wall of sorts, dry and flaky to his touch, and gradually the dizziness passed.

This is no good, he told himself: I'll be of no damn use to her unless I can control myself! To her he said, "Potent stuff, your local wine."

"Only a few more steps," she whispered.

She moved closer and again there came the sound of sliding silk, of garments falling. He put his arm around her, felt the flesh of her body against the back of his hand. The weight of the bottle slowly pulled down his arm. Smooth, firm buttocks—totally unlike Julia's, which sagged a little—did not flinch at the passing of fingers made impotent by the bottle they held.

"God!" he whispered, throat choked with lust. "I wish I could hold on to you for the rest of my life . . ."

She laughed, her voice hoarse as his own, and stepped away, pulling him after her. "But that's your second wish," she said.

Second wish . . . Second wish? He stumbled and almost fell, was caught and held upright, felt fingers busy at his jacket, the buttons of his shirt. Not at all cold, he shivered, and deep inside a tiny voice began to shout at him, growing louder by the moment, shrieking terrifying messages into his inner ear.

His second wish!

Naked he stood, suddenly alert, the alcohol turning to water in his system, the unbelievable looming real and immense and immediate as his four sound senses compensated for voluntary blindness.

"There," she said. "And now you may remove your blindfold!"

Ah, but her perfume no longer masked the charnel musk beneath; her girl's voice was gone, replaced by the dried-up whisper of centuries-shrivelled lips; the hand he held was—

Harry leapt high and wide, trying to shake off the thing that held his hand in a leathery grip, shrieking his denial in a black vault that echoed his cries like lunatic laughter. He leapt and cavorted, coming into momentary contact with the wall, tracing with his burning, supersensitive flesh the tentacled monstrosity that gloated there in bas-relief, feeling its dread embrace!

And bounding from the wall he tripped and sprawled, clawing at the casket which, in his mind's eye, he saw where he had last seen it at the foot of her couch. *Except that now the lid lay open!*

Something at once furry and slimy-damp arched against his naked leg—and again he leapt frenziedly in darkness, gibbering now as his mind teetered over vertiginous chasms.

Finally, dislodged by his threshing about, his blindfold—the red mask and black silk handkerchief he no longer dared remove of his own accord—slipped from his face . . . And then his strength became as that of ten men, became such that nothing natural or supernatural could ever have held him there in that nighted cave beneath black ruins.

Herr Ludovic Debrec heard the roaring of the car's engine long before the beam of its headlights swept down the black deserted road outside the inn. The vehicle rocked wildly and its tyres howled as it turned an impossibly tight corner to slam to a halt in the inn's tiny courtyard.

Debrec was tired, cleaning up after the day's work, preparing for the morning ahead. His handful of guests were all abed, all except the English Herr. This must be him now, but why the tearing rush? Peering through his kitchen window, Debrec recognized the car, then his weary eyes widened and he gasped out loud. But what in the name of all that . . . ? The Herr was naked!

The Hungarian landlord had the door open wide for Harry almost before he could begin hammering upon it, was bowled to one side as the frantic, gasping, bulge-eyed figure rushed in and up the stairs, but he had seen enough, and he crossed himself as Harry disappeared into the inn's upper darkness.

"Mein Gott!" he croaked, crossing himself again, and yet again. "The Herr has been in *that* place!"

Despite her pills, Julia had not slept well. Now, emerging from unremembered, uneasy dreams, temples throbbing in the grip of a terrific headache, she pondered the problem of her awakening. A glance at the luminous dial of her wristwatch told her that the time was ten after two in the morning.

Now what had startled her awake? The slamming of a door somewhere? Someone sobbing? Someone crying out to her for help? She seemed to remember all of these things.

She patted the bed beside her with a lethargic gesture. Harry was not there. She briefly considered this, also the fact that his side of the bed seemed undisturbed. Then something moved palely in the darkness at the foot of the bed.

Julia sucked in air, reached out and quickly snapped on the bedside lamp. Harry lay naked, silently writhing on the floor, face down, his hands beneath him.

"Harry!" she cried, getting out of bed and going to him. With a bit of a struggle she turned him on to his side, and he immediately rolled over on his back.

She gave a little shriek and jerked instinctively away from him, revulsion twisting her features. Harry's eyes were screwed shut now, his lips straining back from his teeth in unendurable agony. His hands held something to his heaving chest, something black and crumbly. Even as Julia watched, horrified, his eyes wrenched open and his face went slack. Then Harry's hands fell away from his chest; in one of them, the disintegrating black thing seemed burned into the flesh of his palm and fingers. It was unmistakably a small mummified hand!

Julia began to crawl backwards away from him across the floor; as she did so something came from behind, moving sinuously where it brushed against her. Seeing it, she scuttled faster, her mouth working silently as she came up against the wall of the room.

The—creature—went to Harry, snatched the shrivelled hand from him, turned away . . . then, as if on an afterthought, turned back. It arched against him for a moment, and, with the short feelers around its mouth writhing greedily, quickly sank its sharp teeth into the flesh of his leg. In the next instant the thing was gone, but Julia didn't see where it went.

Unable to tear her eyes away from Harry, she saw the veins in his leg where he had been bitten turn a deep, dark blue and stand out, throbbing beneath his marble skin. Carried by the now sluggish pulsing of his blood, the creature's venom spread through him. But . . . poison? No, it was much more, much worse, than poison. For as the writhing veins came bursting through his skin, Harry began to melt. It went on for some little time, until what was left was the merest travesty of a man: a sticky, tarry thing of molten flesh and smoking black bones.

Then, ignoring the insistent hammering now sounding at the door, Julia drew breath into her starving lungs—drew breath until she thought her chest must burst—and finally expelled it all in one vast eternal scream . . .

A *THING* ABOUT CARS!

Despite all government planning—the rapid construction of multiple road systems spanning the length and breadth of the country, population transplants of the human spillover from the cities to the previously thinly peopled regions, and the conversion of many areas of wasteland into vast farming concerns—the traveller in England will somewhere, sooner or later, still stumble across the quiet backwater surviving modernity, defying time, and sometimes, when the setting is just right, radiating an aura out of tune with the day and age which, as if in resentment of the slow but ever approaching encroachment of Man's machineries, might in certain perspective appear ominous and even frightening.

There are places like this in the Severn Valley—Goatswood and Temphill spring unpleasantly to mind—and others in the North and North-East, like Harden on the coast and Tharpe-Nettleford on the North Yorkshire border, but between a certain triangle of ancient but updated towns in the Midlands, there exists an area of some hundred square miles simply abounding with tiny villages of hoary antiquity exuding an ancient nastiness, and I cannot think back on my experience in that region without shuddering abominably and knowing again the terror I knew then.

One village in particular—which I drove through on the morning of that fateful June day not so long ago, on what I hoped was to be the final leg of my search for my poor, unfortunate brother,

Arnold Goyle—seemed by its . . . *effusions* . . . to set the mood for
the rest of the day, a mood of foreboding which began the moment
I drove past the village name board and which grew, dark and oppressive, to the moment of the final horror.

The fact that I missed the name on that board hardly surprised
me; as I drove along I reflected deeply on the unhappy events responsible for my brother's withdrawal. It had started while I was
serving with the forces in the Far East. At that time Arnold had
been living in his own house with his small family at Woodholme
in Nottingham. He was a sparse correspondent, not much given to
writing unless there was something really worth saying, so that when
I received that rather bulky letter from him in February of '48 I
knew before opening the envelope that its contents would be of
some import. I could never have guessed, however, of the tale of
grief to be unfolded at the reading. Arnold's marriage to Helen
twelve years earlier had been possibly the most perfect and harmonious union I had ever known. To say merely that they had been
"devoted" to each other would be an utter understatement, and if
anything, when their only child, Alan, came along at the end of the
first year, they grew even closer, and Arnold's happiness seemed
complete. The letter told of the abrupt destruction of that happiness.
Helen had been run down and killed in a car accident, struck down
on a pedestrian crossing by a speeding motorist. Her death had been
instantaneous. The driver had had his licence taken away and been
gaoled for six months; a "blind and total injustice" in Arnold's eyes,
not unnaturally, but the letter went on in what I considered—even
acknowledging Arnold's awful agony—a morbid vein of self-pity
and whining hypochondria. Of course, I immediately sent my con-
dolences, and later a second letter gently enquiring as to the course
my brother intended his now necessarily altered life to take. Neither
of my letters received a reply, nor did the subsequent half-dozen
enquiries which I despatched at regular intervals over the next seven
or eight months.

Then, when I had almost given up hope, I received another letter from Arnold, the contents of which turned out to be no less depressing than those of that other. In horror I read how Alan, Arnold's boy, had been given a lift to school by the father of a school friend in his car, and how the car had been involved in a serious accident. It appeared that there had been oil on the road, and that the car had been travelling a little "over the limit."

I was able to derive nothing further from this second tragic letter, for it had obviously been written while my brother was still suffering from extreme shock. The writing was barely legible, the punctuation bad even for Arnold, and the whole thing—what there was of it other than bare, terrible facts—rambled incoherently. My pity knew no bounds. Again I wrote of my shock and pain on learning of this, the completion of the destruction of Arnold's world, and again my letter went unacknowledged. I tried to get leave of absence, a compassionate flight to England, to no avail. My Company was due to proceed on exercise and all leave, especially that of junior officers, had been cancelled.

Another year passed before the time for my release from service came round. During that period I attempted, ever in vain, to contact my brother on numerous occasions. Only once did I learn anything of his whereabouts or circumstances. That was when a mutual friend in Woodholme wrote to tell me of how Arnold had gone "into a home" for a while to convalesce. Shortly before my discharge I wrote to an address given by my friend and the result of my enquiry was information to the effect that Arnold had lately recovered from what had seemed to be a series of traumatic lapses and had been, to quote the institution, "released back into society on partial recovery." I was supplied with his last known address.

This correspondence did not reach me until a month or so before I was due to return to England, so I made no immediate attempt to write to Arnold. It seemed pointless to do so when I could see him personally in only a few week's time. It goes without saying that I was very worried over his welfare. He had never been a very steady type and I was afraid that the tragic loss of his family might have done him far more permanent harm than that of which I knew.

Back in England I soon discovered that Arnold no longer lived at the address given me by the institution. I was fortunate to learn, however, that he had left a forwarding address, necessary in that he seemed to receive a lot of mail. And so it was that on that morning last June I drove in search of the village of Boresby in the Midlands, and, reflecting on my reason for being there, missed the name on the village name board; but the hedgerows had been tall for many a mile, excluding all but an occasional glimpse of the surrounding country, and the road had been narrow, winding, and bumpy, demanding that I divide my attentions equally between my reflections and my driving and forget all else. Yet in a twinkling, as I passed that name board, everything changed. The condition of the road improved and its width increased slightly; the hedgerows were replaced by tall, gnarled oaks letting through only a minimum of sunlight to weirdly dapple the road; and, as I cut down my speed to adjust to the sudden near-darkness, I felt the first pangs of a lurking and centuried outsidedess. This, I fancied, was one of those places, like Temphill or Harden, where almost anything might happen, an area literally exuding strangeness, to which all manner of strangeness might therefore be expected to be drawn.

The village proper was no more than a quarter mile in length, a single street wherein the oaks in their turn gave way to high, stark garden walls of buttresslike outer proportions suggestive of immense thickness, with shady gates beyond which I could not see; and only rarely I viewed over the tops of those walls the steeply sloping, thatched roofs of the houses beyond. Many of the great walls, moss- and ivy-grown, leaned perilously towards the road with no sidewalks lining them, so that the trees overhanging from the unseen gardens helped create for me the impression of driving between immense

jaws ready at any moment to snap shut. But worst of all was the
fact that in the entire quarter-mile I saw only one living creature—
and then not until I stopped at the ancient village post office to
enquire about the location of Arnold's address.

Inside the dim, dusty office I found a veined and elderly attendant drowsing behind a partitioned counter. He snorted into wake-
fulness when I let the spring-governed door slam shut behind me.
This action of mine was no display of latent aggressiveness, I simply
wished to demonstrate to myself my ability to shatter the leering
silence; like a traveller who whistles on a dark and lonely road. It
was then, from the old man, that I learned I was indeed in Boresby,
and from this beginning I went on to determine the rough
whereabouts of my brother's habitat. Obtaining anything other than
the most rudimentary information—mumbled directions, the mention of a wooded "T" junction and a rough track through the
woods—from the slow-thinking ancient behind the counter,
however, was the nearest I had ever come to extracting the prover-
bial "blood from a stone," and what little he did know was passed
on to me in an old, whistling, sibilant hiss of a voice which vaguely
reminded me of autumn leaves blowing over early-frosted cobbles.
I eventually left the post office with a number of large envelopes of
the magazine-subscription type bearing Arnold's name and address.
The old attendant had reckoned that as I was going to see my
brother anyway, there could be no harm in my taking his mail along
with me. One of the half-dozen envelopes was torn at one corner,
making the title of the publication within—*Motoring Magazine*—
easily read. Perhaps, I conjectured, Arnold was considering buying
a machine? Certainly the size and shape of the other envelopes was
suggestive of like contents. Yes, it could well be, I decided, that
Arnold was giving the purchase of a motorcar some consideration.
And not a bad idea, what with him living in such an out-of-the-
way spot. It did surprise me that my brother had not bought
a machine before; yet the old man had said that Arnold usually

came into the village on his bicycle. I gave the matter no further thought—not then.

Even after leaving the post office and village behind—when the hedgerows again took up their march on both sides of the road, shutting out as before whatever scenery lay beyond them—the feeling of dark, oppressive effusions remained with me, as if all the poisons of unknown centuries had found a temporary outlet in that soul-disturbing region. I barely noticed the great forest growing up on my right, the increasing dappling on the road, the slow shutting out again of the sunlight, but within no more than a mile of leaving the village behind I found myself at the wooded "T" junction mentioned by the gnarled ancient at the post office. There I turned right, as directed, taking the leg of the 'T' and penetrating into the leafy cool of the trees. The old attendant had been unable to state exactly the location of my brother's house—all registered addressees at the post office collected their own mail, precluding any visits to Arnold's place—but he had told me that the track to Arnold's house through the woods was forbidden to all unauthorized motor vehicles, and also that my brother had sole custody, was the gamekeeper and forest officer commissioned by the forestry authorities to protect the creatures of the woods and the woodlands themselves. Indeed, I shortly passed a huge, official notice board fastened to a tree, bearing a legend defining exactly the penalties to be incurred in ignoring the road's restrictions, but then, when one's own brother is the only authority, and when one is in a hurry, as I was, such restrictions do not mean very much. I had no doubt that Arnold would forgive me my laxity in this matter.

The road narrowed to a mere strip of tarmac threading in and out of the trees and shrubs, and again I knew the cobwebby gloom of enclosed and silent places. As I came round the bole of a great tree I saw the fork in the track and made a rapid decision. It was not that I was going too fast, simply that I was not expecting two tracks, and by the time I had taken the left of the forks it was already obvious that I was on the poorer surface. But now the trees were too close together, offering no opportunity to turn, so that I had to carry on or back up. I did not like to reverse if I could possibly help it. I had only to get stuck in a position where I could move neither forward nor back and the rest of my journey would be on foot! And I was not yet sure how much farther I had to go. Still, there was no proof that this was not the track down which my brother had his house, and there seemed only one way to resolve the matter for sure. I drove carefully on.

In another fifty yards the track petered out altogether and I found myself driving through short grass. There remained, though, signs of a trail of some sort, and the trees were thinning slightly, so that soon I was able to turn back the way I had come.

It was there, deep in the woods down that little used trail, as I made the turn to carry me back to the fork in the track, that I saw the old quarry. Those emanations that had bothered me since driving into Boresby were very strong there, disquieting influences which seemed to pulse through the very air. Dust motes danced in the beams of sunlight filtering through the high branches as I stopped my machine and climbed out to go and stand on the lip of the old stone quarry. The silence was absolute, with not even the soft cooing of wood-pigeons to disturb the lethal-seeming hush.

On three sides the quarry's rock face was steep and almost overhanging, but on the fourth, the farther side, a break in the sloping face had let through the mud and stagnant water of a wooded bog. Possibly this had stopped work in the quarry originally. Now the excavation was filled to a level some thirty feet beneath the lip with ooze and reeds, but directly beneath where I stood the water had apparently filtered itself into comparative clarity, so that I could make out mechanical shapes beneath the surface. There was the glint of chromium and the gleam of sunlight on sunken glass. Automobiles!—an unknown number. Perhaps at some time long past, this place had been used as a tip for broken-down cars. Yet from the little I could see the vehicles beneath the quarry water did not seem particularly aged.

Finally, unable to bear the quiet any longer, I gave a loud hoot of derision at my own strange fancies and climbed back into the driving seat of my car. And yet I was glad to pull away from that spot. Even the echoes of my scornful cry had seemed dulled and had died too quickly away.

Soon I was on the right track again and could hardly have penetrated another half-mile into the forest when I saw the obviously homemade sign, with lettering in Arnold's unmistakable scrawly style, nailed to a tree. He had never been much good with a paintbrush:

HOME BREWED BEER—
—ALL DAY LONG

Oh!—that would be Arnold, all right; hadn't he always fancied himself as a bit of a specialist when it came to home-pressed wines and beers? But what on Earth was he thinking of, putting a sign like that here, with this place allegedly "out of bounds" and him the official Preserver of the Sanctity, so to speak? Why! The sign was a positive attraction to trespassers, an invitation condoning woodland offences! Or perhaps the road was only restricted during certain seasons of the year?

The trees were much more thinned-out here, but that oppressive, shut-in feeling persisted in bothering me. Away through the trees, up a grassy track, stood a thatch-roofed cottage with a high, square towerlike building behind. Thin smoke drifted upwards from a brick chimney. I left my car, walked up the track through the trees to the door of the cottage, and knocked. There was no answer, but the weight of my knuckles was sufficient to cause the door, already slightly ajar, to swing fully open.

"Arnold? Are you there?" Inside, a passage split the cottage into two sections. My eyes were immediately attracted to the wall at the far end of the passage, to a massive door with four great hinges down one edge and a small-paned window in its upper section. I made calculations in my head, coming to the conclusion that the door must lead directly into the base of the tower behind the cottage proper. Come to think of it, what would that tall building be? Why, of course! It must be a watchtower for forest fires; it reached easily to the height of the surrounding trees. Yes, that would be the answer. But that aside, where was Arnold?—and what was that sickly, cloying scent that kept wafting to my nostrils? Difficult to place, that smell, yet I knew it from somewhere. One thing for sure, though, whatever the odour was it did not belong here in this setting—or did it?

I walked slowly down the passage, calling Arnold's name once or twice as I went and receiving no answer. He was obviously out, but perhaps would be back shortly. Two doors at the left of the passage were open and I glanced into the rooms as I passed. A toilet and a bathroom. I passed the bedroom next, pausing briefly to stare at a framed photograph on a dusty bedside table which smiled at me with the faces of Helen and young Alan, before coming to a closed door on the right. A few more paces brought me to the great door at the end of the passage. It was locked and had no doorknob. I tried to peer in through the small-paned window, but the glass was stained a dull brown on the other side, so that all I could make out was a gloomy outline or two. That smell I had noticed before seemed to be issuing from somewhere behind the massive door. Possibly Arnold used the base of the tower as a sort of storeroom. If so it seemed to me that something he had stored in there had gone bad. I retraced my steps to the closed room, turned the doorknob and pushed the door open.

"Arnold?" It seemed pointless calling his name again, but nonetheless, out of plain courtesy, I did so as I entered the room. Just inside the door I stopped dead to gaze astonished about me. What on Earth . . . ?

There was a window looking out on the grass track I had walked to the outside door, but the light coming in through that window had to fight its way past disordered stacks of books . . . or rather, magazines! Hundreds of them, all of the same theme, heaped on a dusty table, littered a score deep across the surface of a desk in front of the window, piled on chairs and stacked on the floor; packed bulging into bookshelves along the wall facing the door—car magazines! *The Motor-Car, Racing Machines, Autocar, The Motorist, Man Transport, The British Motorist, Road Travel,* and dozens of others some of which dated back at least five years.

There are fanatics and fanatics, but what kind of a man, for what possible reason, should want so many books—most of them way out of date—on any one subject? Obviously my brother was no collector in the normal sense of the word, for the magazines were simply scattered about indiscriminately, with no sign of sorting or filing. Indeed, some of the publications were still in their brown-paper subscription envelopes, unopened. I threw down the half-dozen envelopes brought from the post office on top of the rest and moved over to a cabinet relatively clear of Arnold's hoard. The cabinet occupied a space roughly in the centre of the room from where I could stare about me in complete bewilderment. The very walls, other than the one with the bookshelves, were literally covered with automobile photographs, the great majority of them showing cars coming head on towards the viewer.

Some warning mechanism ticked away madly in the back of my mind, telling me that something was very wrong here. "Arnold!" I uselessly called out again, "Where are you?" I opened the cabinet to peer in surprise at the tape recorder and amplifier it contained. I could not remember my brother as being much of a music lover. On a second shelf beneath the tape recorder a number of small green bottles stood. Suddenly I felt thirsty. And why not? Home-brewed beer, no less! I pulled the cork from one of the bottles, raising it to my lips. The sweetly acrid smell of beer from the uncorked bottle was appetizing and I almost drank, but there was a second scent, one which—hinting as it did of something far more toxic than mere alcohol—caused me to sniff suspiciously. Drugged? Or was I imagining things again? Possibly the beer had been over-brewed. And anyway, why should Arnold drug his own products? Nevertheless I recorked the bottle and put it back on its shelf without tasting the contents.

I stood there, undecided for a moment, then I decided to get my mind from its morbid turn by sampling Arnold's taste in music. Perhaps, wherever he was, the sound of his tape recorder playing would alert him to my presence. I switched the instrument on. For the first few inches the tape was blank, so that when the recorded section finally came round the sound reproduction system was fully warmed up. I staggered then, as a sudden scream of revving auto engines, a grinding of gears and blast of horns, an utter cacophony of mechanical sounds belched into me from the amplifier with a force which was as physical as it was unexpected. Through the hellish racket I somehow found the volume control and managed to turn the thing down.

As the incredible, mindless noises subsided, a new sound came to my ears. Apparently the tape recorder's wiring was also connected to some outside source—though why that should be I could not even guess—for I could now hear, from the direction of what could only be the upper reaches of the towerlike structure, the sound of a powerful motor and a rattling as of chains moving over pulleys. As the sound from the amplifiers reached a new height—a pitch which would have been unbearable had I not toned the thing down—there came a long scream of brakes and then . . . silence. Having reached the end of the short tape, the machine had automatically commenced rewinding. The sound of the motor high in the tower had also ceased, but now there came another sound from that direction: a rushing of chains and a whirring of well-oiled gears, and the very ground beneath my feet suddenly shook to a tremendous crash that threatened to bring the whole house down about my ears. Then, almost immediately, the recording of motor horns, brakes, clashing gears, and revving engines started all over again as the tape began its second playing, and again the clank of chains and the throb of a powerful motor from the tower added voice to the general clamour.

Inexplicable though it was, the whole thing was too much for merely human nerves. I quickly switched the tape recorder off. Silence fell in the house as the motor in the tower likewise shut down.

What was I to make of it all? I felt keyed up to screaming point; everything was far too odd, too strange. I wanted to see Arnold and the sooner the better! There were many things here for which I would like an explanation. Not that it was really my business, but Arnold was, after all, my brother, and if there *was* anything wrong . . . well, I wanted to know.

I went shakily back out into the passage, noting that the smell from the heavy door seemed to have grown stronger—as if something rotting had been stirred—and made my way to the outside door. I felt strangely relieved to be out of the house, and I called Arnold's name yet again as I walked round the cottage on the uncropped grass to the towering structure behind.

There was another door in the far wall of the tower, a great strong thing similar to the door at the end of the passage, and it was from this massive entrance, standing slightly ajar, that the cloying smell definitely issued. The door opened outwards and I found myself holding my breath as I pulled it a little further open to lean my head and shoulders inside. I had expected a staircase leading up, but none such existed. Instead the floor looked dark and squelchy, the walls were bare and stained; there was nothing, only the bare bricks of the walls and weak light filtering down in dusty beams from above. No, there *was* something. In a small recess in the op-posite wall there was a second amplifier—the twin of the one in the cabinet in the cottage.

My eyes slowly accustomed themselves to the gloom. I twisted my neck to look up into the top of the tower. There was a square of light, its centre mostly blocked off by a slowly turning dark mass which occasionally bumped against the walls . . . like a weight sus-pended on a thread.

Then I gasped in amazement. The turning thing high above me was a car—a badly battered and twisted wreck of a car! Strips of . . . stuff . . . hung from its bent axles and from the splayed, tyreless wheels, and the entire bottom looked clogged with dark lumps of mud or—

The smell! I knew now where I had known that special odour before—in the gutted villages of Germany in the war years!

I jerked my eyes down to stare hard at the pulpy floor, then back up to bulge at the crusher hanging above, down again to the now discernible mass of . . . of . . . *human debris!*

A car hanging in a tower with pulped flesh clogging its underside; a floor slimy with the ooze and filth of God-only-knows how many mangled bodies . . .

Nightmare!

I gagged, jerking my head back out of that monstrous tower, fighting down the waves of nausea and bone-jellying terror which I felt welling inside. What had happened here? What—

The cough was low, polite, enquiring.

I whirled about, shock stiffening the short hairs on the back of my neck, causing my lips to pull back in what must have looked a bestial snarl. I saw him—but not really—my mind still picturing in camera detail the contents of the towerlike structure, making of this intruder on the horror merely a blurred image. A rustic, at least at first glance, trundling a wheelbarrow. He wore Wellingtons, farmer fashion, and his wide-brimmed hat was more a sunshade. Beneath that hat dull blue, almost disinterested pools of desolation gazed out at me from a face I knew of old. But the old character behind that face had gone completely, was replaced now by a sort of gaunt vacancy. Even then I could not accept the truth.

"Arnold," I finally croaked, "terrible accident . . . get help . . . the police . . . bodies, pulped . . . a car, suspended . . ."

"Accident, Nigel?" he asked dully.

"Yes," I replied, noting for the first time the fragments of dried, decaying offal, strips of skin, and bits of gristle clinging to the terribly stained interior of the wheelbarrow's bucket, seeing in sudden clarity the ghastly *state* of Arnold's Wellingtons. "A terrible . . . accident . . . ?"

I lay back limply against the wall. *"My God!"*

"You've caught me at a bad time, Nigel," he told me, listlessly amiable, ignoring my exclamation of horror and loathing, "I was just doing a little house cleaning." Then his eyes brightened hideously and he leaned closer. "Nigel," his voice now sounded clotted and gutteral, "is that *your* car out front?"

RISING
WITH SURTSEY

It appears that with the discovery of a live coelacanth—a fish thought to have been extinct for over seventy millions of years—we may have to revise our established ideas of the geological life spans of certain aquatic animals . . .

—LINKAGE'S *WONDERS OF THE DEEP*

Surname	Haughtree
Christian Name(s)	Phillip
Date of Birth	2 Dec 1927
Age (years)	35
Place of Birth	Old Beldry, Yorks.
Address	Not applicable
Occupation	Author

WHO STATES: (Let here follow the body of the statement)

I have asked to be cautioned in the usual manner but have been told that in view of my alleged *condition* it is not necessary. . . . The implication is obvious, and because of it I find myself obliged to begin my story in the following way:

I must clearly impart to the reader—before advising any un-acquainted perusal of this statement—that I was never a fanatical believer in the supernatural. Nor was I ever given to hallucinations or visions, and I have never suffered from my nerves or been persecuted by any of the mental illnesses. There is no record to support any evidence of madness in any of my ancestors—and Dr. Stewart was quite wrong to declare me insane.

It is necessary that I make these points before permitting the reading of this, for a merely casual perusal would soon bring any conventionally minded reader to the incorrect conclusion that I am either an abominable liar or completely out of my mind, and I have little wish to reinforce Dr. Stewart's opinions . . .

Yet I admit that shortly after midnight on the 15th November 1963 the body of my brother did die by my hand; but at the same time I must clearly state that I am *not* a murderer. It is my intention in the body of this statement—which will of necessity be long, for I insist I must tell the whole story—to prove conclusively my innocence. For, indeed, I am guilty of no heinous crime, and that act of mine which terminated life in the body of my brother was nothing but the reflex action of a man who had recognized a hideous threat to the sanity of the whole world. Wherefore, and in the light of the allegation of madness levelled against me, I must now attempt to tell this tale in the most detailed fashion; I must avoid any sort of garbled sequence and form my sentences and paragraphs with meticulous care, refraining from even *thinking* on the end of it until that horror is reached . . .

Where best to start?

If I may quote Sir Amery Wendy-Smith:

There are fabulous legends of Star-Born creatures who inhabited this Earth many millions of years before Man appeared and who were still here, in certain black places, when he eventually evolved. They are, I am sure, to an extent here even now.

It may be remembered that those words were spoken by the eminent antiquary and archaeologist before he set out upon his last, ill-fated trip into the interior of Africa. Sir Amery was hinting, I know, at the same breed of hell-spawned horror which first began to make itself apparent to me at that ghastly time eighteen months ago; and I take this into account when I remember the way in which he returned, alone and raving, from that dark continent to civilization.

At that time my brother, Julian, was just the opposite of myself, insofar as he was a firm believer in dark mysteries. He read omnivorously of fearsome books uncaring whether they were factual—as Frazer's *Golden Bough* and Miss Murray's *Witch-Cult*—or fanciful—like his collection of old, nigh-priceless volumes of *Weird Tales* and similar popular magazines. Many friends, I imagine, will conclude that his original derangement was due to this unhealthy appetite for the monstrous and the abnormal. I am not of such an opinion, of course, though I admit that at one time I was.

Of Julian: he had always been a strong person physically, but had never shown much strength of character. As a boy he had had the size to easily take on any bully—but never the determination. This was also where he failed as a writer, for while his plots were good, he was unable to make his characters live. Being without personality himself, it was as though he was only able to reflect his own weaknesses into his work. I worked in partnership with him, filling in plots and building life around his more or less clay figures. Up until the time of which I write, we had made a good living and had saved a reasonable sum. This was just as well, for during the period of Julian's illness, when I hardly wrote a word, I might well have found myself hard put to support both my brother and myself. Fortunately, though sadly, he was later taken completely off my hands, but that was after the onset of his trouble . . .

———

It was in May 1962 that Julian suffered his actual breakdown, but the start of it all can be traced back to the 2nd of February of that year—Candlemas—a date which I know will have special meaning to anyone with even the slightest schooling in the occult. It was on that night that he dreamed his dream of titanic basalt towers—dripping with slime and ocean ooze and fringed with great sea mats—their weirdly proportioned bases buried in grey-green muck and their non-Euclidean-angled parapets fading into the watery distances of that unquiet submarine realm.

At the time we were engaged upon a novel of eighteenth-century romance, and I remember we had retired late. Still later I was awakened by Julian's screams, and he roused me fully to listen to an hysterical tale of nightmare. He babbled of what he had seen lurking *behind* those monolithic, slimy ramparts, and I remember remarking—after he had calmed himself somewhat—what a strange fellow he was, to be a writer of romances and at the same time a reader and dreamer of horrors. But Julian was not so easily chided, and such was his fear and loathing of the dream that he refused to lie down again that night but spent the remaining hours of darkness sitting at his typewriter in the study with every light in the house ablaze.

One would think that a nightmare of such horrible intensity might have persuaded Julian to stop gorging himself with his nightly feasts of at least two hours of gruesome reading. Yet, if anything, it had the opposite effect: now his studies were all channelled in one certain direction. He began to take a morbid interest in anything to do with oceanic horror, collecting and avidly reading such works as the German *Unter-Zee Kulten*, Gaston le Fe's *Dwellers in the Depths*, Gantley's *Hydrophinnae*, and the evil *Cthaat Aquadingen* by an unknown author. But it was his collection of fictional books which in the main claimed his interest. From these he culled most of his knowledge of the Cthulhu Mythos, which he fervently declared was not myth at all, and often expressed a desire to see an original copy of the *Necronomicon* of the mad Arab Abdul Alhazred, as his own copy of Feery's *Notes* was practically useless, merely hinting at what Julian alleged Alhazred had explained in detail.

In the following three months our work went badly. We failed to make a deadline on a certain story and, but for the fact that our publisher was a personal friend, might have suffered a considerable loss financially. It was all due to the fact that Julian no longer had the urge to write. He was too taken up with his reading to work and could no longer even be approached to talk over story plots. Not only this, but that fiendish dream of his kept returning with ever increasing frequency and vividness. Every night he suffered those same silt-submerged visions of obscene terrors the like of which could only be glimpsed in such dark tomes as were his chosen reading. But did he really suffer? I found myself unable to make up my mind. For as the weeks passed, my brother seemed to become all the more uneasy and restless by day, whilst eagerly embracing the darkening skies of evening and the bed in which he sweated out the horrors of hideous dream and nightmare . . .

We were leasing, for a reasonable monthly sum, a moderate house in Glasgow where we had separate bedrooms and a single study which we shared. Although he now looked forward to them, Julian's dreams had grown even worse, and they had been particularly bad for two or three nights when, in the middle of May, it happened. He had been showing an increasing interest in certain passages in the *Cthaat Aquadingen* and had heavily underscored a section in that book that ran thus:

> *Rise!*
> *O Nameless Ones:*
> *That in Thy Season*
> *Thine Own of Thy choosing.*
> *Through Thy Spells and Thy Magic,*
> *Through Dreams and Enchantry,*

May know of Thy Coming;
And rush to Thy Pleasure,
For the Love of Our Master,
Knight of Cthulhu,
Deep Slumberer in Green,
Othuum . . .

This and other bits and pieces culled from various sources, particularly certain partly suppressed writings by a handful of authors, all allegedly "missing persons" or persons who had died in strange circumstances—namely Andrew Phelan, Abel Keane, Claiborne Boyd, Nayland Colum, and Horvath Blayne—had had a most unsettling effect upon my brother, so that he was close to exhaustion when he eventually retired late on the night that the horror really started. His condition was due to the fact that he had been studying his morbid books almost continually for a period of three days, and during that time had taken only brief snatches of sleep—and then only during the daylight hours, never at night. He would answer, if ever I attempted to remonstrate with him, that he did not *want* to sleep at night "when the time is so near" and that "there was so much that would be strange to him in the Deeps." Whatever *that* was supposed to mean . . .

After he had retired that night I worked on for an hour or so before going to bed myself. But before leaving our study I glanced at that with which Julian had last been so taken up, and I saw—as well as the above nonsense, as I then considered it—some jottings copied from the *Life of St. Brendan* by the sixth-century Abbot of Clonfert in Galway:

All that day the brethren, even when they were no longer in view of the island, heard a loud wailing from the inhabitants thereof, and a noisome stench was perceptible at a great distance. Then St. Brendan sought to animate the courage of the

brethren, saying: "Soldiers of Christ, be strong in faith un-
feigned and in the armour of the spirit, for we are now on
the confines of hell!"

I have since studied the *Life of St. Brendan*, and have found
that which made me shudder in awful recognition—though at the
reading I could not correlate the written word and my hideous
disquiet; there was just something in the book which was horribly
disturbing—and, moreover, I have found other references to his-
toric oceanic eruptions; namely, those which sank Atlantis and Mu,
those recorded in the *Liber Miraculorem* of the monk and chaplain
Herbert of Clairvaux in France in the years 1178–80, and that which
was closer to the present and which is known only through the
medium of the suppressed *Johansen Narrative*. But at the time of
which I write, such things only puzzled me and I could never, not
even in my wildest dreams, have guessed what was to come.

I am not sure how long I slept that night before I was eventually
roused by Julian and half awoke to find him crouching by my bed,
whispering in the darkness. I could feel his hand gripping my shoulder, and though I was only half-awake I recall the pressure of that
strong hand and something of what he said. His voice had the
trancelike quality of someone under deep hypnosis, and his hand
jerked each time he put emphasis on a word.

"They are *preparing* . . . They will *rise* . . . They have not mus-
tered *The Greater Power*, nor have they the blessing of *Cthulhu*, and
the rising will not be *permanent* nor go recorded . . . But the effort
will suffice for the *Mind-Transfer* . . . For the *Glory* of Othuum . . .

"Using those *Others* in Africa, those who took Sir Amery
Wendy-Smith, *Shudde-M'ell* and his hordes, to relay their messages
and dream-pictures, they have finally defeated the magic *spell* of
deep water and can now *control* dreams as of old—despite the
oceans which cover them! Once more they have *mastery* of dreams,
but to perform the Transfer they need not even break the surface

of the water; a *lessening* of the pressure will suffice.

"Ce'haie, ce'haie!!!

"*They rise even now*; and He knows me, searching me out . . . And my mind, which they have prepared in dreams, will be here to meet Him, for I am *ready* and they need wait no longer. My ignorance is nothing—I do not *need* to know or understand! They will *show* me; as, in dreams, they have showed me the *Deep Places*. But they are unable to draw from my weak mind, or from *any* mortal brain, *knowledge of the surface* . . . The mental images of men are not *strongly* enough transmitted . . . And the deep water—even though, through the work of *Shudde-M'ell*, they have mostly conquered its ill effects—*still* interferes with those blurred images which they *have* managed to obtain . . .

"*I am the chosen one* . . . Through *His* eyes in my *body* will they again acquaint themselves *entirely* with the surface; that in time, when the stars are *right*, they may perform the *Great Rising* . . . Ah! The Great Rising! The *damnation of Hastur*! The dream of *Cthulhu* for countless ages . . . When *all* the deep dwellers, the dark denizens, the *sleepers* in silted cities, will *again* confound the world with their powers . . .

"For that is not dead which can lie *forever*, and when mysterious times have passed, *it shall be again as it once was* . . . Soon, when the Transfer is done, He shall walk the Earth *in my guise*, and I the great deeps *in His*! So that where they ruled *before* they may one day rule *again*—aye—even the brethren of *Yibb-Tstll* and the sons of dreaming *Cthulhu* and their servants—*for the Glory of R'lyeh* . . ."

That is as much of it as I can remember, and even then not at all clearly, and as I have said, it was nothing to me at that time but gibberish. It is only since then that I have acquainted myself with certain old legends and writings, and in particular, in connection with the latter part of my brother's fevered mouthings, the inexplicable couplet of the mad Arab Abdul Alhazred:

That is not dead which can eternal lie,
And with strange aeons even death may die.

But I digress.

It took me some time, after the drone of Julian's outré monologue had died away, to realize that he was no longer in the room with me and that there was a chill morning breeze blowing through the house. In his own room his clothes still hung neatly where he had left them the night before—but Julian had gone, leaving the door to the house swinging open.

I dressed quickly and went out to search the immediate neighbourhood—with negative results. Then, as dawn was breaking, I went into a police station to discover—to my horror—that my brother was in "protective custody." He had been found wandering aimlessly through the northern streets of the city mumbling about "giant Gods" waiting for something in the ocean deeps. He did not seem to realize that his sole attire was his dressing-gown, nor did he appear to recognize me when I was called to identify him. Indeed, he seemed to be suffering from the aftereffects of some terrible shock which had left him in a traumalike state, totally incapable of rational thought. He would only mumble unguessable things and stare blankly towards the northern wall of his cell, an awful, mad light glowing in the back of his eyes.

My tasks were sufficient that morning to keep me amply occupied, and horribly so, for Julian's condition was such that on the orders of a police psychiatrist he was transferred from his police-station cell to Oakdeene Sanatorium for "observation." Nor was it easy to get him attended to at the sanatorium. Apparently the supervisors of that institute had had their own share of trouble the previous night. When I did eventually get home, around noon, my first thought was to check the daily newspapers for any reference to my brother's behaviour. I was glad, or as glad as I could be in the circumstances, to find that Julian's activities had been swamped from a more prominent place of curious interest—which they might well have otherwise claimed—by a host of far more serious events.

Strangely, those other events were similar to my brother's trouble in that they all seemed concerned with mental aberrations in previously normal people or, as at Oakdeene, increases in the activities of the more dangerous inmates of lunatic asylums all over the country. In London a businessman of some standing had hurled himself bodily from a high roof declaring that he must "fly to Yuggoth on the rim." Chandler Davies, who later died raving mad at Woodholme, painted "in a trance of sheer inspiration" an evil black and grey *G'harne Landscape* which his outraged and frightened mistress set on fire upon its completion. Stranger still, a Cotswold rector had knifed to death two members of his congregation who, he later protested to the police, "had no right to exist," and from the coast, near Harden in Durham, strange midnight swimmers had been seen to make off with a fisherman who screamed of "giant frogs" before disappearing beneath the still sea . . . It was as if, on that queer night, some madness had descended—or, as I now believe, had risen—to blanket the more susceptible minds of certain people with utter horror.

But all these things, awful as they were, were not that which I found most disturbing. Looking back on what Julian had murmured in my bedroom while I lay in half-slumber, I felt a weird and inexplicable chill sweep over me as I read, in those same newspapers, of an amateur seismologist who believed he had traced *a submarine disturbance in the ocean between Greenland and the northern tip of Scotland* . . .

What was it Julian had whispered about a *rising* which would not go recorded? Certainly something had been recorded happening in the depths of the sea! . . . But, of course, that was ridiculous, and

I shook off the feeling of dread which had gripped me on reading the item. Whatever that deep oceanic disturbance had been, its cause could only be coincidental to my brother's behaviour.

So it was that rather than ponder the reason for so many outré happenings that ill-omened night I thanked our lucky stars that Julian had got away with so light a mention in the press, for what had occurred could have been damaging to both of us had it been given greater publicity.

Not that any of this bothered Julian! Nothing bothered him, for he stayed in that semiconscious state in which the police had found him for well over a year. During that year his weird delusions were of such a fantastic nature that he became, as it were, the psychological pet and project of a well-known Harley Street alienist. Indeed, after the first month or so, so strong did the good doctor's interest in my brother's case become, he would accept no fee for Julian's keep or treatment, and, though I visited Julian frequently, whenever I was in London, Dr. Stewart would never listen to my protests or hear of me paying for his services. Such was his patient's weird case that the doctor declared himself extremely fortunate to be in a position where he had the opportunity to study such a fantastic mind. It amazes me now that the same man who proved so understanding in his dealings with my brother should be so totally devoid of understanding with me, yet that is the pass to which the turn of events has brought me. Still, it was plain my brother was in good hands, and in any case I could hardly afford to press the matter of payment; Dr. Stewart's fees were usually astronomical.

It was shortly after Dr. Stewart "took Julian in" that I began to study my brother's star charts, both astronomical and astrological, and delved deep into his books on the supernatural arts and sciences. I read many peculiar volumes during that period and became reasonably familiar with the works of Fermold, Lévi, Prinn, and Gezrael, and—in certain darker reaches of the British Museum—I shuddered to the literacy lunacy of Magnus, Glynnd, and Alhazred.

I read the *R'lyeh Text* and the *Johansen Narrative* and studied the fables of lost Atlantis and Mu. I crouched over flaking tomes in private collections and tracked down all sources of oceanic legend and myth with which I came into contact. I read the manuscript of Andrew Phelan, the deposition of Abel Keane, the testament of Claiborne Boyd, the statement of Nayland Colum, and the narrative of Horvath Blayne. The papers of Jefferson Bates fell to my unbelieving scrutiny, and I lay awake at nights thinking of the hinted fate of Enoch Conger.

And I need never have bothered.

All the above delvings took the better part of a year to complete, by which time I was no nearer a solution to my brother's madness than when I began. No, perhaps that is not quite true. On reflection I think it quite possible that a man might go mad after exploring such dark avenues as these I have mentioned—and especially a man such as Julian, who was more than normally sensitive to begin with. But I was by no means satisfied that this was the whole answer. After all, his interest in such things had been lifelong; I could still see no reason why such an interest should suddenly accumulate so terribly. No, I was sure that the start of it all had been that Candlemas dream.

But at any rate, the year had not been totally lost. I still did not believe in such things—dark survivals of elder times, great ancient gods waiting in the ocean depths, impending doom for the human race in the form of nightmare ocean-dwellers from the beginning of time—how could I and retain my own sanity? But I had become fairly erudite as regards these darker mysteries of elder Earth. And certain facets of my strange research had been of particular interest to me. I refer to what I had read of the oddly similar cases of Joe Slater, the Catskill Mountains vagabond in 1900–01, Nathaniel Wingate Peaslee of Miskatonic University in 1908–13, and Randolph Carter of Boston, whose disappearance in 1928 was so closely linked with the inexplicable case of the Swami Chandraputra in 1930. True, I had looked into other cases of alleged demonic possession—all equally well authenticated—but those I have mentioned seemed to have a special significance, as they paralleled more than roughly that case which I was researching and which involved so terribly my brother.

But time had passed quickly and it was a totally unexpected shock to me, though one of immeasurable relief and pleasure, to find in my letter-box one July morning in 1963 a letter from Dr. Stewart which told of Julian's rapid improvement. My joy and amazement can be well imagined when, on journeying down to London the very next day, to the practice of Dr. Stewart, I found my brother returned—as far as could be ascertained in such a short time—to literally complete mental recovery. Indeed, it was the doctor himself who, on my arrival, informed me that Julian's recovery was now complete, that my brother had *fully* recovered almost overnight, but I was not so sure—there appeared to be one or two anomalies.

These apart, though, the degree of recovery which had been accomplished was tremendous. When I had last seen my brother, only a month earlier, I had felt physically sickened by the unplumbed depths of his delusions. I had, on that occasion, gone to stand beside him at the barred window from which I was told he always stared blindly northward, and in answer to my careful greeting he had said: "Cthulhu, Othuum, Dagon: the Deep Ones in Darkness; all deeply dreaming, awaiting awakening . . ." Nor had I been able to extract anything from him at all except such senseless mythological jargon.

What a transformation! Now he greeted me warmly—though I imagined his recognition of me to be a trifle slow—and after I had delightedly talked with him for a while I came to the conclusion that as far as I could discern, and apart from one new idiosyncrasy, he seemed to be the same man I had known before the onset of the trouble. This oddity I have mentioned was simply that he seemed to have developed a weird photophobia and now wore large, shielded, dark-lensed spectacles which denied one the slightest glimpse of his eyes even from the sides. But, as I later found out, there was an explanation even for these enigmatic-looking spectacles.

While Julian prepared himself for the journey back to Glasgow, Dr. Stewart took me to his study where I could sign the necessary release documents and where he could tell me of my brother's fantastic recovery. It appeared that one morning only a week earlier, on going to his exceptional patient's room, the doctor had found Julian huddled beneath his blankets. Nor would my brother come out or allow himself to be brought out until the doctor had agreed to bring him that pair of very dark-lensed spectacles. Peculiar though this muffled request had been, it had delighted the astonished alienist, constituting as it did the first conscious recognition of existence that Julian had shown since the commencement of his treatment.

And the spectacles had proved to be worth their weight in gold, for since their advent Julian had rapidly progressed to his present state of normalcy. The only point over which the doctor seemed unhappy was that to date my brother had point-blank refused to relinquish the things; he declared simply that the light *hurt his eyes!* To some degree, however, the good doctor informed me, this was only to be expected. During his long illness Julian had departed so far from the normal world as it were, that his senses, unused, had partly atrophied—literally ceasing to function. His recovery had left him in the position of a man who, trapped in a dark cave for a long period of time, is suddenly released to face the bright outside world, which also explained in part the clumsiness which had attended Julian's every physical action during the first days of his recovery. One of the doctor's assistants has found occasion to remark upon the most odd way in which my brother had tended to wrap his arms around things which he wanted to lift or examine—

even small things—as though he had forgotten what his fingers were for! Also, at first, the patient had tended to waddle rather than walk, almost in the manner of a penguin, and his recently reacquired powers of intelligent expression had lapsed at times in the queerest manner—when his speech had degenerated to nothing more than a guttural, hissing parody of the English language. But all these abnormalities had vanished in the first few days, leaving Julian's recovery as totally unexplained as had been his decline.

In the first-class compartment on the London-Glasgow train, on our way north, having exhausted the more obvious questions I had wanted to put to my restored brother—questions to which, incidentally, his answers had seemed guardedly noncommittal—I had taken out a pocketbook and started to read. After a few minutes, startled by a passing train, I had happened to glance up . . . and was immediately glad that Julian and I were alone in the compartment. For my brother had obviously found something of interest in an old newspaper, and I do not know what others might have thought of the look upon his face . . . As he read, his face bore an unpleasant and, yes, almost *evil* expression. It was made to look worse by those strange spectacles: a mixture of cruel sarcasm, black triumph, and tremendous contempt. I was taken aback, but said nothing, and later—when Julian went into the corridor for a breath of fresh air— I picked up the newspaper and turned to the section he had been reading, which perhaps had caused the weird distortion of his features. I saw at once what had affected him, and a shadow of the old fear flickered briefly across my mind as I read the article. It was not strange that what I read was new to me—I had hardly seen a newspaper since the horror began a year previously—but it was as though this was the same report I had read at that time. It was all there, almost a duplicate of the occurrences of that night of evil omen: the increased activities of lunatics all over the country, the sudden mad and monstrous actions of previously normal people, the cult activity and devil-worship in the Midlands, the sea-things sighted off Harden on the coast, and more inexplicable occurrences in the Cotswolds.

A chill as of strange ocean floors touched my heart, and I quickly thumbed through the remaining pages of the paper—and almost dropped the thing when I came across that which I had more than half expected. For submarine disturbances had been recorded in the ocean between Greenland and the northern tip of Scotland. And more: I instinctively glanced at the date at the top-centre of the page, *and saw that the newspaper was exactly one week old* . . . It had first appeared on the stands on the very morning when Dr. Stewart had found my brother huddled beneath the blankets in the room with the barred windows.

Yet apparently my fears were groundless. On our return to the house in Glasgow the first thing my brother did, to my great delight and satisfaction, was destroy all his old books of ancient lore and sorcery, but he made no attempt to return to his writing. Rather he mooned about the house like some lost soul, in what I imagined to be a mood of frustration over those mazed months of which he said he could remember nothing. And not once, until the night of his death, did I see him without those spectacles. I believe he even wore the things to bed—but the significance of this, and something he had mumbled that night in my room, did not dawn on me until much later.

But of those spectacles: I had been assured that this photophobia would wear off, yet as the days went by, it became increasingly apparent that Dr. Stewart's assurances had gone for nothing. And what was I to make of that *other* change I had noticed? Whereas before Julian had been almost shy and retiring, with a weak chin and a personality to match, he now seemed to be totally out of character, in that he asserted himself over the most trivial things whenever the opportunity arose, and his face—his lips and chin in particular—had taken on a firmness completely alien to his previous physiognomy.

It was all most puzzling, and as the weeks passed I became ever more aware that far from all being well with that altered brother of mine something was seriously wrong. Apart from his brooding, a darker horror festered within him. Why would he not admit the monstrous dreams which constantly invaded his sleep? Heaven knows he slept little enough as it was, and when he did he often roused me from my own slumbers by mumbling in the night of those same horrors which had featured so strongly in his long illness.

But then, in the middle of October, Julian underwent what I took to be a real change for the better. He became a little more cheerful and even dabbled with some old manuscripts long since left abandoned—though I do not think he did any actual work on them—and toward the end of the month he sprang a surprise. For quite some time, he told me, he had had a wonderful story in mind, but for the life of him he could not settle to it. It was a tale he would have to work on himself, and it would be necessary for him to do much research, as his material would have to be very carefully prepared. He asked that I bear with him during the period of his task and allow him as much privacy as our modest house could afford. I agreed to everything he suggested, though I could not see why he found it so necessary to have a lock put on his door or, for that matter, why he cleared out the spacious cellar beneath the house "for future use." Not that I questioned his actions. He had asked for privacy, and as far as I could assist him he would have it. But I admit to having been more than somewhat curious.

From then on I saw my brother only when we ate—which for him was not any too often—and when he left his room to go to the library for books, a thing he did with clockwork regularity every day. With the first few of these excursions I made a point of being near the door of the house when he returned, for I was puzzled as to what form his work was going to take and I thought I might perhaps gain some insight if I could see his books of reference.

If anything, the materials Julian borrowed from the library only served to add to my puzzlement. What on Earth could he want with Lauder's *Nuclear Weapons and Engines*, Schall's *X-Rays*, Couderc's *The Wider Universe*, Ubbelohde's *Man and Energy*, Keane's *Modern Marvels of Science*, Stafford Clarke's *Psychiatry Today*, Schubert's *Einstein*, Geber's *The Electrical World*, and all the many volumes of *The New Scientist* and *The Progress of Science* with which he returned each day heavily burdened? Still, nothing he was doing gave me any cause to worry as I had in the old days, when his reading had been anything but scientific and had involved those dreadful works which he had now destroyed. But my partial peace of mind was not destined to last for very long.

One day in mid-November—elated by a special success which I had achieved in the writing of a difficult chapter in my own slowly shaping book—I went to Julian's room to inform him of my triumph. I had not seen him at all that morning, but the fact that he was out did not become apparent until, after knocking and receiving no reply, I entered his room. It had been Julian's habit of late to lock his door when he went out, and I was surprised that on this occasion he had not done so. I saw then that he had left the door open purposely so that I might see the note he had left for me on his bedside table. It was scribbled on a large sheet of white typing paper in awkward, tottering letters, and the message was blunt and to the point:

> Phillip,
> Gone to London for four or five
> days. Research. Brit. Museum . . .
> Julian

Somewhat disgruntled, I turned to leave the room and as I did so noticed my brother's diary lying open at the foot of his bed where he had thrown it. The book itself did not surprise me—before his trouble he had always kept such notes—and not being a snoop I would have left the room there and then had I not glimpsed a word—or *name*—which I recognized on the open, handwritten pages: "*Cthulhu.*"

Simply that . . . yet it set my mind awhirl with renewed doubts. Was Julian's trouble reasserting itself? Did he yet require psychiatric treatment and were his original delusions returning? Remembering that Dr. Stewart had warned me of the possibility of a relapse, I considered it my duty to read all that my brother had written— which was where I met with a seemingly insurmountable problem. The difficulty was simply this: I was *unable* to read the diary, for it was written in a completely alien, cryptically cuneiform script the like of which I had ever seen only in those books which Julian had burned. There was a distinct resemblance in those weird characters to the minuscules and dot groups of the *G'harne Fragments*—I re- membered being struck by an article on them in one of Julian's books, an archaeological magazine—but only a resemblance; the diary contained nothing I could understand except that one word, *Cthulhu*, and even that had been scored through by Julian, as if on reflection, and a weird squiggle of ink had been crammed in above it as a replacement.

I was not slow to come to a decision as to what my proper course of action should be. That same day, taking the diary with me, I went down to Wharby on the noon train. That article on the *G'harne Fragments* which I had remembered reading had been the work of the curator of the Wharby Museum, Professor Gordon Walmsley of Goole, who, incidentally, had claimed the first trans- lation of the fragments over the claim of the eccentric and long- vanished antiquarian and archaeologist Sir Amery Wendy-Smith. The professor was an authority on the Phitmar Stone—that contemporary of the famous Rosetta Stone with its key inscriptions in two forms of Egyptian hieroglyphs—and the Geph Columns Characters, and had several other translations or feats of antiquarian deciphering to his credit. Indeed, I was extremely fortunate to find him in at the museum, for he planned to fly within the week to Peru, where yet another task awaited his abecedarian talents. Nonetheless, busy with arrangements as he was, he was profoundly interested in the diary, enquiring where the hieroglyphics within had been copied and by whom and to what purpose? I lied, telling him my brother had copied the inscriptions from a black stone monolith somewhere in the mountains of Hungary, for I knew that just such a stone exists, having once seen mention of it in one of my brother's books. The professor squinted his eyes suspiciously at my lie but was so interested in the diary's strange characters that he quickly forgot whatever it was that had prompted his suspicion. From then until I was about to leave his study, located in one of the museum's rooms, we did not speak. So absorbed did he become with the diary's contents that I think he completely forgot my presence in the room. Before I left, however, I managed to extract a promise from him that the diary would be returned to my Glasgow address within three days and that a copy of his translation, if any, would accompany it. I was glad that he did not ask me why I required such a translation.

My faith in the professor's abilities was eventually borne out—but not until far too late. For Julian returned to Glasgow on the morning of the third day, earlier by twenty-four hours than I had been led to believe, and his diary still had not been returned—a loss he was not slow to discover.

I was working half-heartedly at my book when my brother made his appearance. He must have been to his own room first.

Suddenly I felt a presence in my room with me. I was so lost in
my half-formed imaginings and ideas that I had not heard my
door open; nonetheless I knew something was in there with me. I
say *something*, and that is the way it was! I was being observed—
but not, I felt, by a human being! Carefully, with the short hair of
my neck prickling with an uncanny life of its own, I turned
about. Standing in the open doorway with a look on his face
which I can only describe as being utterly hateful was Julian. But
even as I saw him, his horribly writhing features composed themselves behind those enigmatic dark glasses and he forced an unnatural smile.

"I seem to have mislaid my diary, Phillip," he said slowly. "I'm
just in from London and I can't seem to find the thing anywhere.
I don't suppose you've seen it, have you?" There was the suggestion
of a sneer in his voice, an unspoken accusation. "I don't need the
diary really, but there are one or two things in it which I wrote in
code—ideas I want to use in my story. I'll let you in on a secret!
It's a *fantasy* I'm writing! I mean—horror, science fiction, and fantasy—they're all the rage these days; it's about time we broke into
the field. You shall see the rough work as soon as it's ready. But
now, seeing as you obviously haven't seen my diary, if you'll excuse
me, I want to get some of my notes together."

He left the room quickly, before I could answer, and I would
be lying if I said I was not glad to see him go. And I could not help
but notice that with his departure the feeling of an alien presence
also departed. My legs felt suddenly weak beneath me as a dreadful
aura of foreboding settled like a dark cloud over my room. Nor did
that feeling disperse; rather it tightened as night drew on.

Lying in my bed that night I found myself going again and again
over Julian's strangeness, trying to make some sense of it all. A
fantasy? Could it be? It was so unlike Julian, and why, if it was only
a story, had his look been so terrible when he was unable to find

his diary? And why write a story in a diary at all? Oh! He had liked reading weird stuff—altogether too much, as I have explained—but he had never before shown any urge to *write* it! And what of the books he had borrowed from the library? They had not seemed to be works he could possibly use in connection with the construction of a fantasy! And there was something else, something which kept making brief appearances in my mind's eye but which I could not quite bring into focus. Then I had it—the thing that had been bothering me ever since I first saw that diary: *where in the name of all that's holy had Julian learned to write in hieroglyphics?*

That cinched it!

No, I did not believe that Julian was writing a story at all. That was only an excuse he had created to put me off the track. But what track? What did he think he was doing? Oh! It was obvious: he was on the verge of another breakdown, and the sooner I got in touch with Dr. Stewart the better. All these tumultuous thoughts kept me awake until a late hour, and if my brother was noisy again that night I did not hear him. I was so mentally fatigued that when I eventually nodded off I slept the sleep of the dead.

Is it not strange how the light of day has the power to drive away the worst terrors of night? With the morning my fears were much abated and I decided to wait a few more days before contacting Dr. Stewart. Julian spent all morning and afternoon locked in the cellar, and finally—again becoming alarmed as night drew near—I determined to reason with him, if possible, over supper. During the meal I spoke to him, pointing out how strangely he seemed to be acting and lightly mentioning my fears of a relapse. I was somewhat taken aback by his answers. He argued it was my own fault he had had to resort to the cellar in which to work, stating that the cellar appeared to be the only place where he could be sure of any privacy.

He laughed at my mention of a relapse, saying he had never felt better in his life! When he again mentioned "privacy" I knew he must be referring to the unfortunate incident of the missing diary and was shamed into silence. I mentally cursed Professor Walmsley and his whole museum.

Yet, in direct opposition to all my brother's glib explanations, that night was the worst, for Julian gibbered and moaned in his sleep, making it impossible for me to get any rest at all, so that when I arose, haggard and withdrawn, late on the morning of the 13th, I knew I would soon have to take some definite action.

I saw Julian only fleetingly that morning, on his way from his room to the cellar, and his face seemed pale and cadaverous. I guessed that his dreams were having as bad an effect on him as they were on me, yet rather than appearing tired or hag-ridden he seemed to be in the grip of some feverish excitement.

Now I became more worried than ever and even scribbled two letters to Dr. Stewart, only later to ball them up and throw them away. If Julian was genuine in whatever he was doing, I did not want to spoil his faith in me—what little of it was left—and if he was not genuine? I was becoming morbidly curious to learn the outcome of his weird activities. Nonetheless, twice that day, at noon and later in the evening, when as usual my fears got the better of me, I hammered at the cellar door demanding to know what was going on in there. My brother completely ignored these efforts of mine at communication, but I was determined to speak to him. When he finally came out of the cellar, much later that night, I was waiting for him at the door. He turned the key in the lock behind him, carefully shielding the cellar's contents from my view, and re-garded me curiously from behind those horrid dark glasses before offering me the merest parody of a smile.

"Phillip, you've been very patient with me," he said, taking my elbow and leading me up the cellar steps, "and I know I must have seemed to be acting quite strangely and inexplicably. It's all very simple really, but for the moment I can't explain just what I'm about. You'll just have to keep faith with me and wait. If you're worried that I'm heading for another bout of, well, *trouble*, you can forget it. I'm perfectly all right. I just need a little more time to finish off what I'm doing, and then, the day after tomorrow, I'll take you in there"—he nodded over his shoulder—"into the cellar, and show you what I've got. All I ask is that you're patient for just one more day. Believe me, Phillip, you've got a revelation coming which will shake you to your very roots, and afterward—you'll understand everything. Don't ask me to explain it all now; you wouldn't believe it! But seeing *is* believing, and when I take you in there you'll be able to see for yourself."

He seemed so reasonable, so sensible—if a trifle feverish—and so excited, almost like a child about to show off some new toy. Wanting to believe him, I allowed myself to be easily talked around and we went off together to eat a late meal.

Julian spent the morning of the 14th transferring all his notes—great sheaves of them which I had never suspected existed—together with odds and ends in small cardboard boxes, from his room to the cellar. After a meagre lunch he was off to the library to "do some final checking" and to return a number of books lately borrowed. While he was out I went down to the cellar—only to discover that he had locked the door and taken the key with him. He returned and spent the entire afternoon locked in down there, to emerge later at night looking strangely elated. Still later, after I had retired to my room, he came and knocked on my door.

"The night is exceptionally clear, Phillip, and I thought I'd have a look at the sky . . . the stars have always fascinated me, you know? But the window in my room doesn't really show them off too well;

I'd appreciate it if you'd allow me to sit in here and look out for a while?"

"By all means do, old fellow, come on in," I answered, agreeably surprised. I left my easy chair and went to stand beside him after he crossed the room to lean on the windowsill. He peered through those strange, dark lenses up and out into the night. He was, I could see, intently studying the constellations, and as I glanced from the sky to his face I mused aloud: "Looking up there, one is almost given to believe that the stars have some purpose other than merely making the night look pretty."

Abruptly my brother's manner changed. "What d'you mean by that?" He snapped, staring at me in an obviously suspicious fashion. I was taken aback. My remark had been completely innocuous.

"I mean that perhaps those old astrologers had something after all," I answered.

"Astrology is an ancient and exact science, Phillip—you shouldn't talk of it so lightly." He spoke slowly, as though restraining himself from some outburst. Something warned me to keep quiet, so I said no more. Five minutes later he left. Pondering my brother's odd manner, I sat there a while longer, and, as I looked up at the stars winking through the window across the room, I could not help but recall a few of those words he had mumbled in the darkness of my bedroom so long ago at the onset of his breakdown. He had said: "That in time, *when the stars are right*, they may perform the Great Rising . . ."

There was no sleep at all for me that night; the noises and mutterings, the mouthings and gibberings which came, loud and clear, from Julian's room would not permit it. In his sleep he talked of such eldritch and inexplicable things as the Deep Green Waste, the Scarlet Feaster, the Chained Shoggoth, the Lurker at the Threshold, Yibb-Tstll, Tsathoggua, the Cosmic Screams, the Lips of Bugg-Shash, and the Inhabitants of the Frozen Chasm. Toward morning, out of sheer exhaustion, I eventually nodded off into evil dreams which claimed my troubled subconscious until I awoke shortly before noon on the 15th.

Julian was already in the cellar, and as soon as I had washed and dressed, remembering his promise to "show me" what he had got, I started off down there. But at the top of the cellar steps my feet were suddenly arrested by the metallic *clack* of the letter-box flap in the front door of the house.

The diary!

Unreasonably fearing that Julian might also have heard the noise, I raced back along the passage to the door, snatched up the small stamped and addressed brown-paper parcel which lay on the inside doormat, and fled with the thing to my room. I locked myself in and ripped open the parcel. I had tried Julian's door earlier and knew it to be unlocked. Now I planned to go in and drop the diary down behind the headboard of his bed while he was still in the cellar. In this way he might be led to believe he had merely misplaced the book. But, after laying aside the diary to pick up and read the stapled sheets which had fallen loose and fluttered to the floor, I forgot all about my planned deception in the dawning knowledge of my brother's obvious impending insanity. Walmsley had done as he had promised. I cast his brief, eagerly enquiring letter aside and quickly, in growing horror, read his translation of Julian's cryptical notes. It was all there, all the proof I needed, in neat partially annotated paragraphs, but I did not need to read it all. Certain words and phrases, lines and sentences, seemed to leap upon the paper, attracting my frantically searching eyes:

"This shape/form? sickens me. Thanks be there is not long to wait. There is difficulty in the fact that this form/body/shape? would not obey me at first, and I fear it may have alerted— (?—?) to some degree. Also, I have to hide/protect/conceal?

that of me which also came through with the transfer/journey/ passage?

"I know the mind of (?—?) fares badly in the Deeps . . . and of course his eyes were ruined/destroyed? completely . . .

"Curse the water that quiets/subdues? Great (?)'s power. In these few times/periods? I have looked upon/seen/observed? much and studied what I have seen and read—but I have had to gain such knowledge secretly. The mind-sendings/mental messages (telepathy?) from my kin/brothers? at (?—?) near that place which men call Devil—(?) were of little use to me, for the progress these beings/creatures? have made is fantastic in the deep times/moments/periods? since their (?) attack on those at Devil—(?).

"I have seen much and I know the time is not yet ripe for the great rising/coming? They have developed weapons of (?) power. We would risk/chance? defeat—and that must never be.

"But if (?????? they ???) turn their devices against themselves (??? bring ?) nation against nation (?? then ??) destructive/cataclysmic? war rivalling (name—possibly *Azathoth*, as in *Pnakotic Mss*).

"The mind of (?—?) has broken under the strain of the deeps . . . It will now be necessary to contact my rightful shape in order to rebecome one/re-enter? it.

"*Cthulhu?* (?) triumph (???) I am eager to return to my own shape/form/body? I do not like the way this brother— (the word *brother* implying falseness?) has looked at me . . . but he suspects nothing . . ."

There was more, much more, but I skipped over the vast majority of the translation's remaining contents and finished by reading the last paragraph which, presumably, had been written in the diary shortly before Julian took himself off to London:

"(Date?) . . . six more (short periods of time?) to wait . . . Then the stars should be right/in order/positioned? and if all goes well the transfer can be performed/accomplished?"

That was all, but it was more than enough! That reference about my not "suspecting" anything, in connection with those same horrors which had been responsible for his first breakdown, was sufficient finally to convince me that my brother was seriously ill!

Taking the diary with me, I ran out of my room with one thought in my mind. Whatever Julian thought he was doing I had to stop him. Already his delvings constituted a terrible threat to his health, and who could say but that the next time a cure might not be possible? If he suffered a second attack, there was the monstrous possibility that he would remain permanently insane.

Immediately I started my frantic hammering, he opened the cellar door and I literally fell inside. I say I fell; indeed, I did—I fell from a sane world into a lunatic, alien, nightmare dimension totally outside any previous experience. As long as I live I shall never forget what I saw. The floor in the centre of the cellar had been cleared, and upon it, chalked in bold red strokes, was a huge and unmistakable evil symbol. I had seen it before in those books which were now destroyed . . . and now I recoiled at what I had later read of it! Beyond the sign, in one corner, a pile of ashes was all that remained of Julian's many notes. An old iron grating had been fixed horizontally over bricks, and the makings of a fire were already upon it. A cryptographic script, which I recognized as being the blasphemous *Nyhargo Code*, was scrawled in green and blue chalk across the walls, and the smell of incense hung heavily in the air. The whole scene was ghastly, unreal, a living picture from Eliphas Lévi—nothing less than the lair of a sorcerer! Horrified, I turned to Julian—in time to see him lift a heavy iron poker and start the stunning swing downward toward my head. Nor did I lift a finger to stop him. I could not—*for he had taken off those spectacles, and the sight of his terrible face had frozen me rigid as polar ice.*

Regaining consciousness was like swimming up out of a dead, dark sea. I surfaced through shoals of night-black swimmers to an outer world where the ripples of the ocean were dimly lit by the glow from a dying orange sun. As the throbbing in my head subsided, those ripples resolved themselves into the pattern of my pinstriped jacket, but the orange glow remained! My immediate hopes that it had all been a nightmare were shattered at once, for as I carefully raised my head from its position on my chest the whole room slowly came under my unbelieving scrutiny. Thank God Julian had his back to me and I could not see his face. Had I but *glimpsed* again, in those first moments of recovery, those hellish eyes I am certain the sight would have returned me to instant oblivion.

I could see now that the orange glow was reflected from the now blazing fire on the horizontal grill, and I saw that the poker which had been used to strike me down was buried in the heart of the flames with red-heat creeping visibly up the metal toward the wooden handle. Glancing at my watch, I saw that I had been unconscious for many hours—it was fast approaching the midnight hour. That one glance was also sufficient to tell me that I was tied to the old wicker chair in which I had been seated, for I saw the ropes. I flexed my muscles against my bonds and noticed, not without a measure of satisfaction, that there was a certain degree of slackness in them. I had managed to keep my mind from dwelling on Julian's facial differences, but, as he turned toward me, I steeled myself to the coming shock.

His face was an impassive white mask in which shone, cold and malevolent and indescribably alien, *those eyes!* As I live and breathe, I swear they were twice the size they ought to have been—and they bulged, uniformly scarlet, outward from their sockets in chill yet aloof hostility.

"Ah! You've returned to us, dear brother. But why d'you stare so? Is it that you find this face so awful? Let me assure you, you don't find it half so hideous as I!"

Monstrous truth, or what I thought was the truth, began to dawn in my mazed and bewildered brain. "The dark spectacles!" I gasped. "No wonder you had to wear them, even at night. You couldn't bear the thought of people seeing those diseased eyes!"

"Diseased? No, your reasoning is only partly correct. I had to wear the glasses, yes; it was that or give myself away—which wouldn't have pleased those who sent me in the slightest, believe me. For Cthulhu, beneath the waves on the far side of the world, has already made it known to Othuum, my master, of his displeasure. They have spoken in dreams, and Cthulhu is *angry*!" He shrugged, "Also, I needed the spectacles; these eyes of mine are accustomed to piercing the deepest depths of the ocean! Your surface world was an agony to me at first, but now I am used to it. In any case, I don't plan to stay here long, and when I go I will take this body with me," he plucked at himself in contempt, "for my pleasure."

I knew that what he was saying was not, could not, be possible, and I cried out to him, begging him to recognize his own madness. I babbled that modern medical science could probably correct whatever was wrong with his eyes. My words were drowned out by his cold laughter. "Julian!" I cried.

"Julian?" he answered. "Julian Haughtree?" He lowered his awful face until it was only inches from mine. "Are you blind, man? *I am Pesh-Tlen, Wizard of deep Gell-Ho to the North!*" He turned away from me, leaving my tottering mind to total up a nerve-blasting sum of horrific integers. The Cthulhu Mythos—those passages from the *Cthaat Aquadingen* and the *Life of St. Brendan*— Julian's dreams: "They can now control dreams as of old." The

Mind Transfer—"They will rise"—"through his eyes in my body"—
giant gods waiting in the ocean deeps—"He shall walk the Earth in
my guise"—a submarine disturbance off the coast of Greenland!
Deep Gell-Ho to the North . . .

God in heaven! Could such things be? Was this all, in the end,
not just some fantastic delusion of Julian's but an incredible fact?
This thing before me! Did he—*it*—really see through the eyes of a
monster from the bottom of the sea? And if so, *was it governed by
that monster's mind?*

After that, it was not madness that gripped me—not then—
rather was it the refusal of my whole being to accept that which
was unacceptable. I do not know how long I remained in that state,
but the spell was abruptly broken by the first, distant chime of the
midnight hour.

At that distant clamour my mind became crystal clear and the
eyes of the being called Pesh-Tlen blazed even more unnaturally as
he smiled—if that word describes what he *did* with his face—in
final triumph. Seeing that smile, I knew that something hideous was
soon to come and I struggled against my bonds. I was gratified to
feel them slacken a little more about my body. The—creature—had
meanwhile turned away from me and had taken the poker from the
fire. As the chimes of the hour continued to ring out faintly from
afar it raised its arms, weaving strange designs in the air with the
tip of the redly glowing poker, and commenced a chant or invocation of such a loathsome association of discordant tones and pip-
ings that my soul seemed to shrink inside me at the hearing. It was
fantastic that what was grunted, snarled, whistled, and hissed with
such incredible fluency could ever have issued from the throat of
something I had called brother, regardless what force motivated his
vocal cords, but, fantastic or not, I heard it. Heard it? Indeed, as
that mad cacophony died away, tapering off to a high-pitched,
screeching end—*I saw its result!*

Writhing tendrils of green smoke began to whirl together in

one corner of the cellar. I did not see the smoke arrive, nor could I say whence it came—it was just suddenly there! The tendrils quickly became a column, rapidly thickening, spinning faster and faster, forming—*a shape!*

Outside in the night freak lightning flashed and thunder rumbled over the city in what I have since been told was the worst storm in years, but I barely heard the thunder or the heavy downpour of rain. All my senses were concentrated on the silently spinning, rapidly coalescing thing in the corner. The cellar had a high ceiling, almost eleven feet, but what was forming seemed to fill that space easily.

I screamed then, and mercifully fainted. For once again my mind had been busy totalling the facts as I knew them, and I had mentally questioned Pesh-Tlen's reason for calling up this horror from the depths—or from wherever else it came. Upstairs in my room, unless Julian had been up there and removed it, the answer lay where I had thrown it—Walmsley's translation! Had not Julian, or Pesh-Tlen, or whatever the thing was, written in that diary: "*It will now be necessary to contact my natural form in order to reenter it?*"

My blackout could only have been momentary, for as I regained consciousness for the second time I saw that the thing in the corner had still not completely formed. It had stopped spinning and was now centrally opaque, but its outline was infirm and wavering, like a scene viewed through smoke. The creature that had been Julian was standing to one side of the cellar, arms raised towards the semicoherent object in the corner, features strained and twitching with hideous expectancy.

"Look," it spoke coldly, half turning towards me. "See what I and the Deep Ones have done! Behold, mortal, your brother—*Julian Haughtree!*"

For the rest of my days, which I believe will not number many,

I will never be able to rid my memory of that sight! While others lie drowning in sleep I will claw desperately at the barrier of consciousness, not daring to close my eyes for fear of that which lingers yet beyond my eyelids. As Pesh-Tlen spoke those words, the thing in the corner finally materialized!

Imagine a black, glistening, ten-foot heap of twisting, ropey tentacles and gaping mouths. . . . Imagine the outlines of a slimy, alien face in which, sunk deep in gaping sockets, are the remains of ruptured *human* eyes. . . . Imagine shrieking in absolute clutching, leaping fear and horror—and imagine the thing I have here described answering your screams in a madly familiar voice, *a voice which you instantly recognize*!

"Phillip! Phillip, where are you? What's happened? I can't see . . . We came up out of the sea, and then I was whirled away somewhere and I heard your voice." The horror rocked back and forth. "Don't let them take me back, Phillip!"

The voice was that of my brother, all right—but not the old *sane* Julian I had known! That was when I, too, went mad, but it was a madness with a purpose, if nothing else. When I had previously fainted, the sudden loosening of my body must have completed the work which I had started on the ropes. As I lurched to my feet they fell from me to the floor. The huge, blind monstrosity in the corner had started to lumber in my direction, vaguely twisting its tentacles before it as it came. At the same time the red-eyed demon in Julian's form was edging carefully toward it, arms eagerly outstretched.

"Julian," I screamed, "look out—only by contact can he reenter—and then he intends to kill you, to take you back with him to the deeps."

"Back to the deeps? No! No, he can't! I won't go!" The lumbering horror with my brother's mad voice spun blindly around, its flailing tentacles knocking the hybrid sorcerer flying across the floor.

I snatched the poker from the fire where it had been replaced and turned threateningly upon the sprawling half-human.

"Stand still, Julian!" I gibbered over my shoulder at the horror from the sea as the wizard before me leapt to his feet. The lumberer behind me halted. "You, Pesh-Tlen, get back." There was no plan in my bubbling mind; I only knew I had to keep the two—things—apart. I danced like a boxer, using the glowing poker to ward off the suddenly frantic Pesh-Tlen.

"But it's time—it's time! The contact must be now!" The red-eyed thing screeched. "Get out of my way . . ." Its tones were barely human now. "You can't stop me . . . I must . . . must . . . must make strong . . . strong contact! I must . . . *bhfg—ngyy fhtlhlh hegm—yeh'hhg narcchhh'yy!* You won't cheat me!"

A pool of slime, like the trail of a great snail, had quickly spread from the giant shape behind me, and, even as he screamed, Pesh-Tlen suddenly leapt forward straight onto it, his feet skidding on the evil-smelling mess. He completely lost his balance. Arms flailing he fell, face down, sickeningly, onto the rigid red-hot poker in my hand. Four inches of the glowing metal slid, like a warm knife through butter, into one of those awful eyes. There was a hissing sound, almost drowned out by the creature's single shrill scream of agony, and a small cloud of steam rose mephitically from the thing's face as it pitched to the floor.

Instantly the glistening black giant behind me let out a shriek of terror. I spun round, letting the steaming poker fall, to witness that monstrosity from the ocean floor rocking to and fro, tentacles wrapped protectively round its head. After a few seconds it became still, and the rubbery arms fell listlessly away to reveal the multi-mouthed face with its ruined, rotting eyes.

"You've killed him, I know it," Julian's voice said, calmer now. "He is finished and I am finished—already I can feel them recalling me." Then, voice rising hysterically: "*They won't take me alive!*"

The monstrous form trembled and its outline began to blur. My legs crumpled beneath me in sudden reaction, and I pitched to the floor. Perhaps I passed out again—I don't know for sure—but when I next looked in its direction the horror had gone. All that remained was the slime and the grotesque corpse.

I do not know where my muscles found the strength to carry my tottering and mazed body out of that house. Sanity did not drive me, I admit that, for I was quite insane. I wanted to stand beneath the stabbing lightning and scream at those awful, rain-blurred stars. I wanted to bound, to float in my madness through eldritch depths of unhallowed black blood. I wanted to cling to the writhing breasts of Yibb-Tstll. Insane—insane, I tell you, I gibbered and moaned, staggering through the thunder-crazed streets until, with a roar and a crash, sanity-invoking lightning smashed me down . . .

You know the rest. I awoke to this world of white sheets: to you, the police psychiatrist, with your soft voice . . . Why must you insist that I keep telling my story? Do you honestly think to make me change it? It's *true*, I tell you! I admit to killing my brother's body—but it wasn't *his mind* that I burned out! You stand there babbling of awful eye diseases. *Julian had no eye disease!* D'you really imagine that the other eye, the unburnt one which you found in that body—in my brother's face—was his? And what of the pool of slime in the cellar and the stink? Are you stupid or something? You've asked for a statement, and here it is! Watch, damn you, watch while I scribble it down . . . you damn great crimson eye . . . always watching me . . . who would have thought that the lips of Bugg-Shash could *suck* like that? Watch, you redness you . . . and look out for the Scarlet Feaster! *No, don't take the paper away. . . .*

NOTE

Sir,

Dr. Stewart was contacted as you suggested, and after seeing Haughtree he gave his expert opinion that the man was madder than his brother ever had been. He also pointed out the possibility that the disease of Julian Haughtree's eyes had started soon after his partial mental recovery—probably brought on by constantly wearing dark spectacles. After Dr. Stewart left the police ward, Haughtree became very indignant and wrote the above statement.

Davies, our specialist, examined the body in the cellar himself and is convinced that the younger brother must, indeed, have been suffering from a particularly horrible and unknown ocular disease.

It is appreciated that there are one or two remarkable coincidences in the wild fancies of both brothers in relation to certain recent factual events—but these are, surely, only coincidences. One such event is the rise of the volcanic island of Surtsey. Haughtree must somehow have heard of Surtsey after being taken under observation. He asked to be allowed to read the following newspaper account, afterward yelling very loudly and repeatedly: "By God! They've named it after the wrong mythos!" Thereafter he was put into a straitjacket of the arm-restricting type:

—BIRTH OF AN ISLAND—

Yesterday morning, the 16th November, the sun rose on a long, narrow island of tephra, lying in the sea to the north of Scotland at latitude 63°18' North and longitude 20°36½' West. Surtsey, which was born on the 15th November, was then 130 feet high and growing all the time. The fantastic "birth" of the island was witnessed by the crew of the fishing vessel *Isleifer II*, which was lying west of Geirfuglasker, southernmost of the Vestmann Islands. Considerable disturbance of the sea—which hindered clear observation—was noticed, and the phenomena, the result of submarine volcanic activity, involved such awe-inspiring sights as columns of smoke reaching to two and a half miles high, fantastic lightning storms, and the hurling of lava-bombs over a wide area of the ocean. Surtsey has been named after the giant Surter, who—in Norse mythology—"Came from the South with Fire to fight the God Freyr at Ragnarok," which battle preceded the end of the world and the Twilight of the Gods. More details and pictures inside.

Still in the "jacket," Haughtree finally calmed himself and begged that further interesting items in the paper be read to him. Dr. Davies did the reading, and when he reached the following report Haughtree grew very excited:

—BEACHES FOULED—

Garvin Bay, on the extreme North coast, was found this morning to be horribly fouled. For a quarter of a mile deposits of some slimy, black grease were left by the tide along the sands. The stench was so great from these unrecognizable deposits that fishermen were unable to put to sea. Scientific analysis has already shown the stuff to be of an organic base, and it is thought to be some type of oil. Local shipping experts are bewildered, as no known tankers have been in the area for over three months. The tremendous variety of dead and rotting fish also washed up has caused the people of nearby Belloch to take strong sanitary precautions. It is hoped that tonight's tide will clear the affected area . . .

At the end of the reading Haughtree said: "Julian said they wouldn't take him alive." Then, still encased in the jacket, he somehow got off the bed and flung himself through the third-story window of his room in the police ward. His rush at the window was of such

tremendous ferocity and strength that he took the bars and frame
with him. It all happened so quickly there was nothing anyone could
do to stop him.

Submitted as an appendix to my original report.

Sgt. J. T. Muir

23 November 1963   Glasgow City Police

BIG C

Two thousand thirteen and the exploration of space—by men, not robot spaceships—was well underway. Men had built Moonbase, landed on Mars, were now looking toward Titan, though that was still some way ahead. But then, from a Darkside observatory, Luna II was discovered half a million miles out: a black rock two hundred yards long and eighty through, tumbling dizzily end over end around the Earth, too small to occlude stars for more than a blip, too dark to have been (previously) anything but the tiniest sunspot on the surface of Sol. But interesting anyway "because it was there," and also and especially because on those rare occasions when it lined itself up with the full moon, that would be when Earth's lunatics gave full vent. Lunatics of all persuasions, whether they were in madhouses or White Houses, asylums or the army, refuges or radiation shelters, surgeries or silos.

Men had known for a long time that the moon controlled the tides—and possibly the fluids in men's brains?—and it was interesting now to note that Luna II appeared to compound the offence. It seemed reasonable to suppose that we had finally discovered the reason for Man's homicidal tendencies, his immemorial hostility to Man.

Two thousand fifteen and a joint mission—American, Russian, British—went to take a look: they circled Luna II at a "safe" distance for twelve hours, took pictures, made recordings, measured radiation levels. When they came back, within a month of their return, one of the two Americans (the most outspoken one) went mad, one of the two Russians (the introverted one) set fire to himself, and the two British members remained phlegmatic, naturally.

One year later in August 2016, an Anglo-French expedition set out to double-check the findings of the first mission: i.e., to see if there were indeed "peculiar radiations" being emitted by Luna II. It was a four-man team; they were all volunteers and wore lead baffles of various thicknesses in their helmets. And afterwards, the ones with the least lead were discovered to be more prone to mental fluctuations. But . . . the "radiations," or whatever, couldn't be measured by any of Man's instruments. What was required was a special sort of volunteer, someone actually to land on Luna II and dig around a little, and do some work right there on top of—whatever it was.

Where to land wasn't a problem: with a rotation period of one minute, Luna II's equatorial tips were moving about as fast as a man could run, but at its "poles" the planetoid was turning in a very gentle circle. And that's where Benjamin "Smiler" Williams set down. He had wanted to do the job and was the obvious choice. He was a Brit riding an American rocket paid for by the French and Russians. (Everybody had wanted to be in on it.) And of course he was a hero. And he was dying of cancer.

Smiler drilled holes in Luna II, set off small explosions in the holes, collected dust and debris and exhaust gasses from the explosions, slid his baffles aside and exposed his brain to whatever, walked around quite a bit and sat down and thought things, and sometimes just sat. And all in all he was there long enough to see the Earth turn one complete circle on her axis, following which he went home. First to Moonbase, finally to Earth. Went home to die—after they'd checked him out, of course.

But that was six years ago and he still hadn't died (though God knows we'd tried the best we could to kill him), and now I was on my way to pay him a visit. On my way through him, travelling into him, journeying to his very heart. The heart and mind—the living, thinking organism, the control centre, as it were—deep within the body of what the world now called Big 'C.'

July 2024, and Smiler Williams had asked for a visitor. I was it, and as I drove in I went over everything that had led up to this moment. It was as good a way as any to keep from looking at the "landscape" outside the car. This was Florida and it was the middle of the month, but I wasn't using the air-conditioning and in fact I'd even turned up the heater a little—because it was cool out there. As cool as driving down a country lane in Devon, with the trees arching their green canopy overhead. Except it wasn't Devon and they weren't green. And in fact they weren't even trees. . . .

Those were thoughts I should try to avoid, however, just as I avoided looking at anything except the road unwinding under the wheels of my car, and so I went back again to 2016, when Ben Williams came back from space.

The specialists in London checked Smiler out—his brain, mostly, for they weren't really interested in his cancer. That was right through him, (with the possible exception of his grey matter), and there was no hope. Try to cut or laser *that* out of him and there'd be precious little of the man himself left! But after ten days of tests they'd found nothing, and Smiler was getting restless.

"Peter," he said to me, "I'm short on time and these monkeys are wasting what little I've got left! Can't you get me out of here? There are places I want to go, friends I want to say good-bye to." But if I make that sound sad or melodramatic, forget it. Smiler wasn't like that. He'd really *earned* his nickname, that good old boy, because right through everything he'd kept on smiling like it was painted on his face. Maybe it was his way to keep from crying. Twenty-seven years old just a month ago, and he'd never make twenty-eight. So we'd all reckoned.

Myself, I'd never made it through training, but Smiler had and we'd kept in touch. But just because I couldn't go into space didn't mean I couldn't help others to do it. I'd worked at NASA, and on the European Space Programme (ESP), even for a while for the Soviets at Baikonur, when détente had been peaking a periodic upsurge back in 2009 and 2010. So I knew my stuff. And I knew the men who were doing it, landing on Mars and what have you, and the heroes like Smiler Williams. So while Smiler was moderately cool towards the others on the space medicine team—the Frogs, Sovs, and even the other Americans—to me he was the same as always. We'd been friends and Smiler had never let down a friend in his life.

And when he'd asked for my help in getting him out of that place, I'd had to go along with him. "Sure, why not?" I'd told him. "Maybe I can speed it up. Have you seen the new Space Center at the Lake? There are a lot of people you used to know there. NASA people. They'd love to see you again, Smiler."

What I didn't say was that the Space Center at Lake Okeechobee also housed the finest space medicine team in the world, and that they were longing to get their hands on him. But he was dying and a Brit, and so the British had first claim, so to speak. No one was going to argue the pros and cons about a man on his last legs. And if that makes me sound bad—like maybe I'd gone over to London to snatch him for the home team—I'd better add that there was something else I hadn't mentioned to him: the Center Research Foundation at Lakeport, right next door. I wanted to wheel him in there so they could take a look at him. Oh, he was a no-hoper, like I've said, but . . .

And maybe he hadn't quite given up hope himself, either, because when they were finally through with him a few days later he'd agreed to come back here with me. "What the hell," he'd shrugged. "They have their rocks, dust, gasses, don't they? Also, they have lots of time. Me, I have to use mine pretty sparingly." It was starting to get to him.

In the States Smiler got a hero's welcome, met everybody who was anybody from the president down. But that was time-consuming stuff, so after a few days we moved on down to Florida. First things first: I told him about the Foundation at Lakeport. "So what's new?" he laughed. "Why'd you think I came with you, Yank?"

They checked him over, smiled, and joked with him (which was the only way to play it with Smiler) but right up front shook their heads and told him no, there was nothing they could do. And time was narrowing down.

But it was running out for me, too, and that's where I had to switch my memories off and come back to the present a while, for I'd reached the first checkpoint. I was driving up from Immokalee, Big 'C' Control ("control," that's a laugh!) Point Seven, to see Smiler at Lakeport. The barrier was at the La Belle–Clewiston crossroads, and Smiler came up on the air just as I saw it up ahead and started to slow her down a little.

"You're two minutes early, Peter," his voice crackled out of the radio at me. "Try to get it right from here on in, OK? Big 'C' said ten-thirty A.M. at the La Belle–Clewiston crossroads, and he didn't mean ten-twenty-eight. You don't gain anything by being early; he'll only hold you up down there two minutes longer to put you back on schedule. Do you read me, old friend?"

"I read you, buddy," I answered, slowing to a halt at the barrier's massive red-and-white-striped pole where it cut the road in half. "Sorry I'm early. I guess it's nerves; must have put my foot down a little. Anyway, what's a couple minutes between friends, eh?"

"Between you and me? Nothing!" Smiler's voice came back— and with a chuckle in it! I thought: *God, that's courage for you!* "But Big 'C' likes accuracy, dead reckoning," he continued. "And come to think of it, so do I! Hell, you wouldn't try to find me a reentry window a couple of minutes ahead of time, would you? No you wouldn't." And then, more quietly: "And remember, Peter, a man can get burned just as easily in here. . . ." But this time there was no chuckle.

"What now?" I sat still, staring straight ahead, aware that the—tunnel?—was closing overhead, that the light was going as Big 'C' enclosed me.

"Out," he answered at once, "so he can take a good look at the car. You know he's not much for trusting people, Peter."

I froze, and remained sitting there as rigid as . . . as the great steel barrier pole right there in front of me. Get out? Big 'C' wanted me to get out? But the car was my womb and I wasn't programmed to be born yet, not until I got to Smiler. And—

"Out!" Smiler's voice crackled on the air. "He says you're not moving and it bothers him. So get out now—or would you rather sit tight and have him come in there with you? How do you think you'd like that, Peter: having Big 'C' groping around in there with you?"

I unfroze, opened the car door. But where was I supposed to—?

"The checkpoint shack," Smiler told me, as if reading my mind. "There's nothing of him in there."

Thank God for that!

I left the car door open—to appease Big 'C'? To facilitate his search? To make up for earlier inadequacies? Don't ask me—and hurried in the deepening gloom to the wooden, chalet-style building at the side of the road. It had been built there maybe four years ago when Big 'C' wasn't so big, but no one had used it in a long time and the door was stuck; I could get the bottom of the door to give a little by leaning my thigh against it, but the top was jammed tight. And somehow I didn't like to make too much noise.

Standing there with the doorknob clenched tight in my hand, I steeled myself, glanced up at the ceiling being formed of Big 'C''s substance—the moth-eaten holes being bridged by doughy flaps, then sealed as the mass thickened up, shutting out the light—and I thought of myself as becoming a tiny shrivelled kernel in his gi-

gantic, leprous walnut. Christ... what a mercy I never suffered
from claustrophobia! But then I also thought: *to hell with the noise,*
and put my shoulder to the door to burst it right in.

I left the door vibrating in its frame behind me and went unsteadily, breathlessly, to the big windows. There was a desk there,
chairs, a few well-thumbed paperbacks, a Daily Occurrence Book,
telephone and scribble pad: everything a quarter-inch thick in dust.
But I blew the dust off one of the chairs and sat (which wasn't a
bad idea, my legs were shaking so bad), for now that I'd started in
on this thing I knew there'd be no stopping it, and what was going
on out there was all part of it. Smiler's knowledge of cars hadn't
been much to mention; I had to hope that Big 'C' was equally
ignorant.

And so I sat there trembling by the big windows, looking out
at the road and the barrier and the car, and I suppose the idea was
that I was going to watch Big 'C''s inspection. I did actually watch
the start of it—the tendrils of frothy slop elongating themselves
downward from above and inwards from both sides, closing on the
car, entering it; a pseudopod of slime hardening into rubber, pulling
loose the weather strip from the boot cover and flattening itself to
squeeze inside; another member like a long, flat tapeworm sliding
through the gap between the hood and the radiator grille... but
that was as much as I could take and I turned my face away.

It's not so much how Big 'C' looks but what he is that does it.
It's knowing, and yet not really knowing, what he is. . . .

So I sweated it there and waited for it to get done, and hoped
and prayed that Big 'C' *would* get done and not find anything. And
while I waited my mind went back again to that time six years
earlier.

The months went by and Smiler weakened a little. He got to
spending a lot of his time at Lakeport, which was fine by the space
medics at the Lake because they could go and see him any time
they wanted and carry on examining and testing him. And at the

time I thought they'd actually found something they could do for him, because after a while he really did seem to be improving again. Meanwhile I had my own life to live. I hadn't seen as much of him as I might like; I'd been busy on the Saturn's Moons Project. When I did get to see him almost a year had gone by and he should have been dead. But he wasn't anything like dead and the boys from Med. were excited about something—had been for months—and Smiler had asked to see me. I was briefed and they told me not to excite him a lot, just treat him like . . . normal? Now how the hell else would I treat him? I wondered.

It was summer and we met at Clewiston on the Lake, a beach where the sun sparkled on the water and leisure craft came and went, many of them towing their golden, waving water-skiers. Smiler arrived from Lakeport in an ambulance and the boys in white walked him slowly down to the table under a sun umbrella where I was waiting for him. And I saw how big he was under his robe.

I ordered a Coke for myself, and—"Four vodkas and a small tomato juice," Smiler told me! "An Anaemic Mary—in one big glass."

"Do you have a problem, buddy?" the words escaped me before I could check them.

"Are you kidding?" he said, frowning. But then he saw me ogling his huge drink and grinned. "Eh? The booze? Jesus, no! It's like rocket fuel to me—keeps me aloft and propels me around and around—but doesn't make me dizzy!" And then he was serious again. "A pity, really, 'cos there are times when I'd like to get blasted out of my mind."

"What?" I stared hard at him, wondered what was going on in his head. "Smiler, I—"

"Peter," he cut me short, "I'm not going to die—not just yet, anyway."

For a moment I couldn't take it in, couldn't believe it. I was *that* delighted. I knew my bottom jaw must have fallen open and so closed it again. "They've come up with something?" I finally blurted it out. "Smiler, you've done it—you've beaten the Big 'C'!"

But he wasn't laughing or even smiling, just sitting there looking at me.

He had been all dark and lean and muscular, Smiler, but was now pale and puffy. Puffy cheeks, puffy bags under his eyes, pale and puffy double chins. And bald (all that shining, jet-black hair gone) and minus his eyebrows: the effect of one treatment or another. His natural teeth were gone, too: calcium deficiency brought on by low grav during too many missions in the space stations, probably aggravated by his complaint. In fact his eyes were really the only things I'd know him by: film-star blue eyes, which had somehow retained their old twinkle.

Though right now, as I've said, he wasn't laughing or even smiling but just sitting there staring at me.

"Big 'C'," he finally answered me. "Beaten the Big 'C' . . ."

And eventually the smile fell from my face, too. "But . . . isn't that what you meant?"

"Listen," he said, suddenly shifting to a higher gear, "I'm short of time. They're checking me over every couple of hours now, because they're expecting it to break loose . . . well, soon. And so they'll not be too long coming for me, wanting to take me back into that good old "controlled environment," you know? So now I want to tell you about it—the way I see it, anyway."

"Tell me about . . . ?"

"About Luna II. Peter, it was Luna II. It wasn't anything the people at Lakeport have done or the space medicine buffs from the Lake, it was just Luna II. There's something in Luna II that changes things. That's its nature: to change things. Sometimes the changes may be radical: it takes a sane man and makes him mad, or turns a peaceful race into a mindless gang of mass murderers, or changes a small planet into a chunk of shiny black slag that we've named

Luna II. And sometimes it's sleeping or inert, and then there's no effect whatever."

I tried to take all of this in but it was coming too thick and fast. "Eh? Something in Luna II? But don't we already know about that? That it's a source of peculiar emanations or whatever?" "Something like that." He shrugged helplessly, impatiently. "Maybe. I don't know. But when I was up there I felt it, and now it's starting to look like it felt me."

"It felt you?" Now he really *wasn't* making sense, had started to ramble.

"I don't know"—he shrugged again—"but it could be the answer to Everything—it could *be* Everything! Maybe there are lots of Luna IIs scattered through the universe, and they all have the power to change things. Like they're catalysts. They cause mutations—in space, in time. A couple of billion years ago the Earth felt it up there, felt its nearness, its effect. And it took this formless blob of mud hurtling through space and changed it, gave it life, brought microorganisms awake in the soup of its oceans. It's been changing things ever since—and we've called *that* evolution! Do you see what I mean? It was The Beginning—and it might yet be The End."

"Smiler, I—"

He caught my arm, gave me what I suspect was the most serious look he'd ever given anyone in his entire life, and said: "Don't look at me like that, Peter." And there was just a hint of accusation.

"Was I?"

"Yes, you were!" And then he relaxed and laughed, and just as suddenly became excited. "Man, when something like this happens, you're bound to ask questions. So I've asked myself questions, and the things I've told you are the answers. Some of them, anyway. Hell, they may not even be right, but they're my answers!"

"These are your thoughts, then? Not the boffins'?" This was one of his Brit words I used, from the old days. It meant "experts."

"Mine," he said, seeming proud of it, "but grown at least in part from what the boffins have told me."

"So what *has* happened?" I asked him, feeling a little exasperated now. "What's going down, Smiler?"

"Not so much going down," he shook his head, "as coming out."

"Coming out?" I waited, not sure whether to smile or frown, not knowing what to do or say.

"Of me."

And still I waited. It was like a guessing game where I was supposed to come up with some sort of conclusion based on what he'd told me. But I didn't have any conclusions.

Finally he shrugged yet again, snorted, shook his head, and said: "But you do know about cancer, right? About the Big 'C'? Well, when I went up to Luna II, it changed my cancer. Oh, I still have it, but it's not the same any more. It's a separate thing existing in me, but no longer truly a part of me. It's in various cavities and tracts, all connected up by threads, living in me like a rat in a system of burrows. Or better, like a hermit crab in a pirated shell. But you know what happens when a hermit crab outgrows its shell? It moves out, finds itself a bigger home. So . . . this thing in me has tried to vacate—has experimented with the idea, anyway . . ."

He shuddered, his whole body trembling like jelly.

"Experimented?" It was all I could find to say.

He gulped, nodded, controlled himself. And he sank what was left of his drink before going on. "In the night, a couple of nights ago, it started to eject—from both ends at once—from just about everywhere. Anus, throat, nostrils, you name it. I almost choked to death before they got to me. But by then it had already given up, retreated, *retracted* itself. And I could breathe again. It was like it . . . like it hadn't wanted to kill me."

I was numb, dumb, couldn't say anything. The way Smiler told it, it was almost as if he'd credited his cancer with intelligence! But then a white movement caught my eye, and I saw with some relief that it was the boys from the ambulance coming for him. He saw them, too, and clutched my arm. And suddenly fear had made his eyes round in his round face. "Peter . . ." he said. "Peter . . ."

"It's OK," I grabbed his fist grabbing me. "It's all right. They have to know what they're doing. You said it yourself, remember? You're not going to die."

"I know, I know," he said. "But will it be worth living?"

And then they came and took him to the ambulance. And for a long time I wondered about that last thing he'd said. But of course in the end it turned out he was right. . . .

The car door slammed and the telephone rang at one and the same time, causing me to start. I looked out through the control shack's dusty window and saw Big 'C' receding from the car. Apparently everything was OK. And when the telephone rang again I picked it up.

"OK, Peter," Smiler's voice seemed likewise relieved, "you can come on in now."

But as well as relieved I was also afraid. Now of all times—when it was inevitable—I was afraid. Afraid for the future the world might never have if I didn't go in, and for the future I certainly wouldn't have if I did. Until at last common sense prevailed: what the heck, I had no future anyway!

"Something wrong, old friend?" Smiler's voice was soft. "Hey, don't let it get to you. It will be just like the last time you visited me, remember?" His words were careful, innocent yet contrived. And they held a code.

I said "Sure," put the phone down, left the shack, and went to the car. If he was ready for it then so was I. It was ominous out there, in Big 'C' 's gloom; getting into the car was like entering the vacant lair of some weird, alien animal. The thing was no longer there, but I knew it had been there. It didn't smell, but I could smell and taste it anyway. You would think so, the way I avoided breathing.

And so my throat was dry and my chest was tight as I turned the lights on to drive. To drive through Big 'C,' to the core which was Ben "Smiler" Williams. And driving I thought:

I'm travelling down a hollow tentacle, proceeding along a pseudopod, venturing in an alien vein. And it can put a stop to me, kill me any time it wants to. By suffocation, strangulation, or simply by laying itself down on me and crushing me. But it won't because it needs Smiler, needs to appease him, and he has asked to see me.

As he'd said on the telephone, "Just like the last time." Except we both knew it wouldn't be like the last time. Not at all. . . .

The last time: that had been fifteen months ago when we'd agreed on the boundaries. But to continue at that point would be to leave out what happened in between. And I needed to fill it in, if only to fix my mind on something and so occupy my time for the rest of the journey. It isn't good for your nerves, to drive down a mid-morning road in near darkness, through a tunnel of living, frothing, cancerous flesh.

A month after I'd seen Smiler on the beach, Big 'C' broke out. Except that's not exactly how it was. I mean, it wasn't how you'd expect. What happened was this:

Back in 2002, when we went through a sticky patch with the USSR and there were several (as yet *still* unsolved) sabotage attempts on some of our missile and space research sites, a number of mobile ICBM and MIRV networks were quickly commissioned and established across the entire USA. Most of these had been quietly decommissioned or mothballed only a year or two later, but not the one covering the Okeechobee region of Florida. That one still existed, with its principal base or railhead at La Belle and arms reaching out as far as Fort Myers in the west, Fort Drum north of the Lake, and Canal Point right on the Lake's eastern shore. Though still maintained in operational order as a deterrent, the rail network now carried ninety percent of hardware for the Space Center while its military functions were kept strictly low profile. Or they had been, until that night in late August 2024.

Smiler had a night nurse, but the first thing Big 'C' did when he emerged was to kill him. That's what we later figured, anyway. The second thing that he did was derail a MIRV bogie on its way through Lakeport. I can't supply details; I only know he did it.

Normally this wouldn't matter much: seventy-five percent of the runs were dummies anyway. But this one was the real thing, one of the two or three times a year when the warheads were in position. And it looked like something had got broken in the derailment, because all of the alarms were going off at once!

The place was evacuated. Lakeport, Venus, Clewiston—all the towns around Lake Okeechobee—the whole shoot. Even the Okeechobee Space Center itself, though not in its entirety; a skeleton crew stayed on there; likewise at the La Belle silos. A decon team was made ready to go in and tidy things up . . . except that didn't happen. For through all of this activity, Smiler (or rather, Big 'C') had somehow contrived to be forgotten and left behind. And what *did* happen was that Smiler got on the telephone to Okeechobee and told them to hold off. No one was to move. Nothing was to happen.

"You'd better listen and listen good," he'd said. "Big 'C' has six MIRVs, each one with eight bombs aboard. And he's got five of them lined up on Washington, London, Tokyo, Berlin, and Moscow, though not necessarily in that order. That's forty nukes for five of the world's greatest capitals and major cities within radii of two hundred miles. That's a holocaust, a nuclear winter, the New Dark Age. As for the sixth MIRV: that one's airborne right now! But it won't hurt because he hasn't programmed detonation instructions. It's just a sign to let you all know that he's not kidding and can do what he says he can do."

The MIRV split up north of Jacksonville; bombs came down

harmlessly in the sea off Wilmington, Cape Fear, Georgetown, Charleston, Savannah, Jacksonville, Cape Canaveral, and Palm Beach. After that . . . while no one was quite sure just exactly who Big 'C' was, certainly they all knew he had them by the short and curlies.

Of course, that was when the "news" broke about Smiler's cancer, the fact that it was different. And the cancer experts from the Lakeport Center, and the space medics, too, arrived at the same conclusion: that somehow alien "radiations" or emanations had changed Smiler's cancer into Big 'C.' The Lakeport doctors and scientists had intended that when it vacated Smiler they'd kill it, but now Big 'C' was threatening to kill us, indeed the world. It was then that I remembered how Smiler had credited the thing with intelligence, and now it appeared he'd been right.

So . . . maybe the problem could have been cleared up right there and then. But at what cost? Big 'C' had demonstrated that he knew his way around our weaponry, so if he was going to die why not take us with him? Nevertheless, it's a fact that there were some itchy fingers among the military brass right about that time.

Naturally, we had to let Moscow, London, and all the other target areas in on it, and their reaction was about what was expected:

"For God's sake—placate the thing! Do as it tells you—*whatever* it tells you!" And the Sovs said: "If you let anything come out of Florida heading for Moscow, comrades, that's war!"

And then, of course, there was Smiler himself. Big 'C' had Smiler in there—a hero, and one of the greatest of all time. So the hotheads cooled down pretty quickly, and for some little time there was a lot of hard, cold, calculated thinking going on as the odds were weighed. But always it came out in Big 'C' 's favour. Oh, Smiler and his offspring were only a small percentage of life on Earth, right enough, and we could stand their loss . . . but what if we attacked and this monstrous growth actually *did* press the button before we nailed him? Could he, for instance, monitor incoming hardware from space? No, for he was at Lakeport and the radar and satellite monitoring equipment was at La Belle. So maybe we could get him in a preemptive strike! A lot of fingernails were chewed. But:

Smiler's next message came out of La Belle, before anybody could make any silly decisions. "Forget it," he warned us. "He's several jumps ahead of you. He made me drive him down here, to La Belle. And this is the deal: *Big 'C' doesn't want to harm anyone*—but neither does he want to be harmed. Here at La Belle he's got the whole world laid out on his screens—*his* screens, have you got that? The La Belle ground staff—that brave handful of guys who stayed on—they're . . . finished. They opposed him. So don't go making the same mistake. All of this is Big 'C' 's now. He's watching everything from space, on radar . . . all the skills we had in those areas are now his. And he's nervous because he knows we kill things that frighten us, and he supposes that he frightens us. So the minute our defense satellites stop cooperating—the very *minute* he stops receiving information from his radar or pictures from space—he presses the button. And you'd better believe there's stuff here at La Belle that makes that derailed junk at Lakeport look like Chinese firecrackers!" And of course we knew there was.

So that was it: stalemate, a Mexican standoff. And there were even groups who got together and declared that Big 'C' had a right to live. If the Israelis had been given Israel (they argued), the Palestinians Beirut, and the Aborigines Alice Springs all the way out to Simpson Desert, then why shouldn't Big 'C' have Lake Okeechobee? After all, he was a sentient being, wasn't he? And all he wanted was to live—wasn't it?

Well, that was something of what he wanted, anyway. Moisture from the lake, and air to breathe. And Smiler, of course.

And territory. A lot more territory.

Big 'C' grew fast. Very fast. The word *big* itself took on soaring new dimensions. In a few years Big 'C' was into all the lakeside towns and spreading outwards. He seemed to live on anything, ate everything, and thrived on it. And it was about then that we decided we really ought to negotiate boundaries. Except "negotiate" isn't the right word.

Smiler asked to see me; I went in; through Smiler, Big 'C' told me what he wanted by way of land. And he got it. You don't argue with something that can reduce your planet to radioactive ashes. And now that Big 'C' was into all the towns and villages on the Lake, he'd moved his nukes in with him. He hadn't liked the idea of having all his eggs in one basket, as it were.

But between Big 'C' 's emergence from Smiler and my negotiating the boundaries, Christ knows we tried to get him! Frogmen had gone up the Miami, Hillsboro, and St. Lucie canals to poison the lake—and hadn't come down again. A man-made anthrax variant had been sown in the fields and swamps where he was calculated to be spreading—and he'd just spread right on over it. A fire had started "accidentally" in the long hot summer of 2019, in the dried-out Okaloacoochee Slough, and warmed Big 'C' 's hide all the way to the Lake before it died down. But that had been something he couldn't ignore.

"You must be crazy!" Smiler told us that time. "He's launched an ICBM to teach you a lesson. At ten megs its the smallest thing he's got—but still big enough!"

It was big enough for Hawaii, anyway. And so for a while we'd stopped trying to kill him, but we never stopped thinking about it. And someone thought:

If Big 'C' 's brain is where Smiler is, and if we can get to that brain . . . will that stop the whole thing dead?

It was a nice thought. We needed somebody on the inside, but all we had was Smiler. Which brings me back to that time fifteen months ago when I went in to negotiate the new boundaries.

At that time Big 'C' was out as far as ten miles from the Lake and expanding rapidly on all fronts. A big round nodule of him extended to cover La Belle, tapering to a tentacle reaching as far as Alva. I'd entered him at Alva as per instructions, where Big 'C' had checked the car, then driven on through La Belle on my way to Lakeport, which was now his HQ. And then, as now, I'd passed through the landscape, which he opened for me, driving through his ever-expanding tissues. But I won't go into that here, nor into my conversation with Smiler. Let it suffice to say that Smiler intimated he would like to die now and it couldn't come quickly enough, and that before I left I'd passed him a note which read:

Smiler,
      The next time someone comes in here he'll be a volunteer, and he'll be bringing something with him. A little something for Big 'C'. But it's up to you when that happens, good buddy. You're the only one who can fix it.

                                                        Peter

And then I was out of there. But as he'd glanced at the note there had been a look on Smiler's face that was hard to gauge. He'd *told* me that Big 'C' only used him as a mouthpiece and as his . . . host. That the hideous stuff could only instruct him, not read his mind or get into his brain. But as I went to my car that time I could feel Big 'C' gathering himself—like a big cat bunching its muscles—and as I actually got into the car something wet, a spot of slime, splashed down on me from overhead! Jesus! It was like the bastard was drooling on me!

"Jesus," yes. Because when I'd passed Smiler that note and he'd looked at me, and we'd come to our unspoken agreement, I hadn't known that *I* would be the volunteer! But I was, and for two reasons: my life didn't matter any more, and Smiler had asked for me—if I was willing. Now that was a funny thing in itself because it meant that he was asking me to die with him. But the thought

didn't dawn on me that maybe he knew something that he shouldn't
know. Nor would it dawn on me until I only had one more mile
to go to my destination, Lakeport. When in any case there was no
way I could turn back.

As for what that something was: it was the fact that I too was
now dying of cancer.

It was diagnosed just a few weeks after I'd been to see him: the
fast-moving sort that was spreading through me like a fire. Which
was why I said: sure, I'll come in and see you, Smiler . . .

Ostensibly I was going in to negotiate the boundaries again. Big
'C' had already crossed the old lines and was now out from the lake
about forty miles in all directions, taking him to the Atlantic coast
in the east and very nearly the Gulf of Mexico in the west. Immokalee had been my starting point, just a mile southwest of where
he sprawled over the Slough, and now I was up as far as Palmdale
and turning right for Moore Haven and Lakeport. And up to date
with my morbid memories, too.

From Palmdale to Lakeport is about twenty-five miles. I drove
that narrow strip of road with flaps and hummocks of leprous
dough crawling, heaving, and tossing on both sides—or clearing
from the tarmac before my spinning wheels—while an opaque webbing of alien flesh pulsed and vibrated overhead. It was like driving
down the funnel trap of some cosmic trapdoor spider, or crossing
the dry bed of an ocean magically cleared as by Moses and his staff.
Except that *this* sea—this ocean of slime and disease—was its own
master and cleared the way itself.

And in my jacket pocket my cigarette lighter, and under its
hinged cap the button. And I was dying for a cigarette but couldn't
have one, not just yet. But (or so I kept telling myself, however
ridiculously) that was a good thing because they were bad for you!

The bomb was in the hollow front axle of the car, its two halves
sitting near the wheels along with the propellant charges. When
those charges detonated they'd drive two loads of hell into calam-

itous collision right there in the middle of the axle, creating critical mass and instant oblivion for anything in the immediate vicinity. I was driving a very special car: a kamikaze nuke. And ground zero was going to be Big 'C''s brain and my old pal Smiler. And myself, of course.

The miles were passing very quickly now, seeming to speed up right along with my heartbeat. I guessed I could do it even before I got there if I wanted to, blow the bastard to hell. But I wasn't going to give him even a split second's warning, because it was possible that was all he needed. No, I was going to park this heap right up his nose. Almost total disintegration for a radius of three or four miles when it went. For me, for Smiler, but especially for Big 'C.' Instantaneous, so that he wouldn't even have time to twitch.

And with this picture in mind I was through Moore Haven and Lakeport was up ahead, and I thought: *We've got him! Just two or three more miles and I can let 'er rip any time! And it's good-bye Big 'C.'* But I wouldn't do it because I wanted to see Smiler one last time. It was him and me together. I could smile right back at him (would I be able to? God, I hoped so!) as I pressed the button.

And it was then, with only a mile to go to Lakeport, that I remembered what Smiler had said the last time he asked for a visitor. He'd said: "Someone should come and see me soon, to talk about boundaries *if for nothing else.* I think maybe Peter Lancing . . . if he's willing."

The "if for nothing else" was his way of saying: "OK, bring it on in." And the rest of it . . .

The way I saw it, it could be read two ways. That "if he's willing" bit could be a warning, meaning: "Of course, this is really a job for a volunteer." Or he could simply have been saying good-bye to me, by mentioning my name in his final communication. But . . . maybe it could be read a third way, too. Except that would mean that he *knew* I had cancer, and that therefore I probably would be willing.

And I remembered that blob of goo, that *sweat* or *spittle* of Big 'C,' which had splashed on me when I was last in here. . . .

Thought processes, and while they were taking place the mile was covered and I was in. It had been made simple: Big 'C' had left only one road open, the one that led to the grounds of the Cancer Research Foundation. Some irony, that this should be Big 'C' 's HQ! But yes, just looking at the place I knew that it was.

It was . . . *wet*-looking, glistening, alive. Weakened light filtered down through the layers of fretted, fretting webs of mucus and froth and foaming flesh overhead, and the Foundation complex itself looked like a gigantic, suppurating mass of decaying brick and concrete. Tentacles of filth had shattered all the windows outwards, for all the world as if the building's brain had burst out through its eyes, ears, and nostrils. And the whole thing was connected by writhing ropes of webbing to the far greater mass which was Big 'C' 's loathsome body.

Jesus! It was gray and green and brown and blue-tinged. In spots it was even bright yellow, red, and splashed with purple. It was Cancer with a capital C—Big 'C' himself—and it was alive!

"What are you waiting for, Peter?" Smiler's voice came out of my radio, and I banged my head on the car roof starting away from it. "Are you coming in, old friend . . . or what?"

I didn't have to go in there if I didn't want to; my lighter was in my pocket; I touched it to make sure. But . . . I didn't want to go out alone. I don't mean just out, like out of the car, but out period. And so:

"I'm coming in, Smiler," I told him.

And somehow I made myself. In front of the main building there'd been lawn cropped close as a crew cut. Now it was just soil crumbling to sand. I walked across it and into the building, just looking straight ahead and nowhere else. Inside . . . the corridors were clear at least. Big 'C' had cleared them for me. But through each door as I passed them I could see him bulking, pile upon pile of him like . . . like heaped intestines. His brains? God, I hoped so!

Finally, when I was beginning to believe I couldn't go any further on two feet and would have to crawl—and when I was fighting with myself not to throw up—I found Smiler in his "office": just a large room with a desk which he sat behind, and a couple of chairs, telephones, radios. And also containing Big 'C,' of course. Which is the part I've always been reluctant to talk about, but now have to tell just the way it was.

Big 'C' was plugged into him, into Smiler. It was grotesque. Smiler sat propped up in his huge chair, and he was like a spider at the centre of his web. Except the web wasn't of silk but of flesh, and it was attached to him. The back of his head was welded to a huge fan shape of tentacles spreading outwards like some vast ornamental headdress, or like the sprawl of an octopus's arms, and these cancerous extensions or extrusions were themselves attached to a shuddering bulk that lay behind Smiler's chair and grew up the walls and out of the windows. The lower part of his body was lost behind the desk, lost in bulging grey sacks and folds and yellow pipes and purplish gelatinous masses of . . . Christ, of whatever the filthy stuff was! Only his upper body, his arms and hands, face and shoulders were free of the stuff. He was it. It was him—physically, anyway.

No one could have looked at him and felt anything except disgust, or perhaps pity if they'd known him like I had. And if they hadn't, dread and loathing and . . . yes, horror. Friendship didn't come into it; I knew that I wasn't smiling; I knew that my face must reflect everything I felt.

He nodded the merest twitch of a nod and husked: "Sit down, Peter, before you fall down! Hey, and you think I look bad, right?" Humour! Unbelievable! But his voice was a desiccated whisper, and his grey hands on the desk shook like spindly skating insects resting up after a morning's hard skimming over a stagnant pond.

I sat down on a dusty chair opposite him, perching myself there, feeling all tight inside from not wanting to breathe the atmosphere and hypersensitive outside from trying not to touch anything. He noticed and said: "You don't want to contaminate yourself, right? But isn't it a bit late for that, Peter?"

From which I could tell that he knew—he *did* know—and a tingle started in my feet that quickly surged through my entire being. Could he see it in me? Sense it in me? Feel some sort of weird kinship with what was under my skin, burgeoning in me? Or was it worse than that? And right there and then I began to have this feeling that things weren't going according to plan.

"Smiler," I managed to get started at the second attempt, "it's . . . *good* to see you again, pal. And I . . ." And I stopped and just sat there gasping.

"Yes?" he prompted me in a moment. "And you—?"

"Nerves!" I gasped, forcing a sickly smile, and forced in my turn to take my first deep breath. "Lots of nerves. It was always the same. It's why I had to stay behind when you and the others went into space." And I took out my cigarettes, and also took out the lighter from my pocket. I opened the pack and shook out several cigarettes, which fell on the floor, then managed to trap one between my knees and transfer it shakily to my mouth. And I flipped back the top on my lighter.

Smiler's eyes—the only genuinely mobile parts he had left—went straight to the lighter and he said: "You brought it in, right?" But should he be saying things like that? Out loud, I mean? Couldn't Big 'C' hear him or sense his mood? And it dawned on me just how little we knew about them, about Big 'C' and Smiler—as he was now . . .

Then . . . Smiler smiled. Except it wasn't his smile!

Good-bye, everything, I said to myself, pressing the button and holding my thumb down on it. Then releasing it and pressing it again, and again. And finally letting the fucking thing fall from my nerveless fingers when, after two or three more tries, *still* nothing had happened. Or rather, "nothing" hadn't happened.

"Peter, old buddy, let me tell you how it is." Smiler got through to me at last, as the cigarette fell from my trembling lips. "I mean, I suspect you now *know* how it is, but I'll tell you anyway. See, Big 'C' changes things. Just about anything he wants to change. He was nothing at first, or not very much—just a natural law of change, mutation, entropy if you like. An 'emanation.' Or on the other hand I suppose you could say he was everything—like Nature itself. Whichever, when I went up there to Luna II he got into me and changed my cancer into himself, since when he's become one hell of a lot. We can talk about that in a minute, but first I want to explain about your bomb. Big 'C' changed it. He changed the chemical elements of the explosive charges, and to be doubly sure sucked all the fizz out of the fissionable stuff. It was a firework and he dumped it in a bucket of water. So now you can relax. It didn't go off and it isn't going to."

"You . . . *are* him!" I knew it instinctively. Now, when it was too late. "But when? And why?"

"When did I stop being Smiler? Not long after that time you met him at the beach. And why the subterfuge? Because you human beings are a jumpy lot. With Smiler to keep you calm, let you think you had an intermediary, it was less likely you'd do something silly. And why should I care that you'd do something silly? Because there's a lot of life, knowledge, sustenance in this Earth and I didn't want you killing it off trying to kill me! But now you can't kill me, because the bigger I've got the easier it has become to change things. Missiles? Go ahead and try it. They'll be dead before they hit me. Why, if I got the idea you were going to try firing a couple, I could even kill them on the ground!

"You see, Peter, I've grown too big, too clever, too devious to be afraid any more—of anything. Which is why I have no more secrets, and why there'll be no more subterfuge. Subterfuge? Not a bit of it. Why, I'm even broadcasting all of this—just so the whole world will know what's going on! I mean, I *want* them to know, so no one will make any more silly mistakes. Now, I believe you came in here to talk about boundaries—some limits you want to see on my expansion?"

Somehow, I shook my head. "That's not why I'm here, Smiler," I told him, not yet ready to accept that there was nothing of Smiler left in there. "Why I'm here is finished now."

"Not quite," he said, but very quietly. "We can get to the boundaries later, but there is something else. Think about it. I mean, why should I want to see you, if there's nothing else and if I can make any further decisions without outside help?"

"I don't know. Why?"

"See, Smiler has lasted a long time. Him and the frogmen that came to kill me, and a couple of farmers who didn't get out fast enough when they saw me coming, oh, and a few others. And I've been instructed by them. Like I said: I've learned how to be devious. And I've learned anger, too, though there's no longer any need for that. No need for any human emotions. But the last time you came to see Smiler—and when you would have plotted with him to kill me—that angered me."

"And so you gave me my cancer."

"Yes I did. So that when I needed you, you'd *want* to be my volunteer. But don't worry . . . you're not going to die, Peter. Well, not physically anyway, and not just yet a while. For just like Smiler here, you're going to carry on."

"But no anger, eh? No human emotions? No . . . revenge? OK, so let me go free to live out what days I've got left."

"No anger, no revenge, no emotions—just need. I *can't* let you go! But let me explain myself. Do you know what happens when you find a potato sprouting in your vegetable rack and you plant it in the garden? That's right, you get lots of new potatoes! Well, I'm something like that. I'm putting out lots of new potatoes, lots of new me. All of the time. And the thing is this: when you dig up those potatoes and your fork goes through the old one, what do you find? Just a wrinkled, pulpy old sack of a thing all ready to collapse in upon itself, with nothing of goodness left in it—pretty much like what's left of Smiler here. So . . . if I want to keep growing potatoes, why, I just have to keep planting them! Do you see?"

"Jesus! *Jesus!*"

"It's nothing personal, Peter. It's need, that's all . . . No, don't stand up, just sit there and I'll do the rest. And you can stop biting down on that clever tooth of yours, because it isn't poison any more, just salt. And if you don't like what's happening to Smiler right now, that's OK—just turn your face away. . . .

". . . There, that was pretty easy, now wasn't it?

"All you people out there, that's how it is. So get used to it. As for the new boundaries: there aren't any.

"This is Big 'C,' signing off."

THE FAIRGROUND HORROR

The funfair was as yet an abject failure. Drizzling rain dulled the chrome of the dodgem cars and stratojets; the neons had not even nearly achieved the garishness they display by night; the so-called "crowd" was hardly worth mentioning as such. But it was only 2:00 P.M. and things could yet improve.

Had the weather been better—even for October it was bad— and had Bathley been a town instead of a mere village, then perhaps the scene were that much brighter. Come evening, when the neons and other bright naked bulbs would glow in all the painful intensity of their own natural (unnatural?) life, when the drab gypsyish dollies behind the penny-catching stalls would undergo their subtle, nightly metamorphosis into avariciously enticing Loreleis—then it *would* be brighter, but not yet.

This was the fourth day of the five when the funfair was "in town." It was an annual—event? The nomads of Hodgson's Funfair had known better times, better conditions, and worse ones, but it was all the same to them and they were resigned to it. There was, though, amid all the noisy, muddy, smelly paraphernalia of the fairground, a tone of incongruity. It had been there since Anderson Tharpe, in the curious absence of his brother, Hamilton, had taken down the old freak-house frontage to repaint the boards and canvas with the new and forbidding legend: TOMB OF THE GREAT OLD ONES.

Looking up at the painted gouts of "blood" that formed the

garish legend arching over a yawning, scaly, dragon-jawed entrance-way, Hiram Henley frowned behind his tiny spectacles in more than casual curiosity, in something perhaps approaching concern. His lips silently formed the ominous words of that legend as if he spoke them to himself in awe and then he thrust his black-gloved hands deeper into the pockets of his fine, expensively tailored overcoat and tucked his neck down more firmly into its collar.

Hiram Henley had recognized something in the name of the place—something which might ring subconscious warning bells in even the most mundane minds—and the recognition caused an involuntary shudder to hurry up his back. "The Great Old Ones!" he said to himself yet again, and his whisper held a note of terrible fascination.

Research into just such cycles of myth and aeon-lost legend, while ostensibly he had been studying Hittite antiquities in the Middle East and Turkey, had cost Henley his position as Professor of Archaeology and Ethnology at Meldham University. "Cthulhu, Yibb-Tstll, Yog-Sothoth, Summanus—the Great Old Ones!" Again an expression of awe flitted across his bespectacled face. To be confronted with a . . . a *monument* such as this, and in such a place . . .

And yet the ex-professor was not too surprised; he had been alerted to the contents of Anderson Tharpe's queer establishment, and therefore the fact that the owner had named it thus was hardly a matter of any lasting astonishment. Nevertheless Henley knew that there were people who would have considered the naming of the fairground erection, to say nothing of the presence of its afore-hinted *contents*, blasphemous. Fortunately such persons were few and far between—the Cult of Cthulhu was still known only to a minority of serious authorities, to a few obscure occult investigators, and a scattered handful of esoteric groups—but Hiram Henley looked back to certain days of yore when he had blatantly used the university's money to go in search of just such items of awesome antiquity as now allegedly hid behind the demon-adorned ramparts of the edifice before him.

The fact of the matter was that Henley had heard how this Tomb of the Great Old Ones held within its monster-daubed board-and-canvas walls relics of an age already many millions of years dead and gone when Babylon was but a sketch in the mind's eye of Architect Thathnis III. Figures and fragments, hieroglyphed tablets and strangely scrawled papyri, weird greenstone sculptings, and rotting, worm-eaten tomes: Henley had reason to believe that many of these things, if not all of them, existed behind the facade of Anderson Tharpe's horror house.

There would also be, of course, the usual nonconformities peculiar to such establishments—the two-headed foetus in its bottle of preservative, the five-legged puppy similarly suspended, the fake mummy in its red- and green-daubed wrappings, the great fruit ("vampire") bats, hanging shutter-eyed and motionless in their warm wire cages beyond the reach of giggly, shuddering women and morbidly fascinated men and boys—but Hiram Henley was not interested in any of these. Nevertheless, he sent his gloved right hand awkwardly groping into the corner of his overcoat pocket for the silver coin which alone might open for him the door to Tharpe's house of horror.

Hiram Henley was a slight, middle-aged man. His thin figure, draped smotheringly in the heavy overcoat, his balding head and tiny specs through which his watery eyes constantly peered, his gloved hands almost lost in huge pockets, his trousers seeming to hang from beneath the hem of his overcoat and partly, not wholly covering the black patent leather shoes upon his feet—all made of him a picture which was conspicuously odd. And yet Hiram Henley's intelligence was patent; the stamp of a "higher mind" was written in erudite lines upon his brow. His were obviously eyes which had studied strange mysteries, and his feet had gone along strange ways, so that despite any other emotion or consideration which his appearance might ill-advisedly call to mind, still his shrunken frame commanded more than a little respect among his fellow men.

Anderson Tharpe, on the other hand, crouching now upon his tiny seat in the ticket booth, was a tall man, well over six feet in height but almost as thin and emaciated as the fallen professor. His hair was prematurely grey and purposely grown long in an old-fashioned scholarly style, so that he might simulate to the crowd's satisfaction a necessary erudition, just such an erudition as was manifest in the face above the slight figure which even now pressed upon his tiny window, sixpence clutched in gloved fingers. Tharpe's beady eyes beneath blackly hypnotic brows studied Hiram Henley briefly, speculatively, but then he smiled a very genuine welcome as he passed the small man a ticket, waving away the sixpence with an expansive hand.

"Not *you*, sir, indeed no! From a gent so obviously and sincerely interested in the mysteries within—from a man of your high standing"—again the expansive gesture—"why, I couldn't accept money from you, sir. It's an honour to have you visit us!"

"Thank you." Henley dryly answered, passing myopically into the great tent beyond the ticket booth. Tharpe's smile slowly faded, was replaced by a look of cunning. Quickly the tall man pocketed his few shillings in takings, then followed the slight figure of the ex-professor into the smelly sawdust-floored "museum," beyond the canvas flap.

In all, a dozen people waited within the big tent's main division. A pitifully small "crowd." But in any case, though he kept his interest cleverly veiled, Tharpe's plans involved only the ex-professor. The tall man's flattery at the ticket booth had not all been flannel; he had spotted Henley immediately as the very species of highly educated fly for which his flypaper—in the form of the new and enigmatic legend across the visage of the one-time freak house—had been erected above Bathley Moor.

There had been, Tharpe reflected, men of outwardly similar intelligence before at the Tomb of the Great Old Ones, and more than one of them had told him that certain of his *artifacts*—those items which he kept, as his brother had kept them before him, in a separately enclosed part of the tent—were of an unbelievable antiquity. Indeed, one man had been so affected by the very sight of such ancientness that he had run from Tharpe's collection in stark terror, and he had never returned. That had been in May, and though almost six months had passed since that time, still Tharpe had come no closer to an understanding of the mysterious objects which his brother Hamilton had brought back with him from certain dark corners of the world; objects which, early in 1961, had caused him to kill Hamilton in self-defence.

Anderson had panicked then—he realized that now—for he might easily have come out of the affair blameless had he only reported Hamilton's death to the police. For a long time the folk of Hodgson's Funfair had known that there was something drastically wrong with Hamilton Tharpe; his very sanity had been questioned, albeit guardedly. Certainly Anderson would have been declared innocent of his brother's murder—the case would have gone to court only as a matter of formality—but he had panicked. And of course there had been . . . complications.

With Hamilton's body secretly buried deep beneath the freak house, the folk of the fairground had been perfectly happy to believe Anderson's tale of his brother's abrupt departure on yet another of his world-spanning expeditions, the like of which had brought about all the trouble in the first place.

Now Anderson thought back on it all . . .

He and his brother had grown up together in the fairground, but then it had been their father's property, and "Tharpe's Funfair" had been known throughout all England for its fair play and prices. Wherever the elder Tharpe had taken his stalls and sideshows—of which the freak house had ever been his personal favourite—his employees had been sure of good crowds. It was only after old Tharpe died that the slump started.

It had had much to do with young Hamilton's joy in old books and fancifully dubious legends; his lust for travel, adventure, and *outré* knowledge. His first money-wasting venture had been a "treasure-hunting" trip to the islands of the Pacific, undertaken solely on the strength of a vague and obviously fake map. In his absence—he had gone off with an adventurous and plausible rogue from the shooting gallery—Anderson looked after the fair. Things went badly, and all the Tharpes got out of Hamilton's venture was a number of repulsively carved stone tablets and one or two patently aboriginal sculptings, not the least of which was a hideous, curiously winged octopoid idol. Hamilton placed the latter obscenity in the back of their caravan home as being simply too fantastic for display to an increasingly mundane and sceptical public.

The idol, however, had a most unsettling effect upon the younger brother. He was wont to go in to see the thing in the dead of night, when Anderson was in bed and apparently asleep. But often Anderson was awake, and during these nocturnal visits he had heard Hamilton *talking* to the idol. More disturbingly, he had once or twice dimly imagined that he heard something talking back! Too, before he went off again on his wanderings in unspoken areas of the great deserts of Arabia, the sensitive, mystery-loving traveller had started to suffer from especially bad nightmares.

Again, in Hamilton's absence, things went badly. Soon Anderson was obliged to sell out to Bella Hodgson, retaining only the freak house as his own and his prodigal brother's property. A year passed, and another before Hamilton once more returned to the fairground, demanding his living as before but making little or no attempt to work for his needs. There was no arguing, however, for the formerly sensitive younger brother was a changed, indeed a saturnine man now, so that soon Anderson came to be a little afraid of him.

And quite apart from the less obvious alterations in Hamilton, other changes were much more apparent: changes in habit, even in appearance. The most striking was the fact that now the younger Tharpe constantly wore a shaggy black toupee, as if to disguise his partial premature baldness, which all of the funfair's residents knew about anyway and which had never caused him the least embarrassment before. Also, he had become so reticent as to be almost reclusive, keeping to himself, only rarely and reluctantly allowing himself to be drawn into even the most trivial conversations.

More than this: there had been a time prior to his second long absence when Hamilton had seemed somewhat enamoured of the young, single, dark-eyed Romany fortune-teller, "Madame Zala"— a Gypsy girl of genuine Romany ancestry—but since his return he had been especially cool toward her, and for her own part she had been seen to cross herself with a pagan sign when he had happened to be passing by. Once he had seen her make this sign, and then he had gone white with fury, hurrying off to the freak house and remaining there for the rest of that day. Madame Zala had packed up her things and left one night in her horse-drawn caravan without a word of explanation to anyone. It was generally believed that Hamilton had threatened her in some way, though no one ever taxed him over the affair. For his own part, he simply averred that Zala had been "a charlatan of the worst sort, without the ability to conjure a puff of wind!"

All in all the members of the funfair fraternity had been quick to find Hamilton a very changed man, and towards the end there had been the aforementioned hints of a brewing madness . . .

On top of all this, Hamilton had again taken up his noctural visits to the octopoid idol, but now such visits seemed less frequent than of old. Less frequent, perhaps, but they nevertheless heralded much darker events, for soon Hamilton had installed the idol within a curtained and spacious corner of the tent, in the freak house itself, and he no longer paid his visits alone. . . .

Anderson Tharpe had seen, from his darkened caravan window, a veritable procession of strangers—all of them previous visitors to the freak house, and always the more intelligent types—accompanying his brother to the tent's nighted interior. But he had never seen a one come out! Eventually, as his younger brother became yet more saturnine, reticent, and secretive, Anderson took to spying on him in earnest—and later almost wished that he had not.

In the months between, however, Hamilton had made certain alterations to the interior of the freak house, partitioning fully a third of its area to enclose the collection of rare and obscure curiosities garnered upon his travels. At that time Anderson had been puzzled to distraction by his brother's firm refusal to let his treasures be viewed by any but a chosen few of the freak house's patrons: those doubtfully privileged persons who later accompanied him into the private museum never again to leave.

Of course, Anderson finally reasoned, the answer was as simple as it was fantastic: somewhere upon his travels Hamilton had learned the arts of murder and thievery, arts he was now practicing in the freak house. The bodies? These he obviously buried, to leave behind safely lodged in the dark earth when the fair moved on. But the money . . . what of the money? For money—or rather its lack—patently formed the younger brother's motive. Could he be storing his booty away, against the day when he would go off on yet another of his foolish trips to foreign places? Beside himself that he had not been "cut in" on the profits of Hamilton's dark machinations, Anderson determined to have it out with him, to catch him, as it were, red-handed.

And yet it was not until early in the spring of 1961 that Anderson finally managed to "overhear" a conversation between his brother and an obviously well-to-do visitor to the freak house. Hamilton had singled out this patently intelligent gentleman for attention, inviting him back to the caravan during a break in business. Anderson, knowing most of the modus operandi by now and, aware of the turn events must take, positioned himself outside the caravan where he could eavesdrop.

He did not catch the complete conversation, and yet sufficient to make him aware at last of Hamilton's expert and apparently unique knowledge in esoteric mysteries. For the first time he heard uttered the mad words Cthulhu and Yibb-Tstll, Tsathoggua and Yog-Sothoth, Shudde-M'ell and Nyarlathotep, discovering that these were names of monstrous "gods" from the dawn of time. He heard mention of Leng and Lh'yib; Mnar, Ib, and Sarnath; R'lyeh and "red-litten" Yoth, and knew now that these were cities and lands ancient even in antiquity. He heard descriptions and names given to manuscripts, books, and tablets—and here he started in recognition, for he knew that some of these aeon-old writings existed amid Hamilton's treasures in the freak house—and among others he heard the strangely chilling titles of such works as the *Necronomicon*, the *Cthaat Aquadingen*, the *Pnakotic Manuscripts* and the *R'lyehan Texts*. This then formed the substance of Hamilton's magnetism: his amazing erudition in matters of myth and time-lost lore.

When he perceived that the two were about to make an exit from the caravan, Anderson quickly hid himself away behind a nearby stall to continue his observations. He saw the flushed face of Hamilton's new confidant, his excited gestures, and, at a whispered suggestion from the pale-faced brother, he finally saw that gentleman nodding eagerly, wide-eyed in awed agreement. And after the visitor had gone, Anderson saw the look that flitted briefly across his brother's features: a look that hinted of awful triumph, nameless emotion—and, yes, purest evil!

But it was something about the face of the departed visitor— that rounded gentleman of obvious substance but doubtful future— which caused Anderson the greatest concern. He had finally recognized that face from elsewhere, and at his first opportunity he sneaked a glance through some of the archaeological and anthropological journals which his brother now spent so much time reading. It was as he had thought: Hamilton's prey was none other than an eminent explorer and archaeologist, one whose name, Stainton Gamber, might be even higher in the lists of famous adventurers and discoverers but for a passion for wild-goose expeditions and safaris. Then he grew even more worried, for plainly his brother could not go on forever depleting the countryside of eminent persons without being discovered.

That afternoon passed slowly for Anderson Tharpe, and when night came he went early to his bed in the caravan. He was up again, however, as soon as he heard his brother stirring and the hushed whispers that led off in the direction of the freak house. It was as he had known it would be, when for a moment pale moonlight showed him a glimpse of Hamilton with Stainton Gamber.

Quickly he followed the two to the looming canvas tent, and in through the dragon-jawed entranceway, but he paused at the door flap to the partitioned area to listen and observe. There came the scratch of a match and its bright, sudden flare, and then a candle flickered into life. At this point the whispering recommenced, and Anderson drew back a pace as the candle began to move about the interior of Hamilton's museum. He could hear the hushed conversation quite clearly, could feel the tremulous excitement in the voice of the florid explorer:

"But these are—*fantastic*! I've believed for years now that such relics must exist. Indeed, I've often brought my reputation close to ruin for such beliefs, and now . . . Young man, you'll be world-famous. Do you realize what you have here? Proof positive that the Cult of Cthulhu did exist! What monstrous worship—what hideous rites! Where, *where* did you find these things? I must know! And this idol—which you say is believed to invoke the spirit of the living Cthulhu himself!—Who holds such beliefs? I know of course that Wendy-Smith—"

"*Hah!*" Hamilton's rasping voice cut in. "You can keep all your Wendy-Smiths and Gordon Walmsleys. They only scraped the surface. I've gone inside—*and outside!* Explorers, dreamers, mystics—mere dabblers. Why, they'd *die*, all of them, if they saw what I've seen, if they went where I've been. And none of them have ever dreamed what I *know!*"

"But why keep it hidden? Why don't you open this place up, show the world what you've got here, what you've achieved? Publish, man, publish! Why, together—"

"Together?" Hamilton's voice was darker, trembling as he suddenly snuffed the candle. "Together? Proof that the Cult of Cthulhu *did* exist? Show it to the world? Publish?" His chuckle was obscene in the dark, and Anderson heard the visitor's sharp intake of breath. "The world's not ready, Gamber, and the stars are not right! What you would like to do, like many before you, is alert the world to *Their* one-time presence, the days of *Their* sovereignty—which might in turn lead to the discovery that *They are here even now!* Indeed Wendy-Smith was right, too right, and where is Wendy-Smith now? No, no—*They* aren't interested in mere dabblers, except that such are dangerous to *Them* and must be removed! *Iä, R'lyeh!* You are no true dreamer, Gamber, no believer. You're not worthy of membership in the Great Priesthood. You're . . . dangerous! Proof? I'll give you proof. Listen, and *watch—*"

Hearing his brother's injunction, the secret listener would have paid dearly to see what next occurred. A short while earlier, just before Hamilton had snuffed out the candle, Anderson had managed to find a hole in the canvas large enough to facilitate a fair view of the partitioned area. He had seen a semicircle of carved stone tablets, with the octopoid idol presiding atop or seated upon a thronelike pedestal. Now, in the dark, his view-hole was useless.

He could still listen, however, and now Hamilton's voice came—strange and vibrant, though still controlled in volume—in a chant or invocation of terrible cadence and rhythmic disorder. These were not words the younger Tharpe uttered but unintelligible *sounds*, a morbidly insane agglutination of verbal improbabilities which ought never to have issued from a human throat at all! And as the invocation ceased, to an incredulous gasping from the doomed explorer, Anderson had to draw back from his hole lest he become visible in the glow of a green radiance springing up abruptly in the centre of Hamilton's encircling relics.

The green glow grew brighter, filling the hidden museum and spilling emerald beams from several small holes in the canvas. This was no normal light, for the beams were quite alien to anything Anderson had ever seen before; the very light seemed to writhe and contort in a slow and loathsomely languid dance. Now Anderson found himself again a witness, for the shadows of Hamilton and his intended victim were thrown blackly against the wall of canvas. There was no requirement now to "spy" properly upon the pair; his view of the eerie drama could not have been clearer. The centre of the radiance seemed to expand and shrink alternatively, pulsing like an alien heart of light. Hamilton stood to one side, his arms flung wide in terrible triumph; Stainton Gamber cowered, his hands up before his face as if to shield it from some unbearable heat—or as if to ward off the unknown and inexplicable!

Anderson's shadow-view of the terrified explorer was profile, and he was suddenly astonished to note that while the man appeared to be screaming horribly he could hear nothing of his screams! It was as if Anderson had been stricken deaf. Hamilton, too, was now plainly vociferous: his throat moved in crazed cachinnations and his thrown-back head and heaving shoulders plainly announced unholy glee—but all in stark silence! Anderson knew now that the mad green light had somehow worked against normal order, annulling all sound utterly and thereby hiding in its emerald pulsings the final act in this monstrous shadow-play. As the core pulsated even faster and brighter, Hamilton moved quickly after the silently shrieking explorer, catching him by the collar of his jacket and swinging him sprawling into the core itself!

Instantly the core shrank, sucking in upon itself and dwindling in a moment to a ball of intense brightness. But where was the explorer? Horrified, Anderson saw that now *only one shadow remained faintly outlined upon the canvas—that of his brother!*

Quickly, weirdly, paling as they went, the beams of green light withdrew. Sound instantly returned, and Anderson heard his own harsh breathing. He stilled the sound, moving back to his spy-hole to see what was happening. A faint green glow with a single bright speck of a core remained within the semicircle; and now Hamilton bowed to this dimming light and his voice came again, low and tremulous with emotion:

> *Iä, naflhgn Cthulhu R'lyeh mglw'nafh,*
> *Eha'ungl wglw hflghglui ngah'glw,*
> *Engl Eha gh'eehf gnhugl,*
> *Nhflgng uh'eha wgah'nagl hfglufh—*
> *U'ng Eha'ghlui Aeeh ehn'hflgh . . .*
> That is not dead which can eternal lie,
> And with strange aeons even death may die.

No sooner had Hamilton ceased these utterly alien mouthings and the paradoxical couplet that completed them, and while yet the green glow continued to dim and fade, then he spoke again, this time all in recognizable English. Such was his murmured modulation and deliberate spacing of the spoken sequences that his hidden brother immediately recognized the following as a translation of what had gone before:

> *Oh, Great Cthulhu, dreaming in R'lyeh,*
> *Thy priest offers up this sacrifice,*
> *That thy coming be soon*
> *And that of thy kindred dreamers.*
> *I am thy priest and adore thee . . .*

It was only then that the full horror of what he had seen—the cold-blooded, premeditated murder of a man by either some monstrous occult device or a foreign science beyond his knowledge—finally went home to Anderson Tharpe, and barely managing to stifle the hysterical babble he felt welling in his throat, he took an involuntary step backward . . . to collide loudly with a cage of great bats.

Three things happened then in rapid succession before Anderson could gather his wits to flee. All trace of the green glow vanished in an instant, throwing the tent once more into complete darkness; then in contrast, confusing the elder brother, the bright interior lights blinked on; finally, as he sought to recover from his confusion, Hamilton appeared through the partition's canvas door, his eyes blazing in a face contorted in fury!

"You!" Hamilton spat, striding to Anderson's side and catching him fiercely by the collar of his dressing gown. "How much have you seen?"

Anderson twisted free and backed away. "I . . . I saw it all, but I had guessed as much some time ago. Murder—and you my brother!"

"Save your sanctimony," Hamilton sneered. "If you've known so much for so long, then you're as much a murderer as I am! And anyway"—his eyes seemed visibly to glaze and take on a faraway look—"it wasn't murder, not as you understand it."

"Of course not." Now it was Anderson's turn to sneer. "It was a—a 'sacrifice'—to this so-called 'god' of yours, Great Cthulhu! And were the others all sacrifices, too?"

"All of them," Hamilton answered with a nod, automatically, as in a trance.

"Oh? And where's the money?"

"Money?" The faraway look went out of the younger Tharpe's eyes immediately. "What money?"

Anderson saw that this was no bluff; his brother's motive had not been personal gain, at least not in a monetary sense. Which in turn meant—

Had those rumours and unfriendly whispers heard about the stalls and sideshows—those hints of a looming madness in his brother—had they been more than mere guesswork, then? Surely he would have known. As if in answer to his unspoken question, Hamilton spoke again—and listening to him Anderson believed he had his answer:

"You're the same as all the others, Anderson—you can't see beyond the length of your greedy nose. Money? Pah! You think that *They* are interested in wealth? *They* are not; neither am I. *They* have a wealth of aeons behind *Them*; the future is *Theirs* . . ." Again his eyes seemed to glaze over.

"Them? Who do you mean?" Anderson asked, frowning and backing farther away.

"Cthulhu and the others. Cthulhu and the Deep Ones, and *Their* brothers and kin forever dreaming in the vast vaults beneath. *'Iä, R'lyeh, Cthulhu fhtagn!'* "

"You're quite—mad!"

"You think so?" Hamilton quickly followed after him, pushing his face uncomfortably close. "I'm mad, am I? Well, perhaps, but I'll tell you something: when you and the others like you are reduced to mere cattle, before the Earth is cleared off of life as you know it, a trusted handful of priests will guard the herds for *Them*—and I shall be a priest among priests, appointed to the service of Great Cthulhu Himself!" His eyes burned feverishly.

Now Anderson was certain of his brother's madness, but even so he could see a way to profit from it. "Hamilton," he said, after a moment's thought, "worship whichever gods you like and aspire to whichever priesthood—but don't you see we have to live? There could be good money in this for both of us. If only—"

"No!" Hamilton hissed. "To worship Cthulhu is enough. Indeed, it is *all*! That, in there"—he jerked his head, indicating the enclosed area behind him—"is His temple. To offer up sacrifices while yet thinking of oneself would be blasphemous, and when He comes I shall not be found wanting!" His eyes went wide and he trembled.

"You don't know Him, Anderson. He is awful, awesome, a monster, a god! He is sunken now, drowned and dead in deep R'lyeh, but His death is a sleeping death and He will awaken. When the stars are right we chosen ones will answer the Call of Cthulhu, and R'lyeh will rise up again to astound a reeling universe. Why, even the Gorgons were His priestesses in the old world! And you talk to me of money." Again he sneered, but now his madness had a firm grip on him and the sneer soon turned to a crafty smile.

"And you're helpless to do anything, Anderson, for if you breathe a word I'll swear you were in on it—that you helped me from the start! And as for bodies, why, there are none. They are gone to dreaming Cthulhu, through the light He sends me when I cry out to Him in my darkness. So you see, nothing could ever be proved . . ."

"Perhaps not, but I don't think it would take much to have you, well, *put away*!" Anderson quietly answered.

The barb went straight home. A look of terror crossed Hamilton's face and, plainly aware of his own mental infirmity, he visibly paled.

"Put me away? But you wouldn't. If you did, I wouldn't be able to worship, to sacrifice, and—"

"But there's no need to worry about it," Anderson cut him off. "I won't have you put away. Just see things my way, show me how you dissolve them in that green light of yours—I mean, in, er, dreaming Cthulhu's light—and then we'll carry on as before, except that there'll be money . . ."

"No, Anderson," the other refused almost gently, "it can't work like that. You could never believe—not even if I showed you proof of my priesthood, which hides beneath this false head of hair that I'm obliged to wear, the very Mark of Cthulhu—and I can't worship as you suggest. I'm sorry." There was an insane sadness in his face as he drew out a long knife from its sheath inside his jacket. "I use this when they're stronger than me," he explained, "and when they're liable to fight. Cthulhu doesn't care for it much because he likes them alive initially and whole, but—" His knife hand flashed up and down.

Only Anderson's speed saved him, for he turned quickly to one side as the blade flashed down toward his breast. Then their wrists were locked and they staggered to and fro, Hamilton frothing at the mouth and trying to bite, while Anderson grimly struggled for dear life. The madman seemed to have the strength of three normal men, and soon they fell to the ground, a thrashing heap that rolled blindly in through the flap of the canvas door to Hamilton's "temple."

There it was that finally the younger brother's toupee came away from his head in the silent struggle, and in a burst of strength engendered of sheer loathing Anderson managed to turn the knife inward and drive it to the madman's heart. He was quick then to be on his feet and away from the thing that now lay twitching out its life upon the sawdust floor—the thing that had been his brother—which now, where the top of Hamilton's head had been, *wore a cap of writhing white worms of finger thickness, like some monstrous sea anemone sucking vampirishly at the still-living brain*!

Later, when morning came, even had there been someone in whom he might safely confide, Anderson Tharpe could never have related a detailed or coherent account of the preceding hours of darkness. He recalled only the general thread of what had passed, frantic snatches of the fearful activity that followed upon the hideous death of his brother. But first there had been that half hour or so of waiting—of knowing that at any moment, attracted perhaps by strange lights or sounds, someone just might enter the tent and find him with Hamilton's body—but he had been *obliged* to wait for he could not bring himself to touch the corpse. Not while the stubby white tentacles of its head continued to writhe! Hamilton died almost immediately, but his monstrous crown had taken much longer . . .

Then, when the loathsome—parasite?—had shuddered into lifeless rigidity, he had gathered together his shattered nerves to dig a deep grave in the soft earth beneath the sawdust. That had been a gruesome task with the lights turned down and Cthulhu's stone effigy casting a tentacled shadow over the fearful digger. Anderson later remembered how soft the ground had been—and wet when it ought to have been dry in the weatherproof tent—and he recalled a powerful smell of deep sea, of aeon-old ocean slime and rotting seaweeds—an odour he had known on occasion before, and always after one of Hamilton's "sacrifices." The connection had not impressed itself upon his mind as anything more than mere coincidence before, but now he knew that the smell came with the green light, as did that strange state of soundlessness.

In order to clear what remained of the fetor quickly—having tamped down the earth, generally "tidied up," and removed all traces of his digging—he opened and tied back the canvas doors of the tent to allow the night air a healthy circulation. But even then, having done everything possible to hide the night's horror, he was unable to relax properly as daylight crept up and the folk of the funfair began to wake and move about.

When finally Hodgson's Funfair had opened at noon, Anderson had something of a shaky grip on himself, but even so he had found himself drenched in cold sweat at the end of each oratorial session with the crowds at the freak house. His only moments of relaxation came between shows. The worst time had been when a leather-jacketed teenager peered through the canvas inner door to the partitioned section of the tent, and Anderson had nearly knocked the youth down in his anxiety to steer him away from the place, though no trace remained of what had transpired there.

On reflection, it amazed Anderson that his fight with his brother had not attracted someone's attention, and yet it had not. Even the fairground's usually vociferous watchdogs had remained silent. And yet those same dogs, since Hamilton's return from his travels abroad, had seemed even more nervous, more given to snapping and snarling than ever before. Anderson could only tell himself that the weird "silent state" which had accompanied the green light must have spread out over the entire fairground to dissipate slowly, thus disarming the dogs. Or perhaps they had sensed something else, remaining silent out of fear . . . ? Indeed, it appeared his second guess was correct, for he discovered later that many of the dogs had whimpered the whole night away huddled beneath the caravans of their masters . . .

Two days later the funfair packed up and moved on, leaving Hamilton Tharpe's body safely buried in an otherwise empty field. At last the worst of Anderson's apprehensions left him and his nerves began to settle down. To be sure his jumpiness had been marked by the folk of the funfair, who had all correctly (though for the wrong reasons) diagnosed it as a symptom of anxiety about his crazy, bad-lot brother. So it was that as soon as Hamilton's absence was remarked upon, Anderson was able simply to shrug his shoulders and answer: "Who knows? Tibet, Egypt, Australia—he's just gone off again—said nothing to me about it—could be anywhere!" And while such enquiries were always politely compassionate, he knew that in fact the enquirers were greatly relieved that his brother had "just gone off again."

Another six weeks went by, with regular halts at various villages and small towns, and during that time Anderson managed to will himself to forget all about his brother's death and his own involvement—all, that is, except the nature of that parasitic horror which had made itself manifest upon Hamilton's head. That was something he would never forget, the way that awful anemone had wriggled and writhed long after its host was dead. Hamilton had called the thing a symbol of his priesthood—in his own words: "The Mark of Cthulhu"—but in truth it could only have been some loathsomely malignant and rare form of cancer, or perhaps a kind of worm or fluke like the tapeworm. Anderson always shuddered when he recalled it, for it had looked horribly *sentient* there atop Hamilton's head, and when one thought about the *depth* at which it might have been rooted . . .

No, the insidious gropings of that horror within Hamilton's brain simply did not bear thinking about, for that had obviously been the source of his insanity. Anderson in no way considered himself weak to shudder when thoughts as terrible as these came to threaten his now calm and controlled state of mind, and when the bad dreams started he at once lay the blame at the feet of the same horror.

At first the nightmares were vague shadowy things, with misty vistas of rolling plains and yawning, empty coastlines. There were distant islands with strange pinnacles and oddly angled towers, but so far away that the unknown creatures moving about in those island cities were mere insects to Anderson's dreaming eyes. And for this he was glad. Their shapes seemed in a constant state of flux and were not—pleasant. They were primal shapes, from which the dreamer deduced that he was in a primal land of aeons lost to mankind. He always woke from such visions uneasy in mind and deflated in spirit.

But with the passing of the months into summer the dreams changed, becoming sharper visually, clearer in their insinuations, and actually frightening as opposed to merely disturbing. Their scenes were set (Anderson somehow knew) deep in the dimly lighted bowels of one of the island cities, in a room or vault of fantastic proportions and awe-inspiring angles. Always he kneeled before a vast octopoid idol . . . except that on occasion it was *not* an idol but a living, hideously intelligent Being!

These dreams were ever the worst, when a strange voice spoke to him in words that he was quite unable to understand. He would tremble before the towering horror on its thronelike pedestal—a thing one hundred times greater in size than the stone morbidity in the freak house—and, aware that he only dreamed, he would know that it, too, was asleep and dreaming. But its tentacles would twine and twist and its claws would scrabble at the front of the throne, and then the voice would come . . .

Waking from nightmares such as these he would know that they were engendered of hellish memory—of the night of the green glow, the deep-ocean smell, and the writhing thing in his brother's head— for he would always recall in his first waking moments that the awful alien voice had used sounds similar to those Hamilton had mouthed before the green light came and after it had taken the florid explorer away. The dreams were particularly bad and growing worse as the year drew to a close, and on a number of occasions the dreamer had been sure that slumbering Cthulhu was about to stir and wake up!

And then, himself waking up, all the horror would come back to Anderson, to be viewed once more in his mind's eye in vivid clarity, and knowing as he did that his brother too had been plagued by just such dreams prior to his second long absence from the fairground, Anderson Tharpe was a troubled man indeed. Yes, they *had* been the same sort of nightmares, those dreams of Hamilton's; hadn't he admitted that "Cthulhu comes to me in dreams?" And had the dreams themselves not heralded the greater horrors?

And yet, in less gloomy mood, Anderson found himself more and more often dwelling upon Hamilton's weird murder weapon, the pulsating green light. He was by no means an ignorant man, and he had read something of the recent progress in laser technology. Soon he had convinced himself that his brother had used an unknown form of foreign science to offer up his mad "sacrifices to Cthulhu." If only he could discover how Hamilton had done it . . .

But surely science such as that would require complex machinery? It was while pondering this very problem that Anderson hit upon what he believed must be the answer: whatever tools or engines Hamilton had used, they must be hidden in the octopoid idol, or perhaps built into those ugly stone tablets which had formed a semicircle about the idol. And perhaps, like the electric-eye beams which operated the moving floors and blasts of cool air in the fairground's Noah's Ark, Hamilton's chanted "summons" had been nothing more than a resonant trigger to set the hidden lasers or whatever to working. The smell of deep ocean and residual dampness must be the natural aftermath of such processes, in the same way that carbon monoxide and dead oil is the waste from petrol engines and the smell of ozone is attendant to electrical discharges.

The tablets, the idol, too, still stood where they had stood in the time before the horror. The only change was that now the canvas partition was down and Hamilton's ancient artifacts were on display with the other paraphernalia of the freak house—but just suppose Anderson were to arrange them *exactly* as they had been before, and suppose further that he could discover how to use that chanted formula. What then? Would he be able to summon the green light? If so, would he be able to use it as he had tried to convince Hamilton it should be used? Perhaps the answer lay in his dead brother's books. . . .

Certainly that collection of ancient tomes, now slowly disintegrating in a cupboard in the caravan, were full of hints of such things. It was out of curiosity at first that Anderson began to read those books, or at least what he *could* read of them! Many were not in English but Latin or archaic German, and at least one other was in ciphers the like of which Anderson had only ever seen on the stone tablets in the freak house.

There were among the volumes such titles as Feery's *Notes on the Cthaat Aquadingen* and a well-thumbed copy of the same author's *Notes on the Necronomicon*, while yet another book, handwritten in a shaky script, purported to be the *Necronomicon* itself, or a translation thereof, but Anderson could not read it for its characters were formed of an unbelievably antiquated German. Then there was a large envelope full of yellowed loose-leaves, and Hamilton had written on the envelope that this was "Ibn Shoddathua's Translation of the Mum-Nath Papyri." Among the more complete and recognizable works were such titles as *The Golden Bough* and Miss Margaret Murray's *The Witch-Cult in Western Europe*, but by comparison these were light reading.

During December and to the end of January, all of Anderson's free time was taken up in the study of these works, until finally he became in a limited way something of an authority of the dread Cthulhu Cycle of Myth. He learned of the Elder Gods, benign forces or deities that existed "in peace and glory" near Betelgeuse in the constellation Orion, and of the powers of evil, the Great Old Ones! He read of Azathoth, bubbling and blaspheming at the center of infinity; of Yog-Sothoth, the "all-in-one and one-in-all," a god-creature coexistent in all time and conterminous with all space; of Nyarlathotep, the messenger of the Great Old Ones; of Hastur the Unspeakable, hell-thing and "Lord of the Interstellar Spaces"; of fertile Shub-Niggurath, "the black goat of the woods with a thousand young"; and, finally, of Great Cthulhu himself, an inconceivable evil that seeped down from the stars like cosmic pus when Earth was young and inchoate.

There were, too, lesser gods and beings more or less obscure or distant from the central theme of the Mythos. Among these Anderson read of Dagon and the Deep Ones; of Yibb-Tstll and the Gaunts of Night; of the Tcho-Tcho people and the Mi-Go; of Yig, Chaugnar Faugn, Nygotha, and Tsathoggua; of Atlach-Nacha, Lloigor, Zhar, and Ithaqua; of burrowing Shudde-M'ell, meteor-borne Glaaki, flaming Cthugha, and the loathsome Hounds of Tindalos.

He learned how—for practicing abhorrent rites—the Great Old Ones were banished to prisoning environs where, ever ready to take possession of the Earth again, they live on eternally. . . . Cthulhu, of course, having featured prominently in his brother's madness—now supposedly lying locked in sunken R'lyeh beneath the waves, waiting for the stars to "come right," and for his minions, human and otherwise, to perform those rites which would once more return him as ruler of his former surface dominions—held the greatest interest for Anderson.

And the more he read, the more he became aware of the fantastic *depth* of his subject, but even so he could hardly bring himself to admit that there was anything of more than passing interest in such "mumbo-jumbo." Nevertheless, on the night of the second of February 1962, he received what should have been a warning: a nightmare of such potency that it did in fact trouble him for weeks afterward, and particularly when he saw the connection in the *date* of this visitation. Of course, it had been Candlemas, which would have had immediate and special meaning to anyone with even the remotest schooling in the occult. Candlemas, and Anderson Tharpe had dreamed of basaltic submarine towers of titanic proportions and nightmare angles; and within those basalt walls and sepulchres, he had known that loathly Lord Cthulhu dreamed his own dreams of damnable dominion. . . .

This had not been all. He had drifted in his dreams *through* those walls to visit once more the inner chambers and kneel before the sleeping god. But it had been an unquiet sleep the Old One slept, in which his demon claws scrabbled fitfully and his folded wings twitched and jerked as if fighting to spread and lift him up through the pressured deeps to the unsuspecting world above! Then, as before, the voice had come to Anderson Tharpe—but this time it had spoken in English!

"*Do you seek,*" the voice had asked in awesome tones, "*to worship Cthulhu? Do you presume to His priesthood? I can see that YOU*

DO NOT, and yet you meddle and seek to discover His secrets! Be warned: it is a great sin against Cthulhu to destroy one of His chosen priests, and yet I see that you have done so. It is a sin, too, to scorn Him, but you have done this also. And it is a GREAT sin in His eyes to seek to use His secrets in any way other than in His service—AND THIS, TOO, YOU WOULD DO! Be warned, and live. Live and pray to your weak god that you are destroyed in the first shock of the Great Rising. It were not well for you that you live to reap Cthulhu's wrath!"

The voice had finally receded, but its sepulchral mind-echoes had barely faded away when it seemed to the paralyzed dreamer that the face-tentacles of slumbering Cthulhu reached out, groping malignantly in his direction where he knelt in slime at the base of the massive throne!

At that a distant howling sprang up, growing rapidly louder and closer, and as the face-tentacles of the sleeping god had been about to touch him, so Tharpe came screaming awake in his sweat-drenched bed to discover that the fairground was in an uproar. All the watchdogs, big and small, chained and roaming free alike, were howling in unison in the middle of that cold night. They seemed to howl at the blindly impassive stars, and their cries were faintly answered from a thousand similarly agitated canine throats in the nearby town!

The next morning speculation was rife among the showmen as to what had caused the trouble with the dogs, and eventually, on the evidence of certain scraps of fur, they put it down to a stray cat that must have got itself trapped under one of the caravans to be pulled to pieces by a Great Dane. Nevertheless, Anderson wondered at the keen senses and interpretation of the dogs in the local town that they had so readily taken up the unnatural baying and howling . . .

During the next fortnight or so Anderson's slumbers were mercifully free of nightmares, so that he was early prompted to continue his researches into the Cthulhu Cycle of Myth. This further probing was born partly of curiosity and partly (as Anderson saw it) of necessity; he yet hoped to be able to gainfully employ his brother's mysterious green light, and his determination was bolstered by the fact that takings of late had been dismal. So he closed off again the previously partitioned area of the tent and his spare-time studies now became equally divided between Hamilton's books of occult lore and a patient examination of the hideous idol and carved tablets. He discovered no evidence of hidden mechanical devices in the queer relics, but nevertheless it was not long before he found his first real clue towards implementing his ambition.

It was as simple as this: he had earlier noted upon the carved tops of the stone tablets a series of curiously intermingled cuneiform and dot-group hieroglyphs, two distinct sets to each stone. This could not be considered odd in itself, but finally Anderson had recognized the pattern of these characters and knew that they were duplicated in the handwritten *Necronomicon*; and more, there were translations in that work into at least two other languages, one of them being the antiquated German in which the bulk of the book was written.

Anderson's knowledge of German, even in its modern form, was less than rudimentary, and thus he enlisted the aid of old Hans Möller from the hoopla stall. The old German's eyesight was no longer reliable, however, and his task was made no easier by the outmoded form in which the work was written, but at last, and not without Anderson's insistent urging, Möller was able to translate one of the sequences first into more modern German (in which it read: *Gestorben ist nicht, was für ewig ruht, und mit unbekannten Äonen mag sogar der Tod noch sterben*), and then into the following rather poor English: "It is not dead that lies still forever; Death itself dies with the passing of strange years."

When he heard the old German speak these words in his heavy accent, Anderson had to stifle the gasp of recognition which welled within him. This was nothing less than a variation of that paradoxical couplet with which his brother had once terminated his fiendish "sacrifice to Cthulhu!"

As for the other set of symbols from the tablets, frustration was soon to follow. Certainly the figures were duplicated in the centuried book, appearing in what Anderson at first took to be a code of some sort, but they had not been reproduced in German. Möller—while having not the slightest inkling of Anderson's purpose with this smelly, evil old book—finally suggested to him that perhaps the letters were not in code at all, that they might simply be the symbols of an obscure foreign language. Anderson had to agree that Möller could well be right; in the yellowed left-hand margin of the relevant page, directly opposite the frustrating cryptogram, his brother had long ago written: "Yes, but what of the *pronunciation*?"

Hamilton had done more than this: he had obligingly dated his patently self-addressed query, and the surviving Tharpe brother saw that the jotting had been made prior to the fatal second period of travel in foreign lands. Who could say what Hamilton might or might not have discovered upon that journey? Without a doubt he had been in strange places. And he had seen and done strange things to bring back with him that hellish cancer-growth sprouting in his brain.

Finally Anderson decided that this jumbled gathering of harsh and unpronounceable letters—be it a scientific process or, more fancifully, a magical evocation—must indeed be the formula with which a clever man might call forth the green light in his dead brother's "Temple of Cthulhu." He thanked old Hans and sent him away, then sat in his caravan poring over the ancient book, puzzling and frowning long into the evening until, as darkness fell, his eyes lit with dawning inspiration. . . .

And so over the period of the next few days the freak house suffered its transition into the Tomb of the Great Old Ones. During the same week Anderson visited a printer in the local town and had new admission tickets printed. These tickets, as well as bearing the new name of the show and revised price of admission, now carried upon the reverse the following cryptic instruction:

Any adult person desiring to speak with the proprietor of the *Tomb of the Great Old Ones* on matters of genuine occult phenomena or similar manifestations, or on subjects relating to the Great Old Ones, R'lyeh, or the Cthulhu Cycle of Myth, is welcome to request a private meeting.

Anderson Tharpe: Prop.

The other members of the fairground fraternity were not aware of this offer of Anderson's—nor of his authority, real or assumed, in such subjects to be able to make such an offer—until after the funfair moved into its next location, and by that time they too had discovered his advance advertising in the local press. Of course, Bella Hodgson had always looked after advance publicity in the past, but she could hardly be offended by Anderson's personal efforts toward this end. Any good publicity he devised and paid for himself could only go towards attracting better crowds to the benefit of the funfair in general.

And within a very short time Anderson's plan started to bear fruit, when at last his desire for a higher percentage of rather more erudite persons among his show's clientele began to be realized. His sole purpose, of course, had been to attract just such persons in the hope that perhaps one of them might provide the baffling pronunciation he required, an *acoustical* translation of the key to call up the terrible green glow.

Such authorities must surely exist; his own brother had become one in a comparatively short time, and others had spent whole lifetimes in the concentrated study of these secrets of elder lore. Surely, sooner or later, he would find a man to provide the answer, and then the secrets of the perfect murder weapon would be his. When this happened, then Anderson would test his weapon on the poor unfortunate who handed him the key, and in this way he would be sure that the secret was his alone. From then on . . . oh, there were many possibilities . . .

Through early and mid-April Anderson received a number of inquisitive callers at his caravan: some of them cranks, but at least a handful of genuinely interested and knowledgeable types. Always he pumped them for what they knew of elder mysteries in connection with the Cthulhu Cycle, especially their knowledge of ancient tongues and obscure languages, and twice over he was frustrated just when he thought himself on the right track. On one occasion, after seeing the tablets and idol, an impressed visitor presented him with a copy of Walmsley's *Notes on Deciphering Codes, Cryptograms, and Ancient Inscriptions*; but to no avail; the work itself was too deep for him.

Then, towards the end of April, in response to Anderson's continuous probing, a visitor to his establishment grudgingly gave him the address of a so-called "occult investigator," one Titus Crow, who just might be interested in his problem. Before he left the fairground this same gentleman, the weird artist Chandler Davies, strongly advised Tharpe that the whole thing were best forgotten, that no good could ever come of dabbling in such matters—be it serious study or merely idle curiosity—and with that warning he had taken his leave. . . .

Ignoring the artist's positive dread of his line of research, that same afternoon Anderson wrote to Titus Crow at his London address, enclosing with his letter a copy of the symbols and a request for information concerning them, possibly a translation or, even better, a workable pronunciation. Impatiently then, he watched the post for an answer, and early in May was disappointed to receive a brief note from Crow advising him, as had Davies, to give up his interest in these matters and let such dangerous subjects alone. There was no explanation, no invitation regarding further correspondence; Crow had not even bothered to return the cryptic paragraph so painstakingly copied from the *Necronomicon*.

That night, as if to substantiate the double warning, Anderson once more dreamed of sunken R'lyeh, and again he kneeled before slumbering Cthulhu's throne to hear the alien voice echoing awesomely in his mind. The horror on the throne seemed more mobile in its sleep than ever before, and the voice in the dream was more insistent, more menacing:

"You have been warned, AND YET YOU MEDDLE! While the Great Rising draws ever closer and Cthulhu's shadow looms, still you choose to search out His secrets for your own use! This night there will be a sign; ignore it at your peril, lest Cthulhu bestir Himself up to visit you personally in dreams, as He has aforetime visited others!"

The following morning Anderson rose haggard and pale to learn of yet more trouble with the fairground's dogs, duplicating in detail that Candlemas frenzy of three months earlier. The coincidence was such as to cause him more than a moment's concern, and especially after reading the morning's newspapers.

What was it that the voice in his dream had said of "a sign?"— a warning which he should only ignore at his peril? Well, there had been a sign, many of them, for the night had been filled with a veritable plethora of weird and inexplicable occurrences— strange stirrings among the more dangerous inmates of lunatic asylums all over the country, macabre suicides by previously normal people—a magma of madness climaxed, so far as Anderson Tharpe was concerned, by second-page headlines in two of the national newspapers to the effect that Chandler Davies had been "put away" in Woodholme Sanatorium. The columns went on to tell how Davies had painted a monstrous "G'harne Landscape," which his outraged and terrified mistress had at once set fire to, thus bringing about in him an insane rage from which he had not recovered. More: a few days later came the news via the same organs that Davies was dead!

If Anderson Tharpe had been in any way a sensitive person,

and his evil ambition less of an obsession—had his *perceptions* not been dulled by a lifetime of living close to the anomalies of the erstwhile freak house—then perhaps he might have recognized the presence of a horror such as few men have ever known. Unlike his brother, however, Anderson was coarse-grained and not especially imaginative. All the portents and evidences, the hints and symptoms, and accumulating warnings were cast aside within a few short days of his nightmare and its accompanying manifestations, when yet again he turned to his studies in the hope that soon the secret of the green light would be his.

From then on the months passed slowly, while the crowds at the Tomb of the Great Old Ones became smaller still despite all Anderson's efforts to the contrary. His frustration grew in direct proportion to his dwindling assets, and while his continued advance advertising and the invitation on the reverse of his admission tickets still drew the occasional crank occultist or curious devotee of the macabre to his caravan, not one of them was able to further his knowledge of the Cthulhu Cycle or satisfy his growing obsession with regard to that enigmatic and cryptical "key" from the hand-written *Necronomicon*.

Twice as the seasons waxed and waned he approached old Hans about further translations from the ancient book, even offering to pay for the old German's services in this respect, but Hans was simply not interested. He was too old to become a *Dolmetscher*, he said, and his eyes were giving him trouble; he already had enough money for his simple needs, and anyway, he did not like the *look* of the book. What the old man did not say was that he had seen things in those yellowed pages, on that one occasion when already he had looked into the rotting volume, which simply did not bear translation! And so again Anderson's plans met with frustration.

In mid-October the now thoroughly disgruntled and morose proprietor of the Tomb of the Great Old Ones looked to a different approach. Patently, no matter how hard he personally studied Hamilton's books, he was not himself qualified to puzzle out and piece together the required information. There were those, however, who had spent a lifetime in such studies, and if he could not attract such as these to the fairground—why, then he must simply send the problem to them. True, he had tried this before, with Titus Crow, but now, as opposed to cultists, occultists, and the like, he would approach only recognized authorities. He spent the following day or two tracking down the address of Professor Gordon Walmsley of Goole, a world-renowned expert in the science of ciphers, whose book, *Notes on Deciphering Codes, Cryptograms, and Ancient Inscriptions*, had now been in his possession for almost seven months. That book was still far too deep and complicated for Anderson's fathoming, but the author of such a work should certainly find little difficulty with the piece from the *Necronomicon*.

He quickly composed a letter to the professor, and as October grew into its third week he posted it off. He was not to know it, but at that time Walmsley was engaged in the services of the Buenos Aires Museum of Antiquities, busily translating the hieroglyphs on certain freshly discovered ruins in the mountains of the Aconcaguan Range near San Juan. Anderson's letter did eventually reach him, posted on from Walmsley's Yorkshire address, but the professor was so interested in his own work that he gave it only a cursory glance. Later he found that he had misplaced it, and thus, fortunately, the scrap of paper with its deadly invocation passed into obscurity and became lost forever.

Anderson meanwhile impatiently waited for a reply, and along with the folk of the fairground prepared for the Halloween opening at Bathley, a town on the north-east border. It was then, on the night of the twenty-seventh of the month, that he received his third and final warning. The day had been chill and damp, with a bitter wind blowing off the North Sea, bringing a dankly salt taste and smell that conjured up horrible memories for the surviving Tharpe brother.

On the morning of the twenty-eighth, rising up gratefully from a sweat-soaked bed and a nightmare the like of which he had never known before and fervently prayed never to know again, Anderson Tharpe blamed the horrors of the night on yesterday's sea wind with its salty smells of ocean, but even explained away like this the dream had been a monstrous thing.

Again he had visited sunken R'lyeh, but this time there had been a vivid *reality* to the nightmare lacking in previous dreams. He had known the terrible, bone-crushing pressures of that drowned realm, had felt the frozen chill of its black waters. He had tried to scream as the pressure forced his eyes from their sockets, and then the sea had rushed into his mouth, tearing his throat and lungs and stomach as it filled him in one smashing column as solid as steel. And though the horror had lasted only a second, still he had known that there in the ponderous depths his *disintegration* had taken place before the throne of the Lord of R'lyeh, the Great Old One who seeped down from the stars at the dawn of time. He had been a sacrifice to Cthulhu . . .

That had been four days ago, but still Tharpe shuddered when he thought of it. He put it out of his mind now as he ushered the crowd out of the tent and turned to face the sole remaining member of that departing audience. Tharpe's oratory had been automatic; during its delivery he had allowed his mind to run free in its exploration of all that had passed since his brother's hideous death, but now he came back to Earth. Hiram Henley stared back at him in what he took to be scornful disappointment. The ex-professor spoke:

" 'The Tomb of the Great Old Ones,' indeed! Sir, you're a charlatan!" he said. "I could find more fearsome things in Grimm's Fairy Tales, more items of genuine antiquarian interest in my aunt's attic. I had hoped your—*show*—might prove interesting. It seems I was mistaken." His eyes glinted sarcastically behind his tiny spectacles. For a moment Tharpe's heart beat a little faster, then he steadied himself. Perhaps this time . . . ? Certainly the little man was worth a try. "You do me an injustice, sir—you wound me!" He waxed theatrical, an ability with which he was fluent through his years of showmanship. "Do you really believe that I would openly *display* the archaeological treasures for which this establishment was named? I should put them out for the common herd to ogle, when not one in ten thousand could even recognize them, let alone appreciate them? Wait!"

He ducked through the canvas door flap into the enclosed area containing Hamilton's relics, returning a few seconds later with a bronze miniature the size of his hand and wrist. The thing looked vaguely like an elongated, eyeless squid. It also looked—despite the absence of anything even remotely mundane in its appearance—utterly evil! Anderson handed the object reverently to the ex-professor, saying: "What do you make of that?" Having chosen the thing at random from the anomalies in his dead brother's collection, he hoped it really was of "genuine antiquarian interest."

His choice had been a wise one. Henley peered at the miniature, and slowly his expression changed. He examined the thing minutely, then said: "It is the burrower beneath, Shudde-M'ell, or one of his brood. A very good likeness, and ancient beyond words. Made of bronze, yet quite obviously it predates the Bronze Age!" His voice was suddenly soft. "Where did you get it?"

"You *are* interested, then?" Tharpe smiled, incapable of either admitting or denying the statements of the other.

"Of course I'm interested." Henley eagerly nodded, a bit too eagerly, Tharpe thought. "I . . . I did indeed do you a great injustice. This thing is *very* interesting! Do you have . . . more?"

"All in good time." Tharpe held up his hands, holding himself in check, waiting until the time was ripe to frame his own all-

important question. "First, who are you? You understand that my—
possessions—are not for idle scrutiny, that—"

"Yes, yes, I understand," the little man cut him off. "My name
is Hiram Henley. I am—at least I was—Professor of Archaeology
and Ethnology at Meldham University. I have recently given up my
position there in order to carry out private research. I came here
out of curiosity, I admit; a friend gave me one of your tickets with
its peculiar invitation . . . I wasn't really expecting much, but—"

"But now you've seen something that you would never have
believed possible in a place like this. Is that it?"

"Indeed it is. And you? Who are you?"

"Tharpe is my name, Anderson Tharpe, proprietor of this"—
he waved his hand deprecatingly—"establishment."

"Very well, Mr. Tharpe," Henley said. "It's my good fortune to
meet a man whose intelligence in my own chosen field patently
must match my own—whose possessions include items such as
this." He held up the heavy bronze piece and peered at it again for
a moment. "Now, will you show me—the rest?"

"A glimpse, only a glimpse," Tharpe told him, aware now that
Henley was hooked. "Then perhaps we can trade?"

"I have nothing with which to trade. In what way do you
mean?"

"Nothing to trade? Perhaps not," Tharpe answered, holding the
canvas door open so that his visitor might step into the enclosed
space beyond, "but then again . . . How are you on ancient tongues
and languages?"

"Languages were always my—" The ex-professor started to answer, stepping into the private place. Then he paused, his eyes wid-
ening as he gazed about at the contents of the place. "Were always
my—" Again he paused, reaching out his hands before him and
moving forward, touching the ugly idol unbelievingly, moving
quickly to the carved tablets, staring as if hypnotized at the smaller

figurines and totems. Finally he turned a flushed face to Tharpe.
His look was hard to define: partly awed, partly—accusing?

"I didn't steal them, I assure you," Tharpe quickly said.

"No, of course not," Henley answered, "but . . . you have the
treasures of the aeons here!"

Now the tall showman could hold himself no longer. "Languages," he pressed. "You say you have an understanding of
tongues? Can you translate from the ancient to the modern?"

"Yes, most things, providing—"

"How would you like to *own* all you see here?" Tharpe cut him
off again.

Henley reached out suddenly palsied hands to take Tharpe by
the forearms. "You're . . . joking?"

"No." Tharpe shook his head, lying convincingly. "I'm not joking. There is something of the utmost importance to my own line
of—research. I need a translation of a fragment of ancient writing.
Rather, I need the *original* pronunciation. If you can solve this one
problem for me, all this can be yours. You can be . . . part of it."

"What is this fragment?" the little man cried. "*Where* is it?"

"Come with me."

"But—" Henley turned away from Tharpe, his gloved hands
again reaching for those morbid items out of the aeons.

"No, no." Tharpe took his arm. "Later—you'll have all the time
you need. Now there is this problem of mine. But later, tonight,
we'll come back in here, and all this can be yours . . ."

The ex-professor voluntarily followed Tharpe out of the tent to
his caravan, and there he was shown the handwritten *Necronomicon*
with its cryptic "key."

"Well," Tharpe demanded, barely concealing his agitation. "Can
you read it as it was written? Can you *pronounce* it in its original
form?"

"I'll need a little time," the balding man mused, "and privacy.

But I think . . . I'll take a copy of this with me, and as soon as I have the answer—"

"When? How long?"

"Tonight?"

"Good. I'll wait for you. It should be quiet here by then. It's Halloween and the fairground is open until late, but they'll all be that much more tired . . ." Tharpe suddenly realized that he was thinking out loud and quickly glanced at his visitor. The little man peered at him strangely through his tiny specs, *very* strangely, Tharpe thought.

"The people here are—superstitious," he explained. "It wouldn't be wise to advertise our interest in these ancient matters. They're ignorant and I've had trouble with them before. They don't like some of the things I've got."

"I understand," Henley answered. "I'll go now and work through the evening. With luck it won't take too long. Tonight— shall we say after midnight?—I'll be back." He quickly made a copy of the characters in the old book, then stood up. Tharpe saw him out of the caravan with an assumed, gravely thoughtful air, thanking him before watching him walk off in the direction of the exit, but then he laughed out loud and slapped his thigh, quickly seeking out one of the odd-job boys from the stratojet thrill ride.

An hour later—to the amazement of his fellow showmen, for the crowd was thickening rapidly as the afternoon went by—Anderson Tharpe closed the Tomb of the Great Old Ones and retired to his caravan. He wanted to practice himself in the operation of the tape recorder which he had paid the odd-jobber to buy for him in Bathley.

This final phase of his plan was simple; necessarily so, for of course he in no way intended to honour his bargain with Henley. He *did* intend to have the little man read out his pronunciation of the "key," and to record that pronunciation in perfect fidelity—but from then on . . .

If the pronunciation were imperfect, then of course the "bargain" would be unfulfilled and the ex-professor would escape with his life and nothing more, but if the invocation worked . . . ? Why, then the professor simply could not be allowed to walk away and talk about what he had seen. No, it would be necessary for him to disappear into the green light. Hamilton would have called it a "sacrifice to Cthulhu."

And yet there had been something about the little man that disturbed Anderson; something about his peering eyes and his eagerness to fall in with the plans of the gaunt showman. Tharpe thought of his dream of a few days past, then of those other nightmares he had known, and shuddered; and again he pondered the possibility that there had been more than met the eye in his mad brother's assertions. But what odds? Science or sorcery, it made no difference; the end result would be the same. He rubbed his hands in anticipation. Things were at last looking up for Anderson Tharpe . . .

At midnight the crowd began to thin out. Watching the people move off into the chill night, Anderson was glad it had started to rain again, for their festive Halloween mood might have kept them in the fairground longer, and the bright lights would have glared and the music played late into the night. Only an hour later all was quiet, with only the sporadic patter of rain on machines and tents and painted roofs to disturb the night. The last wetly gleaming light had blinked out and the weary folk of the fairground were in their beds. That was when Anderson heard the furtive rapping at his caravan door, and he was agreeably surprised that the ever-watchful dogs had not heralded his night-visitor's arrival. Possibly it was too early for them yet to distinguish between comers and goers.

As soon as he was inside, Henley saw the question written on Tharpe's face. He nodded in answer: "Yes, yes, I have it. It appears to be a summons of some sort, a cry to vast and immeasurable ancient powers. Wait, I'll read it for you—"

"No, no—not here!" Tharpe silenced him before he could commence. "I have a tape recorder in the tent."

Without a word the little man followed Tharpe through the dark and into the private enclosure containing those centuried relics which so plainly fascinated him. There Tharpe illumined the inner tent with a single dim light bulb; then, switching on his tape recorder, he told the ex-professor that he was now ready to hear the invocation. And yet now Henley paused, turning to face Tharpe and gravely peering at him from where he stood by the horrible octopoid idol.

"Are you—sure?" the little man asked. "Are you sure you want me to do this?" His voice was dry, calm.

"Eh?" Anderson questioned nervously, terrible suspicions suddenly forming in his mind. "Of course I'm sure—and what do you mean, 'do this?' Do what?"

Henley shook his head sadly. "Your brother was foolish not to see that you would cause trouble sooner or later!"

Tharpe's eyes opened wide and his jaw fell slack. "Police!" he finally croaked. "You're from the police!"

"No such thing," the little man calmly answered. "I am what I told you I was—and something more than that—and to prove it . . ."

The sounds Henley uttered then formed an exact and fluent duplication of those Tharpe had heard once before, and shocked as he was that this frail outsider knew far too much about his affairs, still Tharpe thrilled as the inhuman echoes died and there formed in the semicircle of grim tablets an expanding, glowing greenness that sent out writhing beams of ghostly luminescence. Quickly the tall man gathered his wits. Policeman or none, Hiram Henley had to be done away with. This had been the plan in any case, once the little man—whoever he was—had done his work and was no longer required. And he had done his work well. The invocation was recorded; Anderson could call up the destroying green light any time he so desired. Perhaps Henley had been a former colleague of Hamilton's, and somehow he had come to learn of the younger Tharpe's demise? Or was he only guessing! Still, it made no difference now.

Henley had turned his back on Anderson, lifting up his arms to the hideous idol greenly illuminated in the light of the pulsating witchfire. But as the showman slipped his brother's knife from his pocket, so the little man turned again to face him, smiling strangely and showing no discernible fear at the sight of the knife. Then his smile faded and again he sadly shook his head. His lips formed the words, "No, no, my friend," but Anderson Tharpe heard nothing; once more, as it had done before, the green light had cancelled all sound within its radius.

Suddenly Tharpe was very much afraid, but still he knew what he must do. Despite the fact that the inner tent was far more chill even than the time of the year warranted, sweat glistened greenly on Anderson's brow as he moved forward in a threatening crouch, the knife raised and reflecting emerald shafts of evilly writhing light. He lifted the knife higher still as he closed with the motionless figure of the little man—*and then Hiram Henley moved*!

Anderson saw what the ex-professor had done and his lips drew back in a silent, involuntary animal snarl of the utmost horror and fear. He almost dropped the knife, frozen now in mid-stroke, as Henley's black gloves fell to the floor and the thick white worms twined and twisted hypnotically where his fingers ought to have been!

Then—more out of nightmare dread and loathing than any sort of rational purpose, for Anderson knew now that the ex-professor was nothing less than a Priest of Cthulhu—he carried on with his interrupted stroke and his knife flashed down. Henley tried to deflect the blow with a monstrously altered hand, his face contorting and a shriek forming silently on his lips as one of the wormish appendages was severed and fell twitching to the sawdust. He flailed his injured hand and white ichor splashed Tharpe's face and eyes.

Blindly the frantic showman struck again and again, gibbering mindlessly and noiselessly as he clawed at his face with his free hand, trying to wipe away the filthy white juice of Henley's injured hybrid member. But the blows were wild and Hiram Henley had stepped to one side.

More frantically yet, insanely, Tharpe slashed at the greenly pulsating air all about him, stumbling closer to the core of radiance. Then his knife struck something that gave like rotting flesh beneath the blow, and finally, in a short-lived revival of confidence, he opened stinging eyes to see what he had hit.

Something coiled out of the green core, something long and tapering, greyly mottled and slimy! Something that stank of deep ocean and submarine weeds! It was a tentacle—a *face*-tentacle, Tharpe knew—twitching spasmodically, even as the hand of a disturbed dreamer might twitch.

Tharpe struck again, a reflex action, and watched his blade bite through the tentacle unhindered, as if through mud—*and then saw that trembling member solidifying again where the blade had sliced!* His knife fell from a palsied hand then, and Tharpe screamed a last, desperate, silent scream as the tentacle moved more purposefully!

The now completely sentient member wrapped its tip about Tharpe's throat, constricting and jerking him forward effortlessly into the green core. And as he went the last things he saw were the eyes in the vast face, the hellish eyes that opened briefly, saw and recognized him for what he was—a sacrifice to Cthulhu!

Quickly then, as the green light began its withdrawal and sound slowly returned to the tent, Hiram Henley put on his gloves. Ignoring as best he could the pain his injury gave him, he spoke these words:

> *Oh, Great Cthulhu, dreaming in R'lyeh,*
> *Thy priest offers up this sacrifice,*
> *That Thy coming be soon,*
> *And that of Thy kindred dreamers.*
> *I am Thy priest and adore Thee . . .*

And as the core grew smaller yet, he toppled the evil idol into its green center, following this act by throwing in the tablets and all those other items of fabled antiquity until the inner tent was quite empty. He would have kept all these things if he dared, but his orders—those orders he received in dreams from R'lyeh—would not allow it. When a priest had been found to replace Hamilton Tharpe, then Great Cthulhu would find a way to return those rudimentary pillars of His temple!

Finally, Henley switched off the single dim light and watched the green core as it shrank to a tiny point of intense brightness before winking out. Only the smell of deep ocean remained, and a damp circle in the dark where the sawdust floor was queerly marked and slimy. . . .

Some little time later the folk of the fairground were awakened by the clamour of a fire engine as it sped to the blaze on the border of the circling tents, sideshows, and caravans. Both Tharpe's caravan and The Tomb of the Great Old Ones were burning fiercely.

Nothing was saved, and in their frantic toiling to help the firemen the nomads of the funfair failed to note that their dogs again crouched timid and whimpering beneath the nighted caravans. They found it strange later, though, when they heard how the police had failed to discover anything of Anderson Tharpe's remains.

The gap that the destruction of the one-time freak house had left was soon filled, for "Madame Zala," as if summoned back by the grim work of the mysterious fire, returned with her horse and caravan within the week. She is still with Hodgson's Funfair, but she will never speak of the Tharpes. At certain times of the year well known to anyone with even the remotest schooling in the occult, she is sometimes seen crossing herself with an obscure and pagan sign. . . .

BENEATH THE MOORS

I

DISCOVERIES IN CONVALESCENCE
[From the Notebooks of Professor Ewart Masters]

Following the car accident that nearly killed me, causing what seemed at first rather severe brain damage and leaving me almost completely incapacitated for four months, I decided to spend my convalescence in a return to the interests of earlier years, to take up once more my studies of the ancient things of the world, the civilizations and cities of Earth's youth. The decision to do no actual work was taken as a necessity. One cannot lecture when at any second his memory is liable to fail, his very lucidity depart to leave him a mazed and mumbling wreck.

That was the early condition in which my accident had left me; barely capable of concentrating for more than five minutes at a stretch; prone to lapsing at the drop of a hat into shady worlds filled with half-formed visions of dimly remembered scenes and incomprehensible snatches of unrecognized conversations. Shady worlds which were, in effect, spontaneous daydreams, leftovers from my days of total unconsciousness and my secondary phase of semiamnesia—guaranteed, if ever they should occur in public, to make Professor Ewart Masters a figure of ridicule. In such a condition lecturing was out, as was for that matter anything requiring more than a minimum of concentration.

But I could read and even study, so long as I rested myself as soon as I felt a dizzy spell coming on. And so, when finally I left the London hospital—a move allowed me wholly on my assurance that I *would* rest, that I would not yet attempt to work—it was to catch the first north-bound train out of King's Cross and return to my native Harden on the north-east coast, to the home of my bachelor nephew, Jason Masters, where I might resume the restful studies of my youth.

Restful? I could hardly have been more wrong!

Jason had left nothing to chance, laying in a batch of the latest archaeological journals and papers, a copy of Walmsley's *Notes on Deciphering Codes, Cryptograms and Ancient Inscriptions*, a complete report on the newly opened Mediterranean and Ahaggar digs, and two new illustrated paperbacks taking a refreshing look at the old "forgotten civilizations" theme. I suppose he followed the principle that the more reading I did the less tempted I would be towards more strenuous exertions, but the truth of the matter was I had no intention of working. I had been pushing myself for far too long, with never a break in eight years, and doubtless it was the way I had knocked myself about that was to blame for my car accident. The fault was my own; I had been simply too tired to drive. No, relaxation and quiet were for me: no more long hours on the road, no more road maps to consult, no more lengthy lectures in drafty, poorly lit town halls, and no more sleepless nights worrying over tomorrow's programme, not for quite a long time at any rate.

Yet within a fortnight I was bored to tears, even though the uselessness of attempting anything more ambitious had been brought home to me time and time again. On no less than five occasions I had suffered traumalike lapses while sitting at my desk with various papers, and once, while out stretching my legs with Jason, my mind had completely blanked and my nephew had had to lead me home while I mumbled to some unseen companion of my childhood.

Over a further period of some six weeks, however, my "funny turns" slowly petered out and I began to get about more on my own. Jason was delighted with my progress and in the eighth week arranged a trip on which he accompanied me to Radcar Museum, to have a look at some of the newer acquisitions of the antiquities section. The idea of the trip sprang from the interest I had shown in an article in one of the archaeological magazines Jason had got in for me. It seemed that the museum had in its "Wonders of Ancient Britain" showcases an artefact older than any other known item of British historical interest. Carbon dating and the Wendy-Smith Test had placed the thing—a miniature sculpture of some reptilian "god"—as being as much as twelve thousand years old; yet photographs in the magazine showed its features to be as clearly defined as if cut only yesterday. And there was something else about it, a suggestion of latent . . . *existence* . . . which somehow disturbed me strangely.

From the moment I laid eyes on the actual figurine itself, resting behind glass in its museum showcase, I was lost. Oh, my studies had been restful enough until then, until the advent of this tiny bit of unknown prehistory. But now . . . ?

Suddenly I had a purpose. It seems strange, I know, but I found myself so inexplicably fascinated by the thing that I became almost grateful for the accident which had led me to its discovery, and as soon as I got back to Harden I set to work sorting out all the information I could find on it—which eventually came to quite a bit . . .

Yes, now that I had something to do, something to look for, my health seemed to pick up amazingly, and as the weeks passed my lapses into that strange half-world grew less and less frequent until they ceased almost completely. It seemed the doctors had been quite wrong; work was doing me no harm at all. And, as I have said, I surprised myself at the amount of information I was eventually able to turn up.

Not that I had it all immediately to hand, on the contrary, but after some digging around—a peek or two at Wendy-Smith's *On Ancient Civilizations*, a careful perusal of the "spoof" death notes of Professor Gordon Walmsley of Goole (the author of one of those previously mentioned books procured for me by my nephew), a thoughtful examination of the "message" of the translated but still baffling Kith characters, and, finally, a slow scrutiny of the known and charted subterranean streams and rivers of the Yorkshire moors—I was satisfied that I had garnered as much information on the subject as was available without going to a great deal more trouble.

The subject? Well, for me, fascinating though it had been from the start, the figurine itself was only a beginning, a clue, a pointer to . . . well, to something I did not quite understand myself. I only knew I had the feeling that I was on the first step of an amazing archaeological and anthropological staircase, and that at the top there awaited—?

My interest in speleological charts sprang from the fact that the green lizardlike figurine had been found in a stream where it appeared to have been washed from some underground region through a resurgence at Sarby-on-the-Moor. This, plus a mention in Walmsley's death notes of a mythical city named Lh-yib (the location of which the professor had supposedly traced to a well-known but completely bleak and barren area of the moors), intrigued me tremendously. I saw a connection that to me was undeniable. After all, the fact that the surface of the moors at the area mentioned by Walmsley was barren, completely devoid of any prehistoric remains other than the normal fossils one might expect to find, did not prove conclusively that such a city had never existed. Why, with the passage of Lord-only-knows how many centuries since Lh-yib stood, *if* it ever stood, the Earth's natural convulsions—

earthquakes, tremors, erosion, floods, and all the other planet-rending forces of time and nature—could easily have obliterated even the most fragmentary trace of the city! But in that case, why had the figurine not suffered to a like degree from these deteriorative forces? Had it been cached away somewhere underground to be washed out all these centuries later as clean and new as when first sculpted? This seemed to me the only likely explanation; for that a city should crumble to dust while a mere idol, small and quite susceptible to all Earth's disintegrative processes, remained intact and unaffected down the aeons without some sort of protection was simply not reasonable.

From then on I spent a lot of time in Harden's adequate library, and there, over the next week or two, I became a firm friend of the quite knowledgeable lady librarian Miss Samways, who helped me considerably in tracking down numerous books, even going so far as to have a number sent in from other branches. My purpose primarily was to try to trace the reptilian "god" itself, to see if I could find any reference to it, or its worship, in the translated writings of the world's great predawn civilizations. To this and other ends I scanned or requested information on many a book half-remembered from my earlier years, many of them on archaeological subjects—the classical digs of Babylonia, Turkey, Pompeii, Chichén-Itzá, Milcabamba, and Knossos—and numerous others of far more doubtful authenticity, but nowhere, not even in such comprehensive anthropological texts as *The Golden Bough*, could I find mention of a creature or deity of passing similarity to the green figurine.

It was difficult to see how it fitted in, but I soon became so desperate for a clue that I even thought to briefly consider the Melanesian belief of a time "in the beginning" when mythical beings dwelt on Earth—beings that evolved into men—in particular the crocodile god, Nuga. Then there was the mythology of the Shibiuk peoples of the Upper Nile regions of the Sudan. In these legends crocodile-girls came down from the moon to marry men, and the crocodile later became regarded as the patron of birth and—amazingly enough—protector of babies! Still in Africa, the Malagasy clans believe that the dead return (after growing tails in their graves) in the form of crocodiles, and there are numerous tales of witches and witch doctors changing into crocodiles through their practising of Black Magic rites. Nor could I completely ignore the crocodile-headed "god" of Crocodilopolis in ancient Egypt, Sobek, who lolled—jewel-adorned and with his teeth gold-plated—in the sacred pools of his temple. But in more sober frame of mind I had to admit to myself that none of these could be the creature or deity for which I searched.

Despairingly I turned to more truly zoological material in the hope that I might at least find the animal in whose likeness the statuette had been sculpted. I pored over Banfort's *The Saurian Age, Nessiter's Dragons of Myth and Legend*, McGilchrist's *Notes on "Nessie": the Secrets of Loch Ness Revealed!*, and all and any other volumes which I thought might prove valid to my search. It was a stone wall all the way, and more than once I considered giving up an apparently hopeless task.

But then I turned again to Walmsley's "spoof" notes—those writings published after his inexplicable death—in the hope that somewhere he might have mentioned something of use to me, something perhaps to reinforce his theory of a prehistoric city on the moors . . .

How I had missed it before I cannot say, but sure enough there was in his notes a lead of sorts. Quite simply Walmsley had stated that the people of his alleged city were "fancifully described on the *Brick Cylinders of Kadatheron* . . ."

Just where he had acquired this information is difficult to say (Walmsley had died before Angstrom's team smuggled their pirated treasures of time out of Arabia), but certainly such cylinders as the professor had mentioned were in existence; indeed, Walmsley's own book on the translation of ancient languages had been used extensively in the deciphering of the inscriptions upon those relics of the dead past.

From the library I put through a call to the British Museum in London, requesting a brief reading of the translation. At first the gentleman on the other end of the line was a bit short with me—understandably, I suppose—but when I introduced myself as being Ewart Masters he brought the curator's assistant, one Mr. Fleetly, to the telephone and I got my reading.

There was not a great deal to it in all; I had asked only for the portion, if such existed, containing the description of an ancient people. Mr. Fleetly had snorted in answer to my request before telling me:

"People, sir? *Things*, more like! As wildly fanciful as anything the Greeks ever wrote . . ." And after I had heard the translation I found myself agreeing with him, but more intrigued than ever:

> . . . and the Beings of Ib are in Hue as green as the Lake of Ib and the Mists that rise over the Lake; and their Eyes do bulge outward and their Lips do pout and are as Wattles; and their Ears are curiously formed; and they are without Voices, yet unheard they do speak! . . . Lo, they came down from the Moon one Night in a Mist; lo, they and the Lake and Ib; and there did they worship Bokrug, the great Water-Lizard, and did dance most horribly to the full-waxed Moon . . .

So: that then was the description of the people—or rather the "beings"—of Ib as inscribed on the *Brick Cylinders of Kadatheron.* But those cylinders (the seven so far discovered at least) had come out of the east, while Walmsley's city had supposedly stood somewhere on the Yorkshire moors!

Most puzzling, all of it, but rewarding insofar as I had at last apparently placed my figurine, which, or so it seemed, had been godhead to a worldwide cult!—though how that could possibly have been I was unable to even guess.

Well, one thing often leads to another, and with this in mind I spent a few more days trying to find other references, this time in connection with Ib. But now it seemed that the more I searched the less I turned up. Apart from one mention, again supplied by the British Museum (this time from an ancient translation of doubtful literary origin—*The Ilarnek Papyri*—to the effect that Ib's inhabitants had been wiped out en masse by men from another ancient city, Sarnath, and that later a terrible doom had been visited upon Sarnath), there was nothing.

The time had arrived, it seemed, when I should turn my attention to other things . . .

II

EPISODE AT BLEAKSTONE
[From the Notebooks of Professor Ewart Masters]

Apparently then, I had run the thing to earth; there remained nothing to be discovered of the mystery. Oh, true, the mystery itself was as strange and fascinating as ever, but a means to any sort of solution seemed beyond my capabilities. Nonetheless I felt my researches had not been entirely in vain; they had, I was sure, helped my brain combat the damage done by my accident. In support of this belief there stood the fact that those mental lapses of mine had at last completely disappeared (or so I thought) and my physical health, too, had returned almost fully to normal.

It was about this time that I learned of the gravel pits at Bleakstone, determining to journey there at my earliest convenience to see if I could find some of the reputedly many and various fossils with which the area allegedly abounded.

Jason had watched closely my return through the various stages of recovery but was still more than a little worried when I begged of him the use of his car to go out to Bleakstone for a day or two. I argued, however, that the change of scenery could only do me good, that I badly needed the exercise of scrambling over the rocks and pebbles of the gravel pits. Yet in the end, despite all my protests, I had to resort to a promise of calling Jason at least daily on the telephone (to report of my continuing good health and on the results of my expedition) before he would agree to loan me his car— and then he would only agree on the additional guarantee that I never exceeded the speed limits laid down by the highway authorities.

No doubt about it, my nephew had become a decided pest, and it was not without a sigh of relief that I finally took leave of him and commenced the drive through to Bleakstone.

Now this was more like it!—a return to one of the real pleasures of my youth, when I had often used to scramble in the gullies and quarries of the moors in search of centuried relics of Earth's prehistory. I felt actually excited, and as the miles passed beneath the wheels of the car my exuberance grew to a genuine joy in living the like of which I had not known for many a year.

I arrived at the village at about 6:00 P.M., leaving the car in the car park of The George. I booked a room for three days at that same inn and then went out to a nearby stationers. I was fortunate at that hour to find the proprietor still at work, and bought quite cheaply a large-scale map of the local area with the fossil pits and lanes and paths leading to them clearly marked.

By then it was too late to do anything that night, so I ate a hearty meal with a pint of "best" at The George and retired reasonably early—immediately after calling Jason on the telephone—

in order to be up, about, and away on my rock-hounding trip first thing after breakfast.

Now, I am one of those people who very rarely dream, and then little of any extraordinary content, in view of which fact I could only put the fantastically *protracted* contents of my uneasy slumbers that night down to the consumption of too large a meal taken too late . . . in combination, perhaps, with the strength of the local country brew! This, I reflected the next morning, could be the only explanation, for my dreams had been particularly vivid, if fragmentary in parts, quite outré, and extensive in other parts beyond belief!

They had involved my discovery of a long row of many dinosaur fossils, all of them taking on flesh before my eyes to become a marching line of great green monsters resembling in certain respects the creature of the green figurine at Radcar. I stood in the quarry where I had found the centuried bones and watched this line of reincarnated creatures descend into a huge cleft in the rock face, which closed up after the last of them had entered.

In another part of the dream I saw myself as a child again, scrambling over desolate rock piles in search of a "lost Inca city," and there were other brief visions of some vast underwater fortress wherein swam denizens of the most hideous nightmares.

The extended part of my dreams consisted of one long, unbroken and exact *memory* of my early life during the years between my seventeenth and twentieth birthdays. To be more specific, I *relived* while sleeping every single day and night of those earlier years!—even to the extent of having dreams within dreams which were perfect replicas of those I had known of old. And I had relived those three years to such an unbelievable exactitude that the wonder is I did not age by that same period of time in the course of the single night! Yet, deep down, all the while, I had known somehow that I only dreamed. Heaven-only-knows what inexplicable processes my mind underwent to compress the occurrences of three whole years into less than eight hours!

I was relieved on waking—no, *astonished* might better describe my feelings—to find all normal, with bright sunshine streaming in through the windows of my room at The George . . .

But strange though my dreams had been they were soon pushed into the back of my mind. I had things to do other than worry needlessly over the fruits of indigestion ripened by self-indulgence! I prayed that these were the *only* causes of my incredible dreams, that those dreams themselves would not herald a more serious *derangement* in myself.

There was a slight breeze moving the trees and hedgerows, the air was fresh and sweet following a light night rain, and the sun was already high by the time I finished my fruit juice and coffee to set out—armed with my map, a cold chisel, and a hammer—for the nearest gravel pit. Perhaps it was the excitement, perhaps the sudden exercise following my quite long period of physical inactivity, I do not know for sure; I remember only scrambling down the side of a shallow pit and commencing the splitting of a piece of rock . . . and then no more. . . .

When I "came to," as it were, I had no idea where I was, other than that I was certainly not in the original pit of my choice. That I was in a pit was irrefutable, but this one had walls which were quite high and steep, and I must have had the devil of a job getting down them in the state in which I had been. Obviously I had suffered a relapse, but I could remember nothing whatsoever of it except that the palaeontological theme of my previous conscious intentions had predominated throughout.

It took me some time to climb out of the pit, and when I had done so I was quite horrified to discover that my unremembered wanderings had carried me a distance of well over a mile from my starting point! Time, too, had flown, for my watch showed me that the day already was well into its afternoon.

That was the end of my rock-hounding for the day. Why, *anything* might have happened to me! I could easily have broken my neck attempting a climb so venturesome as the steep sides of that gravel pit. Yet, to an extent, I must have known what I was about; there were one or two small, common fossils in my pockets. . . .

Tired and disappointed that my recovery from the car accident was not the complete thing I had thought it, I made my way slowly back to The George. There I telephoned Jason, as promised, but I told him nothing of my setback, for I liked the quiet Yorkshire village and was still convinced that a few more days there would do me good. There seemed little point in worrying my nephew over something which (I fervently prayed) might never occur again.

Later I went into the smoke room where I took an unoccupied corner table. There were one or two customers, regulars, at the bar drinking beer from their own, personal mugs, and a small party of students sat at some nearby tables. Within the half-hour the latter group left the inn and a few moments later I heard their car pull away into the night. Now that the bar was quieter I took my briefcase and removed from it the magazine with the photographs of the figurine. It could do no harm to have another look at the thing.

I had just opened the magazine to the pages carrying those remarkable pictures when the elderly, balding barman, not so busy now, came over to my table to chat. At least, I assumed that such was his intention, but as soon as he saw the open journal his expression changed from one of friendly interest to a frown of puzzlement and surprise. His attention seemed riveted on the photographs. I smiled, folding the page so that he could see the pictures better:

"Rare, isn't it? A very weird thing to look at . . ."

"Weird?—yes, I'll grant you that, Guv'nor—but *rare*?" He cocked his head on one side enquiringly.

"Oh, yes," I confirmed. "Quite rare, unique! So far as is known, there's only one like it. It's in the museum at Radcar, where these photographs were taken—the only surviving fragment of an unknown, early English civilization . . ."

His interest quickened: "You've seen the real thing then, have you Guv'? I mean, not just these photographs?"

"Why, yes—" I answered, "I saw it just a few weeks ago, at Radcar. Why do you ask?"

"Well, I don't like to stick my neck out," he said, "but if you'll just take a short walk down the street to the police station—well, you'll be able to see another! I saw it myself this morning, in the property room, when I went in to pick up a wallet I lost a day or two ago. . . ."

"*Another figurine!*" I leapt to my feet. "Here in Bleakstone? Are you sure?"

"Positive!" he answered, peering more closely at the photographs. "I mean, a fellow's not likely to forget the looks of one of *those* things in a hurry, now is he?"

III

THE SECOND FIGURINE
[From the Notebooks of Professor Ewart Masters]

So there I was back on the trail again!

It would have been pointless to try to go off to bed early as I had planned (I could never have got to sleep with the thought in my head that within a distance of a few hundred yards a second figurine awaited my attention), so instead I returned my briefcase to my room and then left The George to walk down to the police station, bringing myself into the presence of the weighty night-duty constable, PC Edwards.

I got straight to the point and asked the policeman if I might be allowed to see the figurine. I did not need to furnish him with much of a description of the statuette before he nodded his head in recognition of my subject.

"Oh, yes—that thing! Well, I don't think there's any reason you shouldn't see it, sir, but I'm afraid you're not allowed inside the property room. If you'll wait here and sit yourself down, I'll bring it to you."

He lifted his bulky, blue-clad form from behind his desk and disappeared into an adjoining room closing the door after him. In the space of a few seconds—during which time, short as it was, I fidgeted impatiently—he was back again with the figurine.

I had not really known what to expect. It seemed too much of a coincidence—the odds were stacked far too heavily against it— that a duplicate of the green statuette in the museum at Radcar should exist here at the site I had chosen for my rock-hounding, and that I should so easily stumble across it. Of course, the village *was* a backwater, one of those places that perpetually hover on the edge of modernity without ever actually becoming involved, and tucked away in the confines of this tiny village police station— why!—almost anything might vanish, unclaimed, into complete obscurity. The constable carefully placed the object of my enquiries on the desk before me, dusting it down with his handkerchief.

Delighted beyond my wildest dreams and equally excited, I reached out and touched the thing. My fingers trembled as they followed the lines of its contours. Oh, yes . . . there was no doubt about it. From the smooth baldness of the head, with its piercingly intelligent eyes and tiny, almost circular ears; to the folded arms with their flat hands and blunt, webbed fingers; down the lizardlike body to the powerful legs and webbed feet, the greenstone figurine was indeed the duplicate of the piece in the museum.

Even the short tail was there, curving down and back and giving the whole composition an almost natural balance. "Almost" natural? An understatement, that, for the thing, despite its irrefutable alien-age, looked perfectly . . . well . . . *natural*; and once again, as I had with its twin at Radcar, I found myself certain that the figurine had been made in the form of a living model! Yet how could that possibly be?

"Funny story attached to that there," Constable Edwards informed, breaking into my thoughts, squinting wisely at the thing on his desk. "It's been here with some other stuff ever since Dilham police station closed down. Handed in by a Mrs. White, it was, after the case proper was closed. P'raps you'd care to see the original report and notes? I shouldn't let you see any paperwork, really—but seeing as how it's all long done with, and provided you'd swear never to breathe a word as how you've seen it—I'll let you read it. That is, if you've the time to spare? I appreciate a bit of company on late shift."

If I had the time to spare, indeed! "I'd like very much to see anything you can show me with any bearing at all on this . . . *model*," I told him. "And I promise you that any confidences will be strictly inviolable—you can have complete faith in my discretion . . ."

Which was how the following statement, police report, and notes were first brought to my attention.

IV

THE SISTER CITY
[Being the Statement of Robert Krug]

This manuscript attached as
Annex "A" to report number
M-Y-127/52, dated 7 August 1952.

Towards the end of the war, when our London home was bombed and both my parents were killed, I was hospitalized through my own injuries and forced to spend the better part of two years on my back. It was during this period of my youth—I was only seventeen when I left the hospital—that I formed, in the main, the enthusiasm which in later years developed into a craving for travel, adventure, and knowledge of Earth's elder antiquities. I had always had a wanderer's nature but was so restricted during those two, dreary years that when my chance for adventure eventually came I made up for wasted time by letting that nature hold full sway.

Not that those long, painful months were totally devoid of pleasures. Between operations, when my health would allow it, I read avidly in the hospital's library, primarily to forget my bereavement, eventually to be carried along to those worlds of ancient wonder created by Walter Scott in his enchanting *Arabian Nights*.

Apart from delighting me tremendously, the book helped to take my mind off the things I had heard said about me in the wards. It had been put about that I was different; allegedly the doctors had found something strange in my physical makeup. There were whispers about the peculiar qualities of my skin and the slightly extending horny cartilage at the base of my spine. There was talk about the fact that my fingers and toes were ever-so-slightly webbed; and being, as I was, so totally devoid of hair, I became the recipient of many queer glances.

These things plus my name, Robert Krug, did nothing to increase my popularity at the hospital. In fact, at a time when Hitler was still occasionally devastating London with his bombs, a surname like Krug, with its implications of Germanic ancestry, was probably more a hindrance to friendship than all my other peculiarities put together.

With the end of the war I found myself rich; the only heir to my father's wealth, and still not out of my teens. I had left Scott's Jinns, Ghouls and Efreets far behind me but was returned to the same *type* of thrill I had known with the *Arabian Nights* by the popular publication of Lloyd's *Excavations on Sumerian Sites*. In the main it was that book which was responsible for the subsequent awe in which I ever held those magical words: "Lost Cities."

In the months that followed, indeed through all my remaining—formative—years, Lloyd's work remained a landmark, followed as it was by many more volumes in a like vein. I read avidly of Layard's *Nineveh and Babylon* and *Early Adventures in Persia, Susiana and Babylonia*. I dwelled long over such works as Budge's *Rise and Progress of Assyriology* and Burckhardt's *Travels in Syria and the Holy Land*.

Nor were the fabled lands of Mesopotamia the only places of interest to me. Fictional Shangri-La and Ephiroth ranked equally beside the reality of Mycenae, Knossos, Palmyra, and Thebes. I read excitedly of Atlantis and Chichén-Itzá, never bothering to separate fact from fancy, and dreamed equally longingly of the Palace of Minos in Crete and Unknown Kadath in the Cold Waste.

What I read of Sir Amery Wendy-Smith's African expedition in search of Dead G'harne confirmed my belief that certain myths and legends are not far removed from historical fact. If no less a person than that eminent antiquarian and archaeologist had equipped an expedition to search for a jungle city considered by most reputable authorities to be purely mythological . . . why! His failure meant nothing compared with the fact that he had *tried* . . .

While others, before my time, had ridiculed the broken figure of the demented explorer who returned alone from the jungles of the Dark Continent I tended to emulate his deranged fancies—as his theories have been considered—reexamining the evidence for Chyria and G'harne and delving ever deeper into the fragmentary antiquities of legendary cities and lands with such unlikely names as R'lyeh, Ephiroth, Mnar, and Hyperborea.

As the years passed my body healed completely and I grew from a fascinated youth into a dedicated man. Not that I ever guessed what drove me to explore the ill-lit passages of history and fantasy. I only knew that there was something fascinating for me in the rediscovery of those ancient worlds of dream and legend.

Before I began those far-flung travels which were destined to occupy me on and off for four years, I bought a house in Marske at the very edge of the Yorkshire moors. This was the region in which I had spent my childhood, and there had always been about the brooding moors a strong *affinity* which was hard for me to define. I felt closer to *home* there somehow—and infinitely closer to the beckoning past. It was with a genuine reluctance that I eventually left my moors, but the inexplicable lure of distant places and foreign names called me away, across the seas.

First I visited those lands that were within easy reach, ignoring the places of dreams and fancies but promising myself that later— later!

Egypt, with all its mystery! Djoser's step-pyramid at Saqqarah, Imhotep's masterpiece; the ancient mastabas, tombs of centuries-dead kings; the inscrutably smiling sphinx; the Sneferu pyramid at Meidum and those of Chephren and Cheops at Giza; the mummies, the brooding Gods . . .

Yet in spite of all its wonder Egypt could not hold me for long. The sand and heat were damaging to my skin which tanned quickly and roughened almost overnight.

Crete, the Nymph of the beautiful Mediterranean . . . Theseus and the Minotaur . . . the Palace of Minos at Knossos . . . all wonderful—but that which I sought was not there.

Salamis and Cyprus, with all their ruins of ancient civilizations, each held me but a month or so. Yet it was in Cyprus that I learned of yet another personal peculiarity: my queer abilities in water . . .

I became friendly with a party of divers at Famagusta. Daily they were diving for amphorae and other relics of the past offshore from the ruins at Salenica on the southeast coast. At first the fact that I could remain beneath the water three times as long as the best of them, and swim further without the aid of fins or snorkel, was only a source of amazement to my friends, but after a few days

I noticed that they were having less and less to do with me. They did not care for the hairlessness of my body or the webbing, which seemed to have lengthened, between my toes and fingers. They did not like the bump low at the rear of my bathing costume or the way I could converse with them in their own tongue when I had never studied Greek in my life.

It was time to move on. My travels took me all over the world and I became something of an authority on those dead civilizations which were my one joy in life. Then, in Phetri, I heard of the Nameless City.

Remote in the desert of Araby lies the Nameless City, crumbling and inarticulate, its low walls nearly hidden by the sands of un-counted ages. It was of this place that Abdul Alhazred the mad poet dreamed on the night before he sang his inexplicable couplet:

> *That is not dead which can eternal lie,*
> *And with strange aeons even death may die.*

My Arab guides thought I, too, was mad when I ignored their warnings and continued in search of that City of Devils. Their fleet-footed camels took them off in more than necessary haste, for they had noticed my skin's scaly strangeness and certain other unspoken things which made them uneasy in my presence. Also, they had been nonplussed, as I had been myself, at the strange fluency with which I used their tongue.

Of what I saw and did in Kara-Shehr I will not write. It must suffice to say that I learned of things which sent me off again on my travels to seek Sarnath the Doomed in what was once the land of Mnar . . .

No man knows the whereabouts of Sarnath, and it is better that this remain so. Of my travels in search of the place and the difficulties which I encountered at every phase of my journey I will therefore recount nothing. Yet my discovery of the slime-sunken city, and of the incredibly aged ruins of nearby Ib, were major links forged in the lengthening chain of knowledge which was slowly bridging the awesome gap between this world and my ultimate destination. And I, bewildered, did not even know where or what that destination was.

For three weeks I wandered the slimy shores of the still lake which hides Sarnath, and at the end of that time, driven by a fearful compulsion, I once again used those unnatural aquatic powers of mine and began exploring beneath the surface of that hideous morass.

That night I slept with a small green figurine, rescued from the sunken ruins, pressed to my bosom. In my dreams I saw my mother and father—but dimly, as if through a mist—and they beckoned to me . . .

The next day I went again to stand in the centuried ruins of Ib, and as I was making ready to leave I saw the inscribed stone which gave me my first real clue. The wonder is that I could *read* what was written on that weathered, aeon-old pillar, for it was written in a curious cuneiform older even than the inscriptions of Geph's broken columns, and it had been pitted by the ravages of time.

It told nothing of the beings who once lived in Ib, or anything of the long-dead inhabitants of Sarnath. It spoke only of the destruction which the men of Sarnath had brought to the beings of Ib—and of the resulting Doom that came to Sarnath. This doom was wrought by the gods of the beings of Ib . . . but of those "Gods" I could likewise learn not a thing. I only knew that reading that stone and being in Ib had stirred long-hidden memories, perhaps even *ancestral* memories, in my mind. Again that feeling of closeness to home, that feeling I always felt so strongly on the moors in Yorkshire, flooded over me. Then, as I idly moved the rushes at the base of the pillar with my foot, yet more chiselled inscriptions appeared. I cleared away the slime and read on. There were only a few lines . . . but those lines contained my clue:

> Ib is gone but the Gods live on. Across the world is the Sister City, hidden in the earth, in the barbarous lands of Zimmeria. There The People flourish yet, and there will the Gods ever be worshipped; even unto the coming of Cthulhu . . .

Many months later in Cairo, I sought out a man steeped in elder lore, a widely acknowledged authority on forbidden antiquities and prehistoric lands and legends. This sage had never heard of Zimmeria, but he did know of a land which had once had a name much similar. "And where did this 'Cimmeria' lie?" I asked.

"Unfortunately," my erudite adviser answered, consulting a chart, "most of Cimmeria now lies beneath the sea. Originally . . . it lay between Vanaheim and Nemedia in ancient Hyborea."

"You say *most* of it is sunken?" I queried. ". . . But what of the land which lies *above* the sea?"

Perhaps it was the eagerness in my voice which caused him to glance at me the way he did. Again, perhaps it was my queer aspect, for the hot suns of many lands had hardened my hairless skin most peculiarly and a strong web now showed between my fingers.

"Why do you wish to know?" he asked. "What is it you are seeking?"

"Home!" I answered instinctively, not knowing what prompted me to say it.

"Yes . . ." he mused, studying me closely. "That might well be . . . You are an Englishman, are you not? Yes? May I enquire from which part?"

"From the north-east," I answered, reminded suddenly of my moors. "Why do you want to know?"

"My friend, you have searched in vain," he smiled. "For Cimmeria, or that which remains of it, encompasses all of that north-eastern part of England which is your homeland. Is it not ironic? In order to find your home you have left it . . ."

That night fate dealt me a card which I could not ignore. In the lobby of my hotel was a table devoted solely to the reading habits of the English-speaking residents. Upon it was a wide variety of books, paperbacks, newspapers, and journals, ranging from *The Reader's Digest* and *Time* to the *News of the World*, and to pass a few hours in relative coolness I sat beneath a soothing fan with a glass of iced water and idly glanced through the pages of one of the newspapers. Abruptly, on turning a page, I came upon a picture and an article, which, when I had scanned the latter through, caused me to book a seat on the next flight to London.

The picture was poorly reproduced but was still clear enough for me to see that it depicted a small, green figurine—*the duplicate of that which I had salvaged from the ruins of Sarnath beneath the still pool . . .*!

The article, as best I can remember, read like this:

"Mr. Samuel Davies, of 17 Heddington Crescent, Radcar, found the beautiful relic of bygone ages pictured above in a stream whose only known source is the cliff face at Sarby-on-the-Moor. The figurine is now in Radcar Museum, having been donated by Mr. Davies, and is being studied by the curator, Prof. Gordon Walmsley of Goole. So far Prof. Walmsley has been unable to throw any light on the figurine's origin but the Wendy-Smith Test, a scientific means of checking the age of archaeological fragments, has shown it to be over ten thousand years old. The green figurine does not appear to have any connection with any of the better-known civilizations of ancient England and is thought to be a find of rare importance. Unfortunately, expert potholers have given unanimous opinions that the stream, where it springs from the cliffs at Sarby, is totally untraversable."

The next day, during the flight, I slept for an hour or so and again, in my dreams, I saw my parents. As before they appeared to me in a mist—but their beckonings were stronger and more *positive* than in that previous dream and in the blanketing vapours around them were strange figures, bowed in seeming obeisance, while a chant of teasing familiarity rang from hidden and nameless throats . . .

I had wired my housekeeper from Cairo informing her of my return, and when I arrived at my house in Marske I found a solicitor waiting for me. This gentleman introduced himself as Mr. Harvey, of the Radcar firm of Harvey, Johnson and Harvey, and presented me with a large sealed envelope. It was addressed to me, in *my father's hand*, and Mr. Harvey informed me his instructions had been to deliver the envelope into my hands on the attainment of my twenty-first birthday. Unfortunately I had been out of the country at the time, almost a year earlier, but the firm had kept in touch with my housekeeper so that on my return the agreement made nearly seven years earlier between my father and Mr. Harvey's firm might be kept.

After Mr. Harvey left I dismissed my woman and opened the envelope. The manuscript within was not in any script I had ever learned at school. This was the language I had seen written on that aeon-old pillar in ancient Ib; nonetheless I knew instinctively that it had been my father's hand which had written the thing. And of course, I could read it as easily as if it were in English. The many and diverse contents of the letter made it, as I have said, more akin to a manuscript in its length, and it is not my purpose to completely reproduce it. That would take too long and the speed with which The First Change is taking place does not permit it. I will merely set down the specially significant points which the letter brought to my attention.

In disbelief I read the first paragraph—but, as I read on, that disbelief soon became a weird amazement, which in turn became a savage joy at the fantastic disclosures revealed by those timeless hieroglyphs of Ib.

My parents were not dead! They had merely gone away; gone home . . .

That time nearly seven years ago, when I had returned home from a school reduced to ruins by the bombing, our London home had been purposely sabotaged by my father. A powerful explosive had been rigged, primed to be set off by the first air-raid siren, and then my parents had gone off in secrecy back to the moors. They had not known, I realized, that I was on my way home from the ruined school where I boarded. Even now they were unaware that I had arrived at the house just as the radar defences of England's military services had picked out those hostile dots in the sky. That plan which had been so carefully laid to fool men into believing that my parents were dead had worked well, but it had also nearly destroyed me! And all this time I, too, had believed them killed. But why had they gone to such extremes? What *was* that secret which it was so necessary to hide from our fellow men—and where were my parents now? I read on . . .

Slowly all was revealed. We were not *indigenous* to England, my parents and I, and they had brought me here as an infant from our homeland, a land quite near yet paradoxically far away. The letter went on to explain how *all* the children of our race are brought here as infants, for the atmosphere of our homeland is not conducive to health in the young and unformed.

The difference in my case had been that my mother was unable to part with me. That was the awful thing! Though all the children of our race must wax and grow up away from their homeland, the elders can only rarely depart from their native clime. This fact is determined by their physical appearance throughout the greater period of their life spans. *For they are not, for the better part of their lives, either the physical or mental counterparts of ordinary men!*

This means that children have to be left on doorsteps, at the entrances of orphanages, in churches, and in other places where they will be found and cared for, for in extreme youth there is little difference between my race and the race of men. As I read I was reminded of those tales of fantasy I had once loved: of ghouls and fairies and other creatures who left their young to be reared by human beings and who stole human children to be brought up in their own likenesses.

Was *that*, then, my destiny? Was I to be a ghoul? I read on.

I learned that the people of my race can only leave our native country twice in their lives: once in youth—when, as I have explained, they are brought here of necessity to be left until they attain the approximate age of twenty-one years—and once in later life, when *changes* in their appearances make them compatible to *outside* conditions. My parents had just reached this latter stage of their development when I was born. Because of my mother's devotion they had forsaken their *duties* in our own land and had brought me personally to England where, ignoring The Laws, they stayed with me. My father had brought certain treasures with him to ensure an easy life for himself and my mother until that time should come when they would be *forced* to leave me—the Time of The Second Change—when to stay would be to alert mankind of our existence.

That time had eventually arrived and they had covered up their departure back to our own, secret land by blowing up our London home, letting the authorities and I (though it must have broken my mother's heart) believe them dead of a German bomb raid.

And how could they have done otherwise? They dared not take the chance of telling me *what I really was*, for who can say what effect such a disclosure might have had on me, I who had barely begun to show my differences? They had to hope I would discover the Secret myself, or at least the greater part of it, which I have done! But to be doubly sure my father left his letter . . .

The letter also told how not many *foundlings* find their way back to their own land. Accidents claim some and others go mad. At this point I was reminded of something I had read somewhere of two inmates of Oakdeene Sanatorium near Glasgow who are so horribly mad *and so unnatural in aspect* that they are not even allowed to be seen and even their nurses cannot abide to stay near them for long.

Yet others become hermits in wild and inaccessible places and, worst of all, still others suffer more hideous fates—and I shuddered as I read what those fates were! But there *were* those few who did manage to get back. These were the lucky ones, those who returned to claim their rights; and while some of them were *guided* back—by adults of the race during second visits—others made it by instinct or luck.

Yet horrible though this overall plan of existence seemed to be, the letter explained its logic. For my homeland could not support many of *my* kind, and those perils of lunacy (as brought on by inexplicable physical changes), accidents, and those *other* fates I have mentioned, act as a system of selection whereby only the fittest in mind and body return to the land of their birth.

But there, I have just finished reading the letter through a second time—having interrupted my hasty scribbling of this document to do so—and already I begin to feel a stiffening of my limbs! My father's manuscript has arrived barely in time. I have long been worried by my growing *differences*. The webbing on my hands now extends almost to the small, first knuckles and my skin is fantastically thick, rough, and ichthyic. The short tail which protrudes from the base of my spine is now not so much an oddity as an *addition*; an extra limb which, in the light of what I now know, is not an oddity at all but the most natural thing in the world! My hairlessness, with the discovery of my destiny, has also ceased to be an embarrassment to me. I am different to men, true, but is that not as it should be? *For I am not a man!*

Ah, the lucky fates which caused me to pick up that newspaper in Cairo! Had I not seen that picture or read that article I might not have returned so soon to my moors . . . and I shudder to think what might have become of me then. What would I have done after The First Change had altered me? Would I have hurried, disguised and wrapped in smothering clothes, to some distant land—there to live the life of a hermit? Perhaps I would have returned to Ib or the Nameless City, to dwell in ruins and solitude until my appearance was again capable of sustaining my existence among men. And what after that—after The Second Change?

Perhaps I would have gone mad at such inexplicable alterations in my person. Who can say but that there might have been another inmate at Oakdeene? On the other hand, my fate might have been worse than all these, for I may have been drawn to dwell in the depths, to be one with the Deep Ones in the worship of Dagon and Great Cthulhu, as have others before me.

But no! By good fortune, by the learning gained on my far journeys and by the help given me by my father's document, I have been spared all those terrors which others of my kind have known. I will return to Ib's Sister City, to Lh-yib, in that land of my birth *beneath* these Yorkshire moors, that land from which was washed the green figurine which guided me back to these shores, that figurine which is the duplicate of the one I raised from beneath the pool at Sarnath. I will return to be worshipped by those whose ancestral brothers died at Ib on the spears of the men of Sarnath, those who are so aptly described on the Brick Cylinders of Kadatheron, those who chant voicelessly in the abyss. I will return to Lh-yib!

For even now I hear my mother's voice, calling me as she did when I was a child and used to wander these very moors: "Bob! Little Bo! Where are you?"

Bo, she used to call me, and would only laugh when I asked her why. But why not? Was Bo not a fitting name? Robert . . . Bob . . . Bo? What odds?

Blind fool that I have been! I never really pondered the fact that my parents were never quite like other people, not even towards the end . . .

Were not my ancestors worshipped in grey-stone Ib before the coming of men, in the earliest days of Earth's evolution? I should have guessed my identity when first I brought that figurine up out of the slime, *for the features of the thing were as my own features will be after The First Change, and engraved upon its base in the ancient letters of Ib—letters I could read because they were part of my native language, the precursor of all languages—was my own name!*

Bokrug:

Water-Lizard God of the people of Ib and Lh-yib, the Sister City!

NOTE:

Sir,

Attached to this manuscript, Annex "A" to my report, was a brief note of explanation addressed to the NECB in Newcastle and reproduced as follows:

Robert Krug
Marske
Yorks.
Evening—19 July 1952

Secretary and Members,
NECB, Newcastle-on-Tyne.
Gentlemen of the North-East Coal Board,

My discovery whilst abroad, in the pages of a popular science magazine, of your Yorkshire Moors Project, scheduled to commence next summer, determined me, upon the culmination of some recent discoveries of mine, to write you this letter.

You will see that my letter is a protest against your

proposals to drill deep into the moors in order to set off underground explosions in the hope of creating pockets of gas to be tapped as part of the country's natural resources. It is quite possible that the undertaking envisioned by your scientific advisors would mean the destruction of two ancient races of sentient life. The prevention of such destruction is that which causes me to break the laws of my race and thus announce the existence of them and their servitors.

In order to explain my protest more fully I think it necessary that I tell my whole story. Perhaps upon reading the enclosed manuscript you will suspend indefinitely your projected operations.

Robert Krug
Sgt. J. T. Miller
Dilham
Yorks.
7 August 1952

POLICE REPORT M-Y-127/52 *Alleged Suicide*

Sir,

I have to report that at Dilham, on 20 July 1952, at about 4:30 P.M., I was on duty at the police station when three children (statements attached at Annex "B") reported to the desk Sgt. that they had seen a "funny man" climb the fence at Devil's Pool, ignoring the warning notices, and throw himself into the stream where it vanishes into the hillside.

Accompanied by the eldest of the children I went to the scene of the alleged occurrence, about three-quarters of a mile over the moors from Dilham, where the spot that the "funny man" allegedly climbed the fence was pointed out to me. There *were* signs that someone had recently gone over the fence: trampled grass and grass-stains on the timbers.

With slight difficulty I climbed the fence myself but was unable to decide whether or not the children had told the truth. There was no evidence in or around the pool to suggest that anyone had thrown himself in, but this is hardly surprising as at that point, where the stream enters the hillside, the water rushes steeply downward into the earth. Once in the water only an extremely strong swimmer would be able to get back out. Three experienced potholers were lost at this same spot in August last year when they attempted a partial reconnoitre of the stream's underground course.

When I further questioned the boy I had taken with me, I was told that a *second* man had been on the scene prior to the incident. This other man had been seen to limp, as though he was hurt, into a nearby cave. This had occurred shortly before the "funny man"—described as being green and having a short, flexible tail—came out of the same cave, went over the fence and threw himself into the pool.

On inspecting the said cave I found what appeared to be an animal hide of some sort, split down the arms and legs and up the belly, in the manner of the trophies of big-game hunters. This object was rolled up neatly in one corner of the cave and is now in the found-property room at the police station in Dilham. Near this hide was a complete set of good-quality gent's clothing, neatly folded and laid down. In the inside pocket of the jacket I found a wallet containing, along with fourteen pounds in one-pound notes, a card bearing the address of a house in Marske; namely, 11 Sunderland Crescent. These articles of clothing, plus the wallet, are also now in the found-property room.

At about 6.30 P.M., I went to the above address in Marske and interviewed the housekeeper, one Mrs. White, who provided me with a statement (attached at Annex "C") in respect of her partial employer, Robert Krug. Mrs. White also gave me two envelopes, one of which contained the manuscript attached to this report at Annex "A." Mrs. White had found this envelope, sealed, with a note asking her to deliver it, when she went to the house on the afternoon of the 20th about half an hour before I arrived. In view of the enquiries I was making and because of their nature, i.e. an investigation into the possible suicide of Mr. Krug, Mrs. White thought it was best that the envelope be given to the police. Apart from this she was at a loss what to do with it because Krug had forgotten to address it. As there was the possibility of the envelope containing a suicide note or dying declaration I accepted it.

The other envelope, which was unsealed, contained a manuscript in a foreign language and is now in the property room at Dilham.

In the two weeks since the alleged suicide, despite all my efforts to trace Robert Krug, no evidence has come to light to support the hope that he may still be alive. This, plus the fact that the clothing found in the cave has since been identified by Mrs. White as being that which Krug was wearing the night before his disappearance, has determined me to request that my report be placed in the "unsolved" file and that Robert Krug be listed as "missing."

NOTE:

Sir,

Do you wish me to send a copy of the manuscript at Annex "A"—as requested of Mrs. White by Krug— to the Secretary of the North-East Coal Board?

Inspector I. L. Ianson
Yorks. County Constabulary
Radcar
Yorks.

Dear Sgt. Miller,

In answer to your note of the 7th. Take no further action on the Krug case. As you suggest, I have had the man posted as missing, believed a suicide. As for his *document*; well, the man was either mentally unbalanced or a monumental hoaxer, possibly a combination of both! Regardless of the fact that certain things in his story are matters of indisputable fact, the majority of the thing appears to be the product of a diseased mind.

Meanwhile I await your progress-report on that other case. I refer to the baby found in the church pews at Eely-on-the-Moor last June. How are you going about tracing the mother?

V

CORRELATION

[From the Notebooks of Professor Ewart Masters]

I left the police station about an hour before midnight, but I was awake until at least three in the morning. My mind was working overtime, so feverishly in fact that sleep—until I had thought on certain things and sorted them out somewhat—was simply out of the question.

The next day I was up at a correspondingly late hour, walking back down to the police station before lunch. My purpose was to ask the duty constable to put me in telephone contact with Inspector Ianson in Radcar—but here a setback. The young policeman seemed quite well informed, and he was able to tell me that two years previously the inspector (apparently a man of substantial independent means) had abruptly quit his job to go off with a woman! The couple were thought to have gone abroad. A pity, because of course Ianson would have been able to tell me what he had meant by "matters of indisputable fact," with regard to Krug's statement.

All right; I would have to find out on my own!

No doubt about it, Krug's document was an astonishing thing, and I was in full agreement with Ianson's assessment; yet for a man I had never previously heard of, this Krug—hoaxer and all—seemed damnably erudite, formidable, in ancient lore. There seemed to be so many parallels between his work and mine. Perhaps we had simply followed similar leads towards our mutual "discovery" of apparently like civilizations in the ancient lands of East and West. And why not? Gordon Walmsley, too, had obviously stumbled across just such leads not long before his oddly circumstanced death.

Certainly many of Krug's source books had been the same as mine—but where could the man possibly have gained his knowledge concerning the *Brick Cylinders of Kadatheron*? And again, this *before* those relics had officially been discovered! This was positively astonishing! Had I slipped up somewhere? Had Angstrom known specifically what he was looking for before he left for the East, and had he publicized the fact? No, I knew and had followed his work too closely for that, and I was perfectly sure that such had not been the case. Oh! I was not infallible. I had missed the original discovery of the moors figurine, true, but that had been pardonable. For some reason the thing had received but a minimum of publicity. Angstrom's expedition had been a different thing entirely.

The deeper I dug the more puzzling the whole thing became. There were in Krug's manuscript, for instance, those references to R'lyeh and Mnar. Now, I had heard of legendary Atlantis, of course, and of fictional Shangri-la, the Land of Eternal Youth—but R'lyeh? And yet the name rang a bell! Yes, and after a moment's thought I knew where I had heard it before. Many years earlier I had been allowed a glimpse—*only* a glimpse—into the *Necronomicon* of the mad Arab Abdul Alhazred in the library at Miskatonic University in America. And something else had stayed in my mind following that peep into those blasphemous pages: for although even in my youth I had never been a frequent dreamer, I remembered having seen horrors in my sleep for many a night after my glance into the pages of that work. The thing that had bothered me so had been Alhazred's vague description of a creature called a Shoggoth, a monstrous thing not bearing studied description. And Walmsley, at some time, must also have seen a copy of the *Necronomicon* somewhere— that much was obvious. He had mentioned "Shoggoth-tissue," in some connection or other, in his death notes.

Then there was that mention of Sarnath. That made twice I had heard of the place: once in the translation from *The Ilarnek Papyri* and again in Krug's document.

Now, I had seen a Sarnath. I had actually walked in the ruins of a Sarnath! But *my* Sarnath and Krug's were two entirely different places! The ruins I knew stood in the Deer Park in Benares, where Buddha preached his first sermon; and they were not, I knew, covered by any leprous, stagnant pool! Nor did *my* ruins exist in two distinctly separate units, as Krug had suggested with his "nearby Ib" statement. Besides, he had quite clearly stated that "no man knows the whereabouts of Sarnath," which was perhaps simply his way of saying that no such place as *his* city had ever existed! On the other hand, his reconstruction of the newspaper article—regarding the discovery of the moors figurine and its subsequent donation to the museum—was perfectly authentic. His mention of "Cthulhu," too, was something from the *Necronomicon*, but Cthulhu's aeon-extinct cult was not a thing I knew a great deal about; I had always preferred to keep my researches and studies within the realms of possibility. Still, it went to show how remarkably well read the man had been in this sort of thing.

Now, I have said I agreed with Inspector Ianson's assessment of Krug as a madman; yet for the life of me I could not see why he had taken so negative an attitude. Would there have been any serious harm in sending the NECB a copy of Krug's so-called "statement?" And for that matter, the inspector must have been a singularly short-sighted man not to have seen a sinister and rather ominous link between the Krug case and that other he had mentioned—that of the abandoned baby found in the church pews at Eeley. But no, on second thought that was unfair. Each to his own game, and a man holding so high a position in the police force is no fool. The fault was mine in that here I was trying to read significance into insignificant data, data of quite unproven relevance. Nonetheless I would dearly have loved to see that manuscript in "a foreign language" mentioned by Sgt. Miller in his report, but apparently the thing had been lost. Similarly the "animal hide" had also disappeared in the half-dozen years since its discovery in the cave near Devil's Pool.

That brings me up to date in my notes. There are many tangled skeins here, and I promise myself that later I shall look to the unravelling of the more obscure and uncertain matters brought to light by my reading of the Krug case, not the least of them being that mention of certain inmates at Oakdeene! But for the moment, that will have to wait . . .

VI

DEVIL'S POOL
[The Masters Case:
from the Recordings of Dr. Eugene T. Thappon]

First thing the next morning I drove out to Dilham and from the village proper made my way on foot across the moors to the fenced-off area at the base of a line of steep hills called Ellison's Heights.

There, behind a tall, semicircular curve of warning fencing, swirled the treacherous waters of Devil's Pool. The pool marked in fact the end of the surface route of an unimportant outlet of the River Swale. But the quiet waters of the rivulet seemed to gather strength as they approached and passed beneath the fencing, swelling and surging forward, gradually commencing the circular movements which terminated in the unknown sucking vortex of the whirlpool at the foot of the hills.

Devil's Pool, into which—if there was anything at all in the strange manuscript I had read—one Robert Krug, madman, had plunged himself in the lunatic belief that he was a "God" returning to his rightful seat beneath the moors. Devil's Pool, beneath which, at some watery, lightless place, lay the lost remains of three professional speleologists who had vainly tried—using aqualungs and all the usual paraphernalia of the caver—to map the underground path of the disappearing stream.

I ignored the warning notices pasted to the high fence, and not without a deal of difficulty climbed it to have a closer look at the pool. The blackly swirling water reminded me greatly of a huge gramophone record on a massive turntable, spinning half out in the open, half gurgling away beneath the undermined face of the steep hill, and I found myself strangely disturbed by its almost mesmeric motion.

An ominous place, this—a jumping-off place from the comparative congeniality of the moors into the dank darkness of ancient stygia . . .

Suddenly there flashed into my mind something I saw as being particularly relevant yet at the same time paradoxically obscure: some lines by E. P. Derby, from his book of nightmare lyrics, *Azathoth and Other Horrors.*

> *. . . for cleverer Gods by far*
> *dream 'neath the moorland moss;*
> *Whose kin the night-things are,*
> *who scorn the Christ-Child's cross;*
> *Who journeyed from afar*
> *when earth was young and gross*
> *Whose ken is on a par*
> *with Daemon Azathoth's . . .*
> *Who fear the Pentik Star . . . !*

These lines had no sooner passed before my mind's eye than I found myself reeling helplessly at the edge of the rushing waters, tottering on the brink of the known world, and I flailed desperately with my arms as the foreign entity which had been my mind spun me dizzily away into vortices of its own conjuring . . .

VII

UNDERGROUND: DREAM-PHASE ONE

[The Masters Case: from the Recordings of Dr. Eugene T. Thappon]

I do not know how long the attack lasted. I think I must have gone straight from the pool back to Dilham for the car, and from there to Bleakstone, but I cannot be sure. I seem to remember walking—certainly some sort of physical movement—and a terrible fear, but of what I am likewise incapable of saying. The thought is indeed a fearsome one that I actually *drove* my nephew's car during that phase of mental instability; yet it seems I must have done so. Certainly there later remained a picture in my mind of taking a drink in the bar of The George and of talking with the barman again about the figurine, but no more than that . . .

If I had thought my dreams of the first night at The George protracted and strange, what was I to make of those which were yet to come? The trouble was that this time there was no dividing line, no passage from the waking world into that of dream, so that I could not *really* tell if what next occurred was in fact a long-drawn-out dream or simply an extension of the lapse that began at Devil's Pool—that lapse which was nothing less than the harbinger of my brain's rapidly advancing deterioration.

I had suddenly found myself in nighted, chill, and rushing waters! I had not even attempted to swim. Up-rushing currents had kept me on the surface of the water, bobbing me along like a cork down a rain-washed gutter; and though I had taken in an incredible amount of water my lungs still functioned, and I knew that my stomach, in normal reaction to my near-drowning, had been at work for a long time pumping its unwanted contents back into a crooning, unseen stream from which I must somehow have dragged myself.

There had been dank darkness, suffocating silence, the deafness of unconsciousness . . . then water sounds, whispering wetness, the cold gurglings of ancient, weirdly articulate subterranean sumps. It was completely real . . . the black blindness, the lingering lightlessness, the almost amorous, caressing amaurosis . . .

And then I knew that I was underground . . . beneath the moors!

But in fact my prison was not the place of utter darkness I first thought it; for while on coming to my senses (is the expression pardonable?) the blackness had seemed complete, after a while, as my eyes gradually grew accustomed to the deep gloom, I made out high above me what appeared to be a pinprick of light, and it was purely by token of that unknown, crevicelike entry in some equally unknown gorge on the wild moors that my underground prison had any light at all. That thin, filtered glimmer groping down from the safe, sane world above, possibly saved me in my first "conscious" moments from panic and madness.

My position was straight from Poe, yet to me infinitely worse than any premature burial, for a man entombed in a coffin at least knows the extent of his prison and must soon mercifully suffocate; but a man lost underground in limitless depths, yet with ample air and water, might linger on for weeks in a slow torture of starvation and stygian horror!

That minimum of God's light, sent down through what might have been light-years from the high hole in the roof of the cavern, gave my eyes at least something to cling to, and my mind a point on which to conjecture. I suppose I must have "slept" through that first night, for I remember seeing the friendly, dim point of light slowly fade until the darkness was truly complete, and then no more until quite suddenly I found myself "awake," conscious, and with a gnawing hunger inside me.

I *had* slept within my sleep obviously, for again I had known dreams within dreams, and they had been quite as mad as those I had experienced previously at Bleakstone. There had been crooning voices, or at least sounds, noises made by living things at any rate (or were they simply disturbances on the invisible ether of my mind?) which had left me with impressions of great mystery and age, of limitless alienage, of an antiquity beyond conjecture, and an almost supernatural holiness akin to that feeling in the heart—more an ethereal than a physical thing—which one knows when listening to the reverberating echoes of a powerful choir within the sounding walls of a great cathedral.

These voices had at first seemed to be far away, in time as well as space, but they had drifted closer, ululant and throbbing until the stagnant air of my hole in the earth had seemed vibrant with their chanting . . . and then they had ceased. I had known the momentary fumblings of strange hands—or paws—and had felt upon me the scrutiny of eyes unlike the eyes of men.

No lights had illuminated my visitors, yet I had known and recognized them—those habitants of Ib and Lh-yib, those minions of Bokrug—and then, even dreaming, I had been doubly sure I *only* dreamed, for nothing like these creatures of Earth's youth could possibly remain extant anywhere in the normal waking world. Eventually I had been left alone again to my exhausted slumbers, and thus it remained until I awoke.

I say "I awoke," and yet I simply moved from one level of nightmare to another, for outside, high above, it was "day" again, and the friendly beam once more was flickering down to me in my cold stone prison. And in that prison, cold and hungry, I was as far removed as ever from my comfortable room at The George.

It was hunger that prompted me to drag my cramped body from the stream side, to stumble near-blind about the confines of my great coffin.

"Coffin," indeed! When first I found the mushrooms I was so

lost in morbid reverie, a reverie completely in keeping with the chill damp of the place, that I thought they were great grave worms— fat, white, and squamous—waiting for my flesh to die. But the fatness was only their lush depth, and the scales were not scales but the mottling of the pileus-covered domes.

I ate some of them, ravenously, and then I "slept" once more . . .

VIII

BOKRUG: DREAM-PHASE TWO
[The Masters Case:
from the Recordings of Dr. Eugene T. Thappon]

The period of comparative lucidity—if a *condition* such as I was in may be couched in any such terms—in which I eventually found myself following my meal of mushrooms in the cave of the stream was one that I found completely contrary to any previously conceived ideas of mine concerning delusions or dream-obsessions. Of the fact that the condition was psychotic, there could be little doubt, and yet everything had a quality to it of the real and solid. There was none of the fuzziness of dream or nightmare to the edges of the clearly defined visions I saw, none of fever's repetitious phrasing of words and sentences in conversation (oh, yes, this latter still to come!) and when I moved, each motion I made produced a corresponding ache in those areas of my body bruised by my whirling dream-rush through heaven-only-knows what distances of subterranean waterway and by my blundering about the cave. And yet the things I saw, heard, and felt—indeed all my sensations throughout that odd period—were certainly fantasies and figments of my own disorganized mental processes. In short, I *was* still dreaming . . . and my condition was rapidly worsening!

But more of that later. It would be best if I relate my experiences as they happened, in order to correctly define the magnitude of my fantasy.

My first impression was one of lying on my back in the lumpy loam of the fungus patch from which I had eaten and of seeing in the near-distant darkness a glowing luminosity expanding or pulsating towards me. This vision was accompanied by an ululation, muted by distance, as of voices raised in praise, reminiscent of the prayerlike yet sepulchral sounds I had thought to hear in my semiconsciousness before I first "awoke" to the confines of the dark cave.

As the eerie noises faded so the glowing light, now assuming a spherical shape some seven feet above the floor of the cave, further approached, and as it emerged it lit up the entrance to the narrow tunnel along which it had come. *It also illuminated the creature pacing beneath it!*

I jerked bolt upright at sight of the thing, the short hairs on the back of my neck springing to attention, my scalp tingling, my unbelieving eyes taking in the whole of that alien yet strangely regal being!

Oh! I had seen likenesses of this creature before—but *only* likenesses! This was the living, breathing reality (or so my ruined senses would have had me believe), a walking, man-sized replica of the greenstone figurines! In fact, this was Bokrug—water-lizard god of Ib—reptilian lord of a city lost in the dim mists of time!

It kneeled before me, its short tail balancing it solidly in a posture that reminded me of certain Eastern idols, and the piercingly bright eyes in the thin-lipped, hairless face regarded me unemotionally. For a moment the thing sat there silently while I lay, propped up on my elbows, shivering uncontrollably. Then, amazingly, it spoke:

"You need not fear me, I mean you no harm."

"Bokrug!" I whispered, at a loss for words, at which the creature sat up straighter, an almost human frown visibly forming to crease its high forehead.

"You . . . *know* me?"

Suddenly it dawned on me that my conversation was with a creature of my own imaginings, a figment of nightmare and of my sadly impaired senses. I laughed out loud and fell back weakly on my bed of mushrooms, staring up at that alien face and the halo of moving light in which it was framed.

"I know you, yes—you're a little green god in a case at Radcar Museum—you're a figurine in the police station at Bleakstone. Oh, I know you all right! You're an hallucination within a dream— you're my injured brain rotting inside my head!" I flapped my hands uselessly, scrabbling at the loam about me.

On hearing my manner of expression and my mention of the museum, the frown vanished immediately from the creature's face. "You are a man of science then?"

For a while longer I lay there, thinking at first to ignore the hallucination, to let myself drift back into sleep within sleep. But then, as if in defiance of my own lassitude, I spoke:

"What I am makes no difference; I shall soon wake up back in The George at Bleakstone—or remain in this dream till they find me and take me off to some sanatorium or other to rot! You don't exist—and therefore you can't help me. Go away."

I closed my eyes, resting my aching head back in the spongy loam. A second or so passed and then I felt the pressure of powerful but gentle hands pushing under my legs and shoulders. My head fell back and I let my arms droop listlessly as I was hoisted bodily up into the air. Then, feeling the smooth movements of the crea- ture's walking, I opened my eyes again.

"Where are you taking me?"

The piercing eyes gazed back at me for a moment in a kind of cold compassion. "There is a place where you will be more com- fortable—where food other than mushrooms alone, though not of great variety, can be brought to you—where you might live out the rest of your days less lonely than here. For there I shall visit you frequently, and I will tell you of this place while you, in return, can

freshen for me the memory of your own world. But now be quiet.
You are not well. Cold, hunger, and exhaustion have taken their toll
of you. Rest easy while we go, that I might inform you of some
things you should know . . ."

I closed my eyes again then, laughing weakly and mumbling in
my delirium. "My God!—to hold a conversation with a dream—to
receive succour from a vision . . ." Then an idea occurred to me.
"Are we going to Lh-yib?"

For a second the creature paused and the gently flowing motion
of my body through air ceased. I kept my eyes closed.

"You are a very learned man," the voice slowly said. "Yes, we
are going to Lh-yib . . . but understand, that city is forbidden to you.
Only the Thuun'ha and others—that is, others of *my* kind—dwell
there. You will see the city from on high, but never try to regain its
ramparts once we have crossed them over. The Thuun'ha would
destroy you, for your likeness is as the likeness of those who dwelt
in Sarnath . . . and the men of Sarnath knew no descendants . . ."

IX

THE CREATURE'S STORY: DREAM-PHASE THREE

[The Masters Case:
from the Recordings of Dr. Eugene T. Thappon]

"When this world was young—" the thing called Bokrug presently
told me, striding with me in his arms effortlessly down that corridor
along which I had seen his approach, "—my ancestors and their
servitors the Thuun'ha came from their own dying world to settle
here . . ."

"I know!" I said, breaking in deliriously on the being's narrative:
"*Lo, they came down from the Moon one Night in a Mist; lo, they*

and the Lake and Ib; and there did they worship Bokrug, the great Water-Lizard . . ."

"Yes, that is how the coming was seen by certain primitives of the time, but in fact those ancestors did not come from the moon," he corrected me. "No, they came from far beyond the moon. Their journey had been long and they knew that to begin their civilization again here in this new world would be hard. The plan was to settle in two regions, one in the east of this planet and the other toward the west. So Ib was raised in the eastern deserts, at a place where the instruments of my race told of vast amounts of water below the sands, and Lh-yib, the Sister City, was planned to be built at the place where the moors now grow wild and desolate above.

"But while the building of Ib was easy, with none but a handful of wandering, apelike tribesmen ever stumbling over its location in the great desert, the construction of Lh-yib presented serious problems. For one thing the land here was fertile, where already ferocious warrior clans warred to fence in and domesticate the mammoth—clans that later divided the land and gave their holdings names such as Nathis, Cimmeria, and Gun-hlan—and it was seen that these peoples, particularly the early Cimmerians, who were true barbarians, would not allow such as my ancestors and the Thuun'ha to remain unmolested in anything other than a fortress; and those fathers of my race on Earth were not disposed to build a garrison of that sort. Then the instruments of those ancestors discovered for them far underground a series of tremendous caves and hollows, carved by time and capable of supporting—not without certain difficulties—our civilization. And thus was Lh-yib eventually built down here away from the sun, and the surface lands were left to be ruined by the grazing mammoth and the warring clans . . ."

At this point in his tale Bokrug paused, coming to a halt in a part of the tunnel that he obviously recognized. There he directed me to look at something resting upon a natural ledge worn in the side of the passage. At first I had difficulty making out what the thing was, but as the cloud of fire about my doubtful rescuer's head descended to the level of the ledge, I saw that the object of the lizard-thing's interest was a rotting harness with twin air bottles and an arrangement of valves—an aqualung, as used by ocean divers and certain daring speleologists.

"You are not the first of your kind to find the way to Lh-yib," the creature told me. "Others were here before you . . ."

I thought back on the report I had read in the police station at Bleakstone—of those cavers who had tried to navigate the rushing waters of Devil's Pool—and I shuddered . . .

Tirelessly the creature then commenced once more to stride out, and I lay back again to listen as he continued the story of the history of his race:

". . . But while Lh-yib has lain safe here in the bowels of Earth for twenty thousand years, Ib, in its eastern desert, suffered destruction in less than half that time, at the hands of an Arab race that settled on the farther shore of the lake which my ancestors had forced from the desert's depths. My peoples foresaw the massacre, taking steps to visit revenge on their prematurely triumphant murderers—and a doom came to the city of Sarnath such as no doom ever before known in all the lands of men. Now Lh-yib is the last seat of my race, and I and my brothers and our servants are faced with a different problem, one which threatens to swallow us even as Ib was swallowed by those doomed men of Sarnath.

"For even now men of the surface world—of your own kind— plan the drilling of great wells in the moors, and we fear that such interference may well bring about cataclysms which we could not hope to survive. They search for gasses and oils, your brothers, little knowing that an ancient and honourable civilization flourishes here in these caves of rock. It is fortunate indeed for your surface-dwelling brothers that our original sciences are all but forgotten . . .

"Though I once tried, I have since seen the futility of attempting to beg a cessation of such experimental drilling for even were it presented with irrefutable proofs, your race is so narrow-minded as to refuse them; and if your peoples *could* be convinced . . . then such convictions would only make them ambitious of learning Lh-yib's secrets.

"As our ancestors in distant, ancient Ib waited for the destruction they knew was coming, so must we wait in Lh-yib; yet there is still hope that the plans of your brothers on the surface might be abandoned. That would be a blessing.

"But there, soon we shall come to the Sister City! Can you walk now? If so then follow close behind me and do not speak; it is not seemly that I should be heard conversing with one such as you, nor would it be right for a god to be seen slavishly bearing in his arms a creature moulded in the likeness of Ib's ancient foes."

As the creature spoke he lowered me to my feet. I looked ahead—beyond the being called Bokrug and along the tunnel to where a light faintly showed—then followed closely in his tracks as he made for that light.

The darkness quickly dispersed, so that soon even the glowing halo over the lizard-thing's head dimmed and seemed to vanish . . .

X

LH-YIB: DREAM-PHASE FOUR
[The Masters Case:
from the Recordings of Dr. Eugene T. Thappon]

Stumbling closely on Bokrug's heels, I emerged from the tunnel onto a tremendous, steeply terraced escarpment overlooking a cavern whose proportions were quite literally unbelievable. My first sight of the fantastic city beneath the moors was breathtaking. In one instant I thought of Pellucidar, of Mu and drowned Atlantis before those places sank, and of a dozen other such fabled cities of myth and fancy, yet could find little in anything I had read to compare with this!

When I say "first sight," I do not wish to convey the idea of that sight coming to me *immediately* after I left the tunnel; no, for at first I was blinded by the brilliance of a light so bright in comparison with that darkness in the cave of the mushrooms as to make me certain that I had somehow been miraculously transported back to the waking, surface world. But then, as my eyes grew more accustomed to the glare, I saw that this was not so, and even the wonders of the city itself could not fully hold my eye as I surveyed in awe the immensity of the domed cave wherein that city reared its towers and parapets.

It was as if I stood on the steps of an amphitheatre of the gods. Behind me, to right and left, great tiers of stone-hewn slabs sloped up and back, steplike, to a height of at lest two hundred feet, there to join with the towering, inward-curving higher walls; and in front, reaching forward and steeply down, those same steps—broken here and there by stone-balustraded balconies and wide, sweeping landings—plunged another two hundred feet to a great floor that must have been all of a mile across.

Spanning this subterranean vista, stretching in what seemed to me a rather precarious splendour, great grey bridges arched from wall to terraced wall, some of them obviously wrought by nature, others—grafted in places to enormous stalactites depending from the dizzy ceiling—plainly artificial though of unknown architecture.

The centerpiece of this awesome scene was nothing less than fantastic. What could only be the world's greatest stalactite hung from the apex of the titan-spiked ceiling, meeting with an upthrusting stalagmite of equally tremendous proportions looming from the center of the city itself. Even at the "narrow" point where these two primeval pillars met, the diameter of the column they formed could have been no less than one hundred feet, and all the way up the length of that vast column—adorning its vertiginous sides—lines of small, square-cut windows peeped out from behind supported balconies, showing that even within that phenomenal freak of nature lesser builders had been at work . . .

The city itself was of grey stone, with tall, narrow buildings and spires, many of them forming supports for the spindly looking bridges, rearing dizzily up towards the cavern roof. Smaller bridges cojoined many of those buildings, with jutting balconies defying gravity at every hand, and from each edifice small windows looked out over the city in general.

One structure stood quite apart from the city proper: a great pyramidal thing, drawing my eye in wonder of its purpose. A small stream passed under the base of the strangely enigmatic pyramid, to wander unrestricted—yet altered in colour to a deep green— from that place and across the plain to a spot where it vanished into the wall at the right of the cavern.

I traced the streamlet back from the building to its source, see- ing that it sprang from high in the step-hewn wall to my left, down a concourse cut to contain its flow, to the plain below. Even as I watched, silver fish leapt in the sparkling water plunging down the steep channel. I stared again at the great pyramid.

"The Place of Worship!" the lizard-thing said, as if reading my thoughts. "Come."

He led me to the right and upwards, climbing the steps until the arched tunnel of entry lay below, then made for one of the natural bridges whose nearest root stemmed from the perpendicular wall some three hundred yards away. From what I could see at that distance, no steps led up to the bridge's broad back, yet I seemed to sense that Bokrug intended we should cross the cavern by that means. Also, the bridge, unlike many of the others, had no parapets that I could see, and, hastily scanning its length, I saw with alarm that it narrowed frighteningly toward its centre!

Now, the creature leading me on might well have the agility of a mountain goat and an equally unshakable balance, I did not know . . . but *I* simply did not have a head for heights. Indeed, the mere *thought* of a fall from that dizzy aerial pathway, through over three hundred feet of thin air to the spires or streets of the greystone city below, was one which made my stomach turn over!

However, I relaxed somewhat as we passed over a wide landing and began to descend the steps, until, with the curve of the fearsome bridge looming fifty feet above us, we again made a turn to the right. There, cut back into the stone, another tunnel led into darkness.

Once more I was reduced to stumbling in the wake of that halo of alien light marking the lizard-thing's route, but after many rising, spiralling turns and twists, we settled down to a straight if somewhat upward course which somehow filled me with an odd uneasiness. True, my sense of direction had never been reliable (and, taking into account the winding path I had followed in the darkness, that sense might now safely be reckoned to be knocked even more out of phase), yet I could not rid myself of the crazy idea that this new direction in which we headed *lay straight out over the city-floored abyss!* I put this unfounded—indeed, impossible—notion away in the face of other, more puzzling problems.

Somehow it came quite naturally to me to question the strange figure of my own dreams and imaginings now striding out so, well, *positively* along the narrow, climbing corridor in front of me: "How is it that Lh-yib has daylight—or whatever light it is? What's the source?" The answer came back immediately:

"The atmosphere of the great cave is filled—tenuously, so as not to be blinding—with a living, gaseous, light-producing organism—the same . . . *material* . . . that my brothers and I wear above our heads in individual provision of light. An example is the nimbus which lights our path now!"

"*One* organism?" I questioned, puzzled by this apparent blunder of my divided, yet until now ordered even in division, psyche.

"Yes, one organism—and yet many! Polypous, you might say.

It is a by-product of an experiment performed by a great race even before we and the Thuun'ha came to Earth, and we, like that race before us, have learned to harness it to our own needs. Not that the Thuun'ha require light—they are equally at home in the dark— but we have lighted their city even as Ib flourished in the natural light of its eastern oasis, as a monument to that long-dead seat of worship . . ."

"*Their* city? Then Lh-yib belongs to the Thuun'ha?"

"Certainly—did Thor dwell in Oslo, or Tanwahi in Atlantis? The city is of little real use to us, except to provide the Thuun'ha a basis for their worship. They believe us to be gods; have done so—in this world and others—for hundreds of thousands of years. We have no wish that it should be otherwise."

"A million-year confidence trick—" I mused out loud. "How do you carry it off?"

As I said this the illumined, greenly silhouetted creature quickly turned on me. He was frowning and his eyes glittered angrily. In that moment, dream or none, I knew that I was in the presence of a life-form far superior in every way.

"The Thuun'ha need us to no less a degree than your primitive forbears required their sun gods. We are to them, in their limited spheres, as great a source of inspiration as have been and are the great deities of Earth to your species. Without their water-lizard gods they would have nothing to live for, and conversely, what is a god without his worshippers? We supply one another our needs. It is sufficient . . ." Without more ado he turned and again took up the eerie march along the gradually rising corridor.

More questions surged into my mind, demanding answers, but I held them back for the moment lest I perhaps further infringe on the lizard-thing's congeniality. In any case I was somewhat distracted, had been for some little time, by a steadily increasing visibility in the tunnel hinting of an early emergence. Indeed only a little way further, when we had covered perhaps one-third of a mile on our straight, rising course, we came to a flight of a dozen or so rough-hewn steps leading up to an open, lighted area. It was only on mounting those steps that I knew the truth—that for once my meagre sense of direction had not led me astray!

I saw immediately that we were still in the great cavern (to both sides magnificent depending stalactites merged with soaring, windowed spires of rock or precariously arching bridges), but the *proximity* of the weirdly adorned ceiling and the *level* at which I surveyed those topmost ramparts of the city could bring only one vertigo-inducing conclusion!

We were standing on the back of that great natural bridge I had feared to cross—and the tunnel behind us had been carved through the solid rock of the wider root of that span . . .

A narrow, shallow, groovelike track, no more than two feet in width by six inches deep, had been cut down the centre of the bridge's upper surface as a basic pathway, but not even a handrail guarded the naked edges of that path. And looking further ahead, maybe two hundred yards to the centre of the span proper, I could see that the width of the entire structure narrowed to no more than six feet or so, with the sides of the bridge falling away in a steep curve from the rudimentary walkway to the empty air beneath!

Why, crossing that section of the span, one would be able to look down at a steep angle onto the buildings almost directly below! Vertigo grabbed me then, squeezing me tight in its trembling fist, causing a momentary return of the rushing, tumbling sensation I had known at Devil's Pool, and I went shakily to my knees in sick protestation.

Down there, crouching on the solid stone, where the edges of the bridge did not seem quite so close, my head cleared quickly and the roaring went out of my ears. I looked up. Bokrug was staring at me in strange, cold concern. From where I knelt he was silhouetted against a stark background of stalactites, seeming for all the world to be standing on a great rough tongue within a mighty mouth of teeth about to snap shut. I shook my head weakly: "I *can't* go across there!"

"Close your eyes and offer no resistance. I will carry you," the creature told me. "It will only be for a minute or so, then you should be able to walk the rest of the way . . ."

"*No!*—no, I can't . . ." I babbled unashamedly, backing away on all fours. The lizard-thing took four quick steps toward me, flat hands reaching out—

There came an enormous blackness . . . in which I drifted free . . . awash in soothing anaesthesia . . .

I do not know what the creature did to me, but whatever it was I came out of it far too soon. At first I stayed quite still, fearing the result of any unexpected activity on my part, for the supple, swaying motions I felt beneath me made it obvious that Bokrug was as good as his word. He was carrying me across the yawning abyss, over that narrow strip of nature-carved rock! Then sensing a tightening of his grip on me and believing myself about to be sat down, I opened my eyes—

Fortunately the sight froze me rigid, for the consequence of any movement I might have made at that instant was unthinkable. I was being carried in the "fireman's lift" position, slumped across the green creature's back face down—yet my very first thought was that I was actually free and falling! For though at this, its thinnest point, the bridge must have been somewhat wider and sturdier than I had at first calculated, it had plainly been worked upon in anticipation of a grafting with some planned building—and I gazed in pure horror straight through the two-foot-square jointing hole cut *vertically* through its thickness, down at the points of the spires below and farther yet . . . to the narrow streets of the Sister City!

I do not believe I closed my eyes; there was no need, no time; in fact in a single instant there was . . . nothing! My mind seemed simply to shut down—went, as it were, into neutral . . .

My next—conscious?—thought, came when I felt my face being

slapped by the flat, firm fingers of the green dream-being. I put up my hands to protect myself and the universal blur which everything was slowly cleared, outlines sharpening, until my vision—and apparently my other senses—returned to normal.

I found myself slumped at the edge of a wide landing, with the amphitheatrelike steps of the great cavern's outer perimeter marching down from my position to the plain and the city below. Nearby, the natural bridge flung its fearsome arm out over those hideous heights which Bokrug had somehow crossed with me across his shoulders. I shuddered involuntarily as I saw again in my mind's eye the sight I had seen through that hole in the bridge.

Then, detecting an impatience in my weird companion's attitude, I managed to sit up. "A few minutes more and I'll be all right," I said, but the weakness of my voice belied its message.

"That is as well, for it will soon be the Time of the Mist," the creature told me. "You must not be here when that time comes. For then the cavern fills with fumes which to you would be poisonous, but they are necessary to the well-being of the Thuun'ha."

"The Thuun'ha! You keep mentioning them—and you say Lhyib is their city—yet so far I haven't had a glimpse of any other single living thing . . . not even there!" I pointed down the steps and across the plain to the Sister City. "Just where are the . . . the Thuun'ha?"

"They are at worship; it is the Time. But soon it will be the Time of the Mist. Now, can you walk? Then come."

I climbed unsteadily to my feet. "I can try to walk! Lead on."

"Good."

He led off then, fairly loping up the steps to the left in what I took to be unnecessary haste, heading for a dark entrance cut into the vertical rock face at the rear of the next landing up. I followed stumblingly, my legs weak, wearily climbing to the landing where Bokrug had paused to wait beneath the arch of the tunnel.

I had only a few more yards to cover across that flat space when

I saw the creature's posture alter. His interest—not in me but in something behind me, something down on the floor of the cavern—quickened, and for a moment he stared intently. Then he beckoned urgently, indicating that I should join him without delay.

"Come," he called, "—come *quickly!*"

I glanced back over my shoulder, turning to see better, when my attention was drawn to the pyramidlike building and its stream. In fact it was the stream primarily that caught my eye. From its bubbling source high in the wall of the cavern to the pyramid it ran and sparkled as before, but beyond that building its bed lay exposed and already drying.

And then I saw something else. From previously unnoticed holes in the apex of that strange pointed structure, a thick green mist was billowing silently out, rolling down the four smooth sides and rapidly blanketing the plain in all directions. In no more than ten seconds the mist had spread to the outermost buildings of the city, while in the other direction it already eddied about the feet of the curving perimeter steps.

A few seconds more saw Lh-yib's lower quarters completely swallowed, with the green mist billowing about the foot of the steps directly beneath my vantage point. I knew I should do as Bokrug had bade me and go into the opening to join him there, but somehow those curling, rapidly flowing tendrils of green had me utterly hypnotized; I seemed to be pinned to the landing, with feet of lead, incapable of movement! The mist swept eerily upward, reaching for me—and then Bokrug's arms closed about my waist, lifting me bodily and sweeping me into the tunnel in the wall of rock.

From perhaps twenty yards within that gloomy entrance we paused to look back, and there, where the tunnel opened into the cavern, an opaque green wall swirled threateningly, oddly luminous, mysteriously deadly.

"You see?" Bokrug said simply. "It is the Time of the Mist." He pointed at the swirling wall of green. "Fortunately for you, at times such as this, the tunnels are made to breathe outwardly, so that the mist may not penetrate within them. Can you not even now feel the breathing of the tunnel?"

As he voiced his question I could indeed feel a rising breeze issuing from the unknown caves in the rock, and with this refreshing wind there came a sound, a throbbing, ululant echo, beautifully melodious yet utterly weird in its evocation of an alien choir, and I looked enquiringly, apprehensively, at the lizard-thing.

"The Thuun'ha," he answered my unspoken question. "They offer their thanks, their praise, for the provision of the Mist of Life. As it was in Ib, so is it in Lh-yib, the Sister City!"

For a few moments longer the green creature stood there at my side, watching the silently swirling mist and listening to those ethereal "songs"; then, without another word, he turned and set off again, beckoning for me to follow.

Suddenly I felt completely fatigued and leaned myself against the wall of the tunnel. When only the strange halo showed, bobbing eerily away from me through the near-distant darkness, I managed to rouse myself from my weary torpor to follow as quickly as my leaden limbs would allow . . .

We covered most of the rest of the way—about a mile as I judged it, on a slightly downward course—without further talk, the silence only being broken when we came to a large, obviously artificial gallery. There I was led past a number of strangely inscribed tunnel entrances—and cautioned against ever attempting their exploration! I was ordered to shun one hole in particular, with the lizard-thing offering vague but dark hints of grim retribution should I ever disobey.

My only desire by then was to sleep (I was genuinely, terribly fatigued even knowing myself to be already asleep) and I did not bother myself to answer. Indeed, my weariness was such as to make me incapable of total comprehension, so that when finally my grotesque guide ushered me beneath one of the gallery's archways, informing me that the cave within was to be my own personal quarter, I was only too pleased to sink down there and then in the darkness of Bokrug's departure to pass almost immediately into deep, still slumbers within slumbers . . .

XI

REFLECTIONS IN A NEW ENVIRONMENT: DREAM-PHASE FIVE

[The Masters Case: from the Recordings of Dr. Eugene T. Thappon]

It is somehow hard for me now to try to describe my new "home" in that strange cave leading off from the great gallery. There is a hazy patch in this particular area of my memory, which, like the haze that follows close on more orthodox dreams, threatens to blot out the sequence entirely. I remember that lining the walls there were diversely shaped, handy-sized patches of oddly resilient, fibrous, blossomless heather, of remarkably regular surfaces apparently grown by nature to furnish beds, tables, and chairs as proper-seeming and as comfortable to me as any I had known in the waking world.

I found myself on one of those "beds" on rising from my exhausted sleep within that greater sleep, and if I had had any doubts whatsoever before of the fact that I was only dreaming or suffering incredibly detailed hallucinations, well, such doubts had obviously been unfounded. I knew this as soon as I saw the firefly cloud hovering with luminous familiarity above my head and lighting up in subdued but almost friendly phosphorescence all but the most secret corners of my cave. I had somehow "acquired" a halo, exactly similar to that possessed by my Bokrug archetype.

Subsequent exploration led me to the discovery in a smaller adjoining cave of a pool of crystal water lying in a smooth-lined basin of stalagmitic rock. This basin had been formed by the constant dripping of water from the tip of one lone stalactite in the middle of the low ceiling. I remember how at first sight of the pool, with my face mirrored darkly in a patch of reflected firefly light, I became aware of yet another progression of my fantastic dreamstate. For I had a beard and moustache, and I found it amazing that my mind could so "rationalize" as to create for me these "natural" alterations in my dream-physiognomy. Likewise my clothes were soiled and tattered and I had lost my shoes. I remembered having had my shoes in that earlier part of the sequence at the cave of the mushrooms. And all this, I conjectured, was but the delirious fruit of my fever, while, in all probability, I was still asleep at The George or, at worst, motionless on some specialist's couch in Harley Street—"in a condition of extreme shock and nervous exhaustion . . ."

Further exploration only went to substantiate the *extent* of my mental degeneration, for even natural body functions had not been overlooked in the great hallucination, and I found a small-mouthed pit with a raised rim—looking like a small crater or blowhole—in that corner of the main cave most removed from the resilient beds of etiolated heather. So . . . I could wash and answer the calls of nature . . . but what of food? The lizard-thing had said I would be brought food, and having checked my cave over and discovered all there was to know of it, suddenly I found myself hungry.

I believe that it was while I was taking my first wash in the oddly warm water of the rock-basin that I sensed a *presence* in the main cave. By the time I returned through the low, natural doorway to my "living-room," my visitor—whoever or *whatever*—had gone, but resting upon one of the higher, flat-topped, heatherlike clumps of growth I found a laden platter. Well, perhaps *laden* is not the best word, but at least the platter contained food of sorts. There were three poached fish, each about six inches long and quite fat, and half-a-dozen small mushrooms. The platter was garnished with what looked like greyish lettuce. It was the first real food I had taken in—how long? I remember eating the lot with relish.

After my meal I sat on one of the beds and thought one or two things out. To the best of my knowledge at that time, a meal taken in a dream could not possibly be *physically* satisfying, and yet I actually knew the feeling of satisfaction! Could it be that this was my dream-interpretation of a parallel occurrence in the real world? Supposing for a moment that I was in a coma of sorts, under care somewhere— in a hospital, for instance—and supposing further that I was being regularly fed intravenously or by some other means. It would be a simple matter for a mind as far gone as mine to interpret the feeling of well-being derived from such feedings as being actual hunger-relief sensations brought on by *feeding myself* on the fare of this cavern-world. This was a conclusion I could well accept, but I did not like to dwell on the same theory as applied to my answering the calls of nature! Someone, somewhere, must be finding in me a very difficult charge indeed! But of course, all that was sheer guesswork.

And yet (I told myself desperately), my mind must at least be attempting to hold on to a degree of rationality. Otherwise I would not now be able to make these . . . well, these rationalizations!

I went back to square one, right back to my accident, dwelling in detail on the things that had happened to me since.

Surely this prolonged dream, or sequence of connected dream-hallucinations, was no more fantastic than that other dream I had known on my first night in Bleakstone, when I had completely relived three years of my earlier life in one single night! And surely there could be no stranger nightmare than that I had known when the fossilized bones had taken on living flesh before my eyes? And what of my earlier symptoms following hard on the accident, when my mind used to blank completely? On those occasions (I tried to console myself), I had been far worse off than now, for then at times my brain had literally ceased to function, whereas now, horrible though the experiences were, at least I did *know* experiences! Better to dream and be aware of it than to wander mindlessly as I had on that occasion when I had thought to go rock-hounding! Often after that first time—in the "days" that followed—I would sit in my mind-cave and ponder the strangeness of it all. But at other times my lonely ponderings were relieved by the presence of a visitor, Bokrug, keeping his word (or obeying the instructions of my errant Id), coming to talk to me of the waking world and other things, and to bring me food.

Even about these visits I had my own ideas: was the lizard-being in fact a doctor, a psychiatrist, taking me back purposely along the paths of my past in a medically acceptable attempt to correct the malfunctions of my psyche?

During one session with Bokrug, I asked him to explain in greater detail the origin of the underworld's strange lighting system.

"As I have said," he began, "the tiny, living motes that comprise these nimbuses above our heads and part of the atmosphere in the great cave are what you call polypous. They are in fact basic life-tissues, from which, under the right conditions, all sorts of species and forms of life might spring." He paused to peer closely at me. "You are learned—do you know anything of the *Ubbo-Sathla Cycle?*"

"It rings a bell," I answered, "and yet I can't say I specifically remember having heard or read anything of it. What is this cycle—a mythological contemporary of the Cthulhu Cult or something of that nature?"

"Ah! Then you have heard of Loathly Lord Cthulhu? Yes, probably you have come across Ubbo-Sathla in the same connection. Well, Ubbo-Sathla is reputed in myth to have been the source of all Earthly life; according to certain books I know to exist in the surface world, Ubbo-Sathla '*spawned the grey, formless efts of the prime, and the grisly prototypes of terrene life.*' The story goes on to explain:

'And all Earthly life shall go back at last through the great circle of time to Ubbo-Sathla.' Well, it is my own opinion that this—he passed his flat hand through the halo over my head—and Ubbo-Sathla are one and the same, and that you, therefore, are a son of Shoggoth."

"Shoggoth!" I started, recalling those hideous dreams of old, in the nights following my glance into the pages of the *Necronomicon*. "Did you say Shoggoth?"

"Yes, for that is the name given their creation by its original makers—those Great Old Ones, here even before the Earth was fully formed, hundreds of millions of years ago. They called their protoplasmic creation 'Shoggoth-tissue,' and from it carved themselves beasts of burden—to build their cities and perform their heavier duties—beasts that eventually evolved powers which made them extremely dangerous to the Old Ones. The Shoggoths grew ever more clever, more imitative, more ambitious and ever the more sullen, until a time some one hundred and fifty million years ago when they turned in a great uprising on their masters. That the Old Ones managed to subdue them was a mercy . . .

"When we and the Thuun'ha settled here in these caves, we discovered—well, a *cache* of primal Shoggoth-tissue, still living, but in a form harmless as a shoal of lowly amoebas. We created many strains of simple life from this source—the light-clouds are but one form—but as with the Old Ones, so with us. Our slave-cultures quickly developed powers of their own, until we were forced to destroy them. Now, save for this 'lighting system,' as you call it, and for one other form, Lh-yib and its precincts are completely free of Shoggoths."

"One other form?" I repeated him, making it a question.

"Yes, more truly a *Shoggoth*, as pictured in tortured nightmares by certain sensitive dreamers in the surface world. It serves a purpose here—a necessary *function*—and it is in no position to threaten our existence. In the perpetual, barren environment in which we keep it, there exists no opportunity for . . . learning! It has reached its peak."

"But where is this thing?" I demanded to know. "Is it possible I might be allowed to . . . to see it?"

The lizard-creature studied me gravely for a moment before answering: "If you keep my ordinances, you will never have reason to see it—that I promise you—and I pray you never *shall* see it, for that would be your end . . ."

After this conversation, in my next five or six "sleep" periods, I had recurrent nightmares involving Shoggoths: iridescent blackness, the living excreta of nameless, alien super-creatures; viscous agglutinations of bubbling cells, churning and surging through subterrene tunnels like sentient mucus in a cosmic sinus.

The worst of these nightmares saw me in a great pit with a twenty-foot statue of a water-lizard god. The floor of the place was littered with bones, many of them covered with an evil-smelling black slime—a slime that I somehow knew to be the "snail-trail" of a Shoggoth—and even as I shrieked and frantically tried to climb out of that awful pit, I could hear the rumble of an approaching *something*, a something that sent before it a smell so noxious and alien as to make my senses reel from the incredible assault. A jagged hole led into the pit from somewhere down below, and it was from this hole that the smell belched, ever thicker, ever stronger; and it was from this hole that I knew the horror must soon burst in all its monstrous unreality . . .

After dreams such as this it was good to "wake" and find myself still in my now friendly, comfortable cave. But in a little while these terrible nightmares ceased and eventually there came a time when for all the lizard-thing's visits, and for all my ponderings and "rationalizations," I grew heartily sick of the cave and its appointments. Why, the place was no less than a prison, a cage evolved of my own diseased imaginings! And yet, having created the barriers, might I not as easily tear them down?

That was how my wanderings in the subterranean world first began, and soon they became regular excursions, so that after every three or four resting periods (those times when I "slept" on my heather bed) I would be taken by the urge to get out of the cave and explore a little further along the unknown tunnels.

At first I used to worry about what would happen if my firefly familiars should ever leave me, but after a while, when I saw just how faithfully that luminous cloud kept its place above my head, I lost this fear; and then my wanderings became extensive, and in spite of the warning of the lizard-being I took to exploring those passages down which he had specifically ordered me never to venture.

I could only believe later that the "warning" of Bokrug had been my own subconscious reluctance to let myself delve any further down those channels of my mind where Aberration had its strongest hold. Certainly there were far more fearsome places in this dream-world than my comparatively comfortable cave. Just *how* fearsome I was yet to discover . . .

XII

SINGERS OF STRANGE SONGS: DREAM-PHASE SIX
[The Masters Case:
from the Recordings of Dr. Eugene T. Thappon]

Throughout all my dream-adventures "underground" from that time on, within the cave appointed me by the lizard-being or in . . . *other* places . . . periodically I would hear—sometimes quite clearly as if from near at hand, at other times distantly, a mere murmur in my inner ear—strange songs of ululant praise from somewhere in this subterranean complex of my mind. I spent quite a lot of time during the earlier "days" of my entombment wondering about the real source of those sounds, for of course I knew they did *not* issue (as my Bokrug archetype had had it) from the worshipful minions of the water-lizard gods, Bokrug and the like being non-existent except in my own chaotic brain. The sounds were purely imaginary, as was everything else, and no end of puzzling could do me any good; but in any case, they provided me an interesting point of contemplation and conjecture.

I would rouse from fretful dreams or rare hallucinations to their soulful, often elflike timbre, and at other times I would start from the desolate byways of sprawling Hypochondria on hearing the commencement of a new phase of those throbbing—hymns?

With the passage of some time it grew on me that whatever the sounds were they never heralded any change in my environment (I used to fear at first that they were the harbingers of more hideous things to come or even deeper depths of mental degeneration), and with that realization came a stronger urge to rationalize and at least seek some scientific, if incorrect, theory as to their origin.

I had in fact "rationalized" on many things—Bokrug I had seen first as an archetype, as in C. G. Jung, then as a doctor; my presence in this cthonian dream had obviously come about through my deep interest in the possibility that the figurine at Radcar had originated in just such a place; the fever-inducing "mushrooms" represented an attempt by some subconscious *Me* to explain away my decidedly opiatic condition, etc., etc.! But these *sounds* were something else.

It could only be, I told myself, that *my mind* had started to dig out all sorts of obscure bits of information on subterranean subjects from things I had read long ago (and long ago thought forgotten), and that to make my dream-state more complete was inserting these bits and pieces into the greater hallucination.

And this theory fitted in well with respect to certain things I could actually remember having read or heard about caverns. For example: those sounds—

Yes, I had read how strange noises or echoes sometimes issue, even to the surface, from deep underground. Miners in England's north-east coal mines—probably in other regions—quite religiously record and act upon supposed indications of the conditions of their pits coming to them in the form of underground grumblings and groanings, and sometimes even throbbings and whistles. Certain noises convey to them especially bad omens, and it is not unknown for them to refuse to work a shaft which does not behave itself in this respect. In antiquity cavern oracles were frequently consulted, usually by sibyls, and the Cumaean sibyl was most celebrated for her trance-interpretations of "noises" from the bottom of her cave. Other oracular springs, grottoes, and potholes existed everywhere in the Old World, and in Morocco there are still caves where people sleep in the hope of seeing visions believed to be indicative of their futures, visions influenced by the "spirit voices" echoing from unknown vaults beneath. In fact there is a legend in Morocco, regarding one particularly active cavern, wherein it is told a marriage procession once took refuge from a storm. There the members of the procession were transformed into stone, but today people swear they can still hear the songs, chattering, and general gaiety of that long-gone entourage.

Norbert Casteret, perhaps the greatest of all speleologists, has written of a certain "Magic Flute" phenomenon, when he has heard strange, melodious music underground and has explained the mystery away in observing its origin: drops of water, falling from a height into hollow, flutelike channels and tubes—tubes formed by the very droplets themselves!

So then, with all these odd facts and bits of knowledge floating about in my delirious head, was it really so strange that having "dreamt" myself underground in the first place I should now imagine myself to be hearing those queerly disturbing "songs?"

No, it was not so strange; indeed, in my state, it was acceptable—*had* to be acceptable!—*provided that my mind did not carry its fancies too far!* But suppose I should conjure up for myself the Thuun'ha "in the flesh," as it were? I dreaded the thought of finding myself confronted by creatures the like of those described on the *Brick Cylinders of Kadatheron*, for any singers of songs such as those I had heard must be very strange singers indeed . . . !

XIII

THE CALCIUM LABYRINTH: DREAM-PHASE SEVEN
[The Masters Case:
from the Recordings of Dr. Eugene T. Thappon]

On one occasion (I am reduced to the use of this term by the fact that without any means of measuring time—and immersed as I was constantly in this long, fantastic dream—I was left completely disorientated regarding the hour, the day, the week, even the month at any specific dream-moment), I wandered in a direction which I had never taken before. I branched off down strange tunnels, ever leaving my mark on entrance and exit walls, until I came to an area of that underground world literally honeycombed with caves, holes, and burrows of sizes varying from the merest rat hole, through many intermediary grades, to great yawning orifices of about fifteen feet in diameter.

Closer inspection of the walls in this place brought me to a startling and awe-inspiring conclusion. At some time in the remote past there had existed here an unthinkably vast cavern of comparatively low ceiling but tremendous width and length—perhaps a titanic "split" between layers of primeval bedrock—and water seepage over countless aeons had formed stalactites and stalagmites, which depending and ascending projections of rock-hard calcium carbonate had eventually joined up to form the walls and pillars of the great maze through which I now wandered. Perhaps those very formations themselves had finally stemmed the flow of their own genesis, or had some other cause stopped the mineral-rich seepage from completely filling in the tremendous cavity? I could not say, but certainly the place had seen no moisture for many, many centuries. A fine dust lay between the columns, though where this substance had its origin I was likewise unable to guess, and its surface was so even that my footprints made quite clear tracks behind me. It was this fact that caused me to put away my lump of chalky rock. It seemed pointless to mark my route when each step I took left a clear "spoor" by which to make an eventual return. . . .

How far I wandered through that weird calcium labyrinth must remain purely a thing of conjecture. If my time-sense—even dreaming—had been disorganized before, why, now it suffered devastation in those white-walled centuried caves! The silence was so complete (for some reason the magnificent maze was void of echoes) and the lure of unseen caves ahead and seemingly interminable powder-floored passages lulled my mind into an uneasy dullness of thought ignoring time completely.

I was shaken from this stupefaction, this phase of mindless wandering, by suddenly feeling on my face and arms the coolness of a slight draught, a breeze which grew rapidly by leaps and bounds to a wind, a gale forcing my tattered shirt and raggy trousers against me, pushing me irresistibly along the calcium corridors against all my efforts to resist. In a matter of seconds I was stumbling, then running, lurching wildly from wall to wall, blinded and choking in the clouds of dust swirling up from the floor into my eyes and nostrils. Once, in Cyprus, I had been caught in a dust-devil, and now I knew something of that experience again, but this time, rather than a phenomenon of scientific interest, the thing was horrifying, indeed, a threat to my life! Now I knew whence came those passage-refreshing winds at the Time of the Mist, when, as Bokrug had had it, "the tunnels are made to breathe outwardly . . ."

Then, when it seemed there was no air left in the whole of that hideous underworld, as I clawed at my tortured throat and eyes in an agony of suffocation, the wind dropped as quickly as it had risen and the dust again settled toward the floor.

As rapidly as that it was over. I could breathe again. My nimbus of living light re-formed itself above my head and, as my breath came more easily, so my position was more clearly illumined. For as I gathered my buffeted senses, crouching there against the calcium wall for support, I began to realize the horror of my situation. Not a single footprint remained in the freshly settling dust to hint of my whereabouts or of the path I must take to regain the cavern I had made my home. I who had been so vastly amazed by the variety of form and size of the myriad openings around me, now feared them in a like degree.

Which one?—which of these hundreds of aeon-formed doorways offered a safe return to sanctuary? And beyond that first as yet unknown gate, how many more possible combinations of routes must lie within the incredibly complex maze between me and the comparative friendliness of my secluded chamber?

Terror and panic soon defeated logic. After a pause of only a minute or so I began to walk the dusty, silent corridors, then to run, until I left my guardian cloud of St. Elmo's fire behind, stumbling blindly along in a gloom which might well have existed undisturbed from a time predating the mammoth, and in so doing I came as close and closer than ever before to subterranean disaster!

Seconds after the last dancing motes of living light had receded behind me, leaving me lurching along in a midnight panic-flight, I bumped roughly into an unseen wall, careened over a projection jutting up from the floor and fell sprawling, with all the remaining wind knocked from me, full length in the dark. As my reeling senses steadied I found that my right arm, which I had flung protectively before me, and my head, hung limply, unsupported in empty space. As I have told before, I have never been much of a one for heights, so that the sight that slowly unfolded as my cloud of fireflies gathered ranks once more above me caused me to cringe in fear and wriggle desperately backwards away from the yawning chasm into which I had almost plunged.

I had emerged from the calcium labyrinth on to a vast ledge extending to right and left as far as the light from my fiery familiars reached, and beyond which descended with stark, sheer sides, a great black hole going down to unguessed depths.

Curious despite my fear, I edged slowly forward on my stomach until my eyes again peeped over the lip of the chasm, and then, for the first time, I remembered and attempted to use an *ability* that Bokrug had once told me would be mine to command, which I had not yet had occasion to experiment with. I simply squeezed my mind, concentrating, ordering the brightly glowing halo to desert me and descend into the abyss.

And it worked!

So! This told me something at least—that my mind was fully capable of supporting its own fictions!

I forced the glowing cloud down, down into the unknown pit, and the solid dark of the cave-world settled like a shroud about me, so that but for the feel of the hard rock beneath my body I might well have imagined myself a spirit floating free in the vacuous voids of space. Equally ultimate was the *silence*, with the only sound to disturb that singular stillness being the unsteady beating of my own heart—or was that, too, merely my imagination? Often I was to ponder that possibility, that I was in fact dead, a troubled soul wandering alone in a personal and private Phlegethon . . .

After what seemed a long while, when the light from the cloud still receding into the depths had become nothing more than a dim glow far, far down, I was on the point of calling a mental halt to my experiment when I was taken by an idea. I held the cloud stationary, where it was, while I groped with my hands around the lip of the chasm until I found a sharply projecting knob of stone. I managed to prise the stone free, letting it fall vertically from my fingers into the abysmal shaft. I began to count, but stopped to hold my breath in astonishment when I reached a score; yet it was not until some seconds *after* I stopped counting that the glowing speck below suddenly flew apart as the falling stone hurtled through its members!

I listened then, cupping my hand to my ear, and eventually a sound came to me. But it was not the sound of solid striking solid; it was a rush, a roar, a rising growl echoing up to me from regions undreamed of. *It was the magnified sound of the passage of that small stone . . . fleeing ever faster down the limitless depths . . . to the pits at Earth's very core!*

Shaken, in awe of immensities I had never before imagined as existing, oppressed, crushed, and defeated in the recognition of my own insignificance, I let my neon nimbus drift slowly back to its appointment above my head, and then I wandered listlessly back along the way I had come.

It took me a very long time to find the first chalk mark in a tunnel entrance, and almost as long after that to make my way wearily back to my cave . . .

XIV

THE CAVE OF WHITE GRASS: DREAM-PHASE EIGHT

[The Masters Case:
from the Recordings of Dr. Eugene T. Thappon]

On another occasion, wandering down yet another of those corridors pointed out to me by the lizard-thing as being forbidden to me, I eventually came out of a cavern-complex onto a vista so unnatural as to be hideous.

I had emerged into a large cave with a high ceiling, a ceiling spotted with glowing splotches of light, and the floor beneath my feet had turned from one of centuried dust to loam-rooted grass—grass which, excluded from any source of natural sunlight, had yet grown lush and thick . . . but white as death itself!

I had read somewhere of the existence of just such a monstrosity in the chasms of the Moroccan Atlas, deep below the surface, but here, observing the phenomenon for myself, I was appalled. Here was a small field—but growing in no wise as God had intended—trapped down here since seeded, reaching blindly through moist, dripstone-filtered loam towards a light devoid of the chlorophyll of the sane upper world—growing in monstrous lushness and ripening in pallid horror!

The white blades were soft beneath my feet, with the pliancy of fields remembered from years gone by; yet I shuddered inwardly as I walked silently across that alien terrain, forced against my will to recall a fragment from one of Clark Ashton Smith's poems:

> *What clammy blossoms,*
> *blanch'd and cavern-grown . . . ?*

Then, at a place where the ceiling came down to only a foot or so above my head, I paused to scrape at one of the eerie patches of light, discovering the source of that luminescence to be a crust of lichen, a mass of tiny fronds, strangely cross-hatched and intricately threaded. Even as I examined that odd scrap of dream-cave life, I felt the fall of a spot of moisture, quickly followed by a second and then a third, upon my head. I stepped back to peer upward in wonderment at the wounded lichen—apparently "bleeding" from the area where I had scraped—and saw the reason for the stuff's peculiar composition. The tightly intertwined fronds and rootlets formed a trap to catch the seeping water on which the plant fed.

I thought of the mushrooms; of the lizard-thing and the unseen, unknown Thuun'ha; of the fireflies above my head; of the etiolated heather beds in my cave; and finally of this hideous cavern of white grass and the luminous lichens on its ceiling, and was awed. This underworld, dream or hallucination though it must be, was none-theless full of unending wonders and strange cycles of life . . .

I was still thinking on these bizarre things when I heard the noise. It was a . . . a *rippling*, as of corn in a breeze-driven field, a languorous swishing of foliage, but at the sound my hair stood on end and I lowered my eyes to stare in rising terror at the awful grass.

The whole field, over an area as far as I could see, was alive with motion—with the grass bending over in regular waves like the surface of a small sea *but impelled by no wind!*—and in that same instant of time I knew that those grass blades were somehow drawn to lean towards the fresh moisture dripping from the ceiling. Obviously the cave was not normally as moist as I had thought; this awful grass bent toward water as flowers lift their heads to the sun in the green fields above!

Suddenly a horror burst over me the like of none I had ever known before. I only knew I had to be out of that loathsome place, and I turned and ran for the archway of my entry. Then, glancing back over my shoulder as I left the field and entered the complex of caves, I saw a sight that froze the blood in my veins. For disturbed or alerted by my panic-flight, I knew not which, that entire monstrosity of inner earth, that whole etiolated—meadow?—had swished into a new position, a position in which every tip of every blade of grass now pointed in my direction!

It required no more than a second's thought to discover the reason for this freakish and frightening activity: *that hellish herbage had "sensed," by some means I could never hope to understand, the presence of the little rivers of cold sweat springing in spontaneous solicitude from my body's pores!*

I was still running when I reached my friendly little cave, and there I collapsed in shivering terror on my bed . . .

XV

THE FROGS: DREAM-PHASE NINE
[The Masters Case:
from the Recordings of Dr. Eugene T. Thappon]

It was not until a long time after my adventure in the cave of white grass—or so it seemed to my shattered time-sense—that I dared put foot outside my rightful appointments again. I did it after many "sleep" periods, after as many repetitious sessions with the lizard-creature, and after heaven-only-knows how many boring, almost ritualistic meals of fish and fungi.

It was, of course, monotony that drove me out. In my more lucid moments (I mean at those times when my mental images, my dreams, were sharpest and most clearly defined), I had even attempted a little physical exercise in my cave, by the light of my ever-attendant fireflies, but even in this I had discovered ennui, so that in the end I determined to brave the cave of white grass again, and to go on from that place deeper into the calcium labyrinth.

I experienced no difficulty in rediscovering the cave of the morbid meadow, for I simply followed the marks on the walls as I recalled making them from my chamber to that awful place, but once there I knew many moments of dread and indecision before again committing myself to walk over that sea of leper-sprouting loam. In the end I decided simply to skirt the cavern, to move along the walls where the grass grew thinnest, until I found an exit place; there to take up my wanderings and markings again, until either hunger or weariness should drive me back to the boredom of my cave. This, not without much trepidation, I did, but not once did I notice any abnormal motion in that field of pallid grass, a fact that heartened me greatly and strengthened my resolve to explore further.

I left the lichen-ceilinged cavern at a spot, by my judging, roughly one-third of the distance round its irregular perimeter from the cave of entry, choosing an archway of greater dimensions than the norm and finding the tunnel beyond it to be of corresponding spaciousness. I struck out, in a fairly straight line but yet on a course which after some time I decided must be a gradual descent into the deeper bowels of Earth. At first this declivity was barely recognizable as such, but in a little while I noticed a slight pressure on my toes which told of my almost unconscious "braking" of stride against an increasing steepness of descent.

As I went lower I found that the rock floor beneath my feet (here there was no dust) grew damper and almost slimy; indeed, as the distance I covered increased, the way became slippery to the point of treacherous. Shortly I passed a series of small bore-holes, varying from the size of rabbit burrows to openings into which a man might easily crawl, joining into the tunnel from a direction to my rear as I walked. Here then was the explanation for the sudden dampness of the place. Seepage, from somewhere far above, was making its way down these subtunnels into this main passage. Sure enough, when I touched the mouth of one of the smaller burrows, drops of water gathered into a tiny pool round my fingers before flowing in a visible trickle down to the damp floor of the passage. I moved on.

Soon, as the way grew yet steeper, I fancied that I heard ahead an indistinct rushing sound, increasing in volume as I went until the noise was quite audible, clearly recognizable as the rushing and pounding of tumultuous waters. I pressed on eagerly. Here indeed was a diversion! The sight of a subterranean waterfall, or perhaps of a resurgence from some lower level, would be balm to my tired eyes, the nerves of which must, I was sure, be slowly atrophying in the perpetual sameness of my environment.

Soon the dampness was also in the air, soothing to my dry throat, and the vibrations caused by the as yet unseen surgings somewhere ahead became such as to actually set the walls and floor of my tunnel trembling. A few minutes or so more saw me around a final bend in the descending passage to confront an awe-inspiring spectacle of subterrene grandeur.

A great shining spout of water was literally *erupting* from a high rock wall some eighty feet above, to cascade out and down into a swirling, rushing pool which in turn emptied itself mightily, in liquid haste, into a great fault in a distance-shadowed wall. Such was the turbulence of the water that the air was full of moisture, and water particles continually spattered against me.

My vantage point was from a rocky ledge onto which the tunnel had opened, about ten feet above the level of the pool, and there I threw myself belly down to watch in awe the majestic carom of water.

The *sound* was literally deafening, an explosion of noise as of a thousand thundering engines, a cacophony such as to put any ten steel-forging mills to shame, but I chanced the ruin of my eardrums gladly to be able to see the stupendous resurgence and to feel on my face the flung spray of this Chthonian cataract.

It was from this position that I first saw the second ledge at a level some eight feet beneath me, and as my firefly familiars descended to hover above me as I lay there they lit up to a degree the darker surface of that second ledge also. There were *shapes* down there, and I knew immediately that I was seeing living creatures, though of what species I could not be sure. There were dozens of them, of the general size of large house cats, and they seemed to spend their time darting ferociously, with bounding leaps and dripping, slippery cavortions, in and out of the treacherous pool. Then, as more of them leaped, I saw the sleekly shining extended rear legs, noting the strong webbing between the digits of those hind limbs, and I knew that the creatures were some outsize species of frog; but what on earth were they doing, frenziedly hurtling in and out of the rushing waters like that?

The answer came in a flash. I saw one of the frogs emerge from the churning surface of the water to leap to the ledge below me, and in his mouth he carried a flapping, shiny-scaled fish! The things were fishing! And of course, this would be the perfect place: a spot where the fish were dazed by the great fall of the water and the buffeting of powerful currents. So far as I could see the creatures were blind (as are many other forms of cavernicolous faunae), eyeless in fact, and it amazed me the powers of perception they must have achieved since their origin to be able to swim and fish so expertly in these unknown and unlit depths. So thinking, I leaned my head out further over the ledge in order to observe their actions more closely.

I must have disturbed some small, washed pebbles, of which a number littered the floor. Certainly I had felt something slide out from beneath my chest to fall from the ledge, but such was the racket put up by the spouting water and roaring pool that the sound of the dislodged pebbles striking the ledge below was hopelessly lost to me.

Not so the frogs!

If I had wondered at the development of their cavern senses before, I was utterly astonished now, for with one accord, as if commanded by a single governing brain or ganglion, the squatting batrachians stopped their feasting, the leapers quit their leaping, and in unison the entire horde turned to stare sightlessly up at me. Then, after a pause of no more than a second or so, they launched themselves en masse towards my position on the high ledge.

Ghastly terror threw me upright then, sent me flying—shrieking madly, sobbing and gasping between shrieks—up the slippery nightmare corridor of rock. Not merely because of the concerted attack of the giant frogs in their singular unison of monstrous intent nor because of my apparent and shuddersome magnetism for both flora and fauna alike in this awful underworld—no, I fled for another reason, one which unmanned me and terrified me almost beyond endurance. For as those dwellers in the depths had turned to me, the light of my friendly fireflies had been reflected in their faces— not from their eyes, for they had no eyes, *but from great, sharp, curving fangs that gleamed whitely and dripped redly in their evil, wide-slit mouths . . .*!

The floor being so greasy my progress was nightmarishly slow, a pace with which my fireflies could easily cope as I plunged and slithered up the now seemingly interminable corridor, and having at last traversed that bend leading away from the cataract, I gazed fearfully back to see if the frog-things had managed to gain the ledge and follow me. From behind, above the now lowered din of the waterfall, came such sounds of slithering and hopping that I knew, even before the first of those toothy fishers flopped into sight around the bend, that any hope of mine of the passage being inaccessible to them had been in vain.

I waited no longer, but flung myself with all my energy up and along the corridor . . . and it was then that I found myself in what at first appeared a hopeless situation. For with a sudden rush and a roar, surging down the tunnel came a frothing gush of black water almost knee deep as I judged it, quite sufficient if it hit me in my present position to knock my feet from under me and send me flying back into the chomping fangs of my loathsome pursuers!

I had reached a point level with the lowest of those small adjoining burrows, and as the racing water rushed closer upon me and the slavering horde squelched and flopped behind, I hurled myself heedlessly, head and shoulders, into the barely adequate hole. My intention was to crawl completely into the cavity, but, horror of horrors, the burrow tapered down to a veritable mouse hole in a distance of only a few feet!

Then, even as I felt the first slimy snatchings at my legs and winced at a leering mental picture of curving fangs and slavering jaws, the water hit; swirling and threatening to suck me out of the little cave, down to the lower ledge and the great pool below with its fearful, squamous feasters. I hung on for dear life, while the water rushed into my cave and filled it completely, pouring into my mouth and nostrils, ballooning my tattered trousers—my last vestige of clothing—and swilling away, perhaps for ever, my poor drowned fireflies.

I think I came close to drowning myself—certainly I lost consciousness, though probably only momentarily—for the last thing I remembered before finding myself soaked and coughing, spread-eagled on the floor of the recently flooded shaft, was spreading my elbows and humping my back to jam myself against the sides and roof of my small and doubtful refuge. I had obviously been washed from that place, to be left high but not so dry about twenty yards lower down the tunnel.

As I climbed unsteadily to my feet there came to my ears a frantic flapping sound that caused me to gasp aloud and spin about, searching for the frogs which I felt sure must be near at hand. In my terror I hardly noticed the fact that my fireflies had not been drowned but were still there above my head as always, and it was by their light that I quickly discovered the source of the flappings which had so startled me—and also, incidentally, the reason my presence had had so disturbing an effect on the brutish batrachians.

For the corridor was littered with still living fish, stranded now that the subterranean gusher had passed, and I could well understand why the fanged frogs had waited down by the pool for the first sounds of the obviously regular resurgence—sounds heralding the easy pickings of stranded fish! Inadvertently I had triggered that hellish response of theirs, when I knocked down the pebbles from the ledge. They had seen my intrusion as a harbinger of the anticipated feast to come!

But then I heard a sound other than the agonized flapping of stranded fish—a sound that steadily, nastily grew louder—and this time there could be no mistaking the vicious chomp and snapping of ghoulish gluttony, close and coming closer. It would not be long, I realized, before the great frogs had followed the trail of fish back up the shaft to me!

I wasted no more time but set off as quietly and quickly as I could back along the way I had come, towards the upper levels and the comparative safety and sanity of the better-known passages above . . .

XVI

THE SPAWNING PLACE: DREAM-PHASE TEN
[The Masters Case:
from the Recordings of Dr. Eugene T. Thappon]

There eventually came a time when I had all but used up the various exit tunnels from that great gallery of which my own cave was but a small cul-de-sac. That is, I had explored the great majority of them—most, as told, with terrifying or mind-staggering results! But boredom is a tremendous force to be reckoned with, and the *utter* boredom of that small cave of mine would have been quite sufficient to drive the most timid soul (even forewarned by past events of possible disaster) out into the unknown underworld.

"Better the devil you know—" they say, but is it always true? I did not *ever* want to see the cave of white grass again, and the thought of the pool of fanged frogs was more than enough to cause my hackles to rise. Likewise, no amount of urging—had there been anyone to urge me—could have induced me to revisit the bottomless pit down which I had dropped a stone in the folly of believing that by that simple act I might gauge its depth! Nor was the idea of a fresh visit to the calcium labyrinth, with its suffocating winds of change, in the least attractive to me. No, it seemed that in order to stifle my yawning boredom I might be wiser to face the as yet unrealized "devils" of those corridors which so far my feet had never known.

So it was, that with a piece of marking rock tucked into a pocket of my almost completely shredded trousers, I entered the first of those remaining few tunnels branching off from the great gallery and began to make my cautious way into what was to eventually prove a new realm of nightmare.

It made no difference that this was that shaft especially pointed out to me by the dream-lizard as being forbidden above all others; indeed, I believe that his warning was in the main the special attraction!

But it *was* different, this great burrow, with none of the dryness of the calcium labyrinth, nor yet damp like the slippery declivity to the rushing pool of frogs; no, the atmosphere here seemed rather more, well, *livable*—or was it simply that I myself was becoming more conditioned to "living" underground?

There were no side tunnels leading off from this shaft, and when I gave closer examination to the walls I was led to the conclusion that time and nature were by no means wholly responsible for their mechanical regularity. There was no stalagmitic dripstone for one thing, and for another there were marks which could only have been the results of an extensive mining operation.

I had gone perhaps one half-mile along the tunnel, keeping to the main shaft and leaving alone the hundreds of smaller side burrows, when I came to the steps. There were seven of them, cut into the solid rock (a sort of darkish basalt as opposed to limestone), leading me up to a level of the passage on a slightly higher elevation. That higher passage was of basalt, too, having a slow but definite rise to its floor which made me unconsciously quicken my pace. It seemed the closer I got to the surface world, the nearer I came to the *waking* world, and the faster I wanted to go. Hah!—as if there could exist the slightest hope of my discovering a way out of my sprawling mind-prison . . .

It was only when I thought I heard something, a noise from somewhere ahead, that I slowed my pace. I stood still then to listen for a recurrence, and there *was* a sound, receding now but recognizable nonetheless.

It was one of those "songs of praise," as heard often before, echoing back to me from some distant region. I kept still, so that I might catch the last of those ephemeral notes, but too late, for the song had already died. Yet in its stead I seemed to hear an odd whispering, a muted, infinitesimal echo, as it were, of what had gone before—and strangely, again I was reminded of the voices of many young choirboys, singing in unison in some great cathedral.

At first I told myself there could be little doubt that this muted harmony was only the fading echo of the greater sound, but as I wandered steadily on along the basalt passage, so the whispering seemed to grow louder (rather than dying out, as I had thought it might) until soon it was a distinctly audible, ululant *hum* in the air—an effect which might with some difficulty have been attained in more orthodox settings by playing in harmonic phases the lower notes of a guitar in the confines of an echo chamber. And yet, paradoxically, I could not truly say that I "heard" anything. It was more as if some psychologically deep-rooted tuning fork had been struck in my inner self, to reverberate simultaneously in both my conscious and subconscious beings.

That hackneyed term *telepathy* sprang to mind, to be as quickly put away. I was well aware that my mind was in no fit state to rationalize with any accuracy whatever on *any* occurrence, regardless of which of my five stumbling senses—or any combination of them or addition to them—seemed to perceive that occurrence. Far less could I afford to believe in things which I *knew* were fantasies—things I had considered fantasies long before I ever saw the figurine in the museum at Radcar. That was the category in which at that time I placed telepathy.

I might well have gone on thinking along these lines had not my thoughts been interrupted by my abrupt emergence from the basalt passage into a large chamber.

The cavern must have been at least one hundred yards across, making it second only in sheer size to that tremendous vault wherein stood greystone Lh-yib, and its borders would surely have lain undefined were it not for the great domed ceiling—like that other ceiling in the cave of white grass—being liberally dotted with great patches of the same species of luminous lichen.

Stretching up and away that weirdly lighted roof receded, casting down from its curving surface a slowly shifting "fire-light" which illuminated in pale orange and yellow shades the cavern's centrepiece, a huge, square, sunken area with steps leading down to a great bowl-shaped delve at least thirty yards across—and that depression was filled with what looked like a monstrous mass of greyish jelly, quivering with an inward life of its own . . .

At first I was of two minds; should I leave the place without more ado, or should I go on down the steps to examine the curious . . . *matter* . . . in the great bowl? Then I forced myself to recall that none of my experiences here could genuinely be said to be happening at all, that this was simply another sequence in an unending dream or prolonged hallucination, and with this in mind I decided to carry on.

And all the while those noises in my ears (or at least in the ears of my mind) went on, growing in volume, I thought, and tinged now with currents of—fear? Yes, fear! I could definitely sense a discord, an element of apprehension, creeping into what had been a perfect if alien harmony...

I reached the bottom of the steps to peer unenlightened at the greyish, quivering pile of spherical jelly-things in the huge stone basin. The stuff looked for all the world like a mass of outsize frog spawn, with each single egg the size of a football, and—

Frog spawn!

Ye Gods—frog spawn! But what kind of frogs might eggs the like of these produce? Conquering my natural revulsion I stooped and lifted one of the heavy things in my hands, feeling of its sticky texture and discerning through its semiopaqueness a vague outline suggestive of anything but a tadpole. Why!—the unborn creature within that nauseous plasma was shaped more like a foetus than anything else!

I had at first automatically connected the spawn with those nightmare frogs at the pool of the cataract, but now, with that egg warm in my hands and with the weird songs chaotically resounding in a sudden passion of fear in my head, I had second thoughts. No, whatever these beings were they could in no wise be progeny to those batrachian beasts in that lower tunnel, nor to anything like them. What then?

There had for some time been rising in the air a savage, ululant howling, going unnoticed almost as I pondered the odd nature of the glistening spheroids. Now, as the sound (or rather the *experience*) increased in volume so as to be an almost physical force, I was driven by it backwards up the steps to crouch fearfully above that awesome spawning place. There I suddenly realized that the hideous reverberations issued from some source separate completely from those other, softer sensations conveying fear. Simultaneous with this realization came that flash in my mind illuminating the whole experience in a light which was at least logical, given that any sort of logic could be said to be permissible in my situation.

It was simply this: I had suddenly seen the unhatched eggs in the bowl-shaped depression as containing *sentient* creatures—beings that somehow knew of my intrusion and feared it—and if such a wild theory could possibly be correct . . . then what of the parent creatures? Did they, too, know of my presence in this spawning place, and did they also have this ability to project their emotions? In abrupt terror I knew that they did, *that they were even now voicing their protest in those savage howls of demoniacal rage which had rapidly grown so as to shake my whole being!*

And worse than even this terrifying knowledge, what happened next was more than sufficient to send me in a hag-ridden rush away from the place of the eggs to plunge in mind-jellying horror back down the basalt tunnel—to float in a slow-motion nightmare down the seven steps—to pant in an agony of fear, fear of retribution, from the forbidden tunnel to the gallery and from there to my own cave. And in that cave I huddled in a dark corner, sending my fireflies away from me in the vain hope that without their telltale presence I might remain hidden when *They* came to seek me out.

For come they must; I was sure of it—as sure as the murderer who hears the sound of the hounds on his trail, as sure as the prisoner whimpering in his cell with the shadow of the gallows falling on him through the bars. After all, was I not just such a murderer . . . was I not even more a prisoner?

For as the truth had dawned on me atop those basalt steps I had shuddered in an involuntary convulsion, and in so doing *I had dropped that living egg, watching it burst, splatter, and run in liquid katabolism to the bottom step—and as the egg had burst asunder so there came from out the hideous ether the baying, blood-lusting cry of outraged parenthood—the nightmare promise that those singers of strange songs, the Thuun'ha, would be avenged . . .*

XVII

TAKEN BY THE THUUN'HA: DREAM-PHASE ELEVEN

[The Masters Case: from the Recordings of Dr. Eugene T. Thappon]

It was less than half an hour before they came for me, given that for once my time-sense was in good order, but in that short time I had almost frightened myself to death. Sitting there shivering in my dark corner, I had gone quickly over all that had occurred since my fatal discovery of the statuette at Radcar Museum, and my thoughts had led me to some terrible conclusions.

The truth was that I was finding it more and more difficult to believe that everything down there "below ground" was illusory. Points in favour of prolonged hallucination were legion, yes, but likewise points against! It was one thing to have the occasional mental lapse following a bad car accident, but quite another to "dream" this entire subterranean sequence.

Yet what other explanation could there be? Psychologically everything could be explained away, but the damnable thing was that I did not feel in any way, well, *mental*! I felt normal—completely normal—or as normal as I should feel in my extraordinary surroundings. There were none of the—usual?—phenomena of orthodox hallucination. But could I trust my feelings, or for that matter any single one of my senses? Does any paranoiac *feel* like a paranoiac? And there again, by its very definition, "hallucination" was by no means inadmissible.

Let's see now—"hallucination"—yes, if I remembered correctly: "An apparent perception devoid of any externally correspondent object; any sensation or combination of sensations—visual, tactile, or auditory—caused by mental derangement, fever, or intoxication . . ."

Well, that certainly fitted me, to a T in fact! Certainly I was feverish—definitely I had been and presumably still was mentally deranged, and increasingly so. But in spite of all this I did not *feel* to be, well, deranged . . . not until I saw the Thuun'ha, at any rate, and then I *knew* I was mad, and so there was no sense in worrying about anything any longer. I had seen them before, in an earlier sequence of this hellish dream—that first night in the cave of the stream—but at that time my condition had not been quite so fully developed. Now it was!

Oh, my disordered imagination had had plenty to work on in the development of the Thuun'ha, and it had spared no detail in matching them exactly to that description as translated from the *Brick Cylinders of Kadatheron*. They were only small, but I made no effort to fight them off when half a dozen of them lifted me bodily to carry me out of my cave and into the gallery, and from there down that passage leading back to Lh-yib; one cannot fight that which does not exist! Instead of struggling I merely lay limply in their arms and studied them unbelievingly as they hurried me along. My fireflies had returned to me from their banishment, and the air was full of strange songs and a musty, alien odour—but I barely noticed these things in my amazement at my ruined psyche's construction of such fantastic creatures.

The Thuun'ha were hideous, and no other word could adequately fit them. Perhaps four and one-half feet tall, green as Yorkshire beer bottles, bulge-eyed with flabbily hanging, wattled lips and strangely tapering, furred ears—*hideous!* And their touch was soft, their movements sure, and their telepathic songs were unutterably foreboding as they bore me to that incredible cavity wherein stood the Sister City.

It was all a mad rush to me, with my whirling thoughts only adding to the general confusion. *My* confusion, that is, for as I have hinted the Thuun'ha were very purposeful indeed, and each movement my bearers and their thronging escort made seemed in its sureness the ultimate in alien efficiency.

Darkness came quickly. At first, when the Thuun'ha took me in horror from the cave, my firefly cloud had followed to swirl in what could only be likened to dumb bewilderment about my head, but as I was borne more swiftly along the corridor to Lh-yib, those luminescent ranks thinned, until merely a speckling of light remained . . . and then even that vanished.

Once more I lost track of time completely as my lightless rush through the dark bowels of Earth continued, so that it seemed only a minute or so before light returned in blinding brilliance as I was borne out into the dizzy cave of the city. Without pause, closing my eyes against the terror of the journey, I was carried inert and unprotesting across a network of spindly bridges to the great central pillar and then, once again, darkness descended as my bearers hurried me in through a carved entranceway to commence a spiralling downward course.

During the descent within that great stalactite, at regular intervals, light would suddenly stream in to me, and turning my head I saw that the source of this radiance was the occasional window cut to look out over the Sister City. I remembered having noticed just such windows before, when first I had spied Lh-yib from that great landing onto which the lizard-being had led me from the cave of the mushrooms.

Quickly the descent was over, and still dizzy from the corkscrew fall I was borne out from the base of the huge stalagmite and through the lower streets of the city. There, in every doorway and from every window, peered the hostile minions of the water-lizard gods, leaving no doubt in my mind but that had they their way (and it seemed they had) my punishment would be fitting to my crime. Only once did I see what I took to be a group of the "gods" themselves, well apart from the Thuun'ha and seemingly very aloof, but I was hurriedly bustled away from that area to the very outskirts of the city, then out across the grey, sandy plain, and finally I knew that my ultimate destination lay at the great pyramid—the Place of Worship!

Lying partly on my side in the arms of the six Thuun'ha, I was able to see that as before the silver stream ran and sparkled to the base of the pyramid, continuing its green altered course from that building to the hole in the far wall of the monster cave where it vanished again into the bowels of the Earth, but even as I watched, the stream—where it emerged from under the pyramid—began to dry up as I had seen it do before. Inside the pointed building, for a purpose as yet unknown to me, the path of the stream had been rechannelled . . . but by that token I at least knew that it would soon be the Time of the Mist . . .

XVIII

SACRIFICE: DREAM-PHASE TWELVE
[The Masters Case:
from the Recordings of Dr. Eugene T. Thappon]

My mind was morbidly working overtime as I was rushed in through a low entranceway in the base of the great pyramid. Was I to be subjected to the green mist at its source, to choke and die in its poisoned fumes, or was there a yet more terrifying end in store for me in reckoning for my crime in the spawning place? Again I found myself in darkness, carried down, steeply down, in tortuous intestines of unlit earth before the course once more levelled out. Then those alien fingers fastened more securely about me as my bearers tightened their grip. There was to be no sudden escape, that much was obvious, and I guessed that it would not be long before the ultimate, unknown destination was reached.

In a few minutes more there came to my ears the rush of waters dulled by walls of rock, and I remembered how I had seen the stream beyond the pyramid dry up. Was this, then, the place to which the waters had been rechannelled from the pyramid? And if so—why? No sooner had I asked myself this question than I believed I could see the answer. As the dank air of the underworld swept by me (so it seemed in that lightless rush), it brought to my nostrils an acrid odour as alien to my sense of smell as was the touch of the Thuun'ha to my flesh. There were liquid gurgles, too, and the deep thrumming of ponderous machinery. In my mind's eye I pictured black cauldrons and churning paddles, with greenly bubbling concoctions steaming and giving off lethally poisonous vapours.

How good my guess was became apparent when I was borne through an extensive cave lit by dull fires which burned beneath lines of huge stone vats extending into the miasmal darkness. The entire place resounded to the chucklings of boiling liquids and the poundings of mixing or stirring devices. Here and there, shadowy Thuun'ha teams worked at the lips of the vats, pouring vessels of noxious chemicals into the bubbling liquids, and above, great vents in the ceiling sucked away the green mist as it rose from the vats in billowing, thickly opaque clouds. The merest wisp of vapour from one vat set me coughing and choking as I was bundled quickly through the awful place. The whole was a dark scene from Hieronymus Bosch—perhaps his "Hell" from *The Garden of Delights*—and thinking on that artist's nightmare conception, for a hideous moment I believed I was to be thrown into one of the fearsome vats. But then we passed on into the darkness of yet another tunnel.

Down again, ever deeper, to where it seemed the very netherpits must lie, and there in the darkness my fantastic journey came to an abrupt end. I felt myself bundled into a container of sorts, like a basket, and, with a slight swinging motion, there followed the sensation of being lowered into grotesque and even greater depths.

For some time the descent continued, and by groping around I discovered that I was indeed in a kind of basket, with two thick ropes connecting the vehicle to what could only be some sort of pulley system above. Stretching my arms over the side of the basket, I could feel the upward slide of a rough rock wall, and looking down I could make out a red glow not too far below.

Soon the basket swung down into a cave, passing through a ring of flaring, bracketed torches set in the ceiling around the opening of the shaft, so that for a moment I felt their heat on my face. From ceiling to floor the cave was all of fifty feet in height, and from wall to dimly lit wall about twice that distance.

As soon as I saw the place I was filled with a terrible foreboding. Somewhere in my severely damaged mind I dimly remembered having *seen* this cavern before. But there was something out of place, an awful silence which, unremembered from that previous vision, seemed somehow ghastly in its intensity. It was a silence that screamed.

With a grating crunch the basket settled, and though my first thought was to stay exactly where I was, those above had decided that events were to take a different course. One of the supporting ropes began to slacken, coiling as it fell, but at the same time the other rope tightened, turning the basket violently on its side and pitching me out. Before I could scramble to my feet in the shadow-flickered cave, the basket was withdrawn, quickly ascending and disappearing through the circle of torches into the hole in the ceiling.

Then for the first time I noticed the cave's monstrous flooring. I have said that the basket *crunched* when it came to rest. The reason, when I came to look closer, soon became hideously apparent. The place was littered with bones. Indeed, the whole cave seemed a veritable ossuary, in which I could hardly have hazarded a guess at the depth of the skeletal debris beneath me.

The vast majority of the bones were very similar to the skeletons of large monkeys or chimpanzees, and I quickly related their characteristics and proportions to the Thuun'ha. Was this then a burial ground of sorts? Then, seeing a skull far larger than the others and picking the thing up in shaking fingers, I saw that this time my find was indeed human. There were, too, certain other large bones of a *not quite* human nature, and I reckoned them to be the scattered remains of long-dead lizard-things. So, the place did serve as a mortuary—both for the water-lizard gods and their servitors—and, remembering the human skull, occasionally for others! When certain softer remains beneath my feet crumbled, causing me to stagger, I saw something in the grim white expanse that caused the hair of my neck to bristle sharply erect. It was simply a black rubber flipper—of the type used by frogmen—and I thought again of the aqualung in its rotting harness and of those cavers lost in unknown subterranean dimensions. . . .

With only the flickering fire of the high torches to light the place, I had difficulty in making out its more remote corners, and, the better to acquaint myself with my new surroundings, I stumbled flounderingly in the direction of the sheer wall, sometimes sinking to my knees as the bones gave and settled to my step. The feeling that I *knew* this place and the dreadful fear inside me grew by leaps and bounds, and when suddenly a great, rock-carven statue with magnificent cave-pearl eyes appeared in a momentary flare of bright torchlight, I shrieked aloud and bounded backwards as I finally recognized my location. For I was *inside* that cave of the nightmare—the place I had seen in mad dreams within dreams following Bokrug's story of the origin of the light-tissues—the place of the bones and the reptilian statue and . . . the . . .

Madly I stumbled away from the towering figure of stone, across the crackling remains, towards the opposite wall. I had to know for sure . . . *I had to know!*

I pulled up short, my jaw falling to hang slack, my hands going up before me to prevent a sight too monstrous for reasoned thought. For there, looming blackly in the flickering shadows of the wall, a jagged hole led downwards into utter darkness—*and those bones nearer to the opening were covered with a blackly shining film of vile-smelling slime the origin of which only a diseased mind like mine could envisage!*

And with a thrill of ultimate horror I knew that I could and already had envisaged just such an origin. This *filth* clinging to the bony debris was nothing less than the mark of a Shoggoth's passing, and this place was where that "other form" as mentioned by Bokrug was kept imprisoned to serve its "necessary function"—the elimination of the carcasses of deceased members of the Thuun'ha, their gods, and, rarely, those of inquisitive wanderers from the surface world! And no doubt the Thuun'ha were not above the occasional *live sacrifice!* For to them, surely, the Shoggoth would have been explained away as a death-deity, an avatar of their Bokrug gods!

Scientifically the thing was no more horrifying than cremation, as applied to the destruction of wasted and useless tissues—but as a means of sacrifice . . . ? And especially since it seemed I myself was destined to serve just such a purpose . . .

With all these hideous thoughts running through my head, even as I peered in nameless dread into the threatening hole, there came a rush of greenish water from somewhere above. Again I started horribly from the shock of this unexpected deluge, shrieking and flinging myself backwards away from the hole. For a moment I cowered there, digging myself into the bones, then, looking up, I saw that a pipe had been lowered down the entrance shaft, and that the green liquid was rushing from that source. The bony floor had a slight slope in the direction of the black hole, and the water rushed and tumbled over the deeply heaped remains to pour in a swirling flood down that charnel channel.

For perhaps ten minutes the gushing flood continued, while I got myself under a semblance of control and backed away to drier quarters. Shortly the rush turned to a trickle that quickly petered out. The pipe was withdrawn.

It was not long after this that I began to hear again the strange songs of praise of the Thuun'ha. Those ethereal stirrings in my brain had of course been with me all through my nightmare, captive rush through the subterrene labyrinths, but after I had been lowered into the cave of the bones they had faded away and ceased. These fresh songs were altered somehow, different from any I had "heard" before, and they seemed no longer telepathic but actually physical. I found myself for the first time *listening to* rather than feeling the weird vibrations. With this realization came another—one that caused me to recoil and almost faint at its implications. It was simply this: that those newer, more real songs I was hearing were issuing from the black and reeking hole!

Frantically I searched my memory for the things told me by my Bokrug archetype of the Shoggoth menace, and as I did so I noticed how harsh those previously harmonious rhythms had become. In a little while there came another sound, a rushing as of a great wind, and in the space of a few seconds the loathsome vent began issuing a continuous blast of the most awfully offensive gasses imaginable.

I could picture the Shoggoth down there in the earth, a great black viscous mass, pushing before it its own pressured stench as it rushed upwards in answer to the summons of the lately vanished water from the pipe. And then I remembered what Bokrug had told me of the Shoggoths—*how in the old days they had grown ever more imitative*—and I knew then why those new, physical songs, issuing along with the monstrous stench from below, were harsher and unharmonious! Down there, with nothing but the occasional mind-songs of the Thuun'ha to keep it company, this last survivor of the Shoggoth cultures had *learned* those sepulchral sounds parrot fashion, and was even now "singing" them to itself as it surged upwards to perform its "necessary function!"

I completely lost whatever little remained of my mind then, throwing myself madly about the skeleton-floored cavern in a vain attempt to find an exit hole or tunnel of escape. Before I knew it the whole cave had started to tremble like a log cabin in an avalanche. The *Thing* was almost upon me, rumbling up through the poisoned earth in semiplastic horror. Ever denser the hellish gasses rushed from the hole into the sacrificial chamber, and with every other second I expected the monstrosity itself to put in an appearance at the mouth of that vile pit . . . which eventually it did!

I was scrabbling wildly over a heap of bones with my back to the hole when the Shoggoth arrived, but even before I turned I knew that it was there. The loathsome exhalations ceased and in an instant the trembling of the walls and fragile floor, too, stopped short. Once more silence breathed in the cave—hellishly expectant silence in which I slowly turned to face my doom.

Great God . . . ! Huge, lidless eyes forming by the dozen in a semisolid wall of blackly glistening, thickly mobile sludge—eyes that quickly fastened on me! And no sooner had the thing spotted me than it began to form mouths—great slobbering mouths that dripped a fetid coating of slime onto the already shiny-black bones in the mouth of the terrible shaft—that same coating which, in a hardened form, already covered so many of the cavern's skeletal remains!

Man and monster face to face, and then, even as I sensed that the horror was about to surge forward to engulf me, there came the tremendous blast that brought down the roof of the cave in great chunks, completely sealing off the pit of the Shoggoth—the blast that hurled me face down into the scattering bones, that cracked the cave's very walls with its fury.

I was instantly deafened, my eardrums rupturing as the brute roar of that inexplicable explosion slammed me senseless into the skeletal fragments. It was as if an enormous charge of dynamite had been set off nearby in the pressured rock, and even the huge statue had been brought down and broken up by the blast. I found myself clawing at the shattered pieces of the great stone head, at the bulging, pearly eyes in that starkly impassive face. Then the torches above were extinguished as even greater sections of the ceiling continued to rain down, and the wonder is that I was not crushed in that avalanche of rock from the roof.

Deaf, blasted, and mazed, blind in the inky blackness of the shuddering, crashing cave, I found myself picked up in a sudden titanic rush of icy water and swirled around and about amidst black and bony debris.

The rest of my memories are fragmentary and very dim. They are composed in the main of half-remembered sensations: the sensation of heaving, frantically rushing waters; the horrible sensation of drowning; the sensation of hearing, as if from a great distance, the fear-filled mind-songs of the Thuun'ha, awful now in their intense bewilderment and almost childlike disbelief; and finally, the sensation of a wildly erratic ascent through leagues of labyrinthine resurgences on the crest of a frothing deluge . . .

XIX

LETTER OF A HARLEY STREET PSYCHIATRIST

63(a) Harley Street
London
8 September 1959

Mr. Jason Masters
25 Yoden Ave.
Harden
Co. Durham

My dear Mr. Masters,

Further to my last report of the 1st: it is with the greatest regret that I now bring myself to inform you of my complete failure in bringing the Professor's condition under control. As you suggested should such prove to be the case, I am now prepared to place your uncle back in your care—though I feel it only fair that certain facts should be made quite clear to you before you agree to any such undertaking. His delusions and hallucinations are quite the most fantastic I have ever had to deal with, possibly unique in the annals of psychiatric complaints.

For instance: your uncle—even under sedation, hypnosis, the influence of the most modern drugs, or any combination of these devices—refuses to address any person in any term or by any name other than "Bokrug!" He *will not* stay in any brightly lighted room without the application of the greatest restraint, and therefore any attempt to work or reason with him must be carried out by candlelight—and even then he is given to grabbing at the candle flame and snuffing it out! I believe he is quite genuinely suffering from a severe form of photophobia, which is only to be expected if indeed he has spent a year underground. In any case, following such an irrational action (candle-snuffing and so on), he explains that he has only "destroyed another of those damned Shoggoths!"

His personal hygiene until recently left much to be desired—due entirely to his condition of course—and unless he was forcibly bathed he would refuse to take anything other than the merest dab of a wash in barely tepid water. Unless he was watched continuously he would relieve himself in the corner of any room in which he happened to be! Even now he will only sleep on a bare mattress, and I still have not quite managed to wean him off fish and/or mushrooms—still the only food he will readily accept. He will only clothe himself when reminded that *he has* clothes to wear, and then reluctantly. He is, too, apparently almost stone deaf—and all these are but a few of the complications of his disorder. I will supply you with a complete list of these pyscho-idiosyncrasies at your request.

At best, the Professor is erudite but eccentric in his "logic," and barring his hallucinations and other fancies his mind's processes move in quite ordered cycles. The trouble is that these cycles are *not acceptable to us*, for he believes that everything about him is part and parcel of a great dream or nightmare of which he is the author! At its worst (while he never becomes physically dangerous in the sense of a homicidal maniac) his is a horrible condition.

As you requested during our telephone conversation of 23 August, I here enclose a complete typescript of your uncle's recorded "story" as related little by little to me since you placed him under my care a month ago. A letter to Inspector Blaysden at Radcar provided me with the copy of the statement of Robert Krug, which I have incorporated into the typescript in place of the less enlightening version of your uncle as he remembered and related it. The typescript as it stands is of course incomplete; there were many recorded sessions which were so garbled as to be meaningless, and no successful translation could be made.

Should the naturally congenial atmosphere of your home, with which your uncle should be well acquainted, prove of little or no benefit to his condition, then I fear there will remain but one alternate course of action left open to you. There are a number of highly specialized private sanatoriums . . . I can recommend at least four.

In the hope (though admittedly a small one), that at some time in the near future your uncle may be fully returned to you in every respect, I remain . . .

Yours very sincerely,
Dr. Eugene T. Thappon

XX

IN CONCLUSION
[From the Notebook of Jason Masters]

It is difficult to know where to begin. I am left, after all my investigations, with such a collection of bits and pieces, facts and figures and dates, incidents and occurrences and coincidences, that their correlation seems near impossible. I know that it should be beyond my capability to write of the thing coldly and without feeling—love of my uncle should dictate a version coloured by emotion—yet I feel that this is the only way to properly present the facts as I know them. I will only present facts, a chronological list of events *which I know definitely have taken place*, and in this way I hope to avoid voicing too many of my personal opinions; for such as my opinions are they might well cause me to be considered as having inherited my uncle's "madness" . . .

On 12 August 1958 Professor Ewart Masters vanished into the Yorkshire moors. His condition some months prior to his disappearance (he had suffered rather bad head injuries earlier in a car accident) had been unstable to say the least, but his improvement over the month or so immediately preceding that vanishment had almost completely disarmed me—so much so in fact that with hardly an argument I had loaned him my car to drive from Harden down to Bleakstone in Yorkshire. At first all seemed to be going well with his fossil-hunting trip, and he called me daily on the telephone; but then, after a period of three days of silence, when I contacted The George, the inn at Bleakstone where I knew he had been staying, his disappearance was discovered. On the 15th of the month my car was found in a Dilham side street, and attempts were commenced to trace my uncle's movements. He had last been seen on the 12th at about noon, heading across the moors on foot in the direction of Devil's Pool.

For five days search parties covered the moors from Eeley to Dendhope and from Marske to Lee-Hill. I say "covered the moors," but that is of course a gross overstatement, for ten thousand policemen could not have *covered* the moors, let alone the two hundred that tried! There are so very many nooks, crevices, and other unexplored places on the great heath. But the police did their best, and for some six months I periodically received copies of further progress reports, all to no avail. Finally, in late February 1959, Ewart Masters was posted as being a "missing person" . . .

On 5 August in that same year, almost exactly twelve months after he vanished, when I had long since given up hope of ever seeing my uncle again, news came to throw me into transports of hope and wonder. Three days previously, on the afternoon of the 2nd, a naked man had been found in a condition of extreme exposure and ordeal-induced delirium stumbling weakly, mazedly about the countryside near Sarby. His eyes had been closed, apparently against the brilliance of the daylight.

The man, a person in his late forties, had first been taken into a small local hospital, only to be transferred to a private ward in the well-equipped hospital at Radcar when it was seen just how dangerous his condition was. There at Radcar on the morning of the third day, after being asked repeatedly to identify himself, he had finally managed to supply the name of Ewart Masters!

The hospital staff passed this information to the police, and they in turn contacted me. That was how I first came to hear of my uncle's return, and of course I went straight down to Radcar in the hope that I would be able to provide positive identification. There was no doubt about it—the long-bearded, moustached, white-haired, and incredibly *pale* man I found between the white sheets of the hospital ward was indeed the professor.

He was asleep when first I saw him, but his nurse told me that it was decidedly better that way (his condition was not a pleasant one when he was awake), for which reason he had been under sedatives since his arrival. Yet even in his drugged sleep he tossed and turned, groaning and mouthing incoherently of strange and incomprehensible things.

Beside his bed an ashtray sported a huge cave-pearl. The nurse saw me eyeing the thing and told me about it: "He had that in his hand from the time they found him until he was brought in here. He was holding on to it very tightly—mumbling about Ulysses and a . . . a Cyclops with *two* eyes! We had quite a struggle getting him to give it up."

"May I take it? I'll give it back to him later."

"Certainly, though if it tends to remind him of whatever he's been through, it's probably best if you remove it for good—whatever it is!"

"It's a cave-pearl," I told her, tossing the thing thoughtfully in my hand. "Just about the biggest I've ever heard of. Now where d'you suppose my uncle might have got it?" Of course, she had no answer.

I do not intend to write of the professor's . . . activities when finally he did awaken. Suffice to say I immediately contacted the best psychiatrist I could find. That was how I came to place my uncle's care in the hands of the Harley Street specialist Dr. Eugene T. Thappon.

Within a week I was back home again in Harden, and it was only then that I gave any thought to the odd "natural" occurrences which had accompanied my uncle's inexplicable reappearance. I had of course already traced his movements in Bleakstone prior to his disappearance, and almost a year had gone by since I had spoken to a policeman in that village who informed me of the professor's stated intention the day before he vanished of going down to Dilham to have a look at Devil's Pool. I would have been blind not to have given the idea considerable thought that perhaps my uncle had attempted the exploration of the pool's continued course below ground.

In this, apparently, I had been correct. The police, having also spoken to people in Bleakstone and Dilham, had arrived at the same conclusion; nor, I was informed, would the professor be the first person to have vanished into Devil's Pool. It could only have been by a series of miracles that he had managed to survive down there to emerge alive all these months later.

But what of those strange circumstances surrounding his return? For instance: there had been no sudden or heavy rains in the greater Yorkshire area for many months; yet, on the very day my uncle had been found babbling deliriously near Sarby, it had also been reported that three new resurgences had opened up in that same cliff face whence the figurine in Radcar Museum had originated. Indeed it was quite possible that the professor had been borne from below ground by the force of these mysteriously and suddenly rushing waters. But what had caused the necessarily vast alterations in the substrata of the moors which alone might explain the sudden appearance of so great a quantity of water? Had some seismic shock or other—a subterranean earthquake, perhaps—been responsible for my uncle's merciful release?

On 18 August I went to Sarby to have a look at the new resurgences myself. Much of the original cliff face had been broken down by the force of the erupting water and lay in great blocks of lime- and grit-stone, and where once a small stream had chuckled from below ground at the foot of the cliffs there now opened four cavernlike mouths from which rushed veritable torrents of chill water. I spoke to a number of geologists and cavers, there to speculate on the phenomenon, only to discover that they were as baffled as the most uninformed man-in-the-street regarding the cause of the sudden flood.

Yet another group of observers—men I noticed keeping very much to themselves and talking in whispers—turned out to be members of the scientific staff of the North-East Coal Board, but understandably I failed to tie this fact in until later.

Fortunately the out-gushing flood merged with the Thyne less than a mile from the cliffs, and only one small road-bearing bridge had been inundated. A new bridge was already planned, but in the meantime a team of Army engineers had put up a temporary Bailey.

While my brief trip had produced no really useful information, I was hardly back at Harden before reading in the *Hartlepool Mail* of another archaeological "find" in the new tributary of the Thyne at Sarby. An extremely violent jet of water on the 20th of the month had thrust out from the cliffs an eighteen-inch fragment of strangely sculpted stone—part of a reptilian head—from beneath the moors. Equally important were the perfectly preserved bones (presumably prehistoric) of as yet unidentified animals, which the same eruption threw forth in their hundreds. But I was most interested in the sculpture, and I read how the fragment comprised the left side of a face of odd intelligence, lizardlike yet with a high forehead of almost human proportions. An empty socket in the stone face showed where an eye of sorts had once rested. Remembering what the nurse had said of my uncle's remarks regarding the cave-pearl— of Ulysses and a Cyclops with two eyes—I went straight down to Radcar Museum where the new find had been placed beside that earlier figurine in the "Wonders of Ancient Britain" showcases.

I arrived before the fragment went behind glass and, unobserved, was able to place the cave-pearl in the gaping socket in the great stone face. The pearl fitted perfectly; confirming (so far as I was concerned) beyond all dispute, the fact that my uncle had indeed been trapped underground for a year!

Three weeks later, on 10 September, I received a letter from Dr. Thappon in which he admitted his inability to properly improve my uncle's lot, and only three days after that, I had the professor back with me in Harden. There *were* improvements in his condition, I could see that from the first, but he was still in so very bad a way with regard to things I had been warned of by Dr. Thappon that I knew I would be unable to handle him myself. So, to take no chances, I had hired in advance a local male nurse, Harry Williamson, to work nights from 6:00 P.M. to 10:00 A.M.—long hours to be sure, but very well paid indeed.

During those first few evenings and nights I gave my wholehearted attention to Thappon's typescript of my uncle's tape-recorded "story." Much of it, up to the time of his sojourn in Bleakstone, I knew already (though I had *not* known of the attacks he suffered there), but from that time on, well, it was all new and terrible to me. I did pick up one inconsistency, with regard to the professor's claim of having returned from Devil's Pool to The George in Bleakstone. Obviously he had not done so. The barman at The George could quite definitely pinpoint the last time my uncle had been seen there, and then of course there was that other proof—the fact that my car had been found in Dilham. This much of his story at least was certainly only the professor's memory of early hallucinations, and much of the remainder—the great majority of it in fact—could surely only be put down to the same origin.

As I have told, I was quite certain by then that my uncle had been underground for a year, and I believed it possible that he had found the crumbling remnants of a long-lost civilization. In support of the existence of such a city, there was the proof of the figurines at Radcar and Bleakstone, and the additional and stronger proof of the cave-pearl eye of the lately disgorged stone face-fragment. Perhaps the professor *had* lived on fish and mushrooms down there in the dark (indeed, considering that he did not show any appreciable *physical* wastage, such seemed the only likely explanation), but the rest of his narrative—except as hellish dreams or diseased fancies— was quite unacceptable. The greater wonder was that in his state of mind he had survived the terrible ordeal at all . . .

Like my uncle before me, I, too, found it odd that Inspector Ianson, one-time Inspector of Police at Radcar, had not seen grotesque *connections* in the Krug case. On 16 September I again went down to Radcar (I had hired the services of Harry Williamson for the whole day) and set about the task of tracing Ianson or whichever relatives he might have left behind when he forsook the country. But here an important find—a *negative* find—for to all accounts Ianson had had no known relatives; apparently *he had been an orphan!*

I did trace a retired policeman, a man who allegedly had known Ianson as well as any other, and then at last I received the first of those clues which eventually were to signal in me certain frightening reversals of belief.

I had spoken to this gentleman, a Mr. Simpkins, on the telephone from Radcar's police headquarters, and later at a public house, The White Horse, I met him as arranged. He was a jovial, healthy-looking old fellow, whose manner and outlook on life gave me complete faith in the reliability of the facts with which he presented me. Over a pint we first chatted of this and that before settling down to the business at hand. Mr. Simpkins was not a man to gossip of anyone without good reason, and I had to explain my case before he would get down to the relevant details. In short, those details were these:

In the two or three years immediately preceding his "going abroad," Inspector Ianson—a strange, completely hairless man— had suffered increasingly from an obscure form of ichthyosis, a condition he treated himself and of which he would allow no professional medical examination. The disease had not been confined to his skin, for all his bodily movements in the weeks prior to his quitting Radcar and its environs had been stiff and painful. In fact Ianson's appearance had been *not quite human* in those last days, and his attendance at the various police stations had suffered accordingly. Simpkins did not believe that the inspector had gone off with a woman—he had given all the circumstances much thought at the time and had arrived at the conclusion that Ianson, knowing he was dying, had simply gone away, without any fuss, to some private place where he might pass on in peace. That was Simpkins's reckoning. My own . . . ?

From Harden on the morning of the 19th I put through a telephone call to Oakdeene Sanatorium and asked to speak to that institute's director. He was not available, but perhaps the speaker could help me with my enquiry? On learning that I was interested in the possibility that certain inmates at the sanatorium were "so unnatural in aspect" that they were not allowed to be seen by outsiders, the voice on the telephone turned hard and unfriendly:

"I'm sorry, sir, but I can't talk to the Press. There's quite enough in the papers already . . ." With that the connection had been broken. Until that time I had been unaware of any untoward happenings at the sanatorium.

A further telephone call to the offices of the *Sunderland Echo* (a good friend of mine was a reporter there) supplied me with the following information. I copied the words directly over the telephone, which will explain any discrepancies between my text and that which appeared in the *Echo* at the time:

TWO DANGEROUS LUNATICS ESCAPE FROM ELMHOLME

Two Elmholme lunatics, believed to be twin brothers, escaped last night (the evening of the 17th) after being transferred from Oakdeene Sanatorium near Glasgow. For the past six months the two escapees have been undergoing a special course of psychological therapy at Oakdeene as administered by a German psychiatrist of impeccable references, Dr. Ruben Kruger. It was on the advice of Dr. Kruger—following tremendous improvements in what had hitherto been considered hopeless cases—that the two inmates were moved to the low-security wing at Elmholme, but since their escape the authorities have been unable to contact him. The escaped men are of the following description: bald and with no bodily hair whatever; 70 to 72 inches in height; approx. 130 pounds in weight. They are suffering from severe skin and muscular diseases by which they may be most easily recognized, i.e., the skin of their faces and bodies is thick, rough, and scaly, and the speed of their movements is painfully restricted. At a distance, they might easily be taken for old people as their movements suggest severe rheumatic disorders . . .

There was more, but in effect that was the gist of the announcement. I have yet to discover what my friend in Sunderland thinks of the way I ended our conversation (I must think up an excuse for having cut him off without even a word of thanks), but the truth is I simply let the receiver fall before he had done speaking.

Later, when I was able to carry out further investigations, I discovered of the two escaped . . . men? . . . a horrible history of madness, peculiar ichthyic diseases, and an obscurity of origin so like the background of Inspector Ianson and the "fiction" of the alleged madman Robert Krug that I found myself ever more apprehensive of my discoveries and eventually actually trembling with an inner horror. It was too mad, too fantastic—yet item upon item, clue after clue, the whole incredible jigsaw was piecing itself together into a picture of the most awe-inspiring and hideous aspect.

It was on 21 September that yet another piece of the puzzle slipped itself into place. The morning newspaper carried second-page news of an enquiry opened by the Minister of National Economics into an alleged "misuse of authority" by the NECB. Even before reading the thing I remembered that Krug's statement had been supposedly designed to prevent the North-East Coal Board's extension of its drilling operations on the Yorkshire moors; and more . . . I remembered the furtive-seeming crowd of scientists I had seen at the site of the new resurgences at Sarby!

Apparently it had come to the notice of the Ministry of National Economics that the NECB had been carrying out unauthorized experiments on the moors—*experiments involving the drilling of deep shafts into the earth, and the sinking and detonation of powerful explosives!*

The Minister's prime allegation was that these experiments had been directly responsible for bringing about the resurgences at Sarby, the inundation and collapse of a previously quite serviceable bridge, and the destruction of fifty yards of metalled road; but he further pointed out that the results *might* have been disastrous. Had the water forced an outlet at some other spot, whole villages may well have been swamped!

Of course, I was not much interested in these allegations as such—but I *was* interested in the locations at which those detonations had taken place. Had not my uncle mentioned a tremendous blast towards the end of his narrative—a blast heralding the waters which carried him to freedom? Hurriedly I read on to discover that the site of the last and biggest explosion of the series had been a spot just some four miles out on the moors. The bomb had been set off by remote control at a great depth in the earth at 10:00 A.M. on 2 August *only four or five hours before my uncle was found wandering about on the outskirts of Sarby!*

The more I learned the more it appeared that the professor's hallucinations had had at least a foothold in reality, but I found myself praying that was *all* they had had.

The rest of the thing is easy to relate. It happened so quickly—and, to me at least, its proofs were so *positive*—that everything remains in my mind with unbelievable clarity. I only wish I could forget all I know of it . . .

On the evening of 23 September I left my uncle in the capable care of Harry Williamson and went out into the brisk air to walk along the sea cliffs. The shushing of the waves below was soothing to me and I realized how badly, how deeply the occurrences of the last month had affected me. The truth was I had needed to think things over, for I was seriously considering—despite any beliefs I might by then have developed—taking Dr. Thappon's advice regarding the placing of my uncle in a private home. At least an action such as that, harsh though it seemed, would give me time to carry out further investigations. As it happened, I need not have bothered my mind about the professor's future; even as I turned towards home that night, his "future" was already in the process of being taken entirely out of my hands . . .

Now, my house stands at the very outskirts of the village, not many miles from the A19, which of course runs south and to the west of the Yorkshire moors on its way to Thirsk, York, and Selby. I mention this fact in order to illustrate the ease with which a traveller through Harden might make his way directly down to the moors, a journey of no more than ninety minutes to two hours at the outside in a motorcar, especially a car as big as mine.

By the time I reached the garden wall I knew something was wrong. I had set out three hours earlier, at about eight in the evening, and the night was quite dark, but I could see that the house was ablaze with lights and that my car was missing from its garage, the doors of which were swinging open. Passing in through the garden gate at a run, I saw that the front door was ajar. As I skidded to a halt on the gravel path the door opened fully and Harry Williamson staggered out. He was holding his head and there was a mixed expression of shock and bewilderment on his face. Pausing only to ensure that Williamson was not urgently in need of attention, I hurried into the house and made a rapid search of all the rooms. Need I add that my uncle was nowhere to be found?

The statement Williamson made to the police later that night is reproduced in all its important details as follows:

> ... Then, after Mr. Masters went out, I checked again that the professor was asleep and made myself a cup of coffee. I would say that it was about 8:30 P.M. by the time I'd finished my coffee. I cleaned up in the kitchen and went back to my easy chair outside the professor's room. I smoked a cigarette and then sat reading for a while. Just after 9:00 P.M. I heard the professor talking in his sleep. I knew he must still be asleep because he'd had his sedative at 6:30 P.M. and it normally keeps him out right through the night. The light was off in his room—he likes it that way—and when I looked in I saw a cloud of fireflies over his bed. When I switched the light on these fireflies must have gone out the window, which was slightly open; anyway, I couldn't see them. No, not just because it was light in the room ... I mean, I really did *look* for them. They're insects, you know? I sat by the professor's bed then for a while, listening to him talking. He was on about "songs" or something like that, and he kept putting his hands up to his ears in his sleep. Yes, that's it, he kept saying "The songs have started again—they're coming for me ..." A few minutes later he began to go on about "dreams within

dreams" and other things I could make nothing of. At about 9:30 he became very agitated and started to toss and turn on his bed. Then he sat straight up and looked at me. He was awake then, yes. He said: "Dr. Bokrug, I presume?"—he always called me Bokrug—and then burst out laughing. I tried to get him to lie down again and he did, but he kept complaining about the "songs" and putting his hands to his ears. I went to get him another tablet and when I got back to his room he was sitting up again. He said: "Ah, *Herr Ober*! What's on the menu? *Champignons und Fisch?*" I speak a little German so I knew he meant mushrooms and fish. That's his favourite meal. No, I don't know why he spoke in German. A little while later, after getting him on his back again, he started to get violent—but very weakly, because that second pill was getting to work on him. "What's real?" he kept asking me. "What's *real*? Are *you* real? If you are ... then you have to help me! They're coming for me! I tell you—*they're coming for me!*" I asked him whom he meant. I had to shout, he's very deaf, and he told me: "Why, *Them*!" Yes, that's how he said it: "*Them*." He carried on: "And they're bringing the Thuun'ha with them ... for of course, it wouldn't be seemly for one of *Them* to be seen slavishly bearing in his arms the likes of me!" Yes, I remember he said just that. It sounded so odd to me that I took special note of it. A few minutes later he dropped off to sleep, but he was still very restless and kept mumbling to himself. Just after 9:45 (I was back in my chair again outside the professor's door) there was a knock at the front door of the house. I answered the knock and found an odd-looking chap standing on the doorstep. By "odd" I mean that he was queer-looking. He had no eyebrows that I could see and he was as bald as a coot. He told me he was a doctor and a friend of Mr. Masters. I was about to invite him inside, to wait on Mr. Masters' return, when I saw a movement at the bottom of the garden in the shadows near the gate. It was dark down there, and I remember thinking what a lot of fireflies there were about—you don't often see them nowadays, certainly not at this time of year. I asked this Kruger chap—yes, that's what he said his name was—if he had someone waiting for him, at which he beckoned in the direction of the gate. I heard the gate open and then these two . . . well, these two . . . yes, I *will* get on with it, but I don't know if you'll believe me! I swear to God I wasn't asleep and dreaming it all, but . . . they were *Things*! No, they weren't people. They walked upright but they were almost like, well, *crocodiles*! but with humanish faces! They had short tails and they were green. *I told you you wouldn't believe me!* . . . All right. These creatures (I'll call them creatures) each carried what looked like a roll of leather of a sort. I can tell you, I didn't see much of them right then! Quick as a flash I was back into the house and trying to get the door shut. I don't know what happened then. I think that this Kruger chap must have taken hold of my hand as I tried to close the door, but I'm not sure. I found myself flat on my back on the hall carpet. I could hear and think, all right, but I couldn't move a finger. Now, God knows you *can't* believe what happened next—but I swear it's true! This Kruger and the two . . . creatures . . . came in through the door and went to the professor's room. They came out again, looking very satisfied with themselves, and went about the house switching off the lights. In the dark I could see that the place was full of fireflies—especially round the heads of Kruger and the . . . others. Then they left the house and went outside. I thought maybe they'd left for good, but I was wrong. I did notice, though, that those fireflies went with them. In less than five minutes they were back *and they brought some other . . . things . . . with them*! Yes, I know I said they switched off the lights, and so they had, but those damned fireflies seemed to

follow them about so that I could see everything that happened! The other things I mentioned? Oh, yes, well . . . I mean
I can't be sure. Well, they were like . . . children! That is, they
were the same size as kids. Yes, I could see them clearly,
but . . . for God's sake! *You simply won't believe me!* All right,
all right. I'll tell you. There were four or five of them. They
were small, about four feet tall, I'd say, and they . . . *they were
like nothing on Earth!* No, I don't know. I can't describe
them—*I won't!* . . . Well, these smaller things carried the professor from his room and out of the house. The other three
stayed for a while, mainly in Mr. Masters's rooms, and then
they left too. They took something with them—papers, I
think. A few moments later I heard the station wagon drive
away. I think it must have been about 10:00 P.M. by that time.
For the next hour or so I tried to get up, and slowly I felt the
strength coming back into my arms, legs, and body. In the
end I did manage to get up. I put all the lights on, and I had
just made it to the door when Mr. Masters came home . . .

I listened until Williamson had done with dictating his statement
to the police, then I quickly checked my room. Every scrap of paperwork I had collected on my uncle's case was gone. (I later learned
that Thappon's taperecordings had been stolen from his Harley
Street office during the hours of the previous night.)

Then it was my turn—by which time my head was spinning
with the mad thoughts whirling round and around inside it. Dully,
mechanically, I told the police as much as I knew of the evening's
occurrences, which was not a great deal. All the while, I had to fight
to keep myself under control. They were so, well, *professional* about
it all. But then, when they asked me for a description of my car,
my control finally went. I laughed hysterically and told them not to
worry about the car: first thing in the morning I would go down
to Dilham and pick it up myself . . .